PARADOX

PARADOX

Paulie J. Johnson

The Regency
Publishers

Copyright © 2022 Paulie J. Johnson.

All rights reserved. No part of this publication may be reproduced, distributed, or transmitted in any form or by any electronic or mechanical means, including information storage and retrieval systems, without a prior written permission from the publisher, except by reviewers, who may quote brief passages in a review, and certain other noncommercial uses permitted by the copyright law.

ISBN: 978-1-958517-48-2   (PB)
ISBN: 978-1-958517-49-9   (HB)
ISBN: 978-1-958517-47-5   (E-book)

Some characters and events in this book are fictitious and products of the author's imagination. Any similarity to real persons, living or dead, is coincidental and not intended by the author.

Book Ordering Information

The Regency Publishers, International
7 Bell Yard London WO2A2JR

info@theregencypublishers.com
www.theregencypublishers.international
+44 20 8133 0466

Printed in the United States of America

SUMMARY

Born premature, blind and diagnosed at an early age as having a form of autism. A boy was institutionalized and later was subjected to an unauthorized test that was given to him by his doctor. The doctor died and his condition was reassessed by his new doctor that differed with the opinion of the boy's previous doctor and he began taking on a new life that was different from the life he subjected to. At the age of twenty five he was released from the institution and in his world, all things were new.

To complicate matters. He was wealthy and was the heir to his family fortune so he didn't socialize until he walked into his father's firm and announced he would be taking over operations, but not without having difficulty.

Life came at him to fast and he grew weak from his encounters and one day he decided to change his life and by doing so, he met the person that helped him to conquer his troubles and through her, he was able to be the person he wanted to be and not the person he was. He never looked at himself the way he saw himself to be again.

CHAPTER ONE

I began my day preparing to explore my surroundings. It was a totally different environment from which I was accustomed to. When I walked out of my house, I could feel the warmth from the sun and when I stopped to listen, a car could be heard as it passed along the highway up the road every now and then.

It took most of my morning to reach the small town where I moved to and every now and then I would stop and listen to the sounds that the little city gave and smell the odors of its inhabitant's. After I caught a whiff of an aroma that whetted my appetite, I chose to follow my nose.

The sound of a horn alerted me to the presence of a car, so I moved over to get out of its way. When I found the entrance, I walked along the steps until I reached the door and then opened it and eased in slowly.

"Can I help you hon." A woman said.

"Is this a restaurant?" I asked.

"I don't think I would go quite that far" the lady reflected her views "most folks around here call us a diner."

"Are there others?" I asked her.

"Hon, we have three gas stations, one small grocery store, four resale shops, six banks, and ten real estate agents." "We're the only diner this side of Murray, and that's fifty miles away."

"So, you have a monopoly on the customer's huh?" I said smiling.

"Hon, we're at the mercy of tourists." "The drought just doesn't dry up the lake, it dries up customers too." "Would you like to hear what we have?" She asked.

"No ma'am." "A burger and fries and some unsweetened tea will do."

"All right then, I'll be back in about fifteen minutes." She said with a tired voice.

I could hear a conversation between two gentlemen and that gave me a small idea of how the layout of the diner was fitted. Judging by my booth, and the size of the diner, I assumed every table was similar to mine.

I heard a bell signaling the opening of a door, and then felt the seat in the next booth move in front of me.

"Excuse me." I heard a female say with an agitated voice. "Excuse me!" The voice was louder and it now carried a bit of anger to it. "You're a butt hole!" She stated. "Hello, butt hole!" This time her voice had a tone of irritation and I then felt a movement from a seat in the booth in front of me. "People like you really get my goat; you have no shame." I heard her say as she walked my way and stopped.

I didn't hear the conversation between the two men anymore. But I felt the seat in front of me move.

"I'm sorry." I heard her say.

"Oh" "You were talking to me." "I thought you were talking to that waitress." I answered. "It's okay."

I felt the seat move and then I felt the movement of the seat in the next booth again.

After I finished eating, I handed my waitress a twenty and told her to keep the change, and then stood to make my way to the door.

"You need some help, hon." I heard my waitress say.

"No ma'am, I have to figure this out on my own." "I do thank you for asking though." I told her. "Ma'am, can I ask you something?"

"Sure."

"Is the grocery store on this side of the road?" I asked.

"You'll pass two resale shops and two gas stations, and then the grocery store is next." She responded.

"I thank you ma'am." I said reaching outward trying to find the handle on the door. I heard the sound of the bell and moved out of the way, and then I felt a hand take me by my arm.

"You have a step coming up." I heard a voice and then stopped; it was the girl that apologized to me. "I work part time at Barney's" "I can give you a lift if you want."

I listened to what she said and then replied. "No thanks, I have to gather my bearings and memorize my surroundings." "I do thank you for asking though."

"Look, earlier when I was being a jerk." She began.

"Ma'am, you've already apologized for something that didn't bother me, it's okay, really."

"But I still feel like a jerk back there." She said to me. "That's what those old men were thinking when I caused a scene." "I was angry and the next thing I knew I looked up and thought you were staring at me."

"I don't look at it like it was all that big of a deal." I told her as I felt the wooden railing that lined the steps and walked down away from her.

When I stepped down to my final step, I felt the rocky pavement of the parking lot, and then felt a hand take me by my arm again.

"You don't understand this community." "By now everyone in this county has heard about me chewing out a blind man." She resumed. "To your left is the parking lot for the people that enter from this way and beyond the parking lot is the road." "On the righthand side is a parking lot for the people that come in from the opposite direction." "Beyond that lot is nothing but weeds and brush." "It hadn't been mowed since I've been here and that's been three years." "This parking lot is for Becky's diner, where you just ate at." "Be careful walking through here" "people tend to use this as a side road to avoid the caution light if their turning right." "There aren't any businesses between here and the resale shops, so you'll be walking on a grass path after you cross the road to get in here." "After a rain, don't walk this way, it fills up and floods here."

"I can handle this, I'm not helpless." I told her as she walked with me.

"No one said you were." She responded with a soft tone in her voice. "Are you and your wife staying with someone around here?"

"No ma'am" I answered to be polite "I moved here because everything seemed to be changing on me too fast." "A building would go up, and others were torn down." "I was hoping to find a place where everything seemed settled, and I'm not married."

"Look, first off" she began "you have your buttons buttoned uneven; one side of your shirt hangs down lower than the other." She said while redoing my shirt. "As far as things growing here, I don't think you'll have that kind of a problem to worry about." "The only thing that changes in this little town is the ownership of the diner, the resale shops, and the gas stations." "It seems like everything you can buy out of a garage sale becomes a valuable antique when it enters the resale shops and anyone needing a mechanic comes out cheaper if they buy a new car." "You've got a curb coming up." "You'll have to step up to get over it." "You got a name?" She asked.

"Kurt" I said.

"Kurt, my name's Bailey." "I work part time at Barney's because I go to college in Murray." "I've had four interviews for jobs that I applied for and three of them have filled the position." "I just got a call telling me that the fourth job that I interviewed for has postponed their hiring." "Why can't people just tell you that the job's been filled or you don't meet their expectations?" "I'm sorry I took out my frustration on you." She said apologizing again.

"Does helping me make you feel better?" I asked.

"No, I still feel like a jerk." She restated. "You've got a curb coming up to where you'll have to step over the curb and down onto a drive." "You'll have to cross it and another curb will come up for the next gas station." "You'll have to watch for the sign they use to tell you how much gas is, they like to put it where we're walking." "All right, here's our first curb, step up, over and down." She stated.

When she led me into the store, she asked me what I needed. "I'm not settled yet." "The only thing I needed to know was where the grocery store was." "I'm living out of boxes right now." I expressed my problem. "I only wanted to count the steps to each obstacle and memorize them and that way I could learn where I was at if I became disoriented." I opened my watch and felt the needle and then turned around. "We've been walking east."

We were interrupted by a man that walked over and without any hesitation; stated to her that he needed someone that was more dependable.

"Mister Hudson."

"I'm sorry Bailey, I get told what to do just like everyone else that works here." He commented.

"Mister Hudson" "please."

"I'm sorry." He repeated and walked away.

The walk back was a quiet one.

"We're back at my car." She stated. "Maybe I'll see you around."

I heard the door open and then close. "Go ahead." She said in a disruptive utter.

I was a good distance away before she turned her key to start her car. The engine never started, and in her attempt the battery couldn't sustain the load. I stopped and turned back around and began working my way back over to her. There wasn't any problem in finding her; her crying could be heard from fifty feet away. I felt my way along the car until I found the door and opened it. After checking the seat to see if it was clear for me to sit down, I sat there while she cried.

"Bailey, I went to a private school" I started "I was supervised everywhere I went." "I got lost four times." "I know a lot about the way you're feeling now." I said failing in my attempt in trying to calm her. "I came here because I didn't want to get lost anymore." "I wanted to do things on my own, and I'm finding out quickly that I'm not very good at it." "Every day I woke up I encountered some kind of a problem that I had to work my way around." "I wanted to be more self reliant." "You can always get your car fixed, or get another car, but I'm always going to be dependent on someone and I don't want to be." "Do you live nearby?" I asked her.

"No" "I'm two months behind on my trailer." "I'm scared every time I drive home, I'm going to be met by my landlord." "But I ain't got that worry now, I can't even drive home." She said as she started crying again. I let her let it go.

"Are you wearing a band around your hair?" I asked her.

"What kind of question is that?"

"I was born blind." I said to her. "I slid all the way down until I didn't have any place to go but up and I went through all that for twenty five years." "Right now, you feel like that hair band; you can only twist it so far until it snaps and when it does it doesn't do what it was designed to do anymore."

"How do you fight it?" She asked.

"I got a phone call, and the next thing I know, I'm here." "I can't live in a city, not because of me being blind, but because I'm confined there." "I wanted to go for a walk and not have to count how many steps, or what obstacle to look for." "But no matter how hard I try, I know I'm always going to be dependent on someone for something, and like I said, I don't like that." "Bailey, there's a lot of things I can't do." "Every time I go to the grocery store, I have to ask someone for help." "I can't tell the difference of whether it's a can of peas or a can of dog food." "Try buying milk without being able to read the expiration date, two days later, it's soured." "Do you know when milk is sour; the taste buds tell you first, not the nose?" "I hate soured milk." I expressed my disgust. "Where are your parents?" I asked her.

"My mom lives in Florida with her husband, and my dad lives in Washington, with his wife." She began. "I haven't talked to my mother since I was twelve, and I haven't talked to my father since I was seventeen." "They have my number, but I guess they've got other things in their lives that are important." "What about yours?" She asked.

"I was born premature." "My mother was rammed by a fire truck on a training exercise." "They did an emergency operation on her and I was born, she was dead when they operated." "My father said I weighed two pounds five ounces." "He died two years ago."

"Did you ever meet anyone?" She asked.

"You mean did I ever have any girl friends?"

"I didn't want to put it like that." She stated.

"I'm not the kind of man you would want to party with." I answered. "Take a blind man out and mix him with alcohol and you've got nothing but a bundle of trouble that's doing nothing but looking for a safe place to fall down." "Try waking up in a place where you don't know where you're at or which way to go and I don't want to be around people that do drugs, both of them only bring you trouble." "I'm tired of living a life of hell."

"Is that what you think, that you're living in hell?" She asked.

"Isn't that what you were feeling a few minutes ago?" I replied to her. "You were all twisted up and ready to snap." "You go to school." "You drive a car that eats everything up in gas and repairs." "You're behind on two month's rent and you get fired from what little pay you did get." "You have a hell that you live in, and I live in mine." "How much did they say you could get your car fixed for?"

"Seven hundred dollars" she said "that's more than what I paid for it."

"So, you were hoping to get a job in Murray so you could slash driving a hundred miles a day where you could go to college?"

"No, I want a job that pays" she stated "take a look, there's nothing here." She quickly apologized for her remark.

She tried starting up her car, but all it did was click.

"You've got to add a battery to that seven hundred." I told her, and then she started crying again. "Bailey, I need help, and I don't have anyone to ask."

"What"

After a brief pause, I began. "I told you I was dependent on a provider" "I don't like the word caretaker so to speak, but that's what some people refer to themselves as being." "I need someone to help me make my house look like a home." "I need everything, but I don't know what I'm getting when I get it."

"You don't know anything about me." She stated.

"Have you ever heard of the term gold digger?" I asked.

"Are you referring to a woman only loving a man because of his money?" She answered.

"It doesn't necessarily have to mean a woman, it could be a man like me, or a salesman, or a contractor." "I'd have to depend on an interior decorator to get my furniture, and I can't afford that, I can get the furniture for the price I'd have to pay them." "Besides, I'll be the only one that's going to use them."

"You're an easy target." She stated.

"I've been there and done that too." I told her. "Bailey, everybody I meet I have to take a chance on."

"So, what are you proposing?" She asked me.

"I can get your car fixed and pay your back rent, and in exchange, you can live in my house free of room and board." "You pick out my curtains, my furniture, my linen, and everything else that goes in my house." "That way you'll have freedom to go to school, and it'll give you time to find the job you were wanting."

"What if someone calls me up next week to go to work, I won't be able to pay you back, at least not right away?" She asserted.

"Then it'll be a loan and when you get back on your feet, you can pay me back."

"I don't think my boyfriend will go for it." She finally said after hesitation.

"Well, maybe I'll see you around then." I said opening my door and getting out.

"Hey" "hey" "Kurt." "Slow down, stop, you're going to get run over." She was saying as she was trying to catch up to me. I felt her hand grabbing my arm. "Stop" she said with a soft tone. "We just met." "You don't just up and tell a girl you'll give her money if she'll move in with you." "That isn't the way you do things." She scolded me.

"It doesn't appear I've got much choice in the matter, do I?" "I understand." I told her and then was about to begin leaving when she held me back.

"Kurt, I don't think you do."

"Ma'am, everybody has a lifestyle." "Trust me, I understand." I turned and walked away.

After I got out of the city, I stopped to take a breath and felt coolness in the air. I was about to begin again when I heard footsteps behind me. I walked on without giving it any further attention. When I turned down the road that I lived on, I walked a way's and then stopped. I listened and the sounds I heard were silent. I then took several steps back a way's and stopped, and then sniffed the air.

"Hello, is anyone there?" I said not expecting an answer.

I was starting to take a step when I heard footsteps again. A hand held me by my arm as I was being urged to walk.

"I'll agree to this arrangement on conditions." She stated.

"There won't be any conditions." I told her "You can do whatever you want to do when you do it." I paused. "You know, you're right, there isn't anything here."

"What's that supposed to mean?" She asked.

"Well, one day you'll get a degree, and then money will be thrown at you." "You'll understand then." I answered.

"I don't think it works like that." She said as she escorted me. "You've got to climb a career ladder before you make big money." "What did you just mean about nothing being here?" She asked again.

"I was a ward of the state" I spoke "they sent people out to look in on me, and over a period of time, things came up missing."

"Kurt, I lied to you about having a boyfriend." "I was seventeen when I moved to Murray." "My boyfriend at the time was going to school and I worked to help him graduate." "I ended up getting dumped for my reward." "I need you to stop for a minute." She asked me. "My first good job I ever got was being a housekeeper for the people that lived down this road right here where we stopped." "I worked here for two years before I was let go."

"What happened?" I asked.

"They were on a vacation and their plane went down." "When I came here and seen what they owned, I knew right then and there that I wanted to be a doctor." She confessed.

"Do you want to be a doctor or are you going to school to marry a doctor?" I followed.

"I'm not a gold digger" she corrected me "and I know I can't ever be a doctor." "First off, I don't have the smarts, and secondly the money." "I didn't start going to school, until this semester." "I got a grant for my books and tuition."

"I wouldn't think a doctor would be able to live around here." "Where would he be able to work?" I asked.

"He was a heart surgeon and he flew to six different hospitals." "He was the richest man here." She answered.

"It's almost dark" I said "do you think you could take me there and tell me what kind of place it looks like?"

"How do you know it's almost dark?"

"The wind is cool; the warmth of the sun has faded." I responded.

"No, let's go, it's up for sale, its private property, and if the Sheriff saw us in there, he may get the wrong idea." She stated with a hint of being scared in her voice.

"What's he going to do, arrest a blind man?" "I'll tell them that I wanted someone to show me what it looked like, I may buy this place." I told her.

She started laughing.

I started moving my cane back and forth in front of me.

"What are you doing?" "Kurt, get back over here." She tried to keep her voice below a high whisper.

"I want to feel the house." I replied in the same tone.

"Kurt, you're going to get us arrested."

"Bailey, we all have desires in our life, how am I going to set my goals if I don't know what my goals are?" I commented.

"I can tell you everything about that house from right here." She was scolding me again.

"You can tell me, but when I can't feel it, I can't grasp what you're telling me." I stated to her. "Now, are you coming?"

"Why not" she sighed "I lose my job, and my car breaks down; getting arrested would make the little things seem minor."

She took me by my arm and we slid through a hole in the fence gate. "This is the driveway that we're on now." "It's straight and turns to the right up ahead and then circles the front of the house where you can drive back out without having to back up to turn around."

"How long is it?" I asked.

"I don't know, but when I drove up in my car." "I had to park it in the back parking lot."

"Why?" I asked her.

"Let's just say my car was worth about sixty thousand less than the cars that were in front, and I had an oil leak." "Kurt, I don't like being here, let's go back."

"We slid through a hole in the gate." I said to her. "So, there must be a lock on it." "What are the police going to do, go get a key?"

"Hold your voice down." She whispered.

"You see somebody." I said ducking down.

She pulled me back up. "No, I don't want to get caught here, there's a right and wrong, and we're on the edge of wrong."

"You said no one lives there." I stated.

"I don't care, it still feels wrong." "Be quiet." She whispered. "We're almost to the front of the house."

"What does it look like?" I asked her.

"It has two stories" she began "twelve bedrooms, all of them have full baths and walk in closets." "The smallest room can hold my trailer and three more." "There's four study rooms, one game room, one humongous family room, a restaurant style kitchen with six convection ovens, a walk in refrigerator and freezer, and a dining room that is oh so beautiful." "Kurt, they had a dinner table that sat twenty people." "I never saw a table that big." "Working for him was the best job, I ever had." "He paid more money than any of the jobs in Murray." "That's why I drove from Murray to here." "It was worth it." "I thought I was living good, and when they got killed, I lost my job."

"Did they have any kids?" I asked her.

"They were gone and married when I started to work for them." She answered. "It was a good job and the pay was good."

"Did you ever sneak out back and sit in the hot tub and the pool." I asked her.

"No, there were always other maids and the butler and the cooks were always around too." "How did you know about the hot tub, and pool?" She questioned.

"I don't think anyone that has a house this big wouldn't be without luxuries." "I bet it's heated too?"

"I don't think they'll sell it" she said "there isn't anyone around here with that kind of money."

I started working my way over to the door.

"What are you doing, get back over here." She ordered me in a whisper.

"I want to feel the door." I told her.

"Why" she whispered again.

"It'll tell me what the windows look like." I whispered back.

I pulled the key out of my pocket and unlocked the door.

"Let's go Kurt." "I don't like this."

"Bailey, there's no need to whisper." I said in a normal voice opening the doors. "I signed the papers on the house three days ago."

"What"

"I own this house." I stated to her. "It was put up on the auction block because the children were having a dispute on what to do with the house and property." "None of them wanted to move back here."

"What" she stated again.

"I told you I meet people sometimes, but I'll use you as an example." I said to her. "When you meet people, you have a fifty percent chance of that person betraying you, no matter the reason." "You were betrayed and used by your last boyfriend; he was a gold digger; he benefited from you financially." "I need help, and you need help, or you wouldn't have followed me here."

"So, all of that mumbo jumbo about hiring an interior decorator you fed me was just a bunch of crap?" She had anger in her voice.

"Bailey, what do you see in this house?" I asked her.

She held her silence.

"You see money." I told her. "But to me, this is my sanctuary." "In a week or two I'll be able to go anywhere in this house and never get lost." "In a year, I hope to have rope around the whole property; that way I'll know then where my borders are." "But I can't do that unless I have someone to help me spot the markers."

"You knew about Doctor Wilcox, didn't you?" She said to me.

"Yes"

"You really are a butt hole, you know." She once again stated to me with anger in her voice. "You let me carry on the way I did, and played me for a fool."

"Bailey that's not true." "I knew you were lying to me about a boyfriend." "When you helped me down the steps at the diner, you asked me if my wife and I were staying with someone." "You got the answer you wanted to know." "When I offered to help you, you mentioned your boyfriend; I thought you were just looking for a way out, so I chose to give it you."

I could hear footsteps and the door being slammed.

I sat down on the floor with my back up against the wall. A little time later I heard the door open and her voice seemed highly upset.

Paradox

"Where are you at, butthole?" She said in an angry voice.

"I'm sitting over here."

I could hear her footsteps walking towards me and soon I heard her cussing as she fell over my boxes that I had sitting on the floor.

"Welcome to my world." I responded.

Soon, I felt her touch me and then she was sitting next to me.

"I'm mad" she fired "I got down to the gate and I was about to go out, but I couldn't." "I started walking back and forth and trying to find a reason why I shouldn't be mad." "You deceived me Kurt, but then I started asking myself, would I have said "hey" come with me and I'll let you live in the house of your dreams with me." "My answer was no, and I need to know why you did."

"Think for a minute." I told her. "You said that everyone in town will know about you chewing out a blind man when you introduced yourself to me." "Then that means tomorrow everyone in town will know that I bought this place." "I won't be able to walk down the road without someone stopping and wanting to help me out." "When you leave, I'm still going to need help." "I can't drive, and nothing's changed, I need furniture, so I'm dependent on someone for help." "Now, I can guarantee you the next person that sits where you're sitting is going to be sitting there for only one purpose, and that's to do her level best to please my every wish."

"How do you know I won't be that person?" She commented.

"I don't." "Bailey, you followed me." "So, you did it for one or two reasons." "You either need my help or you know about me already."

"So, you think I could be setting you up for a scam?" Her voice had a settled sound.

I began to explain my reasons for my actions to her. "You told me yourself, I'm an easy target." "For starters, you happened to have come into the diner right after I did, and you left when I did." "Bailey there was only two customers in the diner and they were in the back." "I was seated in the middle and you sat down in front of me." "I can only guess that the diner had around fourteen, maybe sixteen other tables that you could have sat down at, but you didn't, you sat down in front of my table facing my direction when you could have sat down facing the opposite direction." "You helped me to the store and now you're here."

"Is that what you were thinking of me?" She asked.

"That's a lot of why's I have to think about." I stated.

"First off" she responded "you were sitting in my seat" "and secondly this was my house, and you took it away from me." "Now what am I going to do?" "Everyone will believe that I'm only helping you because." She stammered a little.

"Because I have money" I interrupted "try putting yourself in my shoes." "Let's say a woman was able to find her way to me, and through her evil ways she managed to manipulate and then seduce me with her love." "And in five years and three children later that love faded." "What do you think my outcome would be?" I said to her.

"You think I would do that to you?" She answered.

"Oh yeah" "that and more." "Trust me, my father made a fortune off of family law."

"Is that where you got your money?" She asked me.

"Well, I'm basking in the success of my ancestor's blood and sweat." "My great, great, great, great grandfather was an indentured servant." "He was given up by his father at the age of eleven." "But records show he was nine." "They shaved two years off of his age so he would have to work longer." "It didn't matter though." "The man that he was in bondage to had a daughter and when his master died, he married his daughter and bought some land in California, and after he died, it was passed down to my great, great, great grandfather and when he died, he passed it down to my great, great grandfather." "And when he died, he passed it down to my great grandfather, and when he died, he passed it down to my grandfather." "When my grandfather found out I was blind, he set up the land to be sold in a trust fund for me." "At the age of twenty five, the land sold and my grandfather's father's father's father's fathers investment was relinquished to me." "My father and mother were both lawyer's." "My father sued the city over my mother's accidental death and my disability and won." "Guess where he put it." "He told me that when he found out my mother was pregnant, he went and had a new sign made." "I felt it myself." "Bryant, Bryant, and Bryant." "That never came to pass."

"I can see why you have a negative view." She confessed. "Kurt, I think your father might have been on to something about you being a lawyer, you would have made a good one."

"It didn't fit me." I uttered. "We were encouraged in school to thrive to be successful." "We were taught to overcome our adversities and never admit defeat." "I always seemed to fall asleep after reading the first page of law."

"Did you ever, you know, work anywhere?" She asked.

"No, not me, I found out what my true calling was." I giggled.

"What was that?" I felt her head turn towards me.

"A gigolo" "I just wave my magic cane around and let it work, it's a chic magnet." I could feel her laughing before I could hear her laughing. "You walked into that one." I told her, and that only made her laugh harder.

"That's healthy for you, you know?" I chuckled from her laughing.

"What"

"Laughter, it's good for the body as well as the soul." I told her.

"Did you ever wonder what I look like?" She asked

"I know you have hair that's past your shoulder's, and judging by the way it felt, it's full of body and it has the feel of satin to it." "I felt it brush up against my arm when you were leading me." "I know you're a well figured girl." "I heard several wolf whistles and people honking at you when they went by."

"How do you know that wasn't someone else that they saw?" She asked.

"If there was, she had to walk to the store with us and back because all the whistles and the horns were always next to us." "But there is one thing that is clearly evident; you wore the wrong shoes today." I told her. "You have a slight favor to your left foot." "Bailey, it's dark, and I'm blind." "I don't care what you look like in your bare feet." "Do yourself a favor and give those paws a rest." I told her.

I could feel her taking off her shoes.

"You're very observant." She stated to me.

"I tend to recognize the little things in a person." I told her.

"Such as?" Her voice was insistent.

"Well, for instance, that perfume you're wearing; that's probably the reason why no one hired you."

"What's wrong with my perfume?" She said perking up.

"It doesn't beg anyone to play vampire." "When you leave, leave your address with me, and when I get some help to take me to town, I'll buy you some real perfume, then I'll ask whoever it is behind the counter, if I could get some help in finding someone to give me some help in choosing some wrapping paper." "Then I'll have to ask for help at the post office in writing down your address on the box so I can send it to you."

"Yeah, you would have made a good lawyer." She quipped.

"And in answer about me wondering what you look like" I said "I find satisfaction in the voice." "You do know that's where the cliché of love being blind was born from."

"I didn't know that." She stated.

"Yeah, I'll show you." "When you came in you tripped over my boxes that was sitting down in front of you." "I would imagine you fell because the moon must be new; so, it must really be dark in here and you couldn't see in front of you." "Now imagine being in a room like this one, and having to touch the people you talk to, to find out what their outstanding features are." "This is my life, here I don't live in darkness, and here I'm protected by the boundaries of my property."

"Will you touch me?" She asked.

"Careful, that's a loaded question." I chuckled.

"You know what I meant."

I put my hands up to her face and began feeling her. "I feel tears."

She pushed my hands away and I could feel her body start to quiver. She was crying the way she was when we were in the car, only she wasn't letting out her emotions.

"Bailey, a wise man once said that the hardest years of his life was his first one hundred." "It seems like life deals us one blow after the other." "You've already shown me your anger twice, and we only met today."

"What am I going to do?" She asked me.

"I think you have a hair band that's stretched." I gave her my opinion.

"So, you want me to be your little love flower, your boy toy?" She once again dispelled her anger.

"That makes three times now." I said to her to make her aware of her mental state of mind. "And no, that wasn't my intention; having any type of a relationship outside of business with anyone would be a huge mistake on my part." "Trust me." "The only outstanding feature people feel on me in the dark is my wallet."

"Are you speaking of all women in particular?" She asked with a calmer tone in her voice.

"No, I'm only referring to anyone that stands in front of me." I commented.

"Are you talking about me?" She asked.

"Where are you at?" I said to her.

"Kurt, I'm right here next to you, you know that." She answered.

"Then you're not in front of me, are you, you're beside me."

"So, you really do need someone to handle your affairs then." She commented.

"I need help." I repeated to her again. "I can't just pick up a telephone and tell them to give me a number to a business without knowing the business that I need the number for."

"You're asking someone to do the impossible" she lectured "no one can give you all those things you ask for, not even a wife." "You're asking someone to be on call twenty four hours out of the day, work all weekends, holidays, and vacations for you." She rebuked. "You'd have to pay good money for someone like that, but if you're willing to listen to my terms, we can negotiate a contract." "Or do I have to see five people for an interview before I can even get considered for the job."

I held my silence waiting for her offer.

"Kurt, I swear I didn't know anything about you before I went into Becky's." "And contrary to your perception, I'm not a whore looking to take advantage of a good opportunity; if I were, I'd take you for everything you have." "I'll work six months under probationary terms for one penny." "At the end of my probation, if you still wish to retain my skills, I request that my salary be doubled."

"Is that what your plan was on climbing a career ladder?" I asked.

"No, it was the can of peas, the dog food, and milk that got my attention." "I don't like sour milk either." "I agree" "it is disgusting and after I taste it, I don't want to drink milk again for a long time." "That's why I stopped at the gate." "I realized when I was upset, you would have been gone if my car would have started, but it didn't, and I found myself to be following you because I didn't want to get a ride back to my trailer, it's probably locked." "I'm still mad at you though for leading me on the way you did." "That was a low blow telling me you were a ward of the state." "I came in here to give you a fight, but those boxes over there put a stop to that." "Kurt, I'm tired, I worked my butt off putting that blankety blank through school." "And all the while he was putting his saddle on another horse while I was working to buy his books and pay his tuition."

"Did you love him, Bailey?" I asked her.

"Yeah" "When I came to work here, I kept telling myself that all my hard work will pay off when he graduated." "This house was the only thing that kept my dreams alive, but instead of his diploma, I went home and found an empty closet." "I shouldn't complain; he did help me lose fifteen pounds that week." "I didn't eat or sleep, all I did was cry." "I hated myself for being a fool and I swore that no man would ever do that to me again." "That's why I got mad at you when you played me, it reminded me of him." "But what really made me mad was I made it easy for you."

"I'm sorry Bailey." I stood up and felt her arm and took her hand. "Come with me." I said as I pulled her up.

I felt along the walls to guide me to the doors that entered my other rooms. After going through several rooms, I stopped. "Do you know where we're at?" I asked her.

"Kurt, it's dark."

"Bailey, we're in my scream room." "In the school I went to, a lot of the kids had problems dealing with the problem they had." "In truth, all they wanted to do was go home, but when they acted out by screaming, they always put them in a room to let them scream." "I know" "I was put in there every day for a long time." "You asked me when I was talking to you in your car, how I dealt with my problems." "This is my scream room, and this is where I go to fight back." "I scream as loud as I can scream, until I can't scream anymore." "Try it."

"I'm not going to do that." She said to me.

I let out several screams and she told me to stop it.

"Bailey, that's the only way I can let it go." "You cry" "I can't." "I grew up without a mother, and the only time I spent with my father was during a holiday, that is if he wasn't busy doing something else and he always was." "Me being diagnosed with a form of Autism gave him the impression that he couldn't talk to me like a normal kid." "Bailey if you weren't here, I'd still be screaming."

She screamed a small scream and I asked her if that was all the contempt, she had for him. Then she screamed a louder scream.

"I think you still love him." I said to her.

She began to let out loud screams and it only escalated from there. I sat down and leaned back against the wall and let her have her peace. When she sat down, she was crying, and when she became silent, I asked her if she felt better.

"I thought all that was behind me." She stated.

"Bailey, you'll never forget anybody that you loved." "Ten years, twenty years, fifty years, you'll still remember him, and you'll wonder what he's doing." "Is he still alive?" "Did he get married?" "How many children did he have?" "You'll always wonder about him." "One day, he'll remember you and he may try to find you." "Maybe he'll regret what he done and tell you how much he loved you."

"If he does, that'll be the first time." She remarked.

"How come you said you'd work for a penny?" I asked her.

"You deceived me." She replied. "I'm not interested in scamming you, I never was, if anybody is being scammed, it's me." "I'm not like those people you described; but I can see why you feel that way and I'm sure you've heard that before." "But the truth was I was willing to accept the agreement you wanted."

"Bailey I was desperate; I can't stand the silence." I said to her.

She began to speak "I'll tell you what, I'll propose a contract with a probationary period." "You can tell me to leave any time you want, or you can ask me to stay, no strings attached." "Those same conditions also apply to you." "If you turn out to be a pickup artist, heaven help you, I know where you live." "Kurt, you don't make moves on a girl, like you made to me." "You don't know anything about me, or anything about anyone else that you meet." "What if I did like to party, I could have a good time and act all proper when around you." "Besides you took my dream away." "As long as no one bought this house, it was still mine; I had hope on my side." "I would have worked sixteen hours out of the day, just to get to rent a room." "I'm not kidding you about four of my trailers being able to fit into them."

"What was the doctor like?" I asked her.

"I only seen him one week out of the month, the rest of the time he was traveling." "That's why I liked working for him." "His wife never bothered anyone; she was always looking for someone to talk to." "It was a look busy and you appear to be busy type of job, and I worked at my own pace." "When they got killed everyone was given a two week's severance pay." "Becky and I are the only ones that stayed here, everyone else got accustomed to the check, and they ended up moving."

"Becky!" I was surprised.

"She was your waitress today." "She owns the diner."

"I didn't know that was the owner."

"Yeah, when we got laid off, she took over ownership and her business hasn't blossomed as well as she had hoped." She said sadly. "These people that live around here are retired and their budgets are spent the first week of the month." "When I worked at Barneys, they had all kinds of sales to keep the customers from driving to Murray to shop." "The rest of the month was slow, that's why I worked part time, they cut my hours, so I thought it was the best time for me to get my education and look for a job in Murray." "Then you came along." "You know, this really bugs me, but if I would have said that I wanted fifty thousand a year, would you have paid that?" She asked.

"I would have said I'll double it." I told her.

"What if I said I wanted a hundred?"

"I would have said I'll double it." I told her.

"Oh" I heard her moan and with a shaky voice, she said. "And what if I said two hundred?" I felt her shaking.

"I would have said I'll double it."

"Why" she asked.

"If you ask a price and I give you double, you'll work twice as hard, you won't require supervision, you won't want someone to come in and undermine what you have." I told her. "You said the reason you came here was to work for the pay." "It was worth the drive, you said." "Now, you're under contract for one penny, but I'm a man of my word, so, I'm going to give you two pennies, for the first six months, and if I retain you, the next six months you'll earn double." "You've obligated yourself to a possible one year term young lady."

"Yeah, you would have made a great lawyer." She admonished. "Where did you sleep at last night?"

"Leaning against the wall, the way I am now." "That's why I was so desperate." "I need a good bed; I can't sleep without one." "So, I thought I would take my magic chic magnet into town and put it to use."

"Here" she said "lie down on the floor, and put your head in my lap." When I did, she put her arm over my chest and started telling me about her life "I lived with my mom till I was twelve, her boyfriend, now husband, was way too much loving for me, so I went to live with my father." "I lived there with him and my step mother until I met Tom, my boyfriend." "My stepmother wasn't a friendly type of woman so I didn't have much of a problem making a decision when Tom asked me to come with him." "He talked a good talk; he was good; he had me fooled." "By the way" she said "he's an amateur compared to you, you're a lot better talker than Tom ever was."

"How long have you been alone?" I asked her.

"Kurt, that's not something you ask a girl." She stated angrily.

I held my silence.

"Tom was my first love, and there hasn't been a romance in my life since he left." "All the boys around here are gone as soon as they graduate, and there's easy pickings if you like sixty year old's, they make the best husbands, all they want is someone to put them to sleep." She chuckled. She began to stroke my hair and feeling my face softly "I feel a smile." She said to me "That's good, I thought your face was glued on." "And you need to shave to." She then felt my cheeks and gave me a light slap. "You deceived me Kurt, you do it again and I won't use an open hand." "I can't work as close as you want me to work without knowing that you're being honest with me." "I won't know where to file all of the paperwork." She then started stroking my hair again "I was just thinking, what if it was me that had money?" "Would I believe you if you said that holding me makes your life complete?" "Kurt, my answer is no."

"I wouldn't know" I said "I've been accused of moving way to fast." "With you, I'm traveling in uncharted waters." "I'm trying to navigate through a channel that's got a lot of sandbars, and I don't want to run aground."

"You ought to run for president." She stated.

"I can't, you have to be thirty five; that leaves me with seven years to go." "You're twenty eight?" "How old do you think I am?" She asked.

"Let's see, you said you were seventeen when you came to Murray." "Usually, a degree takes four years if dedication is involved." "That would put you to be at least being twenty to twenty one maybe twenty two when your boyfriend skipped town." "When we met, you said you lived here for three years." "So, you would have to be a late twenty three or twenty four, or an early twenty five." "I'll take a chance and say that my guess is in a month or two you'll be twenty four."

"I'm impressed." She commented.

I heard her cell phone go off, and I sat up and leaned against the wall so she could take it out of her pocket.

"Hello" "hey beck" "no it wouldn't start" "no, everything's alright" "yeah, his names Kurt" "yeah, you saw him, he's the butt hole" "yeah, him" "no I'm alright, really" "yeah, I got laid off" "no, I don't need a place to stay" "okay, okay, bye." "That was Becky, she seen my car parked in the parking lot and she was checking in on me to see if I was okay." "She said to tell you, thanks for the tip."

"I think I owe her an apology" I said "when I went into her diner, I asked her if it was a restaurant and then I asked if there were others, I hope she didn't get the wrong idea."

"Becky is low key, she's hard to get mad, but when she's mad, I'd hate to be the one she's mad at." "She wouldn't hesitate to tell you to turn around and walk out the door you walked in." "If she didn't then you didn't say anything bad."

"It sounds like she's a good friend of yours." I said to her.

"She's more than that." "Every holiday, Becky would call me up to ask me to come over." "She knew I didn't have anywhere else to go." "The first time, I said no, soon after I heard a knock on my trailer and she told me to get in the car, she didn't have time for nonsense, she had her family at home waiting to eat." "The second time we were driving back over to her place, we got to talking and she told me she didn't like driving over to pick me up when I had a car." "She told me with that stare she gave me, that she didn't like to be turned down on her invitation." "Last Christmas, I got that perfume I wear from her husband, and she sewed me this dress I have on." "She knew I needed something to look good in for the interviews." "I couldn't buy them anything." "Kurt, every time I left their house, I'd get depressed."

"Bailey, what would you give me on Christmas?" I asked.

I didn't hear any reply.

"You have a way of twisting my focus from me to you." She expressed her thoughts. "What was yours like?"

"Oh!" "I had a nice dinner, and then I'd sit and listen to Christmas music, and fall asleep." I said to her.

"That's it?" "That was your Christmas?"

"Yeah" "I'd go into my scream room and unload all my anger." "I wanted to fight." I told her. "But all I hit was air when I swung."

"Where was your father at?" She asked me.

"My father traveled a lot." "I told you he made his fortune off of family law." "His clients were millionaires and billionaires." "Everybody has a lifestyle."

"So that's what you meant when you told me that." "Kurt" "tell me what you want for Christmas." I could hear a quiver in her voice.

"I want someone to sit down and eat dinner with." I told her. "In the school I went to, we didn't celebrate holidays." I could hear her crying so I put my arm around her shoulders in hopes of calming her. "When you get tired of crying, you end up with a face like mine and when people look at you, it looks glued on."

"Kurt, this isn't the way things are done, you don't run into someone, and an hour later, go home with him." She said trying to regain her composure. "They have names for people like that."

"I know" I said "they're called psychologist and they charge about five thousand more than the people you're talking about." "I need someone to talk to." "I told you that I find pleasure in your voice, I don't like being somewhere without knowing where I'm at." "I had troubles today, and it all started this morning when I walked out of this house." "I was lucky, I ran into a girl that talked to me, her voice brought me comfort and I didn't feel lost anymore." "Bailey, you have to live your life as if five years from now it's going to change, your boyfriend proved that." "I'm not anything like your boyfriend, everywhere I go, I go under someone's supervision." "And as far as you being a person that you described yourself as, my chances are heads you are and tails you aren't." "Do you have a coin I can flip?" "You'll have to do the flipping" "I can't"."

I eased her body up and kissed her. I then spoke softly. "I didn't mean to do that." I told her.

She gently kissed me back. "Why did you?" She asked.

"I wanted to find out what your lips really felt like." "That's the only way I can tell what a person looks like, by feeling."

"Me too." She said kissing me back.

She wrapped her arms around me and squeezed. I could feel her crying as I held her, so I held her snug.

She rested her crying and fell asleep in my arms. Time went by and she startled herself out of sleep.

"I'm still here Bailey." "You feel better?" I asked. "It's not a dream."

"Kurt."

"Bailey, we'll talk tomorrow, get some rest." I said, and squeezed her tight.

CHAPTER TWO

I could feel movement and I aroused from my sleep. "Now that you've had enough time to sleep on it" "Would you like for me to walk you back to your car, maybe it'll start?" I said to her.

"How did you know I was awake?" She asked.

"You breathe differently when you sleep." I answered.

"We're in the family room." She stated as she turned her head around to look. "The fireplace is in the corner." She put my hand out to show me the location she was referring to. I felt her moving in all different directions.

"Go ahead, run around and see what you want to see." I spoke to her softly.

"No, I'll walk and tell you what I see." "This is your house, but it's my dream." She commented.

She held my hand as we went from room to room describing the windows and making me feel what she was describing. When we got back down the stairs, I told her that I needed to change and get my utilities turned on.

"Where are your clothes?" She asked.

"In the boxes you tripped over last night." I told her.

She left me and when she came back, she took me by my arm and walked me to where they were. I heard her opening them up and then I didn't hear anything else.

"What's this?" She asked.

"I'm at a loss here." I told her.

"Your clothes; everything you have is blue except for your tee shirts." "You've got blue underwear, blue shirts and blue jeans." "Whoa, I was wrong, your socks are white."

"I can't tell you what color looks like." I informed her. "It's been described to me as being cool, hot, warm, soft, loud, fresh, outdoorsy, smooth, sizzling, fresh air, snow, calm, Bailey there's all kinds of adjectives I can give you, I only know one." "The problem I have is; I didn't know if I was wearing something cool along with the hot, or something soft along with the loud." "I don't know what blue looks like." "It was only described to me as the color of the sky." "I don't know what the sky looks like either." "To me there's only night."

I heard her sigh. "Kurt, did you kiss me for a reason, last night?"

"Yes"

"Did you mean to; because you can quit now before any of this goes any further." She spoke softly.

"Bailey, I'm sorry, but you gave me a contract of six months with the option of retaining you for double your wages." I told her. "I know some real good lawyers and I'm going to hold you to that obligation." "Bailey, you have eyes, you can see the person you're with." "You look for something in a man that meets what you require." "Your voice was mine; it gave me comfort and when it comes to judging someone, all I have is their personality to go by."

"It's your smile." She said to me. "You've got that Mona Lisa smile; it's hard to tell if you're smiling or if you're sad." "When you told me that you weren't married, I got the feeling you were letting me know it was up to me." "That's why I walked you over to Barney's; I wanted to spend a little more time with you." "Kurt, you really would have made a great lawyer." "If you had been my boyfriend instead of Tom, I would have worked harder to put you through school." "I watch T.V, and I see where rich people are being sued by their wife or husband, and you're right." "I know what's going on, I see it happening just the way you described it." "Kurt, I know what a prenup is." "I don't want your money; I swear I didn't know who you were or anything about this." "You can get with all of your lawyers and I'll sign anything guaranteeing you that." "I don't want a relationship with you or anyone else just to find out two or three years later, it's dissolved." "I want someone that'll keep me warm on a cold night, and the only person that's going to do that is the man that loves me." "Don't make me tell you I love you and then find out one day that you were playing me for a fool again."

"Bailey, you and I just met." I spoke to her calmly. "We could date for a set period of time, and then at some point make a decision on our future." "That's nothing but saying we'd like to get together every now and then and then go about our life at our own leisure." "I'm looking for someone to make my house a home." "I don't want that someone getting away from me just because we didn't go through a framework of formalities." "I don't care about your past; my concern is now, if I can take care of now, then tomorrow will take care of itself, today."

I felt her grabbing me around the waist and pulling my head down. She kissed me, and then took a deep breath and spoke "You have a way of talking that makes me melt." "Come on, get dressed." She said as she gave me my clothes.

I started working my way over to the wall to go into the other room.

"Stop" When I did, she walked over and gave me another kiss.

"Did you get your answer?" I asked her.

I heard her cell phone ring and then I heard her speak as I walked into the next room and changed.

"Hey beck" "no, no, Kurt" "yeah, we'll stop by" "maybe in an hour" "because we're walking and he lives outside of town" "alright, alright, alright, see you in a little bit."

She walked into the room where I was changing and pulled up my collar, and straightened out my belt.

"Kurt if any of your girl friends said you were cute, they weren't lying to you." "Now, kiss me and let's go."

We walked out of the door and she made sure it was locked. "You've got the key, right?" She said before shutting the door.

I handed it to her.

"I can't carry it; I might lose it." She said to me.

I put it back into my pocket and after we walked a way's she began telling me what the landscape looked like. "Kurt, I need a tractor, I need to mow, this property hasn't been kept up since Doctor Wilcox died." "It's going to take me a month." When we reached the gate, she opened it up and then shut it. I heard it open and shut again, and then again.

When she held my arm, she held it differently; she had more spring in her step. I reached down and found her lips; she had a smile on her.

"How come you didn't tell Becky where you were at?" I asked as we were walking.

"She was just calling to make sure I was alright." "I don't think she was happy about me going home with you though." She sounded concerned.

"Bailey, you didn't do anything to be ashamed of." I told her.

Late that morning we walked into the diner. "I have to use the bathroom." She said as she sat down, and then got up. I felt the seat move in front of me a few moments later.

"I don't know what's going on in that head of yours Mister." I heard Becky say. "That little girl went through quite an ordeal, and whatever is going on, I want you to put a stop to it, now."

"Ma'am, I apologize, but when she spoke about you last night, she had high praise about you in the words she used, and she told me that you aren't shy about expressing your feelings either." "I have to agree with her on that."

"Did she tell you about her boyfriend and what he done?" She asked.

"She told me that she put him through school, and got dumped for her efforts." I said to her.

"Did she mention what happened after that?" She followed.

"No"

"When he left, he took everything they had in the bank; it was almost five thousand dollars." "She had checks that bounced, her car was repossessed and she was thrown in jail." "It took her almost a year to get straightened out." "I got my eye on you, bozo." She said as she got up.

29

A few minutes later, Bailey sat down next to me and started reading the menu for me.

"Okay, what can I do for y'all, today?" Becky spoke in a friendlier tone.

"Kurt" Bailey said wanting to know what I wanted.

"I'll take a burger and fries and a glass of unsweetened tea." I said to her.

"I'll have the same Beck." Bailey said as she held my arm.

"Do they have a phone book?" I asked Bailey.

"Yeah, it's up on the counter."

"I need you to look up some numbers so I can get my utilities turned on, and I'll need a tow truck to haul your car off." "Bailey, I'm sorry, but I can't ride around in your car." "Yesterday when I sat down in it, I noticed you have a hole in the middle of the seat, and there's a spring in that hole." "I can't be chauffeured in a car with a seat that has a hole." "I have areas of comfort and areas of discomfort." "That seat gives me discomfort."

"Give me a minute." She responded.

When she returned, she was writing down the numbers I wanted to contact. I asked her to get the number of a limousine as Becky was setting our plates down.

"I'm sorry." "Did I just hear you say something about a limousine?" She asked.

"I have to have a ride, and Bailey's car doesn't run." "I need a ride to buy her a new car." I told her.

"Am I missing something here?" Becky said.

"Ma'am" I began "I don't hear any customer's conversations; and yesterday while I was here there were only two people and I came in here around dinner time and I stayed for thirty minutes give or take and no one came in." "You said that you depend on tourism for financial subsidence, but due to the drought, tourism is slow."

"It's a little worse than that." She stated.

"Well, Bailey said you worked for Doctor Wilcox as a cook, and I need someone that can cook for me and Bailey." I asserted.

She laughed. "Honey, I don't think you can afford me."

"Ma'am, when you get off tonight, go home and think about how much you're making here, operating this diner." "I'll be willing to bet that its break even or you end up paying out of your pocket to keep this diner open." "With me you'll get a paycheck." "Bailey negotiated on a contract with me too." "I'm offering you a job on Bailey's recommendation." "I need to hear your minimum offer."

"You're kidding me, right?" She said to me.

"I might be, but I need to hear a number before I can begin to negotiate." I told her.

"Honey, I don't know." She sounded confused.

"I understand." I said taking a bite of my hamburger.

"Are you serious." She asked with a curious voice.

"Let me know when you come up with a number." I stated to her.

"Well, for fifty thousand I'd close my doors now." She began laughing.

"That's awful stiff." I commented.

"I could go lower, a lot lower." She stated.

She started laughing again and I took a bite of my burger. "I'll double that offer," "you do cook a mean hamburger." I told her.

"You had me going there." She began laughing again. "You set the hook and reeled me in the boat."

"Becky" Bailey interrupted "listen to him, he's serious."

"Wait up a minute." She stopped talking and when she began, she stated. "This rides a little too fast for me; I'm starting to get dizzy."

"Becky" "yesterday Kurt asked me to help him furnish his house and get adjusted to Skinland." "He was going to pay my back rent, and get my car fixed so I could go to school and look for a job." "There wasn't going to be anything other than that." "I told him no, and he left." She stated to Becky.

"Okay" "And" Becky was urging her.

"I was in a tight spot and I needed some help, so I followed him to offer him my conditions." "We talked along the way, and when we walked by Doctor Wilcox's house, I stopped him and told him about us working for him."

"I'm following you." Becky told her.

"It turns out that Kurt bought Doctor Wilcox's place." She told her.

"And, you want me to cook for you, for a hundred thousand dollars a year?" Becky said.

"Yep" I said. "You'll be cooking for your family mostly, I don't ask for anything out of the ordinary, I want to eat what you feed your family." "I just need one meal a day."

"Can I ask you, why me?" She stated.

"Ma'am, I've learned that money can't buy loyalty, but it does offer me a solution." "I only want people around me that want to be around me." "I don't want those that don't want to be around me to be with me." "You exercised a thought earlier, now I'd like to give you a little insight about me." "Ma'am, I don't like being alone." "I told Bailey I was always supervised." "For the last three years, I had companions, they were trained to guide me wherever I went, but occasionally I met some people that didn't understand the law." "And there were others that had a fear of dogs." "But none of them companions could tell me how to get home if I became confused." "Can you remember when you found out when you fell in love with your husband, was it a week, was it a month, or was it a year or more after you met him?" I asked her.

"I don't know how to answer that." She remarked.

"I understand." I told her. "Ma'am, can you tell me when you fell "out" of love and then back "in" love with your husband?"

"That's not easy to answer either." She stated.

I then continued. "I told you I needed help; Bailey reached out her hand to give me that help yesterday because she felt shameful of the way she talked to me; she didn't know I was blind." "I would have found my way around sooner or later, but because of her help I didn't have any problems in finding two of the four resale shops, or two of the gas stations, and Barney's grocery store." "That leaves me with one other gas station and two more resale shops." "I don't have any interest in the real estate agents, or five of the banks." I said to her. "Bailey gave me information on obstacles that were in my path, that's when I knew I needed her, and I did my best to get her." "If it turns out that I made a mistake, or she made a mistake, then I can't understand why you can meet someone and fall in love with them without being able to remember when that happened." "I can tell you when you fell out of love, but I can't tell when you fell back in love." "Arguments sometimes hurt for months or years." "I need you, and Bailey was my eyes that led me to you." "Ma'am, we've been here for a while, no one has come in; I plan on making my house my home, so I don't look to be hiring another cook until you retire."

"Are you a lawyer?" She asked.

"No ma'am, but my parents were." I said to her.

"Bailey" she asked her "did he talk like this to you?"

"Worse Becky" she said to her.

"Honey, I think this man is the man I was looking for." Becky started laughing again. "Excuse me sweetie, I need to close these blinds and lock up." She said and then stopped before she started. "You're not pulling a prank on me, are you?"

"No ma'am"

After she finished, she walked back over to us and sat down across from us. "When do you want me to start?" She asked.

"I have to get my utilities turned on first, so will next week sometime be alright with you." I stated.

"What planet did you come from, Mars?" She asked.

Paradox

"Close" "New York" I told her.

"Kurt, about that discussion we had earlier when you walked in, I'd like to pretend that that never happened." She commented. "I'm curious though, you could have gotten me for less."

"I need help, bailey is my eyes." I told her. "If she hadn't have talked about you the way she did, I wouldn't be making you this offer." "I don't want someone looking for another job while working for me because they can't pay their bills with the check they get."

"I never thought I'd say this, but the hamburgers are on the house." "Alright, let's back up a little bit." "What's going on here?" She asked me.

"I have to have a bed; I feel stiff sleeping on the floor." I began "It's going to be four or five days before we start getting furniture, so I was thinking about checking out one of those resale shops." "We need a mattress and some blankets for right now."

"Don't worry about pillows and blankets, I have that covered." Becky said. "Finish eating and we'll see if they have a mattress somewhere." "If they don't, I'll drive you to Murray myself and get you one."

"Ma'am, I need to go to a bank and open an account."

"That's no problem." Becky replied. "What else?"

"I need to go pick up Bailey's clothes at her trailer, she doesn't have anything but the dress she has on."

"That's no problem." She said again. "What else."

"What does your husband do, ma'am?" I asked her.

"He works in Murray for a butcher." She said to me.

"In our talk last night, Bailey said Murray was fifty miles away and the money that Doctor Wilcox paid made it worth her while to drive that distance." "On the way over here, Bailey said she needed a tractor to mow the property." I began. "That made me think about plumbing and the maintenance on the pool and with the other things that can go wrong in the house, I need a maintenance man." "Do you think your husband will be interested for a hundred thousand too?"

"Honey, give me a minute." "I need to call my husband up and tell him to get his butt home now." "What's next?" She asked.

"I think our hands are going to be tied up, today." I told her.

When we walked out of her diner and she locked it up. Becky asked me where to first.

"A bank" I said "preferably one where you do your business at."

When we left, Bailey held my arm on my right side, and Becky held my arm on the left side.

33

I heard the door open and Bailey telling me to step up into the cab. I felt the seat and sat down; Bailey sat in my lap. A few minutes later Becky was pulling into a driveway. "This is the bank." Bailey said.

Both of them walked me in.

"Take me to where I can open an account." I said to her.

A few minutes later, I was being greeted by a woman that sounded pleasant but she was using a business way of speaking. Her voice had a bit of hostility to it.

"Can I help you?" She said as if I was keeping her from taking a break.

"I'd like to open an account please." I told her.

"We require a minimum of two hundred dollars to open an account." She had the same voice of hostility in it when she responded to me.

I heard a voice behind me greeting Becky.

"Miss Roberts" he said sourly "we're going to need a payment on the diner." I turned around to face him.

"I'm going to give you a little education, you won't like what I have to say." "There's a proper way of informing someone that a payment is needed, you don't mix business with others when a client is accompanied." "It's embarrassing and just plain rude." I told him. "Usually a letter is sent, and in an extreme situation a phone call is merited."

"Can I help you with something." I could hear his voice had irritation to it by my response I gave him.

"Yes sir, how much money did she borrow from you?" I asked him.

"That's none of your business." He said argumentatively.

"Ah, I can tell by the tone in your voice that you have a temper" I informed him "you really should learn how to control that temper." "You made it my business when you exposed her to be behind on a payment."

"Is everything all right here?" I heard another voice speak.

"May I ask who you are?" I stated.

"My name is Hurley, Herbert Hurley."

"May I ask what your position is in this bank?"

"I'm president of the bank." He informed me.

"Mister Hurley, I can't see, you can tell that I'm blind." "I do have ears though, and I can tell when someone speaks to me with an attitude what type of person they are." "I'm sorry, but I've met two of your people that have shown me that they aren't the person that they pretend to be, at least that's my perception." "This gentleman here and the lady behind this desk, I bet you lose a lot of your customers because of them." "Banking is a field where hospitality is a must, without it what do you have?" "I'm intolerant of verbal responses that give me an impression that I'm not worthy of attention, it makes me feel like I'm being a bother and wasting someone's time." "Miss Roberts told me that there were six banks here, so I imagine that this is a branch of a larger bank." "I prefer to do business with a bank that has friendlier people that can do business the way business is supposed to be done." "These two people here have shown me that this isn't the bank I was looking for." "I was looking to buy her business, but this gentleman here stated that she was behind on a payment, and that makes me worried, why would I want to buy a business when I hear a banker tell me that a person is behind on a payment." "That type of information should be reserved in a private conversation." "That tells me that the diner can't support itself." "You were going to get your money, but now I'm having second thoughts about buying her business." "Mister Hurley, I wish you a good day." I told him. "Miss Roberts, could you take me to another bank please?" I said to her.

I turned and began to find my way out when Bailey and Becky grabbed my arms and began leading me. I felt the breeze from the door as it opened and Mister Hurley met us at Becky's truck before we got in.

"Can I have your name?" He asked.

"Kurt Bryant." I told him.

"Mister Bryant, I'm sorry about what went on in there." He said to me. "Misses Roberts I'd like to extend my apologies on the banks behalf for the discomfort you just experienced." "Mister Bryant, if you give me a chance, I'm sure we can get off on a better foot, if you'll let me." He said to me.

"I don't think that can happen." I told him. "You have people here that I find to be disrespectable." "I can't do business with a business that has people like that working for them." "It gives me an impression that if my accusations are correct then everyone in this bank has complications when working with people like that, and I really find that to be an environment that I don't feel comfortable in." "Miss Roberts told me business was slow due to tourism being down." "Bailey here walked me around and gave me an idea of how big this town is." "I don't see where loans are being made, and I can't see where six banks are needed." "That means competition for an account to be opened is one out of six." "Sir, I've only met three people in your bank, and two of them have persuaded me to look elsewhere." "How can I trust a bank with my money with people like that working for them, you can see my demise." I said to him.

"Mister Bryant, I can assure you, you won't be dealing with either one of them." He told me. "The actions that they displayed to you are not the policies of this bank." "Becky" I said "this is your call." "Do you want to go somewhere else or do you accept Mister Hurley's apology."

"I'm alright." She said to me.

"Alright Mister Hurley, I'll give you that chance, but if I'm wrong, another bank will be holding my account."

We walked back into the bank and he led us to his office.

"Have a seat please." He stated. "Now, how much did you want to deposit."

"Ten million."

He started chuckling. "I deserved that." "Now, how much did you want to deposit?"

"Ten million" I repeated.

"Excuse me a minute please." He stated calmly. "Miss Maxwell, would you please send Mister Jackson and Miss Atkinson in please."

I heard over his intercom that the two people he sent for was in her office.

"Send them in." He spoke to her.

"John, Brenda," he said as they were standing in front of his desk "this is the third time that I've had a talk with you." "Mister Bryant here has brought it to my attention that that's three times too many." "I'm sorry but Mister Bryant's right, banking is in a field of hospitality, you're fired."

When they left, I gave him a card and told him that I needed him to call that number so I could transfer some money into my account. "Take what Miss Roberts owes you out of my account and give me ten thousand in one hundred dollar bills." "I need a little spending money." "And Mister Hurley, I need to buy a car." "Is there someone I can contact to take care of the transaction?"

"I'll handle this personally." He said to me. "This is my cell phone number, and my home phone number." "If you're ever in need of anything and I do mean anything, please don't hesitate to give me a call."

"I appreciate your courtesy Mister Hurley." "Becky was right about this bank." I said to him.

When we left, Bailey guided me to the truck. We sat there for a minute until Becky started talking.

"I can see why Bailey went home with you." She said to me. "You are one quick thinker." I then heard the truck start up. "Where to now?" Becky stated.

"I need a mattress, and Bailey needs her clothes, and then, if possible, maybe we can drive into Murray and get Bailey a car." "That way I can get my utilities turned on, and we won't be dependent on you."

"Honey" she said "you ain't bothering me none at all." "To me this is a vacation." "I've been running that diner a little over a year, seven days a week

Paradox

from six in the morning till nine at night, and this is the first time I haven't been gone from it during the day for more than thirty minutes." "You go right on ahead and bother me all you want to."

After finding a mattress we headed over to get Bailey's clothes. She was right, her trailer was locked up. I heard footsteps approaching us and then a voice telling her that everything in the trailer belonged to him, and for her to get back in her car and get off of his property.

"I came here to pay her back rent, and get her clothes." I told him.

"She owes six hundred, and if I don't get six hundred in my hand, she don't get nothing in that trailer." He used an authoritative voice towards me.

I handed my wallet to Bailey. "Bailey, give the man what you owe him." "And if you have a purse, get it." I said to her.

I stood against the truck as they loaded clothes into the back seat.

"Take only what you value, you won't need anything else." I told her.

A little while later we were headed to Murray to get Bailey a new car. I pulled out my wallet and handed the money to Bailey.

"What's that?" She said sitting in my lap.

"If you can't see its money then you're blinder then what I am." I told her.

"I can see that!' "What's it for." She asked.

"Every time I go anyplace for whatever purpose it's for, I put my ones in my left pocket, my fives in my right pocket, my tens in my left back pocket and my twenties in my back right pocket." "I never carried hundreds." "This way, I don't have to worry about my change; you'll take care of that for me."

"What kind of car do you want?" Bailey said hugging me tightly.

"You're the one that's going to be driving it." I told her. "But I would like a car that has plenty of legroom, so that leaves out a compact or a sports car." "I'd like something that has leather seats and storage room in case I buy something bigger than what I can put in the trunk, yet able to fit inside the back of the car." "I want you to think along the way to Murray as cars pass, if you would like to own that one." "Or remember about you parking in back because the cars that were parked in front of Doctor Wilcox's house cost about sixty thousand more than the one you drove." "That's the kind of car, I'd like too." "And Bailey, please don't buy something cheap."

We pulled into a driveway and ran across some bumps in the road. When we got out, I heard a man come up and introduce himself. He began his friendly chat with us and asked if we were looking for anything in particular.

"You see anything you like Bailey?" I asked.

"I like everything." She stated. "Can you give us a minute?" She told the salesman.

Bailey and Becky began walking me around the lot and explaining what all of the cars looked like.

After I felt a few of them, I asked. "Are these the kind of cars you like?" "Or are you thinking about the cost." "Bailey, I want to ask you a question, what car do you not see in Skinland?" "That's the car you should be driving." "You get what you pay for." I said to her.

"Come on Becky, I think I know what he wants." She stated.

Soon we were pulling into another parking lot, and another man introduced himself to us.

"I want to see something in luxury with plenty of room in the rear, with more of a SUV style to it." Becky said.

A man walked us over to where the cars were at that Becky asked to see. I felt them and asked Bailey if she liked what she saw. "I like the way the fifth one felt." "It feels spacious." I told her. "Do you like it?"

It's beautiful she answered.

"How much is it?" I asked the salesman.

He started laughing. "If you have to ask how much it is, then you can't afford it."

"That may be, but I still need to know how much it's going to set me back." I told him.

"Let's just say, after your down payment, you'll be spending your social security check and having to find a job to pay for it."

"That much huh?" I said to him.

"Bailey, is this car the one you like?"

"Yes"

"Then we need to go inside and talk to the manager and see if we can come up with some kind of a deal." I told her.

I heard the man's footsteps walking behind me, I stopped and turned around. "We won't need you." "I asked you questions and you didn't give me answers." "Bailey, find someone and tell them that I'd like to speak to the manager."

A short time later, we were introduced to another gentleman.

"May I ask what title you pose to this business?" I asked.

"I'm the sales manager." He responded.

"Well sir, my names Kurt Bryant." "I need to buy a car for a girl." "I'm trying my best to show her that I need her." "She's chosen the car she wants, and when I asked your salesman how much it was." "His response was if I had to ask then I couldn't afford it." "I asked again, and his response was, let's put it this way, by the time I put down a down payment, I would be spending my social security check and have to find a job to pay for it." "I don't like people wasting my time, he's got all day to spend here; I don't." "Judging by the size of this town, I would imagine that there are other dealerships that sell the same car as you do." "I need to know how much the car is that I want to buy before I buy it." "It's the little things that matter to me." "Do I need to ask your boss to help me, or should we go find a dealer that can?" I said to him.

"No sir, if you'd please show me the car, I'm sure we can help you." He said apologetically.

"I'll show him." Becky offered.

When they walked off Bailey hugged my arm.

"I liked the way you talked about me." She said to me.

"Are you starting to fall in love with me?" I asked her.

"I can't explain it." She replied. "Yesterday I met you, my car wouldn't start and I go home with you." "The next day I find you buying me a new car." "And I find that disturbing." "Kurt, it's not supposed to go this way."

"Bailey, let's just say you had all the money you needed to buy anything you wanted." "What dreams would you have left?" "I don't like being alone." "If ever the day was to come that I find you to wanting to be somewhere else, I'll know, I don't need my eyes to know what's going on." "I'm not trying to buy you." "I need you." I told her.

"You know I thought Becky was someone that I wouldn't want mad at me, I don't think she would be anything compared to you." "You tell people what you think." She said to me.

"It's your money until you give it to them." I told her. "Businesses are only open to do business with customers." "If they want your money they will tend to your needs." "You can always go somewhere else and get what you want and I can guarantee you one of them will be more than happy to provide you their full attention."

We were interrupted by Becky and the gentleman.

"If you give me a few minutes I can work up some plans." He stated.

"I only need to know the bottom line in cash." I told him.

After a few minutes he gave me a quote. "I can't let it go for less than sixty seven thousand." He stated.

"Is it ready to go?" I asked.

"Give me thirty minutes or so and it will be."

I pulled out my wallet and asked bailey to call Mister Hurley's telephone number and let this gentleman and Mister Hurley finalize the paper work.

"I'm going home and get my husband." Becky said. "I'll meet you at your house and drop off Bailey's clothes and the mattress."

I reached in my pocket and handed her the keys. "You'll probably be there before we will." I told her. "Take a look around." "I imagine you didn't get to see much of the house from the kitchen." "Besides, if your husband wants the job, he's going to want to look around and see what he's getting into."

Bailey led me over to sit down on a sofa and then sat next to me.

"You asked me if I had enough money to buy anything I wanted to buy, what would I buy." "I always thought if I had money, I'd buy a yacht or a big house or I'd get this or I'd get that." "I didn't put any thought into a man." "After what Tom did to me, I didn't want anyone." "At least, that was what I was feeling when I had those thoughts of having money." "Kurt" "I never thought of myself as being a Cinderella losing her glass slipper." "I tried kissing frogs, but all I got was warts." "Skinland was the last place that I thought I would ever find someone; especially when I swore, I'd never put myself in that position again." "Now you come along and screw up all of those plans." "Being rich never entered my mine." "I wanted someone to love me." "That's all."

"Do you believe in love at first sight?" I asked her.

"That's an unusual remark coming from someone like you, don't you think?" She responded.

"Let's say that me and you were real good friends" I began "we'd be able to talk with one another, and we'd be able to go places and share our laughs with each other." "Now, imagine us as enemies, we wouldn't want to be around each other." "One day, you'll have those kinds of feelings about me." "Being with someone like me is like having an anchor tied around your neck."

"Then we'll have to deal with that day when that day comes then, won't we." She spoke softly. "And as far as me believing in love at first sight, I didn't believe in that." "Now I don't know what I believe in." "You changed my life; how can I top that?" "You changed Becky's life, she was looking at bankruptcy, but you came in and gave her and her husband a future." "You can't just come in someone's life and make changes the way you do without those people wanting to repay you somehow." "Kurt" "you have a way of forcing yourself on someone."

"You are repaying me, only you don't know it." I told her "You're helping me get through a rough period in my life." "A prisoner lives in a cell." "Mine happens to be a little bit bigger." "You can look at it one way though." "Whenever we're out shopping and we eat at a restaurant, we'll be on a date." "I'm sorry but if the food doesn't turn out to be any good, it'll be your fault, you're the one that chose the restaurant."

I got poked in my arm for that comment.

Paradox

"I think the man is coming with our keys." She said becoming excited. Ten minutes later we were headed back home.

"You need to stop at Barneys and pick up some candles, that way you'll be able to find your way around tonight." I told her.

"What do you think?" She asked.

"It feels comfortable; I don't feel confined like I felt in your car." "The ride is smooth and quiet, and there isn't a spring poking me in the butt." "You like it, Bailey?"

"You don't know how many times I saw cars like these parked in front of Doctor Wilcox's and made wish after wish." "Barneys did pretty good when the doctor was home." "They entertained other Doctor's and I even seen a couple of people that had body guards with them." "It feels strange driving it; I mean we can live out of this car if we had to." "Kurt, I keep asking myself over and over and over again." "Why me?"

"Last night" I began "you were sleeping in my arms." "I felt something."

"Kurt, you don't know me; that takes time." She reminded me.

"The car is worthless to me if you're using me." I told her. "Bailey, do you think of yourself as being beautiful?" I asked.

"What kind of question is that?" She stated to me.

"Let's say you met up with a man and he and you got married." "He bought a car and you had to use it in order to take care of the family needs." "Is there any difference between using a family car to handle the odds and ends you meet every day, and using the car you're driving now?" "Now, do you think of yourself as being beautiful?" I asked her again.

"No"

I smiled. "There's one good thing about a blind man." "You don't have to wear makeup around him." "That should make any woman happy."

"Kurt, stop talking like that." "Do you move this fast with everyone?" She asked me.

"You're the first." "All the women that talked to me had a price; and because I was blind, I was offered a handicap discount." "No pun intended." "I need you to ask yourself this question." "Out of all the girls that live in Skinland, how many of them would take advantage of this situation?"

"I can't answer that, I don't know." She said to me.

"Then can you name me one that wouldn't?" I followed.

"No"

"Then that means I can't be with anyone that lives in Skinland." "I might as well have all my groceries delivered to me at the gate to be picked up." "That way I wouldn't have to socialize with anyone at all." "I like Becky, maybe I could get her to drive me around and take care of the little things I need to do." "But when you kissed me last night after I kissed you, I felt something from you, and I was hoping what I felt was an end to my past." "I'm the last Bryant, it ends with me." "When you met me, I was wearing Jeans and a button up shirt that didn't even have the buttons buttoned up right." "You didn't know me either, and you took a chance that I would honor my words."

I felt her driving slow.

"What's the matter?" I asked.

"There's a tractor on the road and he doesn't have a place to pull over." She responded. "People are passing him in no passing zones." "The problem is, there's six cars behind the tractor waiting for the tractor to get out of the way." "So, when they pass, they have to pass six cars and the tractor."

"What are you going to do?" I asked.

"I'm not in a hurry." She commented. "We're going to be the seventh in line behind the tractor" and after a short pause she exclaimed "I'm quitting school."

"When did you decide this?" I asked.

"Last night." "I was thinking with me going to school, I'd be gone from you all day." "Kurt, I don't want to be a mother hen around you." "I don't want you to think you can't breathe."

"Bailey, when Tom kissed you, was he a good kisser?" I asked.

"At first, he was, but after a while he got to where he didn't kiss me anymore."

"Tell me what you felt when I kissed you." I said to her.

"Why do you want to know that" I heard silence for a while. "Kurt, you're talking like a lawyer again." "And in case you're wondering, I could have pushed you back, but I wanted more." "Something's wrong up ahead" she said "I see about six cop cars."

We slowed down and I heard the window being rolled down on my side. When we came to a stop, Bailey asked what happened.

"A blowout, he ended up going off the lip of the road and that caused him to crash into a tree." "It's going to take a few minutes." He said to her. "They're cutting the tree up to remove it from the road now."

"Is he okay?" I asked.

"I'm not supposed to reveal that kind of information sir." "You'll have to call the Sheriff's department."

When we finally got started, Bailey drove slowly and gave me a description of what the scene looked like.

"I don't think anyone can live through something like that." "Usually, that only happens after a rain." "People come from a big city to go fishing, and they drive like they're on a super highway, they end up hydroplaning and going off the lip of the road and when they hit that gumbo mud, they slide right into those trees." "I know, that happened to me, except I didn't hit a tree so, now I drive like the rest of the old people here, ten miles under the speed limit." "This road has crosses everywhere." "We're coming into town." "Barney's is right up the road."

"There's going to be another cross put there." I said to her.

"How do you know that?" She asked.

"That cop would have told me that he was all right, if he was." I replied to her.

We pulled into a parking spot that was close to the entrance. I heard several people commenting to her about her car. When she took my arm, she held me close. Several times she was stopped and chatted with the people that worked there. When we got to the checkout counter the checker commented about seeing her car.

"Where'd you get that thing?" She said to her.

I interrupted the conversation. "College helps you to find a better job, a better job means better pay, and better pay means better cars." I said as we began to walk out the door to the car.

"You handled that pretty good." She said as I was buckling up.

"Bailey, you aren't the person who you think of yourself as." "If I can't trust you, who can I trust?" "Do you know what a confidante is?" I asked her.

"I think so." She answered.

"You have Becky as a friend, and being a friend, you talk to her about a lot of things." "A confidante is a person you can talk to and tell them things that you wouldn't even tell Becky."

"Am I a confidante to you?" She asked.

"That's a question that only you can answer, but I've never been happier than when I'm with you." "I've never kissed someone the way you kissed me." "One reason is because I've never had a girlfriend." "They were like Tom was to you." "Your lips aren't cold, a girl that kisses you good night after going to a dinner don't kiss you like they have feelings for you." "Their kiss feels more like, I had a good time and you never see them again." "No pun intended." "You're the first girl that's kissed me with feelings." "Your lips felt warm."

I heard the car start up and felt us backing up and then moving forward.

"Kurt, I need to know if you think you could learn to love me." She asked me.

"I could, but I'm like you, I don't want to fall in love with a girl that doesn't love me." "I love you, but I don't know if you love me." I told her.

"What do I have to do to prove it?" She asked me.

"That's not an easy answer to give either." "My father handled a lot of divorces where the people had been married for thirty years." "And he handled some where they were married for fifty years." I commented. "I think that's a good number." "If we don't make it fifty years then it's clear, you weren't in love with me." "If we're together longer than those fifty years than I'll apologize for being wrong." "Bailey, I know life is full of surprises, I don't like facing surprises, sometimes they're hard for me to deal with, I'm like you; I only want someone if that someone wants me." "I'm willing to renegotiate our contract and propose to you a fifty year contract." "I don't like spending money training new people."

"Kurt, do you understand anything that you just said to me?" She asked. "We don't know each other." "Damn" "you've got a way with words."

"I'm ready now to take a chance in life" I said "I thought I said that I needed "you"." "I understand people a lot better than you think I do." "Sometimes you just have to throw caution to the wind and let the apples lay where they fall."

I felt the car pulling over and come to a stop. Bailey opened the door and got out and shut the door. I heard my door open and she began kissing me. "I need someone to explain to me what's happened in my life." I then felt my door shut, and when she got in, we continued on our way. "Kurt, you don't know how long it's been since I've felt this good" she began "when I lost my boyfriend everything kinda went south on me." "I moved in with Becky and her family until I found a trailer to rent, I don't know where I'd be now if it wasn't for her." "That was a nice thing you done, give her and her husband a job."

"Bailey, I need to know something." "How long does it take for a person like you to know when they fall in love?"

"That depends on who's asking." "But I'm taking it as if you were referring to you." "Kurt, I can't take a step without you saying something or doing something that knocks me off of my feet." "Anyone else I would have said hit the road." "But you move fast, too fast, and that scares me." "I find myself clinging to you because I let myself fall in love with you already." "We're here." She said pulling in. "I can see Becky's truck parked in front." "They're unloading my clothes and the mattress."

We came pulling up and I heard voices getting closer to us. Becky's kids were opening the doors and getting inside feeling of the interior. Becky was scolding them. I got out and told Becky to let Bailey take everyone for a ride. She argued, but I won.

Her husband stayed behind with me.

"My name's Buchwald" "folks around here call me buck for short." He said to me.

"I'm Kurt." I told him extending my hand out.

He took me by my arm and led me over to the truck to have a seat.

"My wife called me up today and told me to get home, that's all she said, was come home." "I got scared and asked if everything was all right, she said nothing was wrong, but to come home now." "I went to the diner and it was closed, that really made me get worried, she ain't never done that before." "I waited outside on the porch for the kids to come home from school and then I saw my wife driving down the road to the house." "She told the kids to get in the back of the truck and off we went." "On the way here, she told me about the offer you gave her." "I was feeling good, and then she said you wanted me too for the same price." "I'm a grown man Kurt; I came close to busting out in tears." "You can hire three people for that."

"Buck, I'm curious, is everyone around here a bubba, a buck, or a brother?" I asked.

"Naw, I got buck teeth, so most folks got to knowing me by buck." He said laughing.

"I'm sorry; I didn't mean to be offensive." I said with shame.

"You needn't be; I learned how to fight that way." "Becky always called me Buck because she heard other people talking about me and she thought it was my nickname, so I tamed down a little." He said to me.

"Well buck, I bet if I can hire three people for what I pay you, then I bet you'll give me more than those three people combined, it seems like the money just isn't enough for some people" "Your wife said you worked for a butcher, so you must be a butcher." I stated to him.

"Yeah, I made my overtime during deer season." He informed me. "It bought the kids their Christmas presents."

"Are you happy there?" I asked him.

"I live payday to payday." He replied.

"This job I offer" I began "if I was to hire three people for what I'm willing to pay you; then it would seem to me that my offer would be good enough to get you here." "Or maybe not having to drive a hundred miles a day would persuade you." "Here, you work at your pace, and rest, and work, and rest." "The only person that will supervise you is your wife."

"My wife told me to watch out when I talk to you." "She said you were slick." "I don't have the words." His voice was shaking.

"Buck, I prefer a family atmosphere around me." "I don't think you would like it if a lot of people worked for you that came and went out of your house." "I didn't." "No one tells anyone what to do, if something needs to be done; then it'll get done." "Bailey says this is a big house and that means big problems, you can oversee contractors for me, the swimming pool and hot tub needs cleaning." "You know how to contact the right people for that." "I've got sixty seven acres that need to be mowed and when I took a walk around to get a feel of the place, I found out that I need to clear some brush and some trees." "I never had a fireplace where I came from; I made sure there was one here before I even considered it." "I heard a boy's voice earlier." I said to him. "How old are your kids?"

"Ronnie's seventeen, Julies thirteen, and Cindy's nine." He answered.

I heard the sound of a car pulling up and girls laughing and doors slamming.

"Daddy it's got a television in the back seat." Judging by the voice it was the youngest.

"Ronnie" I said out loud.

"I'm right here sir." He said walking over to me.

"Can you drive a tractor?" I asked him.

"Yes sir, I used to bale hay." He answered.

"Have you ever operated a chain saw?" I then asked.

"Yes sir."

"I was telling your father about this house being built on sixty seven acres." I started a conversation with him. "The real estate agent said it was heavily wooden." "I found that to be true." "I need someone to mow my property, and I need firewood, and I need this land cleared of brush so I can walk around." "It's got a catfish pond out back somewhere, and I don't know what shape it's in." "I need someone I can trust, if it's alright with your mother and father, I'd like to offer you five hundred a week to clean this place up the way it's supposed to look like." "Your hours will be after school till six o'clock, and Saturday eight o'clock till four o'clock." "Sunday will be your day off." "In summer you'll work eight a.m. till four p.m., Monday through Friday, Saturday and Sunday will be your days off, and I'll pay a thousand a week." "Will that work for you?" I asked him.

"Mister Bryant." "I don't need to talk to my mother and father." "I'll do it." He answered.

"Ronnie, I don't want people to get in a hurry working." "I asked if you can operate a chainsaw, they scare me." "I don't want you getting an arm cut off because you were careless." "I asked you if you knew how to drive a tractor." "People get killed on them." "Your father said you're seventeen, and you're a young man." "When you work like a man, you act like a man." "That means you respect all equipment you use; those that don't, have missing fingers and arms to show you how not to do something." "Do you have a license?" I asked him.

"Yes sir."

"Do you have transportation?" I added.

"No sir" "I ride the bus home." "My mom can come get me though." He said to me.

"I don't know about that; I need your mom and your dad here." "I'll tell you what; I'm going to need several vehicles for different reasons." "Bailey's car is Bailey's car." "So that means we'll have to get you something of your own to drive." "Your mother and father will be busy here, so that means the best way to do this is have you pick up your sisters at school and bring them all over here, that way your mother doesn't have to pack everything up to take home and feed you, she can cook and clean up in one sitting instead of doing it twice." "Ronnie, when you pick out a truck, I want it to be new, and I want you to like the way it feels." "You're going to be taking it home with you and you'll be taking your sisters to school every morning and picking them up, there won't be any more busses rode on." "Are we in agreement?" I said to him.

"Yes sir."

"How are you doing in school?" I asked him.

"I'm a B average." He stated.

"Bailey and I are going to the utility companies tomorrow, and I need a phone." "If it's alright with your parents, I'd like to get that truck tomorrow, so that means you'll have to miss a day of school." I said to him.

I heard silence.

"I think under the circumstances you can miss one day." Becky answered.

"Can I do something too?" I heard one of the girls.

"You must be Julie?" I said looking down. "I was thinking about finding some help for your mother." "She's got a lot on her hands." "What with cooking an all, she doesn't have time to clean up after herself." "Dishes need to be washed and pots need to be scrubbed." "That's a job there in itself." "But, I'm willing to pay someone good money."

"I can do it." She said to me.

"I was thinking about paying someone two hundred dollars a week to do that." "That's a lot of money." I stated to her.

"I can do it." She repeated excitedly.

"You do know that your mother is the boss when it comes to the kitchen; that means when she gives you an order, you don't question what she asks of you." I told her. "You don't work for me; you work for her." "That means no arguments and no whining." "Restaurants are run by chefs that tell others what to do, here, your mother is the head chef."

"I know." She said to me.

"Alright, it's settled then, I have that out of my way." "Give me your hand and we'll shake on the deal." I told her.

After we shook our hands the youngest one asked if there was something she could do.

"I gave that some thought." I told her. "With everybody working around here, the air gets dusty and I'm allergic to dust." "I'm going to need someone to wipe down my tables and all my other furniture." "I can pay a hundred dollars a week for that." "But sometimes your mother may need some extra help, like taking out trash, or making sure your homework is done." "A big girl doesn't need anyone to tell them that homework is first." "So, if your grades start dropping, I'm going to have to start looking for someone that can handle school work and their job here." "Do you think you can handle it?" I asked her.

"Yes sir"

"Alright, give me your hand and we'll shake on it." I told her.

"Okay everybody, we need to get the truck unloaded." Becky told them.

I heard talking and then there was quiet.

Becky held me back, while Bailey clung to me. "That was a nice thing you did for my son." Becky said.

"When Bailey and I met, she said that all the boys her age moved after they graduated." I explained. "There weren't any jobs around here to keep them here." "Boys that move away get married and then move to wherever they can find a job to raise a family." "Boys that can find a job that supports a family locally tend to marry locally and that means grandchildren are always nearby." "Boys that move away work holidays and the time will come where you'll not see your son the way you see him now." "Giving him something to do, and paying him, makes a boy think hard about moving away." "Your son is at the age where having a job and a truck is important to him." "Judging by the way he was talking, I don't think I was wrong, I think he'll make a good man." "Becky, he's reaching an age where a mother begins to lose her control over her baby." "To me, he's in training for a promotion when he reaches that age."

"Bend down a little." She said kissing me, and then walked away.

"Becky's crying." Bailey said. "Kurt, are you an angel?" "Did God send you here?"

"I was asking God if he sent you to me." I told her. "Yesterday I was alone, now I have people around me, meeting you changed my life too." "That's why I moved here, I had to find my life." "Bailey, it takes more than furniture to make a house a home." "I read some articles where people meet each other on the internet, and get married." "Today, men still marry mail order brides, they don't know anything about the women they marry either." "I need you." I said to her.

CHAPTER THREE

"I see everything is up and running." Becky said. "I've got to go get groceries and get stocked up; you're going to need everything, and I do mean everything."

"Stop by the bank on your way." I told her. "Mister Hurley has three cards for "you", "Buck", and "Ronnie"." "Whenever you need anything like pots and pans, dishes, silverware, groceries, gas or whatever." "Use the card." "If you have to drive to Murray for any reason, use the card for whatever you need."

"Is there anything special you want?" She asked.

"I'm partial to a good cup of hot cocoa." I told her.

"You don't want much, do you?" She replied. "You buy my son a truck, and now, I don't have to go into his room five times to get him up to go to school." "He's up as soon as the alarm rings and rushing his sisters to get dressed so they could go." "You know I walked in on him yesterday, he was talking to a girl on the phone." "That's the first time I've ever seen that happen." "You were right, a job and a truck change's a boy's life."

"If you had a talk with him, do you really think he would listen?" I said to her. "I think this is one of those times that you have to let Ronnie handle things his way, he's grown up and sitting on a ledge, he's changing into a man." "Becky, I don't think anyone would have been able to tell you anything different when you were his age, to you, you were a woman, and as a woman, you were of mind to do what you thought was best." "I bet you had words with your parents on that subject." "Don't be upset when he has those same words you used on your parents aimed at you." "He's a good kid." "He's well mannered and polite." "I don't know if a parent can teach a child that, I think sometimes it's who they are, it's their character." "He's a hard worker; and hard worker's end up with girls by their side."

"Where's Bailey at?" She asked.

"Taking a shower" I said "when the water was turned on yesterday, we ran it for a while because she said it looked rusty." "I think she thinks the water is dirty, so she's trying to wash the water from last night off of her." "So, you might want to let the water in the kitchen run a little more today." "I did all the bath rooms and sinks and the commodes." "But I don't know if I did any good or not; I don't know where all the faucets are." I told her.

"I'll tell buck to get to work on it." Becky stated.

I sensed she was tight, and I wanted to clear the air with her. "Becky, I know a lot of this has been strange to you." "I had trouble when I talked to Bailey, and knowing Bailey being friends with you, I'm pretty sure you and her have had your talks, so I think you think some of the things that

Bailey thinks." "She asks why me." "So, I'm thinking that maybe you have asked that same thing yourself or something close to it." "I told Bailey I led a sheltered life with constant supervision." "I grew up with people always around me." "Bailey thinks I'm using my money to buy her." "That's not true." "And it's not true with you either, you give me an answer and it's what you feel." "The people that were around me never spoke their mind." "They guarded their conversations." "Those people got paid to pamper their clients, not infuriate them." "People, who showed hostility in their field instead of hospitality, didn't stay employed very long." "Because of my attitude as a child, I was more or less protected from other children." "Being born premature, I was diagnosed at a young age of having a form of autism." "They were wrong, but I was kept away from other kids because of my attitude." "Talking to Cindy is like talking to a fifteen year old." "She's smart." "If your husband hadn't have told me she was nine, I don't know if I could have caught on right away." "Julie, she's different, she's bored, I don't think she'll be working for two hundred a week for long, I think she'll hit me up for a raise soon." "That brings us to Ronnie." "I wanted to know what I looked like to other kids when I was seventeen too." "I can't feel my face and give you an answer, it just isn't there." "Ronnie is asking the same questions, what do girls think of me?" "I'm thinking that Ronnie may already have a girl that's working her way in." "Kids talk and Ronnie could be at the top of the topic that's circulating through his school, right now he's getting attention." "Judging by the size of this town, I would think everybody knows everybody." "He could be experiencing a moment where he could be the most popular kid in school, or even in this town." "I'm not used to having people around me, but what you don't see is, I like being around all of you." I went on to say. "I know no matter how anyone looks at this situation, I guess I'll always be an employer." "I don't really like handing out paychecks, it seems to say, don't bite the hand that feeds you." "That doesn't apply to kids; they want to see that cash put in their hands every week, not a check." "I told Mister Hurley to transfer two hundred thousand into your and your husband's account." "That way you can manage your money the way you want to."

"You didn't have to do that." She said to me.

"I know Becky, I told you I don't want anyone here that doesn't want to be here." "And I told you that I need you." "I meant that."

"You do know that Bailey is in love with you, right?" She stated.

"We were two starved puppies fighting over a bone." I replied. "Becky, I really didn't want to get involved with someone." "I have an issue, but I like it when she holds my hand." "I like it when she laughs, but she seems to fight that back."

I felt a kiss on my lips. "I heard that." Bailey commented.

"How long have you been standing there?" I asked her.

"Long enough to hear you say that you love me." "Thanks. you don't know how much I needed that." "What were y'all talking about." She asked.

"Becky was getting ready to go to the store and buy some groceries, and she asked if I had any special requests, and I told her that I was partial to hot cocoa." I told her.

"You like cocoa?" She sounded surprised.

"I tried coffee anyway a person could drink it, but it didn't suit my taste, it was bitter." I told her. "I tried hot tea, but it didn't suit my taste, it was weak." "Hot cocoa wakes me up in the morning, and makes me sleepy at night, but most of all, it suits my taste."

"That's odd," "I like it too." She confessed.

"You two need to be alone, I'm going shopping." Becky said.

"Don't forget to swing by and pick up those cards from Mister Hurley." I spoke to Becky a few decibels above normal tone.

"I need you to dial a number for me." I told Bailey.

"Who you calling?" She questioned.

"I have a staff of business manager's that I have to let know where I can be contacted at." "I couldn't do that without getting a phone." I told her "Six months ago, I put my father's estate up for sale." "I never stayed there more than one night." "That was one of the places I got lost." "Imagine getting lost in your own house." "But it wasn't my house." "When my father died, I thought I would move there, but it didn't feel like my home." "Several weeks ago, a contract was signed on it." "I have to go back to New York and sign the papers when it's finalized."

"How long will you be gone?" She asked.

"I can't say" "it may take one day or two days, maybe three." I replied "I don't know I may not even have to go at all." "The deal could fall through; nothing is for certain until the money is in your hands."

"Are you going to call me?" She said shyly.

"No" "You'll be going with me." I told her "If I leave here without you and Barney's finds out that I'm gone, I'm afraid that someone will come over and try to beat me out of a contract." "I've invested way too much in you to let that happen."

I was attacked and being smothered with kisses.

"Hey, don't count on the deal yet." "The money isn't in my hand." I told her.

"Am I interrupting something?" Buck said.

"No, I was telling Bailey I was going to have to fly to New York and she was coming with me." I told him.

"That's too many people in one town, for me." He stated "Mister Bryant."

"Buck, that's Kurt." I corrected him.

"Kurt, I was looking at that catfish pond the other day." "You know you have an artesian well that's flowing into it." He stated.

"No"

"Yes sir, the way I see it is the doctor drilled a well first and put a shut off valve at the bottom with a valve at top." "From the way it looks, it's never been shut." "It's not coming out fast, so it doesn't have any pressure behind it." "On the low end, there's a screen that blocks a pipe that's buried underground." "I walked in the back to the creek, and found out where the pipe comes out at." "I'd guess it's flowing at a gallon or two a minute."

"How big is the pond?" I asked him.

"I walked off a hundred and seventeen steps lengthways, and seventy four steps wide." "It's rectangular shaped" "Kurt, that's a nice size pond." He exclaimed. "I don't know if there's any fish in there, but the pond is full, and clean." "I took a branch about ten feet long and I couldn't touch bottom with it."

"So, I need to put some fish in there huh?" I stated.

"You can stock it, but you may not have to." "I'd toss me out a few baits, and see if anything bites." He replied. "If there's catfish in there, you'll lose a lot of your fingerlings to the bosses of the pond." "I'd try baiting a hook first." "If you catch three or four, you won't need to stock the pond." "But you will need to feed them to get them fat."

"What do I feed them?" I asked.

"You can use deer corn, or floating catfish food, or hen scratch that's been soured." "Anyone of those will do." "The floating catfish food lets you know really quick if there's catfish in there are not." "They're pretty loud when they come up and take the pellets." He said to me. "The corn is good for all the fish in the pond." "The catfish eat it, and the corn doesn't break down, and another fish comes along and eats it and it goes on like that until it's gone."

"Does Ronnie know where I can get this stuff at?" I asked him.

"They have a marina about fifteen miles from here." "They sell it to the waterfront property owners to draw the catfish in." "When I leave here, I'll swing by and pick you up some." "How many bags you want?"

"About ten bags of the catfish pellets and ten bags of corn will do." I took a guess and stated to him.

"That's a lot of bags." He replied.

"If they're in there, they're hungry." "I'll give them all they want." I commented. "Buck, can you teach me how to fish?"

"You've never fished?" He asked surprised.

"No" "The closest I ever got to a fish was holding it in my hands at my school." I related to him.

"Kurt, you can't do that with a catfish, they have fins that are sharp as ice picks and they'll stick you deep." "I'll bring my rods over tomorrow and we'll see if you need to stock the pond or not." "I'm kinda interested myself." He exclaimed. "Now, my wife said that she wanted me to open all the water faucets and let them run for a while." "She said Bailey said the water was rusty when it was turned on." "Just to be on the safe side, I need to check the meter to see if it's turning." "If it is and you're not using water, then that's a sign that you have a leak somewhere."

He turned and began walking away, and then I heard the door open. "I see furniture trucks coming." He commented.

Bailey met them at the door and as they started pulling out the furniture, she was showing them where she wanted everything to be put. She oversaw the construction of our bed and then made sure that another one was being tended to in its proper fashion. She was running around and checking the status of furnishing the house and soon I felt her hand take my arm and walk me into the family room and sat me down on the sofa. "About ten feet in front of you is the fireplace." She began "There's a love seat that's pulled in a little at the end of the sofa with a recliner at the end." "And on this side of the sofa there's a love seat, and a recliner on the end of it too." "In the middle of the chairs and the love seat and sofa is a coffee table."

"Did you check out our bed?" I asked her.

"Kurt, that bed wouldn't fit in my trailer, it's bigger than my bedroom." She responded. "And yes, Mister Smarty, I did lay down on it."

I heard the door opening and Becky's voice called out. "I need a little help here."

"I can carry two bags at a time." I told Bailey. "But I can't use my cane if I do." "You can steer me in the direction I need to go." "I'm not worthless or useless, but I am helpless, and hopeless."

"Come on" Becky said "y'all can sit and chat all night long, right now there's work to be done; I ended up needing something on every aisle." "All the can good bags are in back of the truck, and the crushable bags and the milk and eggs and meats are in the cab, so be careful handling them." You two start unloading and I'll start putting everything away."

Bailey was guiding me out the door when I stopped, and then started again. "What's the matter?" Bailey said.

"Listen when we go back inside and tell me what you hear." I commented.

I was loaded down with several bags and Bailey had one in her arm, and her other one was wrapped around mine. When we entered, I put my bags down where Becky told me and Bailey and I went to get more. After we walked out of the front door, Bailey said she didn't hear anything.

"You didn't hear her humming as she was working?" I said to her.

"I wasn't paying any attention."

"Listen when we go back inside, she's got a song in her mind." I told her.

After loading up, we were unloading the bags from our arms in the same spot she had told us before, and went back for more bags.

"I heard her that time." Bailey said. "She sounds happy, Kurt."

"Can you remember the last time you saw her or heard her acting the way she is?" I asked her.

I felt her stop for a moment. "Kurt, I don't think I've ever seen her act this way at all."

"How about Buck?" I asked her.

"Buck never got home until around nine or so." "When they closed, they had to cover everything up and sanitize their tables and it's an hour's drive home." She commented. "I'd stop by and keep Becky company sometimes, but I didn't see Buck very much."

"So, the kids have been raising themselves then." I said out loud. "Here, give me some bags and let's get busy." "I don't want Becky coming out here and using her whip on us." I chuckled. "Is the house starting to look like a house?" I asked her when we began walking.

"We have a long way to go." She stated. "Ask me that question again in fifty years."

"So, you're going to wait around just to make me apologize, huh?" I said to her.

"No, it's going to take me that long to fill up that closet of yours." "Kurt, I like you in blue." "But I also like seeing you in slacks, and shorts, and shirts that have life." "I'm sorry, but you look dull and boring wearing blue all the time." "But I want you to hear me, and hear me well." "When I dress you, you better not let some young filly come in and put her rope on you and hogtie you; or me and you are going to go round and round." She fired her warning shot towards me.

We sat those bags down and went back for more.

"Here, these are all can goods." "Hold out your arms and hang on." She ordered.

She guided me to the counter and told me to lower my arms until the bags were touching the top of the counter, and then we went back for more.

"How many more are they?" I asked.

"Seven" Bailey returned my answer.

"Load me up." I told her.

We unloaded those and got the rest, and unloaded them.

I was sitting on the sofa when I heard faint footsteps walking into the room.

"Hold out your hands." Becky said.

I did as she asked and I felt warmth from a mug.

"It's hot cocoa." "I put whipped cream on top." "I didn't know if you liked marshmallows or you preferred it dry." She told me

I took a sip and wiped my upper lip clean of whipped cream and moaned. "Mm" "Perfect" I said. "It's been a long time since I've had a good cup of hot cocoa." She then kissed me on my forehead.

"What was that for?" I asked her.

"I don't know" "I think it's because I feel blessed." She replied.

"Becky, after this cup of cocoa, it's me that's feeling blessed." I told her. "Where have you been all of my life?"

"Bailey was right; you are one helluva silver tongued devil." I heard her say as she was walking away.

Around a minute later I felt Bailey sitting down next to me, and when she sat down, she began giving me the plans of tomorrow. "They said they'll be three more trucks tomorrow and three trucks the day after." "We have two beds ready, with ten to go." "We still need a cabinet for the dining room, and whatever you want to do to the game room." "The dressers and eight beds are on back order." "The pool people are coming out tomorrow to see what needs to be done to get it cleaned." "The man told Buck that if algae was in it, it would need to be hydro blasted." "Also, a lady is coming out to measure all of our windows for drapes and curtains, so I imagine she's going to be here for most of the day." "You were right Kurt; you did need help here." "We've been on the road for four days, and we're not even half way through yet."

I looked in her direction. "Where's the best place to put a Christmas tree at in here?" I asked.

I felt her looking around. "Over in the corner to the right." She let me know what she thought.

"How tall is the ceiling?" I asked.

"I don't know." "Why"

"I want a big one" "And I want a real one too, not an artificial one." I told her. "I want to smell it." "Where I lived, I couldn't have one."

"When the time comes, I'll have Buck or Ronnie measure it, and we'll get you that tree." She said stroking my hair to the back. "Kurt, you asked me what would I get you for Christmas." "Christmas was the worst holiday of the year for me." "It depressed me." "I think that's what's been bothering me, I've been depressed, and I think I was depressed because I didn't have anyone to share Christmas with, except Becky and her family." "I wanted more, I had my dreams too, and this house was one of those dreams." "So, I find being here still comes as a shock to me." "I wanted someone to hold me." "Kurt, for me it's Christmas now." "And come Christmas I'll be depressed all over again." "I won't know what to give a man that's given me my dream."

"I don't find that to be true." I stopped her "You buy me clothes and dress me." "I don't like that; I would rather do it myself, but when I do, I look dull and boring." "You're by my side in every business matter I'm involved in, I like that, if you weren't you'd be somewhere else, and I'd be somewhere else." "I think you know that." "You came in and brought me up to date on where we stand with the house." "If I find you wrapped up in a box under the tree, then there is a Santa Claus."

"You better quit talking like that." "The kids will be coming in soon, and I don't want them knocking on our bedroom door." She commented. "Kurt, being with you makes me feel good." "I don't feel down anymore the way I used to." "When you bought me the car, I thought that was a bit much." "Going into Barney's I saw a lot of the stockers and checkers giving me the eye when we walked by." "I got a bad feeling from them looking at me the way they did." "I don't need presents under the tree." "I'm looking forward to sitting down and having that Christmas dinner with you." "Kurt, I think the last Christmas I had was when I was eight, after that one, I can't remember any of them."

"Bailey, close your eyes and tell me what you see."

"I can't see anything." "You know that." She stated.

"I know" I began, "when people look at me, I don't see them either." "So, I don't know what people are thinking of me, and I could care less." "I'm living in my life, and you're living in your life, and all of those people that live in this world, are living in their life." "Everyone you meet has an opinion on what they think of you." "I know I did, and you had an opinion of me when you met me." "I was a butt hole." "If you really look deep inside a person, you might find that those that have negative vibes about you; are jealous." "You said people turned their heads when we drove by." "They saw the car, they saw money, money breeds jealousy." "At first" I said "this relationship you and I are involved in began as an innocent arrangement." "Dating someone is where you try to determine if both of you are compatible to each other's needs." "Twenty years from now, if Barney's is still there, those people that made you feel down, they'll still be working for Barney's and if they think negative thoughts about you now, then they'll still have those negative thoughts about you twenty years from now." "To them, you are who those people think of you as and there's nothing you can do to change the opinion that they have towards you."

"I hear the kids." She said to me.

"Bailey, I need to talk over a few things with Ronnie." "Ask him if he could go for a walk around the property with me." "You can stay here and have a talk with Becky; I don't want her to think that she works for us." "She thinks of you as a friend and I'd like for her to think of me as a friend too." "She might need to be reminded of that often." I told her.

"You sure you don't need me." "I don't mind, I like being with you." She argued.

"No, I need to let Ronnie get an idea of what his job scope is."

"Alright, I really don't mind though." She commented.

I stood up when she did and began walking with her carrying my empty mug of cocoa. Bailey took it from my hand and when she went into the kitchen, I heard Ronnie's voice.

"Mister Bryant, Bailey said you wanted me to go with you."

"Yeah, I want to get an idea of what we're looking at." I told him.

We were walking out back and he was explaining that branches were broken from the trees and lying on the ground.

"How much wood do I have here?" I asked him.

"Mister Bryant, you can burn wood every day and still have plenty of trees, you'll never have a want for wood in the fireplace."

"Ronnie, I don't like the sound of Mister Bryant, it makes me feel old." "Kurt suits me better." I informed him.

"My momma said for me to respect you." He returned.

"Well, that poses us a problem then, I don't like Mister Bryant and you can't call me Kurt." "I can live with Mister B." "If your mother says anything, just tell her that I wanted you to call me Kurt, but we settled on Mister B."

"Ronnie, I was talking to Bailey earlier, and I found out that your mother and father worked late." "That leaves you looking after your sisters after they got out of school." "Did you want to play sports?" I asked.

"I couldn't." He said softly.

"Ronnie, there are different types of girls." I related to him "There are girls that chase athletes, but I lost out on them, I wasn't the athletic type." "I couldn't see the bar on the high jump and I kept running into it."

He was laughing at my statement.

"Then there's girls that want to be with you because you have a truck and you can take them where they want to go, be careful there, you might find out that there's nothing you can do to satisfy them, their eyes are on someone else's truck." "You've probably talked to other kids about your job." "If you let the wrong girl fool you, you'll end up living the rest of your life in misery, and there aren't any guarantees that you won't be fooled a half a dozen time's either." "Sometimes you feel good about your girl and give her flowers, there are some girls that want more than flowers; you just can't give some girls enough." "They'll leave you and find someone that can." "I think you may know some of those girls at school already." "Chances are you've already met some of those girls that didn't want to be around you before, but now they do, those are the girls I'm talking about." I told him. "I'm twenty eight." "I had girlfriends, but that's all they were, "girl" "friends." "So maybe that might give you an idea of my relationship with girls." "I'm not someone you should model yourself after, I'm no Romeo." "You never really know a girl, and a girl never really knows a boy." "That's why people argue." "They find out something they didn't know about each other and anger turns a good relationship into a bad one." "If you become involved with a girl, I hope you understand you have responsibilities." "I don't know what you want to be later on in life." "I do know you'll have a job here for as long as you live, I can guarantee that." "When you turn thirty, you may find out what it is you want to be, or you may be fifty." "Are you a junior?" I asked him.

"Yes sir"

"Have you already met a girl?" I asked.

"Yes sir"

"Have you asked her out yet?"

"No sir."

"Okay, here's the deal." I started. "If I, was you, I'd be thinking that the worst she can do is say no." "If she did, I wouldn't ever look her in the eyes again." "Girls don't like that."

"How do you know that?" He asked.

"You have eyes, I have ears." "Girls that pushed me away, I never spoke to them again." "They knew I was near and when they talked, they talked in a voice loud enough for me to hear." "They were doing it for one reason, but I ignored them." "I got a lot of phone calls." "But, like I say, I had "girl" "friends", "none of them gave me that feeling of them being a soul mate." "Ronnie, you're old enough to know about marriage." "When you look for a girl, you're looking for someone that makes you feel comfortable being around her; she may be the one you'll want to spend the rest of your life with." "You're not going to have to take care of your sisters anymore, your mother and father will be there for them now." "So, if you find the girl you think is the right girl." "You better go after her." "Remember, the worst she can do is say no." "Now, about this property."

I heard hollering from the kids. "Dinner's ready." Cindy shouted to us.

When we walked in, I could hear the kids at the table and Becky was sitting bowls of food down. Bailey told me she was fixing my plate for me. "Your corn is in a bowl on the left side of your plate, right above your plate is a bowl of macaroni and cheese." "To the right of your plate is a bowl of green beans and on your plate is two pork chops, and some corn bread." "Eat up." She stated to me.

I reached down to get my silverware. "Your fork and spoon are in the bowls." Bailey said.

"What about my knife for the meat?" I asked.

"Honey" Becky interrupted "down here we all use our fingers to eat our pork chops and our fried chicken and such." "We're not proper folks." She chuckled.

We were sitting and enjoying a nice dinner when Cindy asked a question.

"Mister Bryant how come your eyes roll around like that?"

"Cindy" Becky reacted.

"That's alright Becky." "This is how kids learn, they ask questions." I began answering her. "I don't have any control of my muscles in my eyes, so they sort of float around." "That's why I wear sunglasses when I go out and talk to people I don't know."

"What happened to your muscles?" She asked.

"I don't know, I was born this way." I told her. "I guess that's a question I never bothered to ask."

"How do you shave?"

"I don't have any problems there, if I cut myself, it teaches me to shave slower." "Then I feel my face and if I feel tiny stubbles on my chin, I shave that spot again."

"How come you talk funny?" She asked.

"That's enough Cindy." Buck interrupted.

"Becky, Buck, I'd like to bring up a thought and let you two do some thinking about what I have to say." "Becky, I told Buck today that I was going to have to fly to New York." "I have to handle some business." "I don't know when, but from what I gather, none of you have been anywhere in a while." "I was wondering if all of you would like to go to New York with Bailey and me."

"You want us to fly to New York with you?" Becky said.

"It'll mean that the kids will have to miss a day or two of school." "But I think going to the museums would do them a lot better than reading about something out of a book." "There's symphonies, opera's, plays, and the statue of Liberty." "You want more, the Empire state building, grand central park, Zoo's, sidewalk entertainers, Becky, New York is only a six hour flight away."

"You go to those places?" Becky asked.

"Yeah" "In music, you have harmony, each instrument is heard and all together they tell a story." "Operas are a little different, you really have to listen." "Plays are movies without all the explosions and disturbances." "I can't say much about the statue of Liberty though, to me, one elevator ride is the same as all the rest." I had to smile at that remark. "Museums are slightly different." "I can't have a conversation with you about art, but listening to some people tell me what they see tells me that art is a beauty that's in the eye of the beholder."

"All of them people up there seem to act like a bunch of stuffed shirts." Buck inserted his thoughts verbally.

"Not all of them." I commented. "But there are people of prominent wealth that like others to know that they're wealthy." "That happens everywhere, even here in Skinland." "But I was throwing out an offer, and I really wish you would consider it." "That way you'll have a better idea of where I came from."

"I don't know." Buck began.

Becky interrupted him. "Kurt, can I ask you why?"

"I told you I don't consider any of you to be employees, I lean towards close personal business associates." "I don't like the phrase of I work for Mister Kurt Bryant, it doesn't sound correct." "As a personal business associate it tells others that they're talking to the people that's got the authority to tell others that I'm not available." "If a phone rings and someone says that they want to talk to the man of the house, then chances are, I don't need what their selling." "Besides, I was telling Bailey the deal may fall through and this conversation will be moot."

"What does moot mean?" Julie said.

"It means I may not have to leave." I replied. "But if I was going to New York, I wouldn't want to say hey, Bailey and I are leaving in six hours, do you want to go." "This way if I'm contacted your mother and father will have had time to discuss this offer in private."

"I don't know." Buck said again. "There are a lot of people there."

"I want to go with Mister Bryant." Cindy said.

"Now" I followed "Bailey was telling me earlier about our furniture, and she mentioned the game room and that got me to thinking." "I have absolutely no idea of what goes in a game room." "I don't play those kinds of games." "So, Ronnie, Julie, Cindy, I need some help in making the game room a game room." "I know we'll need at least four computers, three in the game room, and one in the kitchen." "That's a must, but I don't know what kids do for entertainment, so I'm going to be needing help in furnishing our game room." "There's a child labor law that say's I can't work you very long without letting you to take breaks." "It's a strict law, but you chose to be my business associates, so now I'm obligated to obey that law." "One day without warning, someone from the child labor force could ring our door bell and ask to see the break room." "What am I supposed to do?" "Tonight, write down the things all of you would like to have, that way the game room can start turning into a game room." "A week from now, something else might come into your head." "Write it down so you don't forget and let me know so I won't get in trouble." "Buck and Ronnie." "Becky has a credit card for each of you, use it." "Ronnie, we need a tractor, and a riding lawnmower, chain saws, and tree trimmers." "Use the card and buy whatever you need, but buy the best."

When they left that night, I heard the bathroom door shut and the shower being turned on and then the water went silent. The door opened and I felt bailey's body moving the bed. "Bailey, when I asked Becky and Buck if they wanted to go with us, I didn't ask you for approval and I should have." I stated to her.

"Why"

"Because you're not one of my business associates." I replied. "You said that you were depressed every time you left from Becky's." "I like having friends, and with the kids around, this house definitely doesn't seem to be really all that big."

Bailey started laughing.

"You know Cindy and Julie watch you when you walk around," she said "they make sure all the furniture is where it's supposed to be." "And I don't know what you said to Ronnie, but he was soaking wet with sweat when he came in." "Kurt, I love this house, but there's no way I could have cleaned it by myself, and I really don't want people coming and going." "I think you might be building yourself a family, and if you are I'm not complaining, I love them, they've been more of a family to me than my own my mother and father were." "Besides, I've never been a leader; I've always been a follower." "You're a quick thinker, and after being with you for a while, I've learned that there's a reason behind everything you do and say."

"Kurt, this bed is gigantic." "It's like two King size beds built in one."

I pulled her to me and squeezed her gently. "All of this almost never happened." I told her.

"I still can't believe it either." "You'd make a great baseball player; you throw a lot of curves." She responded to my comment.

"I'd like to give you a little test." I told her. "You saw something in your boyfriend that appealed to you." "All you saw in him was his good qualities, and you were willing to accept his bad qualities, because you loved him." "My field is narrowed down quite a bit." "When I asked you if there was anyone else in this town I could trust, you said no." "I don't like the smell of smoke, I can't breathe." "When I got into your car, I knew you didn't smoke, if you did, the seats and carpet would have told me before I even got in." "I knew you didn't drink, there again your seats and carpet would have tipped me off, the odor lingers for weeks." "If anyone rode in the car with you, they didn't smoke or drink either, that tells me that you didn't hang around those that did." "That leaves the drugs." "Have you ever been given a lie detector test?" I asked her.

"No"

"A lie detector reads the blood pressure and register's nervousness and pulse, mostly." "If a question is posed to them, their pulse and blood pressure elevates if they're lying; nervousness registers a lie the same way." "If you needed something to help you make it through your day, I would have known about it." "I can feel your pulse in your fingertips when you hold my arm, and you aren't restless or nervous." "But, your right, I don't know anything about you." "I can only guess." "But my guess was that if you did drugs, I believe you would smoke to remove the jitters of needing whatever you needed." "And you would drink because like smoking, it's a drug too, and most of all drug users hang around other drug users." "Sometimes you get a lot of answers just by sitting in a car, it told me a lot about some of those things I needed to know." "Those were all plus's that I wanted in a person." "I saw good qualities in you and I was willing to overlook your bad qualities."

"What bad qualities." She remarked.

"For one thing, that temper of yours." "You need to take some anger management courses at college." I chuckled.

I was struck on the arm for that error.

"Bailey, you're a breath of fresh air to me." "Buck made a comment tonight about some of the people acting like a bunch of stuffed shirts." "I didn't date." "I found girls that were daughters of prominent figures to be cold hearted." "They were looking for love, but you had to qualify first." "You didn't know who I was when we met." "You followed me without knowing I had this house, and this house means money to anyone that sees it." "That's what you saw when you came to work here." "You wanted to be a doctor too; you wanted the luxury that came with it." "Did Tom give you any of that?" I asked her.

"No"

"Then when Tom meets a girl and ends up getting married and having kids, he'll find out that a divorce is costly." "He'll get what he gave you." "Tom is a college graduate, if he gets a good job somewhere, chances are, he won't be making enough money to live a life of his choosing." "That's why I didn't date, I told you the night that we first came here, when I didn't have any lights, that the first thing that a woman felt on me was my wallet." "Tom will experience that." "He used you, and the woman he meets and falls in love with, will use him." "He'll get what he deserves." "Have you ever been on a speed date?" I asked.

"Does it have anything to do with sex?" She chuckled.

I began laughing.

"What's so funny?" She asked.

"Nothing, Bailey speed dating is sitting down and having a conversation with a girl sitting across a table from you." "You have three minutes to exchange a conversation before a buzzer goes off and then you move to the next table, and so on, and so on." "There may be as little as six or as much as a dozen girls." "I went to one wearing the kind of clothes that I have now." "I didn't date any of those girls; I didn't measure up to them." "But, when I wore my suit, I caught the interest of more than a few." "Now, let's take Tom." "If Tom went on a speed date, he would wear a suit to indicate to the girls that he was successful." "It wouldn't be long before Tom would find a girl to his liking and that would be his downfall." "Chances are that Tom will be married a couple of times and he'll have three or four kids."

"I didn't want to get married to Tom." She replied. "I loved him, but he never talked about it, and I never brought it up." "This negligee I have on, I bought it to wear on Tom's graduation night." "I never got to wear it, until tonight, it meant something special to me."

"Bailey being blind has its drawbacks" I said "if I would have seen you walking out of the bathroom." "I would have told you how beautiful you look and our conversation we had earlier would never have taken place."

"That would be hard to do, the lights are off." She commented. "And that's another thing that Tom never did, he never said I was beautiful."

Buck arrived with Becky that next morning. "I've got the corn and catfish food, and the rods." He stated. "Let me get everything unloaded and we'll give the pond a test."

Buck was leading me out to the pond when he struck up a conversation.

"Yesterday before I left to go to the marina, my wife said that you put our salary in the bank in one sum." "Kurt, you don't do that." "That kind of money is water in a pail with a hole in it to these people that live around here." "They'll spend it and then they'll leave for parts unknown."

"I know that, Buck." I said to him. "That decision was made because you have Ronnie, Julie, and Cindy." "They're my associates; they'll keep you under control." "Buck, for the record, what do you think of Bailey?"

"Kurt that boy she had before you put that girl through hell." He began. "I told her she ought to file charges against him." "She wouldn't do it." "I think that might be one of reasons why she hasn't gotten a job; she's got a felony theft on her record for almost two thousand dollars in hot checks." "I told Becky on her first interview to give her a call and see how things went." "Becky told me that if she got the job, she would call and tell her." "The only reason they called was to tell her that they had hired someone else." "They called it a courtesy call." "I guess that was to keep her from calling and asking about the position, and Kurt, putting money in the bank the way you did isn't making things easy." "I'm going to have to talk to you straight up as a man." "If anything happens between you and Bailey, Becky isn't going to be happy here, and that means, I wouldn't be able to work for you either."

"That's a fairly candid response." I told him. "I appreciate that." "And Buck, you don't work for me, you're an associate that supervises my welfare." "A person who works for you doesn't do that, they show up at eight in the morning sometimes, if you're lucky, and then they take a break at ten to ten thirty, lunch at twelve and back at one and then another break at two to two thirty, I'd be lucky to get a total of two hours of work from them by the end of the day." "All that they're interested in is four days a week." "They've got sick leave, vacation, and emergencies that come up." "Bailey told me that you had to stay late." "So, you worked twelve, maybe fourteen to sixteen hours a day." "Working that many hours cause's problems." "You can't call in sick; other people that work with you will have to work harder to take up the slack, and if you did take off sick, your job would be threatened, your boss is dependent on you to show up and if you don't, he would end up replacing you with someone that would."

"My wife said I ought to listen to you." "She told me you were a smart man." "We're here Kurt, take this bucket of corn and take a handful and throw it in the water until the bucket is empty." "Throw it out in a fan motion so you can spread the corn out instead of pouring it all in one spot." "It doesn't matter about the catfish food, it floats."

When I finished, we sat down on the bank. "This is a number three ought hook." He said putting it in my fingers. "And this is a box of night crawlers."

"What is that?" I asked.

"Big worms." He answered. "Take one out and thread it on the hook, and when you do, put the lid back on the worms, or they'll get out and they'll be gone."

After I finished, he gave me an inspection. "That's good enough" he said "not perfect, but you don't have to be." "You want your worm to be able to put off a little wiggle."

I heard a loud sound in the water.

"Oh!" "That's good to hear." Buck said. "Now, let me show you something with the rod." "In order to cast it, you want to push this button on the reel and then pull it back to cock your wrist like this." He said taking my hand and showing me while talking. "And then when you get to this position right here." "You release the button and let the weight of the sinker toss the hook out." "Give it a try."

After I cast it out, he commented. "That's not bad; you'll get the hang of it." "Let it sink to the bottom and start reeling in real slow until you can feel the weight of the sinker." "You'll know when you get a bite; you can feel each little nibble." "Hang onto your rod and if one hits, he'll try to yank it out of your hands, and he will if you're not ready." He advised me.

We heard another loud sound.

"Oh!" "That was a nice one." Buck said softly.

Several minutes later, I had a hard hit and started reeling in my line, but it wouldn't come.

"Hang on to him." Buck said. "Let him do the fighting, you won't do any good reeling, all you'll do is twist the line." "That's a nice one, let him fight, and when he tires, pull up on your rod and as you lower it, keep the line tight by reeling it in, and remember, you have to let the rod do the fighting." "You can't horse a nice catfish in until he's ready to come in."

"Oh yeah, he's a good one." Buck said. "Lower your rod and keep the line tight, that's it, that's it, now raise up the rod a little."

I felt the release of the fight, but I could still feel it.

"Oh yeah, he's a good one all right." "In a month he'll make for some fine eating."

"Can I feel it?" I asked him.

"You be careful, he has a barbed fin on each side of him and one on top." "They're sharp and they'll stick you deep."

I began feeling of it, and then started to put my hand around its head when it decided that it had enough of me touching it. Buck was right, the barb was sharp; he got me in my hand.

"You alright?" Buck said.

"That hurt." I said shaking my hand vigorously and then I tried to squeeze the pain away and when that didn't help, I started shaking it again.

"Yeah, that's the thing about fishing." "There ain't no fisherman that's ever fished, that haven't felt the pain of a fin sticking him, the first time I caught a catfish, he got me too." He responded. "I'll get you a pair of gloves and that way you won't have to try to grip it that hard to hold on to it." "Here, I got him; you can feel along its back and sides down to the tail." "Be careful, if he starts a flopping, move your hand."

"It's smooth." I said feeling it.

"You have to skin a catfish, it doesn't have scales, but down here you'll hurt yourself when it comes to eating a mess of fried catfish." He commented.

"It feels thin."

"Yeah, and if there's more like him out there, you think he gave you a good fight now, wait until he fills out some." He tutored me. "He'll make for a good four, maybe a five pounder."

"He has barbs." I quickly pulled my hand away.

He started laughing. "I found that out the hard way too." "Me and another kid was fishing at a mouth of a creek that drained off into the lake." "I caught one that let me know he was a little one." "I put my hand around him to take the hook out and he flopped out of my hand and landed in my leg." "I grabbed him and did all I could to pull him out." "That's a memory a person never forgets." "There, the hooks out." "Reel it in until you can't reel anymore and then feel along the top and you'll come to the weight first and then the hook." "Get you a worm out and thread it on the hook and let's see if we can catch us another one." "Remember, put the lid on the top of the worms, worms come out of the ground, and they don't have any problems getting back in there, if they escape."

I made another cast and judging by the sound of the weight hitting the water; it went about as far as the other one did.

"Let the weight sink to the bottom before you tighten up on the line." Buck repeated.

We sat and listened to the popping of fish that were now starting to get more active in retrieving the floating catfish food. I heard Bailey's voice above me.

"Becky made you some hot cocoa." She stated to me.

"I have to hold on to the rod." I told her.

"Give it to me, and you can drink your cocoa." She replied.

We were sitting there listening to the fish hit the fish food, and buck made a comment about it being a good sign when I heard Bailey began screaming, I didn't know what to do. I calmed down after hearing Buck giving her instructions on how to land a fish.

"You take it." Bailey shouted to Buck.

"Naw, I can't do that." "You caught it, now you got to fight it." "Let the rod fight him." He said giving her the same guidance that he did me.

"Hold it, hold it, lift your rod a little, oh yeah, that's a nice one there." "He'll make a good five pounder when he fills out." He told her.

"Hold my cocoa and give me the rod for a minute." I said to Bailey as I was pulling out another worm from my box. After I baited it back up, I cast it back out and handed it to Bailey. "I'll trade you for the cocoa." I told her.

I had sat down my cup when Bailey began screaming again, and Buck was once again put back in commission.

After she fought that one and landed it. She picked my mug up that sat beside me. "I got to go back; those people should be here by now." She gave me a kiss. "I love you." "Bye."

Buck opened a conversation. "Kurt, we've caught three catfish, and all of them are thin." "That means that there isn't any bait fish in the pond." He said with his heavy drawl.

"So, I need to buy some fish to feed the fish?" I commented to him

"No" he began "I can set out some traps and catch some perch, and then let them go in here." "I think stocking the pond right now would be wasting money and time, you need to set out some brush so that the fingerlings and baitfish can have a place to hide." "I think that's why they're thin; they ate up all the bait fish." "What with you wanting to feed them corn, and pellets." "I would think with the perch having a place to hide, the bait fish won't come under the heavy pressure they were under." "But this is your pond, Doctor Wilcox may have wanted only one type of fish in here, and he might have wanted it to have a clean bottom for that purpose." "I can understand that, catfish are good eating."

"Buck" I replied "I've only been to one pond." "We went there to feed the ducks, but we were attacked by geese." "It was a frantic situation, where do you run when geese are attacking you." "I went down into a fetal position and covered up." "We had twelve kids with us that day, and three supervisors; it took them and bystanders a little time before they got those geese off of me." "That put an end to my field trips to that pond, so every time the school had a field trip there, I had something else to do; those geese have a bite; I have memories of my own." "They may not have any teeth, but I can assure you they do know how to use that bill." "That little ordeal changed my life completely; I find that when having dinner, goose has moved up to the top of my list, so that should tell you what I know about a pond." "I need to know, what would you do?"

"You're going to have wild geese and ducks coming through, but they'll take flight as soon as you're seen." "You need them to fertilize the pond and to keep a new supply of bait fish coming in from the lake, eggs from fish attach themselves to their feet and when they land here, the eggs drop off and when they spawn, they need shelter." "This is a big pond Kurt, you won't be hurt if you put some trash in the middle; I think that way, not only will these fish get bigger and fatter, but they'll be eating natural foods too."

His conversation was interrupted by the jerk of my pole. I fought him longer than I had fought the other one.

"Let him fight." Buck was giving me his advice. "You'll not bring him in until he's tired." I heard the reel making a noise. "Yeah baby" Buck said with excitement in his voice "run baby run." "Kurt, this one might be the boss hawg here." "Let him run." He said again. "Oh yeah" "listen to that reel sing." "Okay Kurt, start easing the rod down and remember to keep the line tight." "Don't give him any slack, or he'll break the line or pull the hook out." "There you go, a little more, a little more." "Hold it." I then felt the rod go limp. "Oh yeah, I think this one may be the boss."

"Can I feel it?" I asked him.

"Hold on a minute and let me hold him down." He replied. "Okay I have him."

I felt his head and went along the back until I felt the barbs; I avoided those and made my way down to the tail. "He feels longer."

"That's because he is." He stated. "He'll probably make a good seven, or a low eight." "This one will easily feed four adults when he fattens up." "Kurt, I think you definitely need to put some brush in the middle of the pond." "You can feed everything in this pond from right here." He implied.

"Okay, what do I do?" I asked.

"Nothing, I'll have Ronnie picking up the loose branches on the ground and have him throw everything in the middle of the pond." "That way you can fish here and not get hung up on the limbs he throws out." "You could stock the pond if you want, but I really don't think you need to." "I'll set out some traps and we'll see how everything goes from there." He stated.

"Alright, sounds good." I said as I got another bite. "Oh yeah, that sounds like a good idea to me." I restated with a little more enthusiasm. "That corn and floating pellets really bring them in."

"Their hungry, they smell food." He commented as he guided me to where he wanted the fish to be netted.

After I finally landed him, he told me to feel along the side of his mouth. "These are his whiskers; he smells and tastes what he smells with his whiskers." "That's why they call him a "cat" "fish." "I don't think any of them would be alive without that well pumping fresh water in." "The ponds not stagnant, if it was, you'd have a dry pond along with the rest of all of the people around here."

"You must have a freezer full of fish." I said to him.

"Naw, I hadn't been fishing in a while." He proclaimed. "I used to go all the time when I was a kid." "I'd buy my bait and a little extra to appease the fish gods." "I felt it was good luck letting a dozen minnows go, or a box of worms." "An old man told me I had to spit on my worm to remove my scent from him." "That didn't do any good either." "I found out that fish bite when fish bite." "I had to give all of that up." "Becky and I both worked in Murray before she worked for the doctor." "I had to leave by seven, so Becky was usually up around by four so the kids could be fed and have their lunches fixed." "The bus came at around six, so the kids had to be there at the bus stop waiting." "The only day I was off was Sunday, and I spent that day mowing and catching up on the upkeep of my house, and then when deer season came, I worked seven days a week for three months straight." "Ronnie took over the chores I did when I started working my overtime." "It was like that for the last eight years." "When Becky started working for Doctor Wilcox, I had to buy another truck so that she could have transportation."

"That set us back some, but she had steady work." "When she lost that, we were hoping the diner would offset the money she lost from working for Doctor Wilcox." "It didn't." "People around here are a prisoner of their community." "They have to go into Murray to buy everything, so they wait to eat out when they go there." "Without the lake, there aren't fishermen or campers coming through." "I can't see how Barney's is still open." He hesitated and then continued. "Yesterday, she had breakfast made and the lunches were packed, she was always pushing them to eat and get ready to catch the bus." "It was odd watching them as they sat watching cartoons waiting for their brother to take them to school, that's a first." "Even Becky was restless while she sat there drinking her coffee and waiting to come here." "Kurt, with me working in Murray till eight sometimes nine, I never was home six days out of the week." "I didn't sit down to a Sunday dinner until Becky opened the diner." "When she worked for Doctor Wilcox, she had to work all the holidays, and so did I, except I was off Thanksgiving and Christmas." "Somewhere along the way, I lost my family." "The only time we've really ever got to sit down and eat a family dinner was yesterday when we were sitting down at your table, it's been that long." "When Becky opened the diner, me and the kids would mosey on down and we'd eat down there on Sunday, but it wasn't the same." "I couldn't buy Ronnie a truck and with Becky running the diner, he'd heat something up that Becky would bring home for them the night before, or they'd have to eat sandwiches." "Ronnie raised his sister's." He said clearing his throat.

We were interrupted by my rod bending down sharply, Buck was right, I didn't have my mind on fishing and I almost lost it. I fought him in silence. Buck was letting me control the fish, when I started bringing him in, the line broke. "Awe man that was a good one."

Buck started laughing. "Son, you can't catch them all, if you did there wouldn't be any of them left." "Besides, the line might have gotten frayed from those others you fought." "That should tell you that after you catch fifteen to twenty pounds of catfish you can expect that to happen." "I would imagine once they put some meat on them, you'll break a lot of lines." "Kurt, have you been down to the creek?"

"No" I said "I walked around, and around, and around, but I don't remember where anything is at." "I only know how to get to my kitchen, the dining room the family room, and my bedroom inside my house." "Outside, I can't tell where I'm at without a barrier to stop me."

"Well, follow me and I'll give you a rundown on what I saw yesterday, while I was checking out the pond." He said taking my arm.

He stopped for a moment and bent down; I heard his voice. "Deer tracks, their using this trail." "Let's go this way." He said changing the direction. A moment later, he spoke again. "That's what I thought." "The deer are using the surveyor's path as a trail." "Come on, we'll follow the path and it should take us to one of your marker's." He once again took the lead. "We're on the east side of your property now." "Those deer are everywhere in here." About a minute later he stopped me and whispered. "There's three of them looking at us." "One of them is bobbing her head up and down." "Deer's colored blind Kurt, all they can see is one color; so as long as we stay still, they can't make us out." "Uh oh, she's on to us, she stomped her foot, that's a warning to other's that danger is near." "There they go, fly them flags of yours." "Let them fly." "Whoa baby" "you never get tired of seeing that." "They must have winded us" "the tree tops are blowing from the west." He reported.

"What did you mean by flags?" I asked him.

"When they run up against danger, in this case us, they stick their tail up in the air showing the white backside and when other deer see it waving from side to side as they ran, they know to be alert, it's a warning to others." He answered. "When I was young, I used to go to my deer blind early in the morning." "On a full moon, I could see deer moving pretty good, and every now and then I heard them squawk, that was another way of warning others." "Deer can smell a man before he sees him, like those deer did just then." "Sometimes I'd look and then rest, and when I looked again, I'd sometimes see one looking right at me, by the time I got my gun raised, it was gone." "They're like ghost." "One time I sat there and didn't see anything anywhere." "I was ready to go home and when I stood up in my blind, one bolted out from underneath it." "When I got out and looked underneath my blind, he had bedded down there." "He snuck up behind me. "You're the only person I've ever told that to." He chuckled. "I can see a marker that means the creek is up ahead."

When we got to it Buck began describing the creek as we walked along the side of it. "We're down below the pipe that comes out of the pond, there's a trickle of water in the creek." "On the upstream side of the pipe it's dry." "Here's a spot where we can go down in the creek." He replied.

I lost all track of time. It was Ronnie that brought us back to the present. Buck shouted to him to let him know where we were at, and several minutes later, he appeared.

"Momma said come eat." He told him.

"What she got cooked boy?" Buck said.

"Meat loaf" Ronnie informed us.

"Ooh, tell her we're coming." Buck said and then we began walking up the creek trying to find a way out. "This looks like a good place." He helped me crawl up the embankment. It was too steep to walk. "Deer travel along here, and when they do, they dig out the earth with their knees and hooves, that's why it's sloped." "Here's a good track." "Feel this one."

"How much do they weigh?" I asked.

"Judging by the size of the print and the depth of it, I would say that this one would weigh pretty close to what you weigh." He commented and stated "If we had a little rain, it would be deeper." "It might have been a doe that was pregnant or maybe a nice buck" "who knows" "if you ate the meat, you'd probably come out with maybe a hundred and twenty pounds, give or take." "The funny thing about deer hunters is that they think they should have more meat than they got when they brought them in to have them butchered." "Sometimes they do their own butchering and find out the truth, then next year, they bring them in to us."

"Do you eat deer, Buck?"

"Me and Becky used to live on it." He began "Our hamburger meat was deer meat, so that meatloaf we're having tonight was made out of deer meat back then." "I made sausage from it, and smoked it." "The back straps I put on a pit, and some of it was used to chicken fry, and I made jerky too." "When I got a job at the meat market, I cut up deer after deer after deer." "If I never process another deer, I'll say I lived out my life as a happy man." "I haven't hunted in eight years, and I'll not hunt again." "I got some meat from a man that was giving it away and took it home." "Becky told me to take it back; she wasn't going to eat another bite of deer meat." "Kurt, I don't miss it either, I guess that's why I don't hunt anymore." "Back when I was younger, it had a different flavor to it." "It was sort of like Becky's pecan pie." He chuckled.

"What about Becky's pecan pie?" I asked him.

"We were neighbors and we more or less grew up together, except she lived a half mile down the road from me." "I was seven when she was born." "I watched her grow from a baby into a fourteen year old girl." "That was the last I saw of her, I enlisted and in basic training, I broke my leg, and got booted out." "I was working for a roofer, and one day I turned onto my road and saw Becky getting off the bus, she was seventeen." "I always passed by her house, so I stopped and asked her if she needed a ride." "She got in my truck and on the way home; she said she was selling pecan pies trying to raise money for the band." "I ended up buying a slice, and then I bought another slice, and then another, and then another." "That pie was so sweet and after she gave me some sweet milk to wash it down with, I bought another pie and ate that too." "Today I can't eat another slice of pecan pie, I ate so much that it made me sick."

"How did you and her end up getting married?" I asked him.

"Ronnie" He replied bluntly.

"So, you two have been married for seventeen years?"

"Yeah, she was three months pregnant with Ronnie, if I hadn't had picked her up that day, me and her wouldn't have happened." "None of my kids would have been born by her, and I would still be able to eat pecan pie." He said laughing. "We're almost back" "Kurt we've spent all day exploring, I feel guilty not doing anything."

"Let's see" I rebuked "you gave Bailey a break, you took me fishing and then we went for a long walk and now I have a better understanding of what the property looks like than what I had yesterday." "You told me to be careful of Becky's pecan pie; by the way you described it, it could possibly contain a magic potion." "That there alone tells me that my time was well spent." I said to him. "But if Becky starts complaining about something, don't call my name, I can't help you." "The kitchen is hers."

"Kurt" "I need to say something that's been on my mind." Buck stated. "I never got a chance to properly thank you for doing what you're doing for us."

"Buck" "If you want to thank someone, it's Bailey that you need to thank." I told him.

When we entered, Becky told us to go wash our hands; she complained that we both smelled like fish.

Bailey escorted me to my chair when I came back in and started letting me know that my mashed potatoes and gravy was in a bowl on the left side of my plate and at the top of my plate was a bowl of sweet peas and on the right side of my plate was a bowl of fried squash. "You have two rolls on your plate with your meat loaf cut up and you have toothpicks in each bite."

"You didn't have to do that." I said to her.

"I know, Cindy thought it would be a good idea." "She thought you could feel the toothpicks and that way you'll know that you still have meatloaf on your plate, if you didn't feel them then that way you could ask for more if you wanted it."

I felt along my plate, and found a toothpick and then picked it up, put the meat in my mouth, and gave a big smile. "That was easy."

CHAPTER FOUR

I was out by the pool with Buck listening to the pool man telling him how to operate the filters and chemicals that needed to be added when Bailey came and got me. I had a phone call waiting.

I sat down and listened. "Kurt this is Broderick." "We've got the papers ready in my office, and we need a signature."

"What day do you want me to be there?" I asked him.

"Thursday or Friday sounds good." He remarked.

"Let's do it Thursday" I told him "That way if something comes up Thursday, I'll have Friday; I don't want to have a wasted flight." "What time?" I asked.

"Is two thirty all right with you?" He stated.

"That suits me fine." I told him. "I'll see you then." I then hung up. "Bailey."

"I'm right here Kurt." She said to me.

"We'll be leaving in three days." "I'm going to need you to ask Becky if they considered our proposal, I need to make a call and have a plane readied." "She's going to give you a problem, tell her that we don't like to be turned down on an invitation."

"Kurt, you just said we and our." "You didn't say my or I." She stated.

"Yeah, that's because there's more than one person sleeping in my bed." "That makes the bed our bed." "It wouldn't make for a fair relationship between us if I didn't include you." "You know there's one thing that both you and I are mutual on; that's our future, we don't know what it holds and that makes us both worry that something will go wrong." I pulled out my wallet, and handed her some cards. "I have three cards here." I said handing them to her. "One of them is for a jet, one of them is for a limo in New York, and one of them is the hotel where I have a suite." "I need you to call these people for me."

"How come you don't have a cell phone?" She asked.

"It gives me problems." "People that have my number, have people working for them." "My number gets out and I end up having to change my number." "It's a headache having to change numbers all the time, that's why I have business managers." "When we go to New York you'll be introduced to them." "And you'll give them your number on your cell phone." "Nobody but them is authorized to call me, so if anyone, and I do mean anyone calls, and it's not them, then I don't talk to them." "Bailey, you were right, not just anyone could do what I ask of them."

"Give me the cards." She said after she kissed me.

When we finished, she went and got a pad to mark down all of our dates and times.

"We'll need to be picked up and returned, so call information and get the number to the chamber of commerce and find out what limo services they have available in Murray, if any." I said to her.

When I finished, I hung up the phone. "Now, you heard everything I said." I said to Bailey. "You can tell Becky after she gets through arguing with you, that it's too late, we've already told them that there will be seven of us, and we'll be leaving at six P.M., Wednesday." "Bailey, this is one of those times that you may have to remind her that she's a friend, and not an employee."

I began to make my way back out to the swimming pool, and as soon as I walked out the back door. I found myself being given a tongue lashing. Becky was doing what Becky did best.

"Are you through?" I said to her.

"Kurt, we can't go." She said firmly.

"Becky, you're not giving a we can't go answer, it sounds more like a we won't go type of answer." "Have you ever been to New York?" I asked.

"No"

"Have your kids been to New York?" I continued.

"No"

"Has Buck been to New York?"

"No"

"Becky, I'll tell you what, if you can give me a solid reason why you can't go, I'll not pursue the subject." I challenged her.

"Kurt" She began.

"Not good enough Becky." I said stopping her. "Becky if you're worried about the kids missing school, then you need to go down to Barney's and see what a high school education gets you around here." "One thing's for certain, they'll never say I've never been to New York anymore."

"It's not our place to be with you." She exclaimed.

"Is that what you told your kids Becky?" "You saw Cindy feeding me last night." "I hear laughing and I hear the kids playing like kids." "Now go back in that kitchen and see if you can come up with a better answer, I don't want to tell the kids that we wanted them to go, but your mother sees us differently than what they see us as." "But Becky I would feel compelled to tell them that; they're my leverage against you."

"Kurt"

"Not listening." I said to her.

"Kurt" She once again called my name.

"Becky, the limo will be here Wednesday at four o'clock, that's usually when the kids get here." "We'll have dinner in flight and I need you to dress

Paradox

light; I have to get Bailey some perfume I promised her." "So, Thursday morning will be spent shopping, and Thursday evening we'll be dining and taking in a musical." "Come Friday, the kids will always remember their trip to the Statue of Liberty, and Friday evening we'll dine, and then depart, Saturday morning we'll wake in Maine, we'll do a little shopping and come evening we'll be dining on Lobster." "Sunday morning we'll depart after breakfast and be back here by six." "Now, please don't tell me that I wasted my time making arrangements."

"I don't know what to say." She stated.

I hesitated before I replied and then stated to her. "Becky, I'd like for you to ease up a little." "From what I gather, you've always been a cook." "It's either what you like to do, or it's the only thing you know how to do." "One of the hardest tasks a person can perform is to cook every day of the week, every day of the month, and every day of the year." "That leaves you with very little time to relax." "You have a television set where you can watch cooking shows to help give you your ideas, and a computer so you can order anything you wish and have the convenience of having it delivered right to our doorsteps." "All of it fresh," "You see something, and you think you might want to do that, then you can get on the computer and type up whatever they're cooking and you print the recipe out." "You want cake, find the recipe and print it out." "You want pie, no problem, print it out." "Beef, pork, chicken, mutton, sea food, all of it can be ordered and delivered right here, from anywhere in the world." "Give me four days, and the next time we travel you won't be giving me the resistance that you're giving me now."

"The next time?" She queried.

"Becky, Bailey asked me if I ever worked." "I told her no." "It was the truth, I didn't."

"I don't follow." She returned.

"Earlier while we were making the arrangements, Bailey asked me how come I didn't carry a cell phone." I stated. "Three years ago, my life began" "I had people saying that they were secretaries and personal assistants and all kinds of titles that were bogus." "I was asked from them if I would attend a fund raiser, luncheon, dinner, or participate in a social event." "Two years ago, there were some commercials that aired with my voice declining those invitations." "I never got involved in politics." "I don't carry a cell phone anymore; I found out it's not that hard to doctor a conversation." "So, sometimes I'm forced to stand up in front of people and tell them that what was said by the way it was worded implied that I supported a candidate that I didn't support, and I was there to correct that error." "I had to tell them that any candidate that approves any advertisement with my endorsement had to be doing so knowing it was a lie." "There's no way out." "By me standing up and correcting that error, it gave others the impression that I supported the other candidate." "They ran advertisements showing me discrediting their opponent so the opposite party made it look like I supported them." "Becky, papers don't always print what was said the way it was said."

"I don't follow you." She replied.

I began to explain what I was telling her. "All it takes is to have a picture of someone, it could be ten years old, and you have a story that's taken ten years to unfold." "None of it has to be true, but the people that read that story think it is, or the paper would be sued for libel and slander." "When you sue a paper, it takes time, a long time." "The judicial system has an appeal process and nothing is resolved until you've ran out of appeals." "In the meantime; the paper sells their papers, and profit from the battle through the court system." "They settle out of court without claim of malicious misconduct or willful intent, and by doing so they admit no wrongdoing, all the while netting a profit of fifteen to twenty million; depending on damages." "There's no retraction and the paper end's up making millions writing a story proclaiming a victory." "If you don't have stories in papers, then papers aren't read." "After a while, you get to where you don't go anywhere." "I've had four paternal lawsuits." "None of them were impregnated by me." "All they wanted was hush money, a billionaire doesn't miss fifty million." "But, when a person makes an accusation, the papers pay handsomely for exclusive interviews." "Stories are printed and papers are sold." "The papers aren't liable because they aren't making the accusation." "After a while, people begin to believe that with so many accusations, all of them can't be lying." "Becky, it only takes one member of a jury to find you guilty."

"I'm sorry." She said to me. "Did you just say Billionaire?"

Bailey interrupted. "Is that what you were talking about when we met?"

"Yeah, three of them were found guilty of attempted extortion after the test was done." "Bailey, there's only one way to get someone pregnant, I never met those girls."

"What about the fourth?" Bailey asked.

"That one got ugly." I started. "She aborted the baby, and claimed that I had her kidnapped and a doctor took the baby to keep me from being convicted." "When she woke up, her stomach hurt, and she didn't remember anything, all she knew was she lost the baby." "She was a good actress, she could cry on demand, but she had a past, and it came back to haunt her." "It turned out that she had an abortion two years earlier." "Her boyfriend and her were in on the scam; he broke rank and testified on my behalf." "She ran into a snag when she said we had dinner and after dinner we left, what got her was the restaurant she said we were at had surveillance cameras that proved she was lying." "Her boyfriend didn't want to go to jail." "So, he testified and was found guilty and his plea was honored, he got probation." "His girlfriend was convicted of attempted extortion, and perjury." "Papers had a field day saying that I bought her boyfriend out."

"Is that why you came here?" Becky asked.

"Becky, have you ever been anywhere away from here?" I posed her question with a question of my own.

"No" She replied.

"I've been to seven states." I asserted. "I can't tell you anything about those states, I'm like you; I've never seen them." "I can tell you a little about this house, and I can tell you a little about the path I take to the pond." "But outside of that, it's like you never going anyplace over an hour's drive away." "That's the way I lived." "Business always and retreat back to my studio." "Becky, you can search for whatever you look for, and never find it." "Maybe it's too far out of reach, I don't know, but I do know for the first time in my life I don't feel confined." "I come from somewhere else; maybe you need to go somewhere else in order to find out that you live in a better place than what you thought, or you may find out that you prefer to be somewhere else, instead of here." "This is my retreat, but it may be a prison for you, this house is my sanctuary; it may be a cell for you." "In New York, I walk outside my door and get into an elevator and walk outside the building one way to five miles of business after business, after business, after business, with countless crosswalks and not any of the cafes make cocoa the way you do." I told her. "The best time to take a stroll was nine to ten in the morning, and two to three in the afternoon; you only had to deal with the crosswalks, and delivery men." "If you go any other time, you'll not get to where you're going as quick as what you hoped." "Do you know when I ate at your diner that was the first time that I ever got a hamburger that fast." I said to Becky. "And I'm sorry, but that was the first time that I was able to dine without having twenty conversations going on around me." "I enjoyed the peace."

"That's because business was slow." She said acknowledging my compliment.

"That may be, but in New York there's a saying, no line, new business coming soon, watch for grand opening." I commented "Let's say you had a steady flow of customer's, the more money you make the more it takes to operate your diner." "You may find out that you were working for all of your employee's, they brought home a steady paycheck, but you had to work the books, order the food, and you did their work for them while they took a break." "It's the same everywhere, if you need more people, then it will cost you more money to operate that business."

"Did you talk with my husband about this?" She asked.

"No ma'am, I didn't think I needed to." "Buck and you get along pretty good." "In a marriage like that, I would assume if Buck came in and said we're going somewhere, you might get mad, and you may throw one huge tantrum, but you would do it in the airplane on the way to New York." "Becky, that's called love." "On the other hand, you can be the one that tells Buck that we're going somewhere and Buck might get mad and throw one huge tantrum, but Buck will do it in the airplane on the way to New York." "He wants to be with you, and you want to be with him." "I believe if Bailey and I had one tenth of what you and Buck have, then neither one us will ever say we made a mistake." "Trust me; you aren't the only one that has trouble falling to sleep at night."

"He's not going to be happy." She stated.

"I know, but I think he needs to understand that your children are going to benefit from this more than you two ever will." "And somehow, hearing that coming from your lips, he'll see it too." I told her.

"I don't understand you" she said "you've changed everything in my life."

"Becky, money does things to people." "What if you were born with it?" "Would you be here doing what you're doing now?" "You don't have to answer that." "I think both of us know that answer." "Becky, I need you, and I need Buck and Ronnie and Julie and Cindy." "All of you are here because of Bailey, and I'm glad you are, she's shown me that I made the right decision in letting her make my house a home." "So, I'd like for you to relax a little, and try to enjoy life a little more." "The laughter of kids isn't heard if you don't listen."

"Where did you hear that from?" She said to me. "That cut pretty deep."

"It's all mine, you can have it if you use it." I responded.

"Let me go talk to Buck and smooth things over with him." She muttered.

I heard footsteps walking away, and then a kiss was felt.

"Kurt, it seems that I have a "Billion" reasons why I should love you." "But I can't really find one reason why you should love me." Bailey said.

"Bailey, you took a chance on Tom and look what it got you." "That can happen to anyone, and you know that." "But there's one big factor you've got in your favor." "I need you."

I felt her kiss again.

That evening I was getting ready to feed the fish in the pond when I heard footsteps running to catch up to me, and then I heard Ronnie's voice.

"Mister B, my mother said we were going to New York."

"Yeah, we'll be leaving Wednesday after you and your sisters get here." I said to him.

"Mister B, I don't know if I want to go." He said in a way that made me draw suspicion.

"Ronnie, with an answer like that, there's got to be a girl involved." "Have you found yourself a girl?" I asked him.

"Yes sir." He answered shyly.

"So, you find it hard to sleep at night thinking about her, huh?"

He didn't give me an answer.

"Did you know this girl before you started working for me?" I asked.

"Yes sir."

"How come you never asked her out?"

"I didn't have a truck; I couldn't get away with my sisters, and besides I didn't have any money to go anywhere." He said softly.

"So, you've been sitting back watching someone else with her, huh?" I said to him.

"No sir, she isn't like that." He stated.

"Ronnie, with your parents working and you watching your sisters, have you ever even been on a date?"

"No sir."

"Do you like her?" I asked him.

"Yes sir."

"The important thing is does she like you?"

"I met her in sixth grade." He stated to me. "She always sat down next to me in the lunchroom." "Momma always put an extra slice of pie in my lunch kit for her when she made pies." "She got kicked by a horse in her head and I didn't see her for the rest of the year." "Come seventh grade, I looked for her in the lunchroom, but she never came there anymore." "About two months after school started, I saw her again." "She had trouble walking and I helped her a little." "We talked some but that was it."

"Ronnie, has anyone ever asked her out, that you know of?"

"I don't know." "She calls me up sometimes and we talk, Mister B, she has trouble with her homework." He told me.

"How old is she?" I asked.

"Seventeen" "but Mister B she failed the seventh grade and had to stay there." "When she moved up into the eighth, she failed the eighth and had to stay in the eighth another year." "She's upset because she's scared that she won't pass." He said sounding distressed.

"So, she didn't get to sit in the lunchroom with you anymore then, huh?" I stated to him.

"No sir, and when I became a freshman, I went on to high school and she was just starting eighth grade, and when I went to the tenth, she was starting the eighth all over again." "Mister B, the kids that are in her class are fourteen and fifteen." "When you gave me my truck, I asked her if she needed a ride home instead of riding on the bus, then I asked her if I could pick her up." "She was crying when we were in the truck because she has problems sometimes." "Mister B, I don't think she's going to get out of the eighth grade." "I don't think she can pass the finals." "If she fails another year, it's going to be bad for her."

"Does she have a small limp to her?" I asked.

"She did in the seventh grade when I saw her again." He said to me.

"Can you see a scar on her?"

"Her hair is long now, but back when it was shorter, you could see it." He confessed.

"Ronnie, back when I was in school, I met kids that had a brain injury; some of them never learned how walk or talk again." "I later found out that pressure sometimes built up and they had to relieve it and the only way to do that was open the skull and drain the fluids." "Some of them were like the girl you're speaking of." "They needed help doing the things that I didn't have any problems with." "The point is, maybe she's lost a year of her life and she can't remember that year." "It could be that she didn't even know her mother and father when she woke up." "In school, a lot depends on what you learned the year before and the year before that." "Math, English, and History are all dependent on the ability to remember the basics." I lectured. "In math, a formula is used; and in English, she has to be able to read and remember what she read." "History is a study of the past; it's not easy living in the present when you can't remember part of the past." "She had to learn all of this all over again." "By failing the seventh and eighth grade, she would have been a better student if she would have been put back in the third or fourth grade to begin with." "Let's say you were to ask her out, where would you take her?" I asked.

"Maybe a movie."

"Then what?" I followed.

Paradox

"I don't know, maybe dinner?" He said not sure of himself.

"Ronnie, I know what it's like to want to be with someone." "If this girl is that special to you, I'd be the first one to tell you to stay here." "But, let's give this some thought." "Let's say you were to ask her out on a date." "You could say, hey, I've wanted to ask you out, but I was always scared that you would say no." "Then you could say." "My boss wants me to fly with him to New York, and I would like to take you with me." "Then you tell her that we're leaving Wednesday after school, and if you want me to talk to your parents I will, because I really want you to go out with me on a date in New York."

"We're here Mister B." He said to me.

"Ronnie, I didn't start dating until I was twenty five." I said throwing corn out. "That's when my father died." "Even then a date wasn't actually a date, they were more like escorts." "I never felt that feeling until I met Bailey, when I did feel that feeling, I let her know, and now Bailey is by my side." "I was scared too, that's why I told you to be careful." "The point I'm trying to make is, you'll never know about someone until you tell that someone how you feel." "I think if it was me, I'd get in my truck and go over to her house and knock on her door and say, hey, my boss is flying to New York, and he wants me to fly with him." "I want you to go with me, and if I need to talk to your parents, I will, because I really want you to go with me." "Ronnie, don't let ten years go by and have you wishing that you took that chance." "All she can do is say no."

"They're not going to let her go." He fought back.

"Maybe not, but it sure does sound like this girl likes you." "Ronnie, she may be afraid to say something because she fears you may reject her, the same as you fearing that she may reject you." I argued. "Besides, the point of interest is does she want to go with you." "If she does then you have to be polite and give her parents reasons why they can trust you." "You can tell them that your sisters are coming too." "And if that doesn't satisfy them, you can drive them over here tonight, or tomorrow, I'll be more than happy to talk to them for you." "But I want you to remember this, Ronnie; no one is for certain how their life is going to play out."

All I heard was silence.

"Are you still here Ronnie?" I asked.

"Yes sir, I'm right here."

"Why" I asked "you should be headed towards your truck and driving over to that girl's house right now." "You have something you wish to say to her, don't you?" "Ronnie, I met Bailey at your mother's diner." "She walked me to Barney's grocery store." "We talked and two hours later, she was standing in my door calling me a butt hole." "You've known that girl since sixth grade, and through all of her ordeal, she came back to school and fights every day to be the same as everyone else." "Ronnie, something has to be there, she remembers you." "I only knew Bailey for two hours, and that was all I needed."

I heard silence again.

"Are you still here Ronnie?"

"Yes sir."

"Why, go boy, go get that girl, tell her how you feel about her and how much you need her." "If you don't, you'll be living the rest of your life with this regret." I said to him.

I heard silence again.

"You're not gone yet, Ronnie?" I concluded.

He took me by my arm and started walking me back.

"Ronnie, I know my way to and from the pond, go get that girl, this is your moment." I said with a determinate tone.

"Thanks Mister B." He said as he began running.

I resumed my stroll back to the house. Ten minutes or so later, Julie met me and took my arm to assist me.

"Is your dad mad at me?" I asked her.

"No sir, he said you said something that made him think." "What's New York like Mister Bryant?"

"I can't describe it to you." I told her. "It's a place where people go and fall in love with it, or when they leave, they find themselves finding a way not to ever go back."

"Do you like it?" She asked.

"I lived there all of my life, and I found myself moving here, I was in search of a princess, I got lucky, I found three of them." "You, Cindy and Bailey." I said to her.

"Do you love Bailey?" She asked bluntly.

"How old are you again?" I asked her.

"I'm thirteen."

"Yeah" "Thirteen going on twenty one." "Julie, do you know what love is?"

"I love momma, and I love daddy, and I love my brother and sister." She replied.

"That's a good love" I said "but one day a boy will come along and he's going to ask you to leave all them here." "And you'll do it." "That's love."

"What about you?" She followed.

Paradox

"I'd like to think that this is my home." I began. "I'd like to think that you thought of it as a home too." "But what if I took Bailey away from here and decided that New York was where I thought I really wanted to be." "I gave that a lot of thought, and I put it out of my mind." "I wouldn't be able to go to your graduation; I wouldn't know what college you were at so I could come and visit you and most of all, I really do like you as a friend." "Julie, it would get awful lonely in my house without you."

"Mister Bryant, I love you too." She stated.

"Oh!" "Does Bailey have competition?" I asked her.

"NO" "Not like that." "I mean, I love you."

"I love you too." I told her.

She held my arm to stop, and then pulled me into the door and stopped me to shut it.

"Hold out your hands." Becky said handing me a mug full of cocoa.

"And what do I owe for this auspicious moment to?" I said to her.

"First off, I don't know what that word means." She chuckled. "And secondly, I feel good, okay." "Did you send Ronnie to Barney's?" "He came in and left in a hurry."

"He didn't want to go to New York." I responded to her.

"Why"

"Let's just say, when you see Ronnie again, don't ask him anything about where he went." "I told you that Ronnie is turning into a man." "Becky, if he goes with us, he'll remember New York for the rest of his life."

"What do you mean if?" She shot back.

"Ronnie wasn't going to come with us." "He's found himself a girl, and he doesn't want to be away from her." "So, I told him to invite her along." "It was either that or Ronnie was going to stay, he had his mind already made up." "The odds aren't in his favor, so don't be asking him questions, he may be hurting instead of rejoicing." I stated. "But, if I get a telephone call, and you answer it, and it's Ronnie, then her parents are calling to talk to you or me." "I'd rather you talk to them, I'm sure you know them." "Becky, if they call your son is going to need your help; they won't let her go without it." "If he doesn't call, then he won't feel like talking, and if they come here, you'll know why they come."

"Who is it?" She asked.

"I never asked him." "He said he knew her since sixth grade." I told her.

"I bet its Cheryl." "Did he say anything about her?" She was inquisitive.

"I don't feel comfortable discussing Ronnie's conversation." "That causes problems but I can say he told me that he's been picking her up in the morning to take her to school and bringing her home." "If you have questions, Julie and Cindy can probably tell you what you want to know." "Becky, if she says she wants to go with him, but her parents won't let her, he's not going to come with us; he'll stay here and take her to school with him and pick her up, he wants to be with her."

I felt a hand holding my arm, it was Bailey's.

"You've been gone for almost an hour." She chided me. "I don't like it when you're not with me."

"You weren't talking to me like that when we met." I teased her back.

"Let's not go quite that far back." She stated "Let's start off somewhere in between, like later that night when you kissed me."

"Y'all two need to get a room somewhere else other than my kitchen; I've got things to do." Becky said getting the last words in.

Bailey walked me into the family room and sat me down on the sofa and sat next to me.

Later, Becky and Buck were about to leave with the kids when the doorbell rang. It was Ronnie with the girl and her parents.

Becky walked them into the family room to sit down with the rest of us. After introducing ourselves, Ronnie introduced the girl he liked to us, Becky was right, it was Cheryl.

"I guess we all know why we're gathered here tonight." I said opening the conversation. "Ronnie, would you take Cheryl and your sister's out back and have them help you show her around, and tell me if that pools warm yet, I need Julie and Cindy checking it out tomorrow to make sure it's the right temperature, I don't like the water cold."

When they left, I opened the conversation again. "I assume you're here because Cheryl wants to go with us." "I'd like to explain something." I said to both of them. "I told Becky I was diagnosed at an early age with a form of autism, and because of that I was labeled as institutionalized." "Basically, that meant that my comfort zone was breached beyond the walls of the school." "My only form of education came from books and teachers." "No book can tell anyone what it feels like to ski, or skydive, or compete against a competitor in an event." "I still can't ski, or skydive without assistance, and I don't like it." "I don't know where I'm going to end up after I stop." "One thing I do know" I spoke to their parents "your daughter is a lot like me, she's struggling to keep up, and I'm sure you've exercised all avenues of exploration in helping her to do just that." "I think you may be overlooking a valuable variable." "Your daughter is seventeen and she's like all other seventeen year old's; they seek independence." "Ronnie wasn't going to go with us to

Paradox

New York because he wanted to stay here, to be with Cheryl." "I think you remember the play that was written by Shakespeare of Romeo and Juliet."

"I thought it was girl stuff." The girl's father said.

I continued. "Romeo was sixteen when he met Juliet at a party, she was thirteen." "But it was love at first sight." "Their love was forbidden; their family had been feuding for years before they were born." "Juliet ended up taking a sleeping potion to make it look like she had died, it was a fake death." "She sent word to Friar Lawrence about what she was going to do, but he never got the message, and when Romeo saw Juliet in her casket, he became so despondent that he swallowed poison, he couldn't live without her." "When Juliet awoke, she saw Romeo dead, and she took his knife and stabbed herself, she couldn't live without him." "I'm sure you both remember the good times you had when you were young, you were a Romeo and Juliet too." I said to them "I learned that by listening to a play, not from a book." "I was like you sir." "I thought it was girl stuff." "I thought it would be best if I let you know that if you find that this trip isn't right for her, you could witness her breakdown." "She's tried so hard, and come so far, for what?" "Will she ever get a good job somewhere, or will she be forever bound by her limitations?" "I think those are the answers that Cheryl's seeking."

"Are you a lawyer?" The girl's father asked.

"No sir, my parents were." I answered.

Buck interrupted.

"Elrod, I was against going too, but Kurt brought it to my attention that my kids would learn more in four days then what they taught them in school for the whole year." "No matter what kind of fuss I posed, I couldn't speak against it." "He's right."

"I'd like to ask a question." I stated "Who helps Cheryl with her homework?"

"I do." Her mother said.

"Do you understand the work she brings home?"

I heard her take a deep breath.

"That pretty much says it all." I said to her. "Ma'am, with Ronnie, your daughter might have the teacher she needs." "Sometimes you and her might have difficulty connecting, I don't mean as a mother, I mean as a teacher." "There might have been times where your patience was stretched thin and you vented frustrated responses." "If you have, then imagine how she feels; she works in her books at school all day long, and when she comes home, she works on her homework." "Is there no rest for her?" "Ronnie said that she was crying in his truck because she was scared that she was going to fail, that's a symptom of stress." "Can you fathom the weight she's carrying around on her shoulders?" "Now, I want to ask another question." "When was the last time you heard her laughing?" "That's the simplest way to gauge whether you're pushing her too hard or pushing her just right."

I then heard nothing but silence again.

"What I do know is" I began "the next time she sees a picture of New York, she'll look at it and say I saw that, and I bet that she'll be able to tell you everything about what she saw." "It's not what she learns; it's how she learns to learn it." "Once she finds a way, then it gets easier for her, until then it's nothing more than a struggle for her to overcome a hurdle, and she does have her hurdle's, the same as you have yours." "In order for the mind to grow, it has to be nurtured, but if you feed it the same food all the time, then, it won't hunger." "To me it's simple; it's an option to explore another avenue, and I'm sure that when it comes to Cheryl, you won't leave any stones left unturned." "You'll make the right decision; after all you're looking after her best interests."

"A little while ago," the girl's father said "I wasn't even thinking about letting my daughter go; it was totally out of the question." "Mister Bryant, my wife and I had a talk on the way over here, my daughter was riding with Ronnie, so we were able to discuss this without Cheryl." "We came over here to basically have an informal chat, and then I was going to say I apologize but I think it's a little too early for this." "I thought Cheryl needed her education to be able to catch up." "To tell you the truth, I don't know how I even let Ronnie talk me into coming over here."

"Mister Jessup, how come you don't help your daughter with her homework?" I asked him.

"Ouch, that hurts." He said "I can't do it."

"Honey" Becky said "don't feel bad, I can't help Cindy, and she's in the third grade." "Julie has to help her." She said laughing.

"Mister Jessup." I inserted.

"Could you please call me Elrod, that's what everyone around here calls me, and my wife goes by Patricia." He stated.

"Elrod" I injected "Cheryl has a troubled time in front of her." "She has uncertainty as a guide for her future." "Due to an accident, your hope of raising a child to grow up in a normal atmosphere has been thrown off its course." "There aren't any doctor's that can give you any of the answers you ask them, if they do, they're formulating a professional guess, not an opinion but a guess." "They spent hundreds of thousands of dollars to be able to tell you that they spent hundreds of thousands of dollars on becoming a doctor so that they could charge you a fee for that professional guess." "Here's a tip I'll give you." "Not all of them know what they're doing in the field they're in, the brain is an organ that man doesn't have much knowledge of how it operates." "Do they have a cure for Alzheimer's or Parkinson's or tremors or any muscle in your body that jerks without control?" "Ronnie said he sat down at the lunchroom and shared his pie with her that his mother made, and after that, she got hurt." "Ronnie's in the eleventh grade, so that means it was roughly five years ago that this incident happened." "The first year involved healing, the second, third, fourth and fifth years, began a rebuilding process, but you didn't see her growing up and learning anything." "Elrod, I didn't start school until I was twelve and trust me, nobody could teach me anything; I absolutely refused to listen." "One day, it was like I woke up." "I couldn't get enough, I wanted more." "Kids don't go to school to learn, they go to school to prepare themselves for the day to come when what they studied will be recalled, that's when I learned and remembered what I learned, and so I had to go back to school all over again." "Cheryl's had a minor setback and she needs to go to school all over again like me." "She doesn't remember a part of her life." "She started her schooling back over in the seventh grade and I think that was a mistake." "Elrod and Patricia, I need you to close your eyes for a moment if you will." I gave them enough time to do as I ask. "When I met Becky, she made a comment about a drought that this community is under" "and Buck showed me the layout of the land." "My way of learning was putting things in a material form and use comparisons to remember, so if you will, try to envision what I say." "We were walking down in the creek that bordered the rear of the property, and I noticed the banks on the creek were close to ten feet tall or more." "We had to crawl down an embankment to get down in it, and then crawl back out another embankment." "Now this is the part that I need you to listen to." "One day it's going to rain, and due to the ground being dry, it'll suck up all the moisture it can." "That's the brain side of the equation." "After the ground becomes saturated, it can't absorb any more moisture, and it runs off into the creek and the creek overflows its embankment and rushes away from where it fell as fast as it can." "The brain can only absorb just so much and the rest isn't heard and my belief is if wisdom isn't read, then it's wasted." "A brain injury is like the ground; it can only absorb so much." "The creek represents knowledge, when a child loses focus, that knowledge can't be absorbed; it rushes away as fast as it can." "Oh," "but that creek doesn't go to waste totally, it drains into the lake." "It may take a while, but that lake will come back up." "You can't tell me when, it may be this month or a month from now, or even a year or two, or more." "You can ask meteorologists and you'll get professional guesses." "But, none of them can tell you when it's going to rain, you'll only get procrastinations." "If you want to find out who's right and who's wrong, then I think you need to slow down some, it's going to take you fifty years to find that answer." "Cheryl is like that lake, the lake won't fill up without a flow to the creek from rain, one day all that knowledge will be stored away and your daughter will wake up like I did." "The rain will come again, and knowledge will be absorbed, and what isn't absorbed is recycled to be used at a later time." "I told you I like using comparisons." "Elrod, if I was to give you a book of Romeo and Juliet, would you be able to write an essay on the book after you read it?" "Don't answer that, it's not a question, I stated it to make a point and the point is, I couldn't, but when I heard the play, I could." "That play opened my doors and I was free." "Cheryl has her doors." "I can't promise you anything except it gives you another tool that could be useful to her."

"Mister Bryant." He said to me.

"That's Kurt." I politely responded.

"Kurt" "I can see why Ronnie had me talk to you." He said "I have to say though; you hit me with some pretty good punches." "Rumor had it that you were a spoiled brat, and I think I came in here expecting you to behave like one." "I need to apologize to you for that."

"There's no need." I told him. "There's nothing anyone can say to sway the minds of the curious." "It's fueled by inaccuracies, and inaccuracies are repeated to others that listen to what is said, and those others repeat what they hear with their own version of the story, and a new rumor is born with more inaccuracies."

"Do people talk about me?" Bailey asked.

There was silence.

"Bailey" I began "there's other questions you should ask to go along with that one." "You should ask if they talk about Buck, and Becky." "Then, you should ask, do they talk about Ronnie, and Julie, and Cindy." "The answer is yes." "Kids spread the rumors they hear from a parent like a cold." "After tonight, rumors will begin circulating about Ronnie and Cheryl." "I'm sorry Elrod and Patricia; you're going to become an object of attention through your daughter, whether you want it or not." "They'll be talk tomorrow night about Ronnie asking her to go to New York with him." "If you socialize, you can expect a casual visitor or a telephone call where a subject happens to come up involving your daughter going to New York with Ronnie." "As long as Ronnie and Cheryl are dating, they'll be rumors, and if they stop dating, they'll be rumors." "Elrod and Patricia, does it bother you any about what I just said?" I asked.

Patricia was the first to speak.

"I don't see where it's anybody's business." She commented.

"Ma'am, you're right, it isn't anybody's business, but when you talk to someone that's not going to repeat what you say to others, then it's all right to talk, at least that's what people think." "Maybe you can appreciate why I choose to keep a low profile." I told her.

I heard the kids coming into the room laughing.

"Ronnie, you want to give Cheryl a grand tour of the house." I said to him.

"Sure Mister B."

"Would you mind if I go with them?" Patricia asked.

Bailey jumped up and told her that she'd come with her.

"I'm going to put on some coffee, and some cocoa." Becky said. "Kurt, you got my kids hooked on cocoa." "They have to have it every morning and night now; they've turned into cocoa fiends." "Julie and Cindy like it with marshmallows, and Ronnie likes whipped cream the way you do." "Buck likes his dry; me, I still like my coffee."

When she left, everything became quiet.

"You do any fishing, Elrod?" I asked.

"I hadn't been fishing since I was a boy, I was always too busy." He replied. "When Cheryl got kicked, I found out that nothing matters." "I sold my business and rounded up every cow and horse I had and took them all to the barn; I didn't have time to take care of them anymore." "Cheryl stayed in the hospital for almost three months before she got to come home." "Kurt, I heard my daughter laughing when they came in, that made me think about what you said, and it hurt; she was laughing when she got kicked." "I never heard her laugh since then, that is until now."

"Well, I think you can let that part of your life go now." "Elrod, when your daughter suffered her injury, you and your wife suffered an injury as well." "No parent can sit for hours on end watching their baby in a hospital bed with tubes attached to her." "It's quite a strain." "You may not realize it, but you and Patricia need emotional strengthening just like Cheryl does." "By letting Cheryl be with Ronnie, it's going to do her good, and it's going to do both of you good too." "I told Becky Ronnie was becoming a man, I'm sorry, but I have to tell you the same thing, your daughter is growing into a young lady, and she needs someone right now that she can talk to." "As a parent, you should know that, and Elrod, that day has come, she wants to go with us or you and Patricia wouldn't be here."

CHAPTER FIVE

"Awe man, cool, it's as long as our bus." I heard Julie exclaim when they got out of the truck.

"Ronnie get Cheryl's suitcase and put it in the limousine." Becky told him. "Buck, check and make sure everything is locked up."

"I've checked it three times already." He stated.

"Then check it once more then." She was nervous, but she was ready to go.

"You can relax Becky; we're not on any set time frame." I told her.

"That's not it, I've never flown, and it scares me." "I keep thinking about Doctor Wilcox." She admonished.

"Doctor Wilcox went down over water" I commented "we have airstrips in every county." "We've got plenty of places to land in an emergency." "Becky, how many people have been killed on that one road that you drove every day to Murray, and back home." I asked. "If you think about it, your chances are worse driving on "it" than flying in that plane." "Tonight, when you lay down to go to sleep, can you guarantee me that you'll wake up tomorrow?" "I can only say we live on borrowed time, so relax, and watch the kids have fun, if we make it, then it wasn't our time to go, and no one knows when that is."

"I definitely had you figured all wrong when you came into my diner." She relinquished.

"That happened for a purpose." I replied. "When you figure it out, come talk to me, until then, I really wish you would loosen up a little." "You and I are going to be together for a long time, unless you find a better offer somewhere." "If I was to tell you how I feel about you." "I would say, if I was having a picture made of a family portrait, I would want Bailey on my right side, and I would want you on my left side."

She ran away crying.

"You do have a way with words." Bailey said.

"Perfume is going to be the first thing on my list." I told her. "I can't smell you when you sneak up on me."

"Kurt, you made me fall in love with you." "The kids are ready; they're in the limo waiting." "They're having a good time and they haven't even left yet." "To be honest with you, I've never rode in one either."

"I know; that's what separates some people from others." "Bailey, I hope you never change, you're beautiful just the way you are."

"What brought that on?" She asked.

"Nothing, I was just recalling why I moved here." I replied.

"We're ready." Becky shouted.

We were about to get into the car when I asked the limo driver to stop by the grocery store, I had a few items I needed.

We soon were pulling into the parking lot of Barney's.

"Ronnie and Cheryl would you mind running in for me and get us some chips and dips?" I said to them. "I don't like Caviar, it's too salty." "Julie and Cindy, you might as well go with them, I like a variety, and it seems like everyone likes what I like."

"There's plenty of stuff in here." Becky commented after they got out. "And you ain't gonna get no Caviar in Barney's."

"You've got a computer in the kitchen" "if I wanted some" "I'd order some." I chuckled. "Besides this is their moment, take a look around, are there people looking at us?" I asked.

"Yeah" she said. "Everybody"

"Now, think like a seventeen year old." "What kind of feeling does a seventeen year old have when everyone is watching you?" "Elrod said these people like to talk, so why not give them something to talk about." I confronted her.

"Kurt, you're difficult to argue with." She complained.

"Becky, there's something you need to know." "I don't like going places where I don't I know anybody." "I'm sort of shuffled off and put in the care of one individual to another." "I don't feel comfortable." "I have to travel on occasion, and when I do Bailey will be by my side, she's my security, when I call her name she's there, that's devotion, much like you and Buck." "But that poses a problem." "Bailey needs time to be alone; she can't live with me twenty four hours a day, seven days a week."

"Hey, don't start speaking for me." Bailey said.

"It's true Bailey, maybe not now, or maybe not in a few months, but a time will come when you'll need rest, I can be quite a handful." "Becky, that's where you and Buck, Ronnie, Cindy, Julie, and now Cheryl come in, I've never been around a family atmosphere, and I find it to be enjoyable." "But I talk with Ronnie, and we have discussions that he says things to me that he doesn't feel comfortable talking to you." "Julie isn't shy at all; she'll come right out and say I love you." "Honesty spoken from a child is truth without thinking about what was said." "Cindy, now she's a difficult one." "I can't push myself away from the table without being forced fed the last of my dinner." "Now Buck, that brings me to you." "Take a real good look at that house." "No house that big can go without its problems, so I would imagine that sometimes you might need Ronnie to assist you." "You could hire someone to do it, but you don't, there's only one reason, nothing is done right unless you do it yourself, you have a lot of pride." "In my travels from time to time, I've had escorts, I couldn't talk around them." "Bailey will accompany me at all times, that is, unless she chooses to be somewhere else."

"There you go again." Bailey said.

"Let me get this straight, you want us to travel with you?" Becky interrupted.

"It causes me less problems." I said to her. "Besides, I learn a lot by listening to what the kids know today." "I missed out on that stuff."

"How" She asked.

"You get punished when you're a problem child." I told her. "They'd put me in my scream room and let me get all of my aggression out of my system." "That went on for quite a while, so, interactions with other kids were totally out of the question."

"What do you mean, scream room." She asked.

"Talk to Bailey, she'll tell you." "So, when I talk to Cindy, Julie, Ronnie, Cheryl, you, Buck, and Bailey, it's an enjoyment that I cherish."

"Shh, here come the kids." Becky said.

When the driver continued on the kids began telling everyone about what was going on. They talked about people asking them where they were going, and what was they going for.

"What did you tell them?" I asked Ronnie.

"I told them that I didn't know." He said to me.

"Ronnie, a while back we had a discussion on what the description of your job title was, and I told you that you were a personal business associate." "From now on, that's the way you'll address and present yourself to anyone." "I do that for a reason, I see you as a very intelligent man that has maturity far beyond his years." "There are some things that people don't need to know, and that's our personal life." "You listen and you use good judgment, that's evident by Cheryl here." "I think she's quite a beautiful young lady." "And to choose you shows me that she's a smart girl." "I hope everyone here heard what I said." "I don't want to hear anything other than I'm a personal business associate." "If you do, people won't look at you as an equal, they'll look down on you." "Cindy, and Julie, this applies to you especially, when you have something to say, don't be afraid to speak your mind, I want to know what you're thinking." "I need the honesty you have, and sometimes that honesty turns out to be the best solution." "Now, reach in the cooler and pass the cold drinks around and open the chips and dips." "Let's celebrate the beginning of a good weekend." I stated.

"Open up your mouth." Cindy said sitting on my lap. "Are you ready for another one yet?" She asked.

I opened my mouth and snatched it from her fingers.

"I love you." She said to me.

I heard silence from everyone.

"That was a nice thing to say." "I love you too." I returned her compliment.

We pulled up next to the jet and departed the limo. The driver took care of our luggage, and I told Bailey to tip him five hundred.

I heard a lot of moans coming from everyone except Bailey.

I tried to calm their fears by relating my first experience in an airplane.

"I was picked up one time and we flew for what seemed like hours." "In reality it wasn't any more than about thirty minutes." "I never understood why I lived away from my father, so I was constantly asking myself one question after the other." "He was a busy man, and he was a business man, and having a kid around, especially a blind one, must have been too much of a burden for him to carry."

The pilot reported we were cleared for takeoff. I don't think anyone was prepared for the quick ascent; I heard a lot of groans.

When he leveled off, I continued on where I left off.

"I don't remember flying on too many trips when I was young, I might have been with my father maybe a half dozen times, I don't know." "We didn't bond that well." "I think maybe me being diagnosed with autism could have played a role on his mind that I wasn't capable of understanding emotions." "I can't ask him those questions now, he's dead." "I've always wondered if he was alive, what would he tell me." "But, years of separation tend to erode the positives you hold onto."

I was awoken from my slumber by Buck's voice. "Naw" "that's way too many people down there." "Look at them buildings, every one of them would come down if they had an earthquake." "I'm telling you; this is a big mistake." He stated his fear.

"Hush" Becky told him. "We're here; let's make the most of it."

"But look how big this place is." He related his thoughts again.

The pilot came on the intercom to tell everyone to fasten their seat belts, we were landing. The moans and groans began all over again.

When we landed, the chauffeur began loading our suitcases, and we were off to our hotel. We were met at the gate by the news media.

"What's going on?" Buck said.

"What happening?" I asked.

Bailey spoke. "There's a bunch of reporters stopping the car."

"Buck, newspapers have to sell their papers, it doesn't matter how they sell them." "What does matter though is who leaked information about me coming here." I said to them.

"Stop driver." I ordered and rolled down the window to a crowd of reporters thrusting microphones and all of them asking questions. I put my hand up. "I can't possibly answer all of your questions" I pointed my finger in a direction. "Ask yours." I stated.

"Mister Bryant channel seven news" a reporter began "it's been rumored that you're eyeing a seat in the senate, can you verify that." He questioned.

"I can only verify that what you heard is true, it is a rumor."

"So, you don't deny it then." He further stated.

"I can only verify that it is a rumor." I repeated. "Next question." I said ignoring the other reporter's comment.

Again, questions were inaudible, so I pointed my finger in another direction. "Ask your question."

"Mister Bryant." "The Daily sun, sir it's been rumored that you've been meeting secretly with several drug manufacturers in the Caribbean, is that why you invested seven hundred million in pharmaceutical stocks." A lady asked.

"I can only tell you that they're rumors." I once again stated.

"Can you explain your absence then?"

"I'm sorry but I'm on a tight schedule." I said as I rolled up the window.

"What was that all about?" Buck said.

"It started when I made some people mad." I told him. "Buck, this is election year and politicians said things about me to make it sound like I was on their side." "I wasn't." "Now, all that's changed."

"But why all the people?" He asked.

"Do you read the financial news?" I replied.

"It never did me any good." He responded.

"Well, maybe that's a good thing." I told him. "See, it's filled with innuendos and inflated numbers." "You have to know what's going on internally in a company; so, if you read the financial news, you would find out one day that all you got was a lot of double digit, double talk." "In the game of stocks, you have winners and you have losers, the trick is not to invest in the losers." "I get a lot more out of a conversation than what other people get, I think it's because most people can't hear what's said, they have eyes so they put more faith on a visual perception." "Buck, when I ask a question, I get my answer." "That reporter asked me about my investment in the pharmaceutical sector." "When her newspaper prints her article along with the other news media's that were present, that sector has moles looking for which investor invests in what." "My stocks go up, and I sell for a profit, so, to assist that speculation I'll invest more and hopefully the sector will see me doing more investing and the stocks will go even higher." "I'll sell when it levels off and when I get out" "investors get nervous and the stocks go down and then the cycle will start all over again." "When I rolled up my window after she asked if I invested in the pharmaceuticals." "I did on purpose." "By me not answering her question, speculators will begin to ask questions." "I'll invest more and that sector will increase in value." "Other's will invest and I'll sell when the price is right." "Now that first reporter asked me if I had eyes on the senate." "That won't be the last time I'll hear that." "Tomorrow, news will be reported that when asked, I didn't deny it." "I get my information from those kinds of questions."

"What information?"

"Buck, I don't support either party." "I invest on futures, and the future clearly points which sectors are going to benefit, and I invest in those sectors."

"What are you saying?" He asked.

"There's got to be a flip." I said to them. "I bet on what politicians are elected, and if the wrong person is elected, I'll liquidate my assets in certain sectors."

"Would somebody tell me what he just said." Buck exclaimed.

"They're following us." Bailey said.

"Yeah, the problem is, I'm worried that they'll find out I bought a home in Skinland." I said "Then we won't even be able to take a trip to Murray without being followed."

"We're here sir." The chauffer said.

"All right." "I need everyone to listen to me." I said before we got out. "These people are behind what you hear on the news, they have absolutely no respect." "No question is taboo to them." "They'll try to anger you and make you react with hostility, it's their job." "I handle it by ignoring them, to me they don't exist, but they do get in my way."

I opened the door to resistance and kept pushing until I got out. I held out my hand and helped each one of my guests out of the limo, all the while holding onto them.

The gauntlet of questions the media were asking were personal and some of them pertained to me and Bailey and the rest of my staff, but I held my silence. The hotel security came and held them back for us to enter, none too soon for me.

"Do you go through that all the time?" Ronnie said.

"Somebody told the media I was going to be here." "The question I have to ask is who." I told him.

"Mister Bryant, I'm Steven." "I'll be your valet for your stay." A young man said.

"Steven, are you married?" I asked him.

"Yes sir." He replied.

"You have kids?" I asked.

"No sir."

"I need a little help." I began. "I've got plans to entertain my guests." "I was wondering if you could see to our needs personally." "I find that when under certain circumstances, my goals end up wasted when a lot of people are involved." "Are you interested in my proposal?" I asked him.

"I'm confused sir." He stated.

"Steven, what do you think would happen when I walk out those doors tomorrow to show my guest around?" "I wouldn't be able to do much entertaining would I." "I was hoping to get a van and have someone help me show my guest what Times Square looked like tomorrow morning; all I wanted to do was do a little shopping in peace." "The problem I have is someone told the media that I'm here."

"You want me to get a van and be an escort?" He asked.

"Steven, did you see those reporters when we came in here?" I asked.

"Yes sir."

"They shouldn't be here, but they are." "That puts a chink in my plans." "I need you to ask yourself this question, how do you think I'd be able to do anything with them all over us?" I said to him.

"I see your point sir."

"Steven, no one other my guest that's with me knows anything about what was said between us." "If I have to fight the media tomorrow, I'll know how they got the information."

"Sir, I've been a valet for three years." He spoke. "I understand." "What time would you like for me to pick you up sir?"

"Nine, I have a meeting at two thirty, and after that we'll have dinner, and I thought we'd take in a musical." "Steven, does your wife work?" I asked.

"No sir."

"Then, you'll need to bring her with you." "I need you." I stated to him.

"Your bags are here sir." "If you'll follow me, I'll prepare your suite." He said to me.

Bailey took me by my arm and led me to the elevator. When we got off Steven unlocked the door and had the porters unload our baggage.

He began showing everyone their rooms, and then stopped to talk to me.

"Mister Bryant, I learned a long time ago to keep my mouth shut." "But I think maybe you should know something." "I was told around eight o'clock that you were coming, and I knew how many people were coming with you." "When you start looking at people and wondering about them, then, I wouldn't underestimate the manager." He stated to me.

"Do you have facts?" I asked him.

"Mister Bryant, I don't see anything, and I don't hear anything." "But the advertisement is free and its worth millions." "Sir, some people come here wanting that kind of treatment they gave you."

"That explains the lapse in the hotels securities attention." I said "Steven, I want you to go home and get a good night's rest." "I've got a lot to do, and no time to do it in."

I shook his hand and then I heard the door shut.

"You've got a way of talking that doesn't leave much room for guessing what you're trying to say." Bailey commented "You know when I first met you; you said a lot of things that didn't make much sense to me." "What we ran into tonight didn't make any sense to me at all." "This is a part of you I've never seen." "What's happening?"

"This is election year" I told her "I've been accused of bribery, and insider trading, all in the name of trying to paint a picture of why you shouldn't vote for the other man." "The problem is I don't do anything without documentation, this is a legal world we live in." "Bailey, what all of you encountered tonight was feinted, it was staged." "Take a look around this apartment." "I lived here undisturbed for almost two years." "I came and went as I liked." "No one met me at the front doors stopping me." "But, when I started protesting the use of my name in an unauthorized advertisement, I became a soldier fighting for justice, at least that's what one article said about me, but other articles didn't care about facts, they printed what someone said, so, it became news." "In Skinland, no one knew me." "I was overwhelmed and I was really tired, but I'm not a quitter." "If I don't verbally respond to a comment, I'm guilty by not responding and trying to correct a false allegation and then at that point if I react with criticism, I'm fabricating statements to distort the truth." "That's one of the reasons I didn't answer that reporter's question about me investing in the pharmaceutical sector."

"What's a valet?" She asked.

"A valet is a person that keeps up with every minute out of your day." I stated to her.

"You don't think I could make a good valet?" She questioned.

"First off, do you know anything about New York?" I asked her.

"No"

"Then, I'll answer that question with a question." "Do you see where you're at now?"

"Yeah, sitting next to you." She answered.

"Well, as a valet, you wouldn't be." "You'd be making reservations, and talking to secretaries." "Bailey, your place is beside me, and that's where I want you, not away working on my itinerary."

"That's a beautiful sight." Becky said coming into the living room from their bedroom.

"It's been my home for almost three years." I said to her.

"We're awful high up." Buck made mention. "Have they ever had earthquakes here?"

I had to laugh.

"I need everyone to be quiet." I said, and after a few minutes I spoke. "What did you hear?"

"I didn't hear anything." Becky said.

"That's all I heard since I moved here." I stated.

We were interrupted by the kids coming into the room.

"Did you live here by yourself?" Julie asked.

"Yeah, I had troubled times and I needed to be alone" I said "but I found out that that wasn't what I wanted at all, it made me feel worse."

"Why" she asked.

"I was lonely, so, I bought a house and fell in love." I told her. "I told you I can't live anywhere else; I wouldn't be able to see you anymore." "You remember that little talk we had about me wanting to know what college you were at so I could come and visit you."

"All right, that's enough." Becky said. "You kids need to go to bed, we have to be ready to go by nine and it's past ten now."

"Becky it's past eleven, we advance an hour." I stated to her.

"That's it, everybody to your rooms." She quickly told them.

"Mom, can me and Cheryl stay up and watch T.V?" Ronnie asked.

I could sense Becky's feelings by the gasp of air she expelled.

I whispered. "Becky, I don't have a right to say anything, this is not my matter." I stated "But, I feel that I need to speak on Ronnie's and Cheryl's behalf." "They're in my suite, they'll be sitting on the sofa, you'll be in the next room, as well as his sister's." "Sometime in the middle of the night they'll both fall asleep and wake up better friends."

"Don't worry Miss Roberts; my momma said boys cause trouble." Cheryl giggled.

"Do you believe that Ronnie is your friend?" I asked Cheryl.

"I like Ronnie."

"Well Becky, Bailey and I are calling it a night; it seems you've got a decision to make."

Early morning, I awoke.

"Are you okay?" Bailey said feeling me move as I was waking up.

"I think the alarm is about ready to go off." I said, and seconds later, it did.

She wrapped her legs around me and squeezed me tightly in a bear hug.

"Last night you told Julie you fell in love, were you talking about me?" She asked.

"Last night, Ronnie wanted to be with Cheryl." I began my answer "I felt the same way about you when you were sitting down next to me in my house." "You ended up in my arms." "If you sneak over to the door and look outside, you might find Cheryl in Ronnie's arms, the way you were in mine."

"You're not a self centered person." That's one of the good things about you." She stated.

"I wouldn't say that" I told her "I do want you all to myself."

We heard a light tap at the door. "Time to get up." Becky said. "We need to be ready."

"For a woman that fought so hard not to come, she's ready to go." I chuckled.

"I love you, Kurt."

"I must be starting to grow on you, huh." I told her.

"You are" she said "I was thinking the other night about you." "I always heard about women wanting a man that wanted her for her mind and not her body." "You don't even know how I look."

"Bailey, as far as me and you are concerned, I wasn't living until I met you." "Becky is finding out what it means to be a mother with a son that has a girl that likes him." "I know how he feels; I have a girl that says she likes me too."

"Take a shower big boy." She blocked my advances "Becky doesn't like having to knock on the door twice."

I heard the bathroom door open and the water from the shower hitting the tub.

"Your shower's ready." Bailey said. "Your clothes will be on the counter next to the sink." "Your towel is hanging on the rack and don't turn the water off when you get out."

"You look handsome." Bailey said tucking my shirt in my pants and adjusting my collar.

She took my arm and walked me out the door into a waiting group.

"I went down to the lobby this morning." Buck commented. "I wanted to get a paper." "I took one step outside to take a look around and stopped and then I turned back around, and came back up here." "I can tell you right now, I don't like it here, no sir, not one bit." "There is way, way, way, way too many people here."

A knock came at the door, and Ronnie answered it. It was Steven and his wife. After introductions were passed around, I struck up a conversation.

"Sarah, I have a meeting this afternoon at two thirty." "I told your husband I wanted to do a little shopping for my girls here." "Cindy is nine, Julie is thirteen, Cheryl is seventeen, and well I don't have to tell you the ages of Bailey and Becky." "I don't know where businesses that cater to women of ages are located."

"I'm assuming we're not talking about the damage." She said with a sour voice.

"Nope"

"What do you want?" She asked bitterly.

I paused for a few moments and then began telling her of my plans. "I want perfume" "clothes" "all I can get till I have to go to my meeting." "After that, I thought we could all take in dinner, and then a musical." "Tomorrow, I'd like to do some shopping before we flew to Maine." "That was my wish, but it's not going to turn out that way." I stated to her.

"Excuse me." She stated.

"Sarah, I asked Steven to take care of me personally." "I'm blind as you can see, but I judge people by perception." "It's all I have." "And judging by my suspicion, you and him are at odds with me because I asked your husband for help."

"What makes you think me and Steven are having problems?" She asked.

"I hear a tone in your voice." "I assume when Steven came home and told you about my plans; you probably didn't like hearing that I invited you along." "I did it for one reason." "I told your husband that I don't like too many people involved in my plans." "I have a life and all of my personal business associates here have a life." "You have a life, and so does Steven." "Neither of you will fight tonight over making our lives pleasant at your expense." "You can go home now." I told her. "I won't be responsible for an argument between you two tonight." "Or will I?" "See if you leave, Steven will have thoughts of his own." "I think it doesn't matter what happens now." "I think you and him are destined to have words and when you do, I want you to remember one thing." "This was my fault, not his." "So, if what I say turns out the way I said it will, then ma'am, I don't think you and your husband will be married very long." "I don't think you fully understand what he goes through, and I find that you're not giving him any support."

"Wait a minute, let's back this up a little bit." She remarked.

"You know me, don't you?" I said to her.

"Yeah, I've heard of you." She responded to my question.

"Buck, did you get that paper this morning?" I asked him.

"Yeah" He responded.

"Did it have anything about our arrival last night?" I asked.

"Yeah"

"Did you read the article?" I asked.

"Yeah"

"Would you get the paper and show the article to Sarah here, and let her read it." I asked him.

After a few minutes, she said she read it.

"Would you give it to your husband and let him read it." I asked her.

After he read it, he said he was through.

"Becky, did Buck show you the article too?"

"Yeah"

"So, everyone has read that article except me and Bailey and probably the kids." I told Sarah.

"Buck, in the article, did it read the way it happened?" I asked.

"No"

"Steven, did the article have anything in it that you saw once we got here?"

"Yes sir" He responded.

"Did they write the article the way it happened in what you saw?"

"No sir." He answered.

"Now Sarah, see how easy it is to formulate a perception of someone by reading a paper." "Your husband is a valet; he's in a position to where he has to please his supervisor; that means he has to cater to his guests on their every whim." "Do you serve him his breakfast in bed?" I asked her.

"No"

"That's odd" I said "if your husband was asked to, he'd do it." I told her.

"Do you iron his shirts and pants?" I asked.

"No"

"That's odd, if your husband was asked to do it, he would." I continued. "So, when you two have that little talk that you're going to have." "And you will have it, maybe not today, or next week." "It might be three months from now, or a year, but one day, you will have a talk." "You're going to hear my words I have to say straight from my mouth, and you'll remember them, you won't need to read any lies that way." "Your husband is in a field where he's a yes man." "He pampers all of his charges." "I'm sorry Sarah, but if he took care of you the way he has to take care of his clients, you'd be a spoilt brat like all of those guests he has to please." "He'd be better off leaving you at home; you don't bring what he brings." "It's his job, not yours."

"You're a rude man." She verbally struck out a blow.

"Yeah, I know, but when you and him have that talk that you're going to have, I want you to remember this conversation we're having." "You aren't on board with your husband, and when the time comes, and it will, I want you to remember my words." "I asked your husband if you worked and he said no." "One day, you'll find a job." "Something may come up to where you may need your husband's help." "I want you to remember coming here, and then I want you to remember when you ask him for help, you'll remember my words of shame on you." "And do you know what the funny part of that is, you'll be recalling my words before you make your call, but you'll be forced to make that call anyway." I stopped my comments and calmed down and then turned my attention to Steven. "Steven, I apologize to you for insulting you." "I should have used more restraint." "If you don't mind, could you call us a limo?" I asked him.

"Mister Bryant." Sarah said. "Is that what you see me as?"

"A lot of people don't care for the way I talk." I said to her. "That's okay; I don't invite them over for dinner." "You said you heard of me, but you said it in a way that sounded as if you had a negative view about me." "Cindy, when you heard this lady speaking to me when she came in, what did she sound like to you?" I asked her.

"Momma said if I don't have something nice to say about someone, then I shouldn't say anything." She stated.

"Your mother's right Cindy, and I should have used that advice." I told her, turning my attention back to Sarah. "Ma'am, all of us here have drawn our own conclusion about this conversation that you and I have been having." "Even your husband has chosen his side." "You're the only one that's going to go home fuming about what I said." "Your husband uses honey to catch flies, your using vinegar." I told her. "You're unhappy, and it shows." "Sarah" I continued "I've been saying things to you that any husband would take offense to." "I'm sure you're questioning why your husband hasn't said one word in your defense." "On your way home, you'll ask him that question." "He's going to say that he's a valet, his job is to please people, and if he doesn't then he'll be looking for another job." "The first question he'll be asked is why were you released from your last job, that's going to hurt him there?" "Then, he'll be worried about what his superiors will say about him." "Then there's the future you'll have to contend with." I told her.

"What about our future?" She asked.

"There won't be any future." I said to her. "Your husband brings home a sizeable sum of money for his services." "If he loses his job because he lost his temper, he wouldn't be able to afford you." "So, it seems he has a struggle ahead of him."

"Is everyone ready?" She asked. "Steven, go down and give me a call and let me know when everything's clear."

I heard the door shut.

"I had that coming." She said to everyone. "Mister Bryant I was mad when I came in here." "I'd like to apologize to everyone for the way I acted." She stated.

"Honey, we've all been standing right where you're at." "Kurt has a way of talking to you in a convincing manner." "You were beaten before you even said hello, only you didn't know it." Becky said. "Now you just calm yourself, I don't know what it is that you think of Kurt, but he's been nothing but good to all of us folks."

There was a casual talk until her phone rang. "Let's move quickly." She told us.

After we left the garage Sarah told Steven we'd hit "Clementine's" first stop.

I felt the shifting of bodies around me. They were checking out all of the sights.

"It looks like on the T.V." Cheryl said.

"Wow, look at that, holy smokes, awe "Naw" "Naw" there's way too many people here." Buck commented. "Wow" he said again.

"Pull in right up there." Sarah said to Steven. Then she turned and explained to everyone.

"There probably aren't any parking spaces around, so when you see a space, get it." "We'll have to walk a couple of blocks." She said to him and then stated "Call me and I'll tell you where we're at."

"Mm, something smells good." Buck said when we got out.

We walked on for a way's and then I told everyone to stop.

"Buck, this is where the smell came from that you smelled earlier, is this a Bakery?" I asked.

A few moments later we entered the establishment. I heard all kinds of moans.

Becky commented. "You wouldn't happen to have cocoa by any chance, would you?"

"Yes ma'am." 'Would you like whipped cream or marshmallow cream."

"One dry, four whipped cream and two marshmallow cream, and one cup of coffee." "What do you want?" Becky said to Sarah. Then I heard her say, come on I ain't got all day. Sarah's phone rang and she told Steven where we were.

"Two cocoas with whipped cream." Sarah told her.

"Make those two extra cocoas with whipped cream." Becky told the clerk.

"Will that be it?" The clerk said.

"No, while you make the cocoa's I'll have everything ready to order." She told him.

I heard laughing, and it made me smile.

"What's wrong with you?" Bailey commented.

"Sarah, would you mind doing me the honors." I said to her.

"All of you have that southern twang to your voice, that's why their laughing, they know you're from the south." She stated. That's when Steven came walking in.

"They all talk funny to me." Cheryl said.

We were interrupted by the clerk handing Becky her order, and she was dispersing the drinks as she received them. Then she started ordering Danishes, muffins, along with éclairs and creamed horns, we were carrying four boxes along with us after we left. It was my job to carry the boxes while everyone else sampled the pastries. Every now and then we stopped, Cindy was adamant about tending to my needs.

"Kurt this is an awful lot of people." Buck said with a mouthful of food.

"Buck, back where you live, you drove every day to Murray." "I found out after riding with Bailey the second day that you can only go as fast as the slowest tractor on the road." "These people are a lot like that traffic, if you're walking to slow; they'll go around you, if not, he's a pickpocket." I heard Sarah laughing.

"We're here." I stated.

"Where?" Sarah said.

"This has to be "Clementine's." "I can smell what I'm looking for." "Follow me." I replied.

"Buck, hold these boxes for me." "Bailey, give me my cane."

I started sniffing the air and pulling the odor in with a constant wave of my hand. Then I found the path to the perfume. Several more waves of my hand had me bending down sniffing the glass of the counter.

"What are you doing?" Bailey asked.

"They spray samples on small pieces of cloth, what isn't sprayed on the cloth, falls on the counter." I told her. "I'm trying to find the one I like; I've smelled a lot of perfumes that wasn't very pleasant to smell."

I began sniffing along the counter again, and then stopped. "Hello, hello, anybody here." I asked.

I'll be right with you, a lady's voice said.

Several more minutes passed. "Hello, hello, anyone here." I asked again.

"I'll be right with you sir." She stated.

"Ma'am, I apologize, but I don't hear you having a conversation with anyone, so I know you're not attending to a customer or talking on a phone." "That means you're doing business other than the business that you're getting paid to do." "I want to see the manager." I told her.

A few minutes went by when a gentleman introduced himself to me.

"I'd like to buy some perfume, but it appears that this company is trying to be run on a tight labor budget." "I approached the counter and worked my way around until I found the area I was looking for." "No one asked if I needed any help while I was doing that, or contacted me in any way." "I assume that you have only one lady present, and she chose to make me wait." "I say assume because I don't hear any other voices helping other customers." "She called you up because I told her I wanted to see the manager." "I have a tight schedule and I don't have the time to wait." "If I did, I wouldn't have asked to see you." "Now, I want to buy some perfume, that lady didn't seem to be too concerned about my needs, if you're like that lady, I need to speak to your supervisor and I can guarantee you, someone will take care of my needs."

"I apologize for your inconvenience sir; how can I assist you?" He quickly replied.

"I need a sample of each bottle in this section, one at a time, and not heavy on the sample, I just need a light touch." I said to him.

He sprayed samples of each bottle like I asked of him. I found one and double checked it.

"Give me six bottles of this." I told him.

"Sir, these bottles are six hundred a piece." He stated

"Give me six bottles and show me the next sample." I said to him.

Each one had five different bottles of perfume for each lady by the time I was through. While the manager was taking care of the payment, I smelled one of the bottles and told Cindy to stick out her arm for me.

"Let me show you something." I told her. "This perfume is powerful; how do you think I found it?" I sprayed a small amount on her wrist and told her to rub it in with her other wrist and then rub it on her neck. "That's all you need, it's that strong." "You put too much on, and I can't breathe." "Julie, you're next, which one do you like?" After waiting a few moments, I smelled the perfume she was applying to her wrist. "You did good." "I can smell the perfume, and it's a good choice too." I told her.

"Bailey, stick out your wrist." I said and then gave her a light spray. I began sniffing along the side of her neck. "Yeah, that's the one." I told her. "It says vampire."

"Becky, stick out your wrist." I sniffed around and chose her bottle. "After she applied it to her neck, I began sniffing along the side of her neck too. I began whispering as I sniffed. "You know Buck is going to be nibbling on your ear tonight." I said as I quickly took a bite of her neck. She couldn't stop laughing.

I took several small whiffs and told Cheryl to hold out her wrist. When I sprayed hers, Ronnie gave her a compliment and told her that she smelled nice.

"That brings me to you Sarah." "You're a trapped wild tiger in a cage." "Bailey was like that, but she's tamed down some now." I sniffed the bottles and selected one for her. "Hold out your wrist." I said as I smelled her perfume and took my hand to wave the aroma in. I smiled.

"What's that grin on your face for?" She said to me.

"Oh nothing, I just smell the same thing your husband smells." I told her.

"And what's that?"

"Steven, would you close your eyes and use your nose to tell her what you smell?" I said to him.

We were interrupted by the manager. "Will that be all?" He asked.

"That'll do, and sir, I appreciate your quick action." I told him.

"Mister Bryant, I apologize for the inconvenience you were shown earlier."

"That's all right; you more than made up for it." I said to him.

"Where to next?" I asked Sarah.

"Daniels," she said.

"Honey go get the van and come pick us up." Sarah told Steven.

"I'll be right back." He stated.

"Take your time" I told him "I didn't get a chance to finish my cocoa."

"Open your mouth." Cindy said.

"Mm, what was that?" I asked her.

"A piece of cheese Danish, you want to try the blueberry one?" She asked.

"You bet" "I never had a blueberry Danish."

"They're good, I ate a whole one." She answered.

"What are you, tourists; only tourists stand in the middle of a walk?" A man commented.

"Keep moving jerk." I said to him "I pay my taxes, and I choose to sit and eat my pastry right here." "How far would you have been if you hadn't of stopped to pollute the air by opening your mouth?" "You must not be in all that big of a hurry to begin with, so keep your mouth closed; when it's opened it tells people you didn't graduate from grade school."

"If you weren't blind, me and you would be."

I stopped him. "Yeah, I wouldn't let that stop you, everyone that's listening already knows you didn't graduate." "Oh, but that may be the reason you made your comment, you can't fight anyone else so you seek out someone you can punch without fear, you must have been abused as a child and this is your way of striking back." "I bet if you went to a doctor all of them would tell you that you hated your mother?" "Move along jerk, no one invited you into our conversation."

I heard him give verbal insults as he walked away.

"Woo," "I thought there was going to be trouble." Buck said.

"Buck, no one has a right to tell anyone what they should do." "That man there didn't own this walk; it wasn't built for him to walk without some type of delay." "He was angry about something or he wouldn't have said a word." "Look around, do you see anyone watching us to see what's happening?"

I waited and he responded. "Maybe a few."

"That's only because they wanted to see action." "They had spectators that came to the coliseums to see the Christians being fed to the lions too." I spoke.

"You know he's right." Sarah said. "You do take offense easily." "Let's go." Sarah began urging everyone into the van. The sounds of horns and insults filled the air when we entered traffic.

About thirty minutes later, we pulled into a garage and rode an elevator.

"This is "Daniels." Sarah said. "If you need anything call me on the phone or come into the store." "Other than that, get lost." She said to us men.

"Well, we can check out what's inside this place, or we can go sit on a bench and watch chic's as they go by." I stated. Both Buck and Steven erupted in laughter. "I need a coin." I said "Heads we go right and tails we go left." "Ronnie, you haven't said much, do you see anything you'd like to check out."

"No sir, I was thinking what if I had to live here, I couldn't, and I was trying to understand how you did." He replied.

"I'm assuming you're referring to me being blind."

"Yes sir."

"I didn't" "I was confined to four walls." I responded to him.

I heard Buck repeat a comment. "I'm like you son, I couldn't live here either, there's way too many people for me."

"Then we go with the coin." I said "Someone flip it."

"Heads" Buck said. "We go right.

"You can get anything you want right here, in Times Square." Steven said. "We'll take a walk and I'll tell you what every shop has in it, and if anyone wants to look around, then we'll stop and take a look."

We were almost back when Steven got a phone call from Sarah telling him that they were ready to go.

Everyone was waiting for us at the garage when we arrived. After they loaded all the clothes in the back, we left to go sign the papers on the house.

"Tenth floor." I said to no one in particular after we got on the elevator.

When the door opened, I gave instructions for us to turn to the left and we'll go to the end of the hall where we have to enter two more doors. When we got to the doors, I opened one and we all walked in.

"Mister Bryant, you're expected." The secretary said. Bailey held me back and then led me in.

"Can the rest of you wait outside?" She asked.

"They're with me." I told her. "They're my personal business associates."

"Yes sir."

I walked around and shook everyone's hand; I stopped and spoke to one of my staff. As I shook his hand, I put my other hand over his wrist.

After the introductions, a member of my staff was about to start the meeting when I stopped him.

I stood up from my seat. "I apologize for my behavior, but in order to prevent a possible future lawsuit, I have to intervene and halt this transaction." "Mister Reynolds, I need lab work done on you." "Mister Laree please notify the lab that Mister Reynolds will be there in around thirty minutes."

"I just had a physical." He rebutted.

"You have thirty minutes to report to the lab." I told him.

I heard his chair slide back quickly. There was silence in the room.

When I heard the door shut. I began to explain my actions to the attorneys for the buyer of my father's estate, as well as everyone else in the room. It was the only way.

"Normal pulse of an adult is around sixty to eighty beats a minute." "Mister Reynolds pulse was over a hundred." "That was strike one." "Strike two was he was constantly trying to keep his nasal passages clear." "That told me that his nasal membranes are damaged." "He used mouthwash, but you don't wear mouthwash on your clothes unless you're trying to cover something up." "That was strike three." "Once again I apologize, but I would rather everyone here know what went on." "You were ready to sign the papers on the house." I told the buyers. "I would imagine that you being ready to sign, your lawyers would have checked everything out and found it to be a binding contract." "If you want to proceed, I'll sign the paper's and if you want to put it in writing that if any legal matters come up on the house, I'll refund all monies to all parties." "I'll sign that too."

"Mister Bryant, I'm Jared Conally, and this is my wife, Anne." "I'm curious, you could have signed everything and then after we left, you could have done all that stuff."

"I brought my personal business associates with me." I told him. "These kids here are in training to become my future business managers." "Mister Conally, twenty million dollars isn't any money to me." "Your lawyers will tell you that." "I'll sign the papers and when you're satisfied, your lawyers can get with my lawyers and the deal will be done when you're ready, the estate isn't going anywhere, and what's in the contract has been read." "This is being done for your sake." I paused. "By the way Mister Conally, I respect your attorneys, but my knowledge of attorneys is I know that either one of them would be eager to fight me in court." "It's good publicity for them." "Besides the outcome would be rewarding to them if they won one case, or settled out of court." "I apologize gentlemen." I said to his lawyers. "I don't hold a high opinion of any attorney I don't know, and I don't hold that high of an opinion with the ones that I do." "You can understand that by my actions I initiated with Mister Reynolds." "Mister and Misses Conally, I apologize if I've offended either one of you." "I didn't expect any of this to happen."

One of the attorneys spoke for Mister Conally.

"Mister Conally" I answered after he finished "you can take that copy of that contract with you, and after further review, you'll find that there will be an additional hundred to a hundred and fifty thousand added in legal fees, and then you'll find that the contract won't have any changes that were made to it" "not one word will be added or deleted." "But you hired them to protect your investment, and it costs dearly for that protection." "I wish you a good day." I said to them.

"We'll sign the papers." The gentleman's wife Anne said with their attorneys protesting.

"I have to be truthful ma'am." I responded. "You know you would be going against your attorney's professional advice."

"I love the estate." She commented. "I fell in love with it as soon as I saw it." "And I don't think any man would sit down in a court of law and lie in front of children."

"I wouldn't do that to you ma'am." "When you leave, ask your lawyers if they've been recording our conversation and you'll find that they are, and they know that we are too." "Show me where to sign." I was given a bunch of papers and a gentleman put my finger on the spot where I signed and then he signed his name along with all of the attorneys for the Conally's.

After sealing the contract with a handshake, they left and I began speaking again.

"Mister Laree, I want to unload every share of stock we have in the markets, and reinvest it." "For right now, put one third in fossil fuel and one third in gold." I paused for a moment. "Put another seven hundred million in the pharmaceuticals and keep the rest idle."

"Kurt, if you'll excuse me, our analysts are predicting that the markets will rise another fifteen percent." He stated.

"I don't see it the way you do" I told him "I hear politicians saying I'm for it, but, I'm against it." "That tells me we've got lobbyist paying heavy contributions to campaigns for a reason, we've got a juggling act going on and I don't want to be invested right now." "If you have inflation that rises one hundred percent, what does that do to the value of stock." "I'll make it clearer for you, if you have ten apples and take away five apples, how many apples are left." "Mister Laree, you say that the markets are primed to rise fifteen percent." "At a hundred percent inflation, you'll lose fifty percent net worth of stock and businesses will take a hit."

"Kurt, I don't usually mix with your decisions, but in this matter, I think I need clarity." He stated.

"Listen to the radio, or the news, or read the paper." "All of it reports that the economy is doing well and growing healthily." "Speculators are priming their projections, and that's the only thing driving the market." "Mister Laree, I don't want to be in the markets right now." I reiterated firmly. "Please do as I ask."

"Yes sir." He said with a somewhat disapproval of my vision.

"Mister Floyd, I need interviews." I said to him.

"Yes sir." He responded quickly.

"Richard, all correspondence between us will be handled by" "what is your last name Bailey?" I asked.

"Simons" she said.

"Miss Simons" I then said to him. "If it's not you, then she'll know it's not a legitimate call."

"Yes sir"

"Now is there any old business we need to attend to." I heard silence.

"Richard, I need for you and Bailey to get together and exchange numbers." I told him. "And gentleman, by the way, I'm moving my residence from New York." "If I'm not needed here, then I won't be here." "That's why I brought in and introduced my personal associates to you." "I pay for loyalty, and it comes at a high price." "But the price is doubled the cost when I don't get the loyalty I pay for." "I'm sorry to say" "there's going to be some changes in the future and Mister Laree will be taking over as head of operations temporarily." "Richard, you'll work directly under Mister Laree." "Are we clear?" I asked.

Yes sir, they all said.

"Mister Laree" "could you call down to the lab and tell me if Mister Reynolds showed up." I asked.

I heard nothing while he made the call. When he hung up, he reported that Mister Reynolds didn't report.

"Then gentlemen, let's call it a day." I said to them.

When my staff stood, all of my guests stood as well. I heard Bailey and Richard exchanging information, and then the door shut leaving us alone.

"Dinner anyone?" I asked.

We walked out of the doors and entered the elevator to go down to the lobby.

"I don't get something Mister Bryant." Sarah said.

"What's on your mind?"

"You didn't know Bailey's last name." She sounded confused.

"I didn't find it necessary until now." I told her. "Sarah, I don't know your last name." "I never found it to be needed." "My name's Kurt to you, not Mister Bryant." "This is Bailey, not Miss Simons, then there's Buck, Becky, Ronnie, Julie, and Cindy, not Mister or Misses or Miss Roberts." "Cheryl here, is Cheryl, not Miss Jessup." "When you're with people that are close to you, you don't need last names." "Those people in that room work for me." "These people beside me work with me." "Mister, Misses, or Miss isn't used between us."

The doors opened to the lobby and when we were walking out, I felt a sharp pain and lost consciousness.

CHAPTER SIX

"**D**on't move" I heard someone say.

"Who are you?" I asked.

"You're in the ICU, you were stabbed and you were in the operating room for ten hours." "Please remain still." She asked me.

Somewhere I lost consciousness again.

"Mister Bryant, Mister Bryant, can you hear me."

"What do you want?" I stated confused.

"I'm Doctor Marshall; do you understand me Mister Bryant?"

"I hear you." I told him.

"Mister Bryant, your attacker did serious damage to your stomach and intestines, but luckily it was confined, no other organs were affected." "Do you hear me Mister Bryant?"

"I hear you." I said making a muffled sound through an oxygen mask.

"Can I talk to Bailey?" I asked.

"Bailey?" He responded.

"Miss Simons." I said to him barely able to talk.

"Miss Simons is in her room recovering."

"What do you mean, recovering?" I slowly injected my question.

"Calm down." He said "From what I have obtained Miss Simons and another lady stopped your attacker until he was subdued by the other members of your party."

"When can I talk to someone?" I asked.

"Let's give it a little time first." He said "I'm going to give you a little more morphine drip; I don't like your blood pressure this high."

I was being awoken to sip some broth. "How you feeling today?" Someone said.

"What day is this?" I asked.

"Saturday, and you have the pleasure of having me as your nurse." She stated "First, we have rules." "They'll be no jumping on the bed."

"I need to know what happened to the people that were with me." I said to her.

"Mister Bryant, I need you to calm down please." She asserted.

"If you were lying here, wouldn't you want to know the questions I ask?" I argued.

"Mister Bryant, I only know what I read in the paper and heard on the news about the attack." "Supposedly, the attacker was a man that you had words with earlier." "My understanding was you fired him." She stated.

"What about Miss Simons?" I asked.

"She was released from observation." "Mister Bryant, I've been told not to say anything, this place is crawling with news medias and reporters from god knows where." "Your doctor was in earlier and he told me to call him back when you came to." "You didn't hear this from me, but I think he's being pressured to bring you out of here." She said "If it doesn't turn out that way, then I shouldn't have said anything."

"You've given me hope." I told her. "That's something I didn't have earlier."

"Can you feel this?" I heard her say as I felt tingling on the bottom of my foot.

"You're messing with my foot." I told her.

"Good" "I think I can give the doctor a call now." She said to me.

Time passed slowly, and I dozed off.

"Mister Bryant, Mister Bryant." I heard a voice.

"I hear you."

"How you feeling?" He asked me.

"Better than I did yesterday, I don't remember it." "I feel doped up."

"The morphine works differently on people." He lectured. "I need you to listen to what I have to tell you." "It's going to take some time before you're healed." "I don't think I have to tell you that." "I could tell you my professional opinion, but everyone heals differently, that part is largely up to you." "If you push it and those wounds you got get infected, you'll go into Septic shock." "Do you understand what I'm saying?" He asked.

"Yeah, you're saying I could get Gang Greene, and you'd be operating on a man that's going to die." I said to him.

"Well, at least that tells me that you're alert and oriented." He commented. "Mister Bryant" "My kids are being hounded by the news media wanting to know if I've said anything to them about you." "They're all loving it." He stated. "My wife isn't too happy though." "She disconnected the phones so we could sleep."

"How are you handling it?" I asked him.

"From the way I see it," He said "I wouldn't want to be you." "I know this may sound a little strange, but, I didn't really enjoy my vacations whenever I went anywhere." "Now, I'm beginning to feel like I need to take a long one." "Three days of glory, and I already wish everything would just go back to the way it was."

"I could ask to be transferred." I told him.

He started laughing. "Are you kidding, my wife and kids watch all the news channels to see if they're on T.V now?" "My wife loves the attention too." "She's been outside working on her rosebushes." "She complained, but she

Paradox

was out there the next day pruning her rose bushes, and I bet tomorrow she'll be out there pruning them again." "There's something about seeing yourself on television and your neighbors that you don't normally see wave at you."

"I wouldn't know." I smiled.

"I'm sorry for that comment." He stated.

"It's alright doc." "Maybe you can introduce me to them in a few days." I told him.

"No, no, no."

"Well, it won't be that hard to find out where you live" I said "I know the mayor, and he knows somebody that knows where you live." "Of course, I'll have to come uninvited." "I don't think I would be able to concentrate wondering if I harmed someone unintentionally."

"Mister Bryant, that wouldn't be professional." He replied.

"Well doc let's look at it this way." I told him. "Let's say one day all of your kids and your wife sees me again on television, and they will." "And let's say, you have family or guests over, or maybe the kids will be married and gone." "They may want to prove to their friends that their father was one of the people that was responsible for saving my life." "What would that mean to a kid?" "Doc, I'm afraid you're going to have to relent on that professionalism." "One day, they'll be old, and I'll be dead." "I may be famous someday." "Think about it, how much could they get if they went into a pawn shop with them posing next to me in bed?"

"I see you have a sense of humor." He stated.

"I know, just trying to lighten up a tense moment, but I'm not kidding doc, I would like to meet your family." "After a couple of days this will begin to get old, you said so yourself, three days of glory." "After a few weeks, things will begin to settle back down for you, or maybe it won't." "But you and your family's personal lives are going to be disrupted for a time." "Let's say things got rough for you and I asked for a transfer, do you know what papers print about doctors?" "Imagine how your family would react to those types of articles." "Trust me; they would go to all lengths to humiliate you." "Can you fathom what would have been printed about you if I had died under your hand?" "You and your family would be going through the same ordeal that you're going through now, only with a twist." "Do you know how many doctors would have spoken up against you in an attempt to assassinate your credibility?" "Doc, I don't think you really understand yet, what would have happened to you and your family if I died." "The news medias don't care anything about you or your family." "Tell me, were pictures taken?" I asked him.

"Tons" he related. "They've got all kinds of videos of you on cell phones, on the news."

"You ever read a tabloid?" I asked him.

"No, I read some of the headlines while standing in line at the grocery store, they caught my eye, but I never read any." He replied. "Why do you ask?"

"Where do you think they get all their stories from?" I said "Doc, they have pictures of you and your family." "They can print anything they wish to print without any concern about you or your family's welfare." "A snazzy headline about you, accompanied by a photo of you is all it takes." "You gave a progress report on me to the media after I was admitted into the ICU, didn't you?" I said to him.

"Yes"

"Now they're out there waiting for you to make another report, aren't they?" I said to him once again.

"Yes"

"Doc" I began "look for the new issues of those tabloids the next time you go into the store, don't be alarmed to find out that you were intoxicated and because of your botched surgery, I've been put on life support, and my last rights were given to me." "When I entered this hospital, and you first began sewing me up, you were put in a damn if you do, and a damn if you don't type of situation." "I need to see your family; I have to let them know that I think their father and your wife's husband performed a miracle." "Doc, you seem to be in another damn if you do and damn if you don't type of situation." "When you go out there, they'll listen to anything you have to say." "The majority of them will hear everything except the truth." "You can quote me on this" I told him "I would have much rather to have met you somewhere else other than here, but you have to understand, I've gone through this before." "If I die, for any reason, all these things that I told you will come to pass." "Bring your family to me" I said "you never know what'll happen, they need to hear me tell them you did nothing wrong." "That way you have insurance." I told him.

"Mister Bryant, to be truthful with you I never thought about any of that until you brought it to my attention." "I need you to rest; as soon as a room is available, you'll be transferred to where your guests can be with you." "Just don't overdo it, okay."

When the door shut behind him, I heard the nurse beside me. "I couldn't help but overhear your conversation." She said "I didn't think of anything like that either."

"What's your name?" I asked her.

"Charlotte"

"Charlotte" "you would have been one of the first to be questioned if I died in this room." "Everything that happened in here would have had to be conveyed to the jury, or the police, or a Judge, or someone, questions have to be satisfied." "You would have been considered a prime suspect." "You said you watch the news; how many nurses have killed their patients intentionally?" "Records can be obtained through subpoenas; your name would have been on the records as calling the doctor." "An autopsy would have been performed to see what actually killed me." "Was it the man that did this or was it you, or was it that doctor that operated on me." "The man that stabbed me would be facing a murder charge." "His attorneys would fight anyway and every way they could to prove that you did it, or the doctor did it and not their client." "Yeah, he stabbed me, but allegations would be aimed at you saying it was your fault." "The records will show that you were aware of an abnormal reading, but no records show that you called anyone." "You think all of this is over with?" I said "Let's say in six months, or a year, or even two years pass and I die." "Everything I said can happen." "That's why people keep records; a finger has to be pointed at someone and it doesn't have to be the one that's guilty."

"You're scaring the hell out of me." She stated.

"Charlotte, everyone that works for this hospital has a target put on them." "It doesn't matter who or what causes a wrongful death." "The simple fact is this hospital is going to be sued." "I bet if you ask the right people, you'll find out that there are probably a dozen lawsuits that are in litigation right now against this hospital or the doctors or nurses, as we speak." "I've been involved in a lot of them, and I haven't lost one yet." I told her.

"You must have some good lawyers." She commented.

"No" I said "this conversation you and I are having, could you remember what I said if what I said could happen, were to happen?"

"Sure"

"Why" I said.

She paused and there was silence.

"Charlotte, I live my life without any fear of not knowing what happened in a meeting or when I was involved in contracts." "I do so because whatever I do, I remember the truth."

"I'm going to miss you." She said to me. "I need someone like you to talk to."

"Are you married?" I asked.

"Yeah, but jobs don't pay much, my husband joined the service to get training in being an airplane mechanic." "He's in Germany right now with nine months to go." "I told him we could survive off of my paycheck, but, he's in Germany." Her voice quivered at the end of her comment.

"Charlotte, I found a motive." I told her.

"Excuse me."

"I found out why I died." I said to her. "I can see the headlines now, Nurse Charlotte despondent over depression of being lonely, charged in Kurt Bryant's death." "See how easy it is to put doubt in someone's mind." "Charlotte, I can't give you help, whatever your outcome is to be, is going to involve you and your husband." "It's hard to write a letter when all you can say is I love you, and I miss you."

"You're smooth" she said.

"It must be the morphine, I usually growl." I said sleepily.

"Mister Bryant, why did he join?" She asked me.

"I wish you hadn't of asked me that." I said to her. "I could lie to you and tell you that men have something they have to do, and let it go at that." "That wouldn't be doing you justice though." "This temporary separation that you're going through with your husband is a test." "Whatever happens between you and him will make you stronger." "Charlotte, when you write him his letter, you tell him you love him, when you see him again, you tell him you love him." "But if he doesn't treat you the way you treat him." "You may be the one that wants another separation." "I don't know anything about your husband except what you say about him." "You know sometimes men grow up and become what they want to be." "I might be wrong; he may think that being an airplane mechanic will bring in enough money for you two to enjoy a lifestyle that'll make you and him happy." "No one knows the truth except your husband."

"That's what my mother said." She stated. "The military was a test."

"Are you really in love with him?" I asked her.

"Yeah"

"Then, if you let the devil talk to you" I commented "he'll tell you all kinds of ugly things that you don't want to hear." "He'll replace your dreams with nightmares." "The day will come when you'll be reunited again, and you'll have the same worry that you have now." "Ma'am, you asked me a question that will take me ten years to be able to tell you the answer." "But you said you were in love with him, maybe that'll be enough to sustain your happiness." "Now, let's go the other way." I told her. "What if your husband is the one having nightmares and hearing ugly things; you may not be the only one suffering depression here." "But, like I say, I don't know anything about your husband, and if you listened to anything I just said, then maybe now you have a better understanding of how easy it is to write an article." "You don't know what's going on over there, and he doesn't know what's going on over here." "All it takes to ruin a new car is to have a flat." "In a marriage all it takes is suspicion." "You asked me if I had good lawyers." "I do." "I have a firm of lawyers dealings strictly with divorce." "I've discovered that in every divorce, there's a reason."

I felt her stroke my hair back. "I'm going to miss you." She stated.

"It's the morphine." I told her. "Talk to me after they take me off of it, and you'll pretend we never had this conversation."

I heard her chuckling and then a door opened.

"Mister Bryant, your room is ready." "Give us a few minutes and we'll have you moved onto your new bed." The nurse said.

The nurses coordinated their movements to where I didn't suffer any pain.

When they opened the door I smelled perfume, not aftershave.

"Bailey?" I spoke.

"I'm right here." "Let these men finish." She said to me.

When I heard the door open again, I felt her kiss, and then I felt more.

"The doctor told me you saved my life." I said to her.

"It didn't happen that way." She began. "Sarah saw him first, she dove over the top of you as I grabbed him in a bear hug, had she not of drove him to the floor when she flew over you, I don't know what would have happened." "Kurt, she kept him from stabbing me, as it was, he got me in my shoulder." "Buck and Ronnie were trying to keep him from hurting us, and Steven put an end to it by grabbing his hair and slamming his head on the floor and knocked him out." "Kurt, everything happened so fast." "Twice, the news reported you died."

"Where's everybody?" I asked her.

"Sarah and Steven took everyone to get something to eat." "They had to sneak out the back of the kitchen."

"Are you okay Bailey?" I asked.

"I hurt bad when they said you died, and to hear it again, scared me; I thought they were keeping something from us." Her voice broke at the end.

"I'd put my arm around you and show you how I really felt about you, but I have a bunch of tubes sticking out of me."

"Rest" she said.

I did.

I awoke to voices.

"I'm awake" I said. "Is everyone here?"

"We're all here Kurt." Buck spoke.

"Is this Saturday?" I asked.

"Sunday evening." He informed me.

"I guess I ruined a good trip huh." "And I thought everything was going so well too."

"Kurt, you were right, that man did have drugs and alcohol in his system." He stated.

"He's already out on bail, isn't he?" I said to him.

"Yeah"

"I guess it's a good thing Steven didn't kill him, they'd probably have him up on murder charges." "Steven are you here?" I asked.

"Him and Sarah are at home asleep." "They've been down here while we slept, at your hotel." Becky said. "The kids were tired."

"Bailey, if I fall asleep again, ask the nurse to get my valuables." "I need you to charter a jet to take everyone back; the cards are in my wallet."

"Kurt" Becky interrupted.

"Becky, you and I both know that there's nothing anyone can do here." "The kids can't afford to miss school without a good reason." "I'll be home in two or three weeks." "Cheryl, I need to call on you for some help." I said to her.

"Yes sir" she said to me.

"Ronnie's going to be busy, and Buck has things that he looks after." "Julie and Cindy help their mother with chores around the house." "I'm worried about my catfish not getting the food that they're used to." "I was wondering if I could depend on you to help me out until I got back."

"Yes sir"

"That would mean you'd have to ride home with Ronnie, and do your homework at the house, and then he could take you home later." I told her.

"I'll do it Mister B."

"Look" I said "we had a bad fall here."

"Kurt, we've all already talked about this trip." Buck said.

"Let me interrupt you." "Those men that I talked to, work for me; they take orders, you and everybody here, work with me, there's a big difference." "Now, about the way I talked to those men." "Mister Laree is now my director of operations, that job belonged to Mister Reynolds." "I put Richard directly underneath him." "Mister Laree thinks I put Richard underneath him to spy on him, I did." "That's why I told Bailey to exchange numbers with Richard to make Mister Floyd think that he's being watched too, and he is." "That way everybody keeps everybody else in line." "Every once in a while, just to shake everyone up, I have an internal audit." "It costs me, but it saves me ten times what it cost me." "Buck, back in Murray at the butcher shop, did your boss ask you to do something every time, or did he tell you?" "When I told Mister Laree to sell my stock, he questioned me." "He's been in this business a long time, but he's one of those stuffed shirts you were talking about." "He likes being in charge, but Buck, there comes a time when you have to make decision's you're not proud of." "I can't renew his contract, so when it's up he's going to retire." I said to him. "He knew what I was talking about when I told everyone he was filling a temporary position and that there would be changes made."

"Why, I don't understand." Buck commented.

"Mister Laree likes to follow statistics, and he doesn't get out very much, so, Mister Laree is optimistic when he should be pessimistic sometimes." "That's where Richard comes in, I tell him what to do, and in turn, he tells Mister Laree what I tell him to do." "When I talked to them the way I did, I was reassuring Mister Laree that I was confident and comfortable in my decision." "This is business Buck, he's nothing more than a figurehead" I said "you can't have a bunch of people all running around thinking somebody is working on a project when nobody is, it gives you a problem, because everybody thinks that somebody is working on it when no one is." "You have to have accountability, and delegation is a part of that accountability." "None of those men can do the work that Ronnie does, so, I wouldn't be wise delegating them for that purpose."

"How do you know who the right man is then?" He said to me.

"It's not a man, you remember the secretary that stopped you at the door?" I asked him.

"Yeah"

"She does all four of their jobs for them." "She's the person that all of them give the responsibility to, she carries the keys; so that makes her the frontrunner when it comes to choosing the best candidate." "Buck, there's only one way to find out the true measure of a man, or in this case, a woman, and that's to put them in charge." "She was a shipping clerk when she first hired on in my father's firm."

"Hello, I see we're all here." Sarah said as I felt a kiss on my forehead.

"Bailey said you saved my life."

"Nah, Bailey's being humble; she had him wrapped up so tight, all I did was knock him back." "Buck and Ronnie had his arms."

"Steven that was some quick thinking, he could have killed someone." I told him.

"Mister Bryant."

"I'd like for you and Sarah to call me Kurt, like the rest of my friends." I said to him.

"That's difficult." He responded. "I'm out of my zone, my wife calls it."

"Sarah and Steven, I was sitting here boring my friends with my thoughts." I stated. "I'm getting tired so if I nod off along the way, I need to talk to you again." "But I need you; I have areas where I can't do what I have to do."

Later I was awakened by the nurse taking my blood pressure, and then I heard Bailey shuffling in the chair.

"I thought when the mayor was admitted here; we had problems, Mister, you're causing us more problems than what the mayor did." She said releasing the cuff from around my arm.

"Can you feel this?" She asked me.

"You're messing with my foot." I reported.

"That's always a good sign." "Mister Bryant, I need to change the dressing on your abdomen." She stated. "You shouldn't feel anything, but if you do, let me know, okay."

"Give me your head." I told her.

"What?"

"That's the only way I'll be able to get your attention, if I feel pain, you will too." I said to her.

"Oh, you're a funny man." "I was going to be easy with you, but I can see you like it rough." She said with a maniacal laugh. "You want to see honey?" I heard her say to Bailey.

"It looks bad." I heard her say.

"The body is a lot tougher than you think." She said "I know, my fourth kid took three minutes and he popped out." "I'm talking about the sex dear."

"Awe please, don't make me laugh." I said to her.

"I told you honey, I was going to be easy on you, you know I'm a standup comic, right?" She stated.

"No"

"Yeah" she said "I do my best work when I have a captured audience, and since you've got no place to go, I thought I'd come in here and try out my new routine on you." "You do know, I'm not really your nurse right, I dress this way to let everyone think I am?" I then heard that maniacal laugh again. "Now that I have your attention." She said "You've got twenty nine staples on the outside, and on the inside, your heart is now where your appendix used to be."

I tried to fight it, but I hurt from laughing.

"They say that laughter is the best medicine." "It really is you know." "In this case, you exercise stomach muscles and you get a good feeling from it." "I'm sure that your doctor went over all of the don't overdo this or don't do that stuff with you." "Where was he at when my grandmother came in from the field and had my mother, and was back in the field that evening?"

"That's terrible." Bailey said.

"Tell me about it, but she said that wasn't the worst she had ever been through." "And being me, I had to ask." She said putting tape on my dressing.

"What was the worst part?" Bailey asked after waiting.

"That woman had to walk barefooted to school in the snow and she said it was uphill both ways." She delivered.

"Oh, morphine, give me morphine." I commented.

"Oh no honey, I'm not done yet." She said "My grandmother lived to be ninety six; we stopped putting candles on her cake because by the time she got those all blown out the kids were at school."

"Buddha, bump, bump." She sounded like a drum. "All kidding aside." She said "You need to take it slow, but you have to get up out of that bed tomorrow." "Your energy is going to be drained and your muscles will get stiff, so a few steps are going to take a lot of effort." "Mister Bryant, I need to tell you that there's a secret service man at the nurses station."

"I figured as much." I stated "He wants a report directly from you so that he can make a report, right?"

"Yes sir"

"Open the door and motion for him to come in." I told her. "When he does, I want you here." "Questions come up sometimes, and trouble causes more trouble." "I'm not the only one here that needs protection."

"Yes sir."

I heard the door open.

"Nurse" I said.

"Yes sir"

"Don't let your license expire." I joked.

"Oh, you do like it rough." "Welcome to my chamber of horror." She let loose that maniacal laugh again, and soon I was being talked to by the agent.

"Mister Bryant I apologize for this inconvenience in light of your situation, but."

"I understand" I told him interrupting him. "That's why I told the nurse here to tell you to come talk to me; you need a one on one verification." "You can report that I personally said that I'm being well cared for and that this staff that's taking care of me have boosted my esteem." "You can report that I said I was in good spirits." "Do you understand?" I told him.

"Yes Sir" he said.

"Now" "you can do something for me." I stated.

"Sir" He responded.

"Tell me how Mister Reynolds was able to post bond so quick?" I asked him.

"I'm sorry sir; I can't answer that question, his case in under investigation." He said politely.

"What case?" "What investigation?"

"Sir, he was killed." He stated.

"When" I was surprised.

"I'm sorry sir; I'm not at liberty to discuss this matter with you."

"Then they sent the wrong man to talk to me, get out of here and don't return, tell the man that sent you here, I won't allow anyone to talk to me except him, and if I don't get the answer I want from him, then, we'll see how far up the echelon it goes until someone calls you up and tells you to answer my question."

"Mister Bryant you have to calm down." The nurse said.

"You're not gone yet?" I said to the agent.

After I heard the door shut, I heard my nurse.

"You aren't very tolerant of people, are you?" She stated.

"He didn't make me laugh." I responded and her comment was appropriate.

"You should come down to the laugh house with me; you might have a future in being a comic." She said as she left.

"Bailey, squeeze in next to me." I said to her.

"Kurt, I can't do that." "You're all cut up bad."

"Go slow" I told her. "But I have to have you lying next to me."

"Kurt"

"Do I have to get my cane out?" I said to her.

"Kurt"

"Bailey hand me my cane." I ordered.

"Dad gum you Kurt, I can hurt you." She was scolding me as she eased alongside the bed with me and laid her head down on my arm.

"I feel a lot better now." I told her "I was cold, now I feel warm."

"You know that nurse is right, you're not a very tolerant man." She said to me. "I thought when you got in to it with those people at the bank; I was seeing a dark side to you." "It turns out I was right." She kissed me. "Everyone waited around a few minutes after you passed out." "Sarah wanted to know if we knew what you needed." I then felt her kiss me again. I gave her all the attention she was giving me back to her, and then some.

"Are you having a side effect to those drugs?" She said "You tell the doctor to talk to me, and when he tells me it's all right, then, we'll take this further, until then, it stops here." She said putting her finger on my lips. "Kurt, I need you." "Don't ever scare me like this again."

I heard a knock at the door.

"Mister Bryant, someone wants to see you." The nurse said when she opened it.

"Can you leave us please?" I heard the agent say.

"It's all right nurse." I said to her.

"Ma'am" he said to Bailey.

"She stays." I told him.

After a few seconds he began.

"Mister Bryant, it's believed he supplied others with cocaine." He stated "And it's believed someone wanted him silenced for that purpose."

"Ahh" "so that makes me a prime suspect of retaliation." "You can call back whoever sent you here and make out your report that I understand the process, I'll comply with protocol." "What's your name?" I asked him.

"Bruce, sir."

"Bruce, tell your superior that Mister Reynolds made a comment to me when I told him that I wanted lab work done on him." "He said he just had his physical." "Only "one" man knows when physicals are scheduled and that's my scheduler." "He handles all the random drug tests and vacations."

"Yes sir."

When I heard the door shut, Bailey spoke up again. "That's strange."

"What was said just now was between us." I said to her. "We don't need others involved, that's why the agent asked you to leave." "When you have money and do drugs, you become a transporter for other people who have money and do drugs; it's used as a stepping stone to success." I told her. "At some point in time, Mister Reynolds made friends with the wrong people and he paid a price for that friendship." "Now, where were we?"

I was awakened again by the nurse. "You know I'm not going to get accurate vitals on you with your girlfriend laying there." She said, and then Bailey eased up from the side of me. "I'll give you a few minutes for everything to calm down; I have to take three readouts."

"How long have you been married?" I asked her.

"Twenty three long, long, long long long years." She replied.

"I need to ask you a personal question, if you don't mind?" I told her.

"I won't answer it if it's too personal." She said to me.

"I'm sorry ma'am, but I need a little education in a professional way, and in this case, I believe you might be the only person I can ask and get the truth."

"What's the question?" She asked.

"You said you've been married for twenty three years." "At what point did you consider yourself married to your husband when you weren't, or did you?"

I heard silence. "We had a fight one day when he drove me home from school, and I didn't sleep a wink that night." "I waited for him to call, that sorry no good" "well" "I didn't get any sleep that night, and I wasn't going to call him up." "I was waiting for him to pick me up the next morning." "He didn't show up, and when he did, I missed school." "We went at it again when he finally showed up, and I wanted to fight." "Oh, I was mad, and when I started in on him, he reached in his pocket and pulled out this beautiful little ring on my finger." "Here" "feel it" she took my finger and rubbed it on her ring. "It wasn't an engagement ring; he bought the ring to say he was sorry." "This one on my other finger, he gave it to me for our engagement." "She once again took my finger to touch it." "But this one here, he gave it to me at the altar." "I was doing to it what I was doing to the others." "Why did you ask that?" She asked me.

"Ma'am if two people get married, can those two people be married as soon as they know that they're in love?" "That is assuming that the love they were in was a true love." I said to her. "You've been married for twenty three long, long, long, long long years?" "I thought you would be able to tell me how you feel about love and marriage." "In a professional way of course."

"Mister Bryant, I don't think you needed my opinion on anything." She commented. "You're right; I need to edit out that part about my marriage." "It's not that way." "I love my husband."

"If you do" I said "I would call him up when he gets up and tell him that." "Bailey and I were talking and in the course of a conversation, it came to my attention that he could end up here, like me one day." "I didn't expect to."

"Mister Bryant, I didn't mean to offend you." She stated.

"You didn't, I need to know when you and your husband was married in "your" mind." I said to her. "I ask because I was thought to have autism and I was in an institution for twenty five years." "I knew nothing of love and with Bailey, I don't want to make a mistake." "Bailey here, has brought it to my attention of what love feels like." "But I'd like to know what love means to other people."

"When I walked up to him and told him I wanted a date with him." She boldly exclaimed. "I had to; he wouldn't have asked me."

"But you've been together." I said to her.

"I had to take a pot to him every now and then; my grandma showed me that quick." "My pawpaw griped all the time, but when he seen my grandma reaching underneath the sink, for the pot, he'd go and chop wood." "You're not anything like I hear people say you are Mister Bryant."

"That's because you're a miracle worker." I told her. "I was an ogre before you came in here and cheered me up with laughter." "It is the best medicine." "You've made me a better man." "Me being blind, I have to learn how to control my temper because I won't be able to see a pot coming at me."

"You would do good at the laugh shop, now give me your arm, and let me go take care of sick people." She commented.

When she left, Bailey eased back up in the bed to be with me.

"You always talk about me and you as a couple." Bailey whispered.

"I'd like that." I said "Bailey it doesn't matter what I want, I could want the moon, but I know I can't have it." "It's like my sight, I want it, but I can't have it." "This is your life too."

"Would I be here now if I didn't love you?" She said to me.

"That's my point." I told her. "That's why I talk about you and me as a couple, I want that wish to come true, I want to share my life with you, and I want you to share your life with me." "We need mutuality."

"No" she said "I need to take some classes on being a legal assistant, I don't understand you sometimes when you talk like a lawyer." "Marriage scares you, doesn't it?"

"Yeah" "but not the way you think." I said "But still it scares me."

"How" She asked.

"I'm going to be out traveling when I can get back on my feet." "You remember me telling Mister Laree that I wanted to be out of the market?" I said to her.

"Yeah, I didn't quite understand a lot of that stuff, but I remember that."

"This is election year" I told her "This is when decisions of the future are made." "I have research to do." "There's a taste of tension in the air."

"What did you want Sarah for?" She asked.

"Have you noticed similarities between Sarah and Becky?" I questioned.

"Ronnie said something like that too." She returned.

"Who took charge of seeing to it that everyone was taken care of?"

"Sarah" She stated.

"Did Steven ever show any display of being anything else other than a servant to anyone?" I asked her.

"Ronnie said something about that too." "I know Julie likes him." She commented. "She said he treats her like her butler."

"What does Cindy think about him?" I asked.

"I don't think she likes anyone taking care of you except her." She chuckled. "Are you thinking Sarah and Steven will fit in your plans?"

"I don't know who they are Bailey." "But Steven knows his way around bookings and reservations."

"She was a receptionist." Bailey said. "She quit because Steven and her job had them working separate hours." "And their last name is Bishop." "We had a talk while I walked the floors." "She said she was curious and asked me about you and how come you didn't know my last name." "I told her that you moved fast." "Kurt if you're asking me for my input, you told me that you didn't work." "You don't work like I did, or Becky and Buck." "We did it because we had bills to pay." "I like getting out and working in the garden on a beautiful day, I like cake." She said "You like doing what you like doing because you like it." "That's good enough for me; I'm like that too, I like doing whatever I want to do because I like doing it." "I believe in you." "Now, get some rest, and Kurt, I love you."

I closed my eyes for what seemed like only a few minutes before my nurse woke me.

"You again, don't you have a home?" I said to her.

"You're a lucky man." She commented. "I have a four day swing shift, and my shift ends this morning." "You won't have to put up with me until I get back." "Hold out your arm." Bailey began to get up, and the nurse told her to be still, she could get her readings.

When she finished, she informed me that my doctor would be in sometime this morning, if she knew the time she'd tell me, but doctors don't have a time. She stated.

"Is the agent still out there?" I asked.

"He's waiting on the doctor, that's why I don't know when he'll be here." "Normally, he makes it here by seven, seven thirty, but something tells me that you may be his first visit of the morning." "I thought I'd give you a little warning before I came back, I got some new routines I've been working on." She said with a maniacal laugh as she walked away.

I was once again awakened. I never knew I had fallen asleep.

"I see our rules don't mean much." I heard the doctor.

"I get warmth." I told him. "Without it, I'd rather be dead."

"I can't let that happen." He replied. "You painted quite a vivid picture the other day."

"Doc, one day I'll be taken to a hospital and that doctor won't be able to do anything for me." "Here's the secret," I told him "You'll suffer the same fate." "I won't be concerned with anything, but the people that live will." "Because of who I am money will circulate long after I'm dead." "Maybe my body will even be exhumed to satisfy an accusation." "You and I may be dead but your children won't be." "You need to do what I told you that you need to do."

"Can you tell me what I'm doing?" He said to me.

"You're messing with my foot." I told him. "Do all Doctors and nurses have a foot fetish?"

"I see that you've met our local comedian on the floor." He chuckled. "How are you feeling?"

"Is the answer for you or whoever sent the agent?" I asked him.

"Both of us." He said "I need you to stand up for me."

Bailey got up slowly and both she and the doctor helped me to stand.

"Can you take a few steps for me?" He asked. "You're doing good." "Now" "a few more."

Then I was being helped back into bed.

"I guess I can go home now; I've made my pay for my car note." He commented. "Mister Bryant, I'd like to keep that invitation open and under consideration."

"Either way you want it." I told him. "In this room or at your house."

"I never thought I'd be so tired from standing up." I said to Bailey when the doctor left.

When I aroused from my state of mind, I didn't feel Bailey next to me, but I soon felt a kiss.

"You're not Bailey." I said "Bailey doesn't wear lipstick; I hope you're not my nurse."

"My husband took her back to your studio." "She needed a shower and something to eat, she hasn't eaten anything since all of this happened." Sarah said. "We had a little talk about you and how you and she met." "Kurt, I want to clear something up." "I looked you up on the internet, and I was surprised to find out very little about you until a couple of years ago." "When my husband told me about what you wanted him to do, I envisioned you as a short chubby man out to get his jollies anyway he saw fit." "You surprised me by that tongue you snap." "I owe you an apology."

"No, it was me." I told her. "Sarah" being in an institution for twenty five years does something to a man." "I could hear screams coming from other kids that had problems." "I don't know what they were for, but they scared me because no one seemed to be concerned about them."

"Mister Bryant, I don't know if this is my place or not, but I find you to be a controlling man." She replied. "Did Bailey tell you anything about me and my husband?" She asked.

"No, I don't think I held a conversation very long, I was in and out, if she did, I don't remember any of it." I uttered.

"Well, I was working one day at the hotel." She started.

"The hotel?" I responded.

"That's where I met my husband." "He applied for a job and when he came in for an interview, we met." "He isn't anything at all like you." She said "That's what attracted me to him." "He wasn't a New Yorker, he was like a puppy, if I talked mean to him, he'd tuck his tail under his butt and slowly ease away, and as soon as he saw me again, he'd act like nothing ever happened." "We lived together for three weeks before we split up." "It was my fault." She said to me.

I waited for her to continue.

"I was a bitch." "That talking you gave to me about not being supportive to him was true, only I didn't see it until you made me aware of what was happening." "Mister Bryant, I really didn't see it." "And you buying me four thousand dollar's worth of perfume didn't help any either." She stated. "That was nice of you, but I didn't feel right letting you do it."

"Sarah you've got a lot to learn and I don't think that you're going to be able to do it, I don't believe you have it in you." "Steven has a very rare quality instilled into his beliefs, he's a young man; so sometime recently he's been a valet before he applied for the job at the hotel." "He likes it, so, you'll either have to accept his manners, or you'll end up splitting with him again."

"He joined the army." She said "He was in boot camp and a Colonel needed someone to cater services at a party." "He volunteered to get out of KP he told me." "After that, he ended up in Korea with the Colonel." "When he got out, he hoped to use his experience." "He's worked for the hotel for three years; I don't think he's going to move up." She stated.

"Sarah, do you know why people get divorced?"

"I guess there's a lot of reasons." She answered.

"Yeah" "maybe so" "but out of all of those reasons, it only takes one." "People get divorced because one day they wake up and say, I'm not in love with that person anymore." "You already faced those feelings in the past, so what's to keep them from resurfacing?" I stated to her.

"Bailey must have really had a hard time dealing with you." She commented. "You're not an easy man to talk to."

"What about your husband's job?" I asked.

Paradox

"He was forced to take a vacation." "I don't know if he'll be working there very long." Sarah commented. "The manager found out that we went out the back door of the kitchen." "One of the chefs told him." "They had words and the manager told him that he had vacation coming, and that he was going to use them."

"Just like that huh, that sheds some light on why they didn't give him time off." I said to her. "I talked to Bailey earlier, Sarah, I need you, and I need Steven." "You both get along better when you're with each other." "I don't expect an answer soon." "You need to talk this over with Steven, tonight." "I need personal managers."

"That's quite an offer." She stated.

"Sarah, I'd like for you to keep this conversation between us." I told her. "If either of you find it's not in your future, I wouldn't like Steven applying for a job thinking he got it on his own merits." "If he found out I put in a word for him, he'd be mad at me and he wouldn't take the job." "But, if he found out that you knew about me doing it, Sarah, he wouldn't be the man you know him as?"

"What do you want me to do?" She asked.

"Marriage is two people agreeing on a future." I told her. "A marriage is two people supporting each other." "As far as I'm concerned this conversation never existed between us." "What was said was said in private between friends."

"Why" she asked.

"Steven doesn't have any friends." I told her. "Steven is Steven because that's his character." "You can't change him from being who he is."

"That's a strange thing to be saying. She answered.

"I do a lot of listening to a person's way of talking Sarah." I said to her "You love Steven, but you give me the impression when you talk to him that he gets on your nerves." "That your character." "You get mad at Steven sometimes, but you don't know why." "You were edgy when we met." I told her. "I could tell by the way you spoke." "What you don't understand is that Steven is an introverted man, if you speak to him with a disparaging remark or represent yourself to him in a demeaning way, then I don't think you really love Steven that much, a person in love with someone doesn't talk to the person they love that way." "You can't change him." "So, if you're really like you say you are, in love with Steven that is, you'll give this meeting between us some thought."

"Bailey said you're a talker." She commented. "Now I know why she loves you, and that bothered me for a while." "I don't know why, but, it did." "I thought you two were, you know."

"You mean me being involved in a relationship of convenience?" I asked her.

"Yeah, something like that." She commented.

"What changed your mind?" I asked.

"After we got the perfume, we went shopping for clothes." "I watched her." She said "I thought she would." And then she paused trying to speak without offending me.

"Spend a lot of money?" I answered for her.

"Yes sir" "But that's my problem, she didn't buy anything for herself." "Mister Bryant, a man that talks to people the way you do, I would have thought I would have read more about you."

"Sarah, when I walked out of the institution I was in, I was twenty five, I caught a taxi." "And over a period of time, I got hired on as a mail room clerk working for my father's firm, no one knew me." "You hear little comments like if I didn't steal something every day; I'd feel like this company is getting over on me." "Or, clock me in Joe; I've got some side business I need to take care of." "A person learns a lot by listening Sarah." "Six months later, forty four employees were downsized." "That don't seem like much, but my profits increased thirty three million that year, to put it simple, the men I let go weren't working and after the downsizing, productivity increased, it made the ones that were left think they were next, so, they worked." "Sarah with some people the only work they do is when they reach out their hand for a paycheck." "Now" I said "as far as the last two years." "There were some people that used my name to get elected or reelected." "They shouldn't have been." "I feel sorry for the people they represented, but I'm sorry, I made millions off of them." "Sarah, politicians own businesses, and all elected politicians that own businesses, prosper." "An investment sometimes pays off with huge rewards, especially if that politician gets along well with other people that have attained a certain social air." "It's more of if you scratch my back, I'll scratch yours type of friendship." "I told Bailey this is election year and because of that, there's going to be people elected that's going to make decisions that's going to change our future, that's how progress works, sometimes it goes forward and sometimes it goes backwards." "I need to see what the future holds, and I need personal business managers."

I heard the door open.

"I see you're up." Steven said.

"This stuff is funny." I told him. "I can be talking to you one minute and the next the nurse is waking me up wanting to know if I have feeling in my foot."

Paradox

"Everybody left around ten, sir." Steven said.

"I guess I didn't leave them with a good impression of New York." I spoke. "Sarah" I told her "I'm going to be here for a while." "Baileys going to need some help getting to and back from my apartment, and she needs someone to take her to some nice restaurants to eat." "And Sarah" "Bailey Idolizes you." "I would like for you to take her to some nice places and dress her up." "Steven, I'm going to need my apartment cleaned out." "I need my clothes sent to me." "The rest of my stuff I don't need." "So, if you don't mind, I'd like to ask you for a hand." I said to him.

"What about pictures?" Sarah said.

"I don't have any." I told her. "I apologize if I brought either of you discomfort, especially to you Sarah." "When I asked your husband to help me, I told him to invite you along." "I thought with us taking up his time, I was asking a lot from him, and you." "I caused problems by doing that, and for that I'm sorry."

"Steven" Sarah said "Mister Bryant wants you to be his personal manager." "I think you should listen to what he has to say."

I smiled and heard Sarah taking in a deep breath; she didn't want me to bring her name up.

"I have twelve bed rooms in my house, only one of them is occupied, that leaves eleven, empty." "You came into my life not knowing much about me, all I was to you was a client for the hotel." "You still don't know that much about me and you know nothing at all about Bailey, or any of the rest of my entourage that was with me." "None of them take orders from me, but they do take orders from each other, and if you accept my offer, you'll never hear me give you one." "You won't be working for me; you'll be like the rest; they work with me." "And Sarah, that's Kurt, Steven this involves Sarah as well." "So, take your time, I'm not going anywhere."

"What do you want me to do?" He asked.

"I don't do radio, and I don't do talk shows." "I need reservations at hotels and I need transportation bookings." "Whenever I travel Bailey will be my side, and hopefully all the rest of my associates." "Buck complains a lot about big cities." "But Becky has control over Buck." "I want Sarah to travel with us, both of you work good together." "Sarah is well adjusted at handling my associate's affairs, the same as you." "Like I said" "I don't do radio and I don't do talk shows." "You on the other hand have an attentive personality." "So, if you don't mind, I'd like to ask that both of you work together as a team." "I need you Steven, and I need Sarah too." "Without the both of you, I don't have a whole team." "There's one thing you should know, I'm not a used car salesman, if you love New York; you won't like Skinland." "Take your time and think about what I say, both of you have been around, your decisions are subject to change at any given date or time, and I'm okay with that." "I don't want either of you with me, if you don't want to be with me." "I'm not naïve and neither are you." "When you talk, money is going to come up." "It won't do you any good to put it on paper." "Bailey would have to tell me."

"I don't know what to say." Steven said.

"Steven, I'm sorry but I'm starting to get a little groggy." "Just think."

I felt my arm move and a cuff being put around it.

"Don't worry" the nurse said "I'm not a comedian." "How you feeling?"

"I don't have any energy." I told her.

"That's the drugs." She said "Without them, you wouldn't be a very pleasant person."

"How's the circus outside?" I asked her.

"It's dying down." "The doctor gave statements that you're recovering better than expected." "Everyone's been ordered not to make any comments." She said to me.

"Are you married?" I asked her.

"No, divorced."

"You have a boyfriend?" I continued.

"Yeah, but that's as far as it's going to go." She stated.

"I was just going to say that you said that the administrator's told everyone not to comment on me." I muttered "If everyone is married or has a boyfriend, or parents, children, cousins, aunts, and so on and so on." "They talk and in their talks my name happens to come up." "Ma'am, you don't have to talk to the media to start a rumor." "Do you know me?" I asked her.

"I saw you once." "You were supposed to be the guest speaker for a charity group I volunteer for." She said to me. "You left without speaking."

"I remember that." I told her. "If you also remember it turned out to be a political rally when a certain member of congress just happened to show up too." "What you don't know is he wanted my endorsement, and for me to be seen shaking his hand, it would have given the people the impression that I was doing just that." "If you watched the news that night, I'm sure he was on television, and I'm sure my face was also shown, it wasn't anything except free subliminal publicity."

"We were told you had an emergency come up." She stated.

"It did, I don't like politicians using a charity event as a makeshift soapbox." "I'm not an activist; I don't support any member of any party, that's up to the people to decide." "I just don't want them using me for leverage; that's why I left that fund raiser." "No one told you that, you were told I had an emergency." "Don't you find it strange that the person that told you that I had an emergency come up was the same person that contacted the congressman to let him know I was going to be there." "I'd like to ask you a question?" I said to her.

"Go ahead."

"Let's say you and I had a difference of opinion and you felt uncomfortable around me." I stated. "Have you ever traded patients with other nurses?"

"We don't do that." She said to me.

"Yeah, how do I know that" I questioned "someone else could have been assigned to me and that other person could have traded me for your patient?"

"Mister Bryant we don't do that." She restated.

"I'm trying to make a point." I told her. "When you don't feel comfortable around someone, you usually find yourself moving away from them or leaving them entirely."

"You're talking about my ex." She stated.

"I'm not any different than anyone else." I continued. "I don't like politicians to call me a friend, when they aren't." "In that incident, I chose to leave to avoid a confrontation." "He wasn't a friend of mine." "I don't like it when politicians lie to the people, a lot of men have died in wars so that politicians can betray the people." "And when they see me at a fundraising, that a congressman happens to show up at." "They see me as supporting that politician." "So that cliché about believing half of what you hear and nothing of what you see, is nothing more than propaganda because those people that quote that cliché, don't follow that advice."

"I didn't know that." She stated.

"That's because you're not political and I doubt that you vote." "You know the funny thing about all of this." I chuckled. "You can't tell anyone any different, you've been given orders not to comment on me." "Can you see the humor?"

"Kathy said you were a good talker." She stated.

"Kathy?" I responded.

"Kathy was the nurse you had on the graveyard shift."

"Oh!" "The comedian." I had to smile.

"I've got to change the dressing." She informed me.

After a few minutes, she was putting the sheet back over me.

"Mister Bryant, you can't afford to lose twenty pounds, you're a thin man already." "I've seen people like you that came out of surgery and suffered a loss of appetite." "Two hundred and fifty pound men and women dropped their weight down to the size you are." "It may have taken them a year, but the anesthesia affects people the same as any drug, it has side effects." "If you have to tighten your belt a notch, that's one notch too many for you."

"You sound concerned about my welfare, was that an omen or have you changed your opinion of me?" I told her.

"I don't talk to a lot of my patients other than the questions pertaining to their vitals." She commented.

"Is it because some of these people you see aren't going home?" I asked.

"When I got out of college, I applied for a position here and got hired on." "Two weeks later, I went in to check on one of my patients and she was dead." "I had to go through therapy for that, it hit me hard." "There was an investigation, but it was nothing more than a formality."

"What's your name?" I asked.

"Rhonda"

"Rhonda, have you ever given thought that maybe Kathy acts the way she does because that's the way she deals with being a nurse on this unit." "You can try as hard as you can not to, but every nurse establishes some form of bond with they're patients."

"That never entered my mind." She stated.

"Maybe that's why you're a volunteer." I told her. "You needed some sort of a vent."

"I never thought of it like that either." "Mister Bryant, you are a talker." She said to me.

I heard the door opening and the sounds of several pairs of feet and then a kiss.

"How was dinner?" I asked Bailey. "I smell perfume and onions."

"I'll check back in on you later." My nurse said.

"We ate at the best restaurant this city has." Bailey said. "We got a hot dog from one of them vendor's, he had everything in his cart." "Kurt, that hot dog costs us eight dollars apiece."

"That's all she's talked about since we left." Sarah said laughing.

"I see you've accepted my offer." I said to her.

"How do you know?" Sarah commented.

"You're laughing, that means you're happy, if you weren't you'd be acting differently." I told her.

"You're a "very" observant man." She replied.

"Bailey said that too." I informed her.

Paradox

"When you nodded off yesterday, Bailey said you had a rough night." Sarah began "We had a lot of questions and we went out to eat, Bailey smelled the hot dogs and we ended up having hot dogs by the fountain." "You remember asking us if we loved New York."

"I remember." I mumbled.

"We were driving to the restaurant and got caught in a traffic jam." "Bailey said that never happens back home." "I asked her about where you live." "And without hesitation, she said out in the middle of nowhere, and right now, she would give anything to have you back there." "That only led to more questions that caught my attention." She commented. "I told her we'd have to set conditions, and she said that there wouldn't be any conditions." "You don't like them."

"She's right." I said "You won't work for me; you'll work with me." "Then between me and Bailey, and Buck and Becky, and the kids we can handle things." "They'll be times where you'll have to have your me times" "just like Bailey and everyone else." I told them.

"I gave her a number." Sarah said.

"How much?"

"Three hundred." She was a little tentative in her answer.

"That's steep" I said "what did she tell you?"

"She doubled my offer."

"She's a tough negotiator." I chuckled. "She learns quickly."

"You mean you'd pay us six hundred thousand?" She shot back with her comment.

"Can you and Steven do what I ask?"

"Yes sir"

"Sarah when I first met Bailey, she was looking for a job fifty miles away, that was the nearest town." "Becky owned the only diner." "I bought a house there and fate intervened, I asked Bailey to help me make my house a home; you and Bailey can have a talk about that, or you may have already, you can pretty much see what takes place when I'm not there." "I told Bailey it was my sanctuary, but she didn't understand me at the time." "Cindy, Julie, and Ronnie answer the phones, if it's not important, it doesn't go any higher." "And Sarah, in case you're wondering, Bailey doesn't get paid." "She's not my mistress, but being a small town, people look at her and talk." "Skinland has a population of six hundred and thirty eight people." "The whole county has a total of less than twenty five hundred people." "That's why I said if you love New York, you'll not like Skinland, you'll get bored easily." "But I can guarantee you that you'll never have to wait in another traffic jam again, and Steven will never have to worry about finding a parking space." "And when it comes to the highway, I found out by experience that you can only go as fast as the slowest tractor." "That leaves you with two options." "The first one is you can give it some time and see how things work out for you." "The second one is I don't have to tell you about New York, some people can't leave." "That's why I told you about the first option of trying it out to see how it goes." "You may not think of it the way I do, and if you don't, you'll get your answer then."

"Bailey's right, you do move fast." Sarah said." "Mister Bryant." "I don't see how we can turn down your offer." She stated.

"First off" I said "my name is Kurt, not Mister Bryant." "I introduced all of you to my business managers as my personal business associates." "Never call me Mister Bryant again, it shows you as an inferior, and you won't get respect, if asked, you are my personal business associate." "You represent me on my behalf." "Cindy can give you some good pointers, if you don't believe me, call my house and if she answers ask for Mister Bryant." "She'll ask you what do you want, and if you treat her like a nine year old, you'll find out really quick she knows how to cancel your number from calling again." "All of them know that if it's a recording, don't bother, just hang up." "Bailey will go with you to your bank and transfer six hundred thousand into your account with you." "The kids are the only ones I give money to." "They like cash."

"Mister Bryant, that's highly irregular." Sarah said.

"Buck told me the same thing." I told her. "Sarah, there's a saying that you spend what you make, I bet your savings account in New York is borrowed from occasionally, and never paid back." "And, that's Kurt, not Mister Bryant." I told her again.

"You don't leave a person much room to breathe, do you." She commented.

"If I did, Bailey would be with someone else by now, and she would hate me for the rest of my life." I told her.

"Why" Sarah asked.

"I took her dream away from her."

"I'm surprised you remembered that." Bailey said.

"How could I not forget?" I told her. "You weren't in one of your best moods."

"Kurt, that was what four hours after we met, come on, you don't put a saddle on a bronc and expect to ride it without getting bucked." I then heard silence. "It's a long story Sarah."

CHAPTER SEVEN

"You're looking chipper this morning." The Doctor said. "Have you been walking?"

"Everyday" I answered "I walk to the nurses' station and then I walk to the end of the hall." "My arms are giving me a little trouble though; they feel like someone's trying to break them."

"That's the side effect of the morphine" he said "I had to wean you off of it." "Have the pills been helping you?"

"I'm fine except for my arms, especially my wrist." I replied.

"Theoretically speaking" he said "you're looking at nine months to a year before you're back to feeling a hundred percent." "I don't think you need a doctor to tell you that." "But you won't get there in that amount of time unless you take action and get some form of exercise." "Once again, you don't need a doctor to tell you that." "You seem to be quite a hit with the nurses." He commented.

"Yeah Doc." "I want to talk to you about that." "Everyone around here seems to have a foot fetish." I chuckled. "Doc, I'm not doing anything here." "I'm ready to leave."

"Mister Bryant, you've had a major surgery." "I've done all I can and truthfully the rest is up to you." "If you lift something and rip your intestines back open, you'll find yourself to have a serious infection."

"I can do that here too." I told him. "Doc, I can sneeze and the results would be the same." "I could bend over to put on my pants or tie my shoes and feel a pain." "If I do, I know where you work." "I stayed in my room at the hotel for months sitting on my couch listening to the financial news all day long." "I can't lay in this bed another day and go through that again." "I have to leave." "I can't breathe here."

"Mister Bryant, are you okay?" He stated.

"Yeah Doc." I spoke "I bought a house and met some people, and I find myself missing them."

"Mister Bryant, I'm aware of your history." He said "I'll look in on you tomorrow and if you still feel the same way, I'll sign the release." "But I'm warning you, I don't think you should enter any marathons, or go skiing right now."

"Oh!" "You should team up with Kathy." "You and her would make a good team at her comedy shop." I said to him.

I heard the door open.

"I'm through here." I heard the doctor say shutting the door behind him.

I felt a kiss and smelled perfume, and then bit Bailey on the neck.

"Hey, we have company." She stated.

"I can't help it, that perfume drives me out of my mind."
"I can leave." Sarah said.
"No" "I'll be good, I promise."
"Kurt" Sarah said "I want to bring up something about your clothes."
"I'm listening."
"Bailey doesn't think they fit right on you, and I agree." "When did you get them?" Sarah asked.

"November first, three years ago, I graduated from school." "I bought them then." "I brought pieces of cloth in to show the clerks what I wanted." "One of my assistants told me it was the color of the sky on a warm sunny day." "She said it looked good on me, she described the color as neutral so that's how I buy my clothes."

"Bailey told me why." She said "Kurt, those clothes have got to go." "Bailey and I did a little shopping while Steven slept."

"Where is Steven, I don't smell him."

"He's at the hotel." Sarah said. "I saw the manager when we were walking out of your suite and he asked if he could talk to Steven." "I told him I was his wife, and he knew me, if he had something to say involving him, I wanted to hear it." "Kurt, he turned to me without showing any expression at all and said, he's fired."

"You can contact Richard and tell him I said to get my legal team involved." I said to Bailey. "Sarah" "Your husband is a victim of wrongful firing." "His superior was seeking inside information." "Tell Richard to tell them I said to sue them for a hundred million." "You won't get it, but you will get millions, they'll settle out of court." "If that manager received a bonus, then he was rewarded; and a bonus represents his superiors had prior knowledge of his actions, so there were other people involved as well." "That's where it stops." "They'll settle out of court." "Sarah, that's how business works, when proper ethics aren't used, you violate a thin line where you expose a corporation that wants a good reputation, but when you tell them by a lawsuit that they'll be engaged in negative advertisements, they take matters completely differently." "At least that's what my deposition is going to read when I'm called to testify." "But I won't be." "Sarah, that manager didn't just use Steven, he used me and everyone else that were with me." "I had to ask Steven for his silence and it cost him his job." "You're going to be a rich woman." I said "That Corporation doesn't just own that chain of hotels, they own restaurants, and malls too." "The CEO made fifty million in salary, and with his bonus, he made two hundred and fifty million." "Do you think that man is going to fight me?"

"But you wanted Steven to work for you." She argued.
"I wanted both of you." I stated. "Did Steven give him a notice?"
"No"
"Then that settles it." "He was still employed up until the time he was fired." I stated.

I heard the door open and close.

"She's crying." "Kurt, you really should have been a lawyer." Bailey commented.

"I think the doctor is going to let me out tomorrow." I said to her.

"Home" she sighed "I want to click my heels." She followed with another comment. "Buck was right; there are way too many people here." "Sarah took me to the Empire State Building." "Kurt when we got to the top, it was beautiful." "That's when I thought about Buck and what he said about if any earthquakes happened here." "My knees started shaking and I asked Sarah if we could go." "When we walked outside, I looked around and everywhere I looked, I saw nothing but tall buildings, and then I thought if an earthquake did happen, I'd be just as dead from the buildings falling on top of me." "That's when Sarah said we needed to go shopping." "Kurt, a ride in a taxi cost a hundred dollars, and he called me cheap when I gave him a five dollar tip for doing what he was being paid to do anyway."

"I see your going to bring home some memories." I commented. "Bailey, they'll be more, this is my headquarters."

"So, we'll be coming back now and then?" She asked.

"Not unless I have to." I told her. "But, now and then we will."

"So that means we'll be coming back over and over." Bailey said again.

"I wanted you to hear one of the best orchestras in the world." I told her. "I wanted to take you to some plays." "I didn't get that opportunity."

"You like orchestras?" She asked.

"Yeah, I like listening to elevator music." "Sometimes I would ride up and down on the elevator until the end of the music." "One day my doctor and I were talking and music was playing on her radio in a low tone." "I told her it was Bach, and she argued with me." "I told her that it seemed that we no longer could talk in a doctor patient relationship." "I know Bach's music, and that's Bach." "The next day, I was brought to her and she told me she was sorry, I was right." "She pulled a slick one on me; she played Mozart, Chopin, Beethoven, and Brahms." "When she played other music, I told her I didn't listen to that stuff." "I can't hear anything except everyone trying to play over everyone else." "I knew she was testing me and I told her my reasons." "In symphonies, you have control." "Every note is heard by each instrument, and every instrument compliments each other."

"Kurt, I find myself scratching my head trying to figure you out, and just when I think I have a handle on things, boom, you hit me with something else that blows my mind."

"Music is the salvation of man." I told her. "People sing when they're happy, and when they're not." "A lot of people like music I don't like, or records wouldn't be sold." "Maybe if I grew up differently, I'd be listening to the music of today." "That's something I'll never know."

"I'm glad you didn't" Bailey commented "I love you just the way you are."

I could feel a draft before I heard the door.

"Are you, my nurse?" I asked.

"Yes sir." She commented.

"Do you know you wear your husbands after shave." "Maybe you should hug him before he puts it on instead of after." I said to her. "I thought you were a man when you entered." "Your voice told me otherwise."

"You're kidding?"

"Ma'am, I can tell you exactly what brand he wears." "He can't smell it, so he slaps it all over his body." "You have it on your uniform; your skin, and the left side of your cheek." "So, you hug him on his left side of his face, and a few kisses later, you share his after shave." "Do you find me as being rude?" I said to her.

"You're a scary man." "How much do I weigh?" She asked.

"You're about five foot four, and judging by your breathing when you talk, you weigh around a hundred and fifty."

"Okay smart guy, what color is my hair."

"Dyed" I said.

"That ends that." She began. "I was going to tell you that you are a rude man, but I can't." "All the girls told me to watch myself with you." "I got what I expected." "But I didn't get it the way I expected it." "Mister Bryant, I've worked here almost ten years, and none of those girls ever said anything to me."

"I bet it's not they're fault." I told her. "First, no one wants to tell someone they like that kind of information." "I bet you wouldn't either." "Second, maybe they never paid attention." "I'm not that kind of a person to keep a secret like that." "To me it would have been rude not to." "I don't like people laughing at me behind my back, and I don't like people laughing behind other people's back either." "So, I choose to be helpful, but I end up sounding rude when I do." "If I appeared to have come off to you that way, I apologize." "But ma'am, I can't breathe."

"I'm sorry Mister Bryant." "I'll call my daughter and have her bring me another uniform and wash up." She stated "Hold out your arm."

She was taking my blood pressure and pulse and changing my dressing. "Have you looked at your scar in front of a mirror yet?" She asked.

"I didn't like what I saw." I told her chuckling.

"I'm sorry for that, I wasn't thinking." She stated.

I chuckled again. "What's your name?" I asked her.

"Sharon" she replied.

"Sharon, people don't bother to be concerned with other people, they have their own worries." "I have my inabilities, but I don't see myself with a disability." "We all have something that's going to cause us problems as we age." "Arthritis cripples, and a common cold kills." "The problem is, the people that see other people with inabilities don't see themselves becoming like the people they see." "If you eat food, you can be poisoned and suffer from that poisoning for the rest of your life, you've probably already consumed arsenic and mercury in small traces from eating fish and never know it." "If you're allergic to any kind of a drug, you may buy water from a store that contains that drug." "What you don't know is that water is filtered water." "It's the same water you get out of a tap, only it's been filtered." "Cosmetics contain toxic chemicals." "Some shampoos contain Benzene." "The problem is, with some people that small trace is enough to cause them to get Leukemia." "You watch the news and they report contaminations of a lake or a river like that every day." "The worst place to have a mistake made is in a hospital." "People don't see themselves in the people they see with inabilities until it either strikes them or someone they know." "Never say I'm sorry to someone, they'll learn to thrive off of pity." "Sharon, sometimes when you go shopping, do you ever see panhandlers?" I asked.

"All the friggen time." She stated.

"Have you ever been to any of those places you shop and see the same panhandlers?" I followed.

"Yes sir"

"Then I bet the next time you go to those stores you'll see them again, and they'll be holding out that hand." "Do you know they have a school that teaches people how to beg and not take no for an answer?" "People get tired of them and give them change." "That's what they're taught to do." "Do you know they followed one of those panhandlers and caught him getting into a limo?" "That was his job." I told her. "And he was good enough to have a butler and a chauffeur." "Sharon all people are a lot like me." "I know I have limitations, and you have them too." "Try lifting up fifty pounds, I bet you'll say I need help, so you go and get your husband." "Now, let's say, you need to lift two hundred pounds, your husband will say, I need some help." "So, never apologize for saying something that might sound offensive." "After all, I sounded offensive to you when we met."

"Missy" she said to Bailey. "Is this your man?"

"Yeah"

"You in a whole lot of trouble girl." She said walking away.

"Are you always so outspoken?" Bailey said.

"I lived in my suite, ate in my suite and slept in my suite." "When I came out of the institution, all kinds of odors filled the air." "My lungs felt like they were on fire." "I couldn't breathe, so I sat in my chair thinking." "I confined myself because others think they have a constitutional right to impose on my rights." "I don't think like that anymore, now I express my views to inform them that I have rights as well." "I speak out my opinion." I said to her.

"Is that why you had a hard time dealing with people in school?" She asked.

"No, it was a totally different situation." I stated. "I had problems and I had the wrong people in charge of me." "That's in the past now."

"Kurt, what happened?" She asked.

I heard the door open and a chair being sat down in.

"Have you calmed down?" I said to Sarah.

"You gave me a shock." She said to me.

"Sarah, I'm blind, but I don't need eyes to see you want to be rich." "You said you didn't think Steven was going to move up." "So, you're more interested in success." I stated. "Money makes people act strangely." "You said you left Steven after three weeks, I bet money was involved in that decision somehow, maybe not directly, but I bet it had something to do with it." "Sarah, I listen to the news a lot." "I've heard more than once about lottery winners filing for divorce." "One of them or both of them were using each other because they didn't have enough money to go anywhere else." "Money gave them the dream they really dreamed."

"You think that about me and Steven?" She asked.

"I don't know; we'll find out though." "Bailey, could you get Richard on the phone, I want to talk to him." I said to her.

Several minutes passed and I was talking to him. "Richard, I need you to have Broderick to contact me." "I'm filing a suit against Shelton's corporation for a hundred million." I listened for a few moments. "When" "tell them I'll accept." I replied.

When I hung up, I informed Bailey we were flying to California in two weeks.

"Kurt, you need rest, you look like a walking skeleton." She gave me a sound of her being scared.

"I'll have plenty of time to rest later." I told her. "You can't let the apples rot on the tree before you pick them."

Both of the girls simultaneously said. "What"

"It means that time waits for no one." I informed them.

"Kurt, I need to know about Steven." Sarah said.

"Sarah, I've heard about homeless people die on the streets, investigations revealed that several died wealthy but they lived poorly and no one ever knew they had a penny to their name." "In due time, you'll receive a sizable sum of money." "Money does strange things to people." "Where do you think you'll be in ten years?" I said to her.

"No one knows that answer." She replied.

"You're right" I told her. "But if you were to ask me, I would say I'd like to be at my house, and I'd like for Bailey to be where she's at now." "We were who we were when we met." "We didn't know anything about each other." "Since then, I'm still the person she met, except she's seen a little more of me." "She's still the same person I met, and I hope she never changes." I said "That's the girl I fell in love with."

"You sound confident" she said.

"That's because that's where I want to see myself ten years from now, and I'll work my hardest to see that it happens." "Sarah, maybe you and I hold different values." "Bailey and I get along together, that's important." "We're adults and I think we both know that if we find out that we made a mistake, we'd go out and eventually we'd find ourselves another and we would probably make the same mistake with someone else, so we try our hardest not to get in each other's way." "I'm sure you had boyfriends before you met Steven." "What happened to end those relationships?"

I heard Bailey's cell phone.

"Hold on." "It's Mister Broderick." She whispered.

"Mister Broderick, it's an honor to talk to you again." I said to him. "Yes, that's correct."

A good time had passed with me filling in all of the details. "Mister Broderick, I need you to slip a leak to Mister Shelton about the lawsuit." I listened as he talked and then commented. "Tell your mole to tell him I'm going to end up costing him a billion by the time I'm through." I said and then hung up.

"Well, the balls rolling." I told Sarah.

"Mister Bryant I don't know what to say."

"That's Kurt" I corrected her. "Sarah, it appears that you're a lot like Steven." "You always call me by using Mister when you speak my name." "Sarah, Steven helped me when I needed help." "Look what it got him?" I told her. "Fired." "I won't turn my back on that kind of a man." "Steven is quite a remarkable person." "And Sarah, please call me Kurt."

I heard the door open. "How you feeling?" Steven said.

"The doctor's going to release me tomorrow." I told him. "Steven, I need you to find out where he lives, I'm going to pay him a surprise visit." "I hear his family was bothered and I need to apologize for their lives being disrupted." "I figure around seven, that way we won't interrupt their dinner."

"Yes sir"

"I'll need a charter jet; we'll be leaving around nine." I told him.

"Yes sir."

"Steven, we need to talk." Sarah said, and they both went out the door.

"Do you know how many times you said you loved me when you were talking to Sarah?" Bailey stated.

That was the longest kiss she ever gave me. I have to admit I did hold her from getting away.

"What's happening in California?" She asked.

"I've got an interview." "If you make noise, others make noise." "The easiest way to find out where a person stands is to make them lose their temper, and then they'll tell you everything they plan on doing." "I read a book on poker." I told her. "It had a little under three hundred pages." "I read it from start to finish, and all I got from it was that you play the hand you're dealt." "The problem was the person that wrote the book lost all of his money playing poker." "Politics is like a poker player; you have politicians that are lying to you and you have politicians that are telling you the truth." "If you bet against the politicians that's lying to you, you'll go home a winner."

"What do you see in me now?" Bailey said.

"I think you're tired and ready for a long sleep." I told her. "You're worn out and this bed isn't your bed." "I've learned one thing from being here." "You like to sleep close."

"You know this bed is small." She defended herself from my comment.

"Yeah, I'm thinking about buying one just like it for the house." I replied.

"Kurt, you have to eat." Bailey shared her feelings again. "I looked it up the other day; you're supposed to weigh at least thirty pounds heavier." "Kurt, you look thin and pale."

"Look who's talking." I said to her. "You've lost weight too."

"How can you tell? She asked me.

"I can feel your ribs." I told her.

"That's your fault; I always lose my appetite when I'm upset." She lashed out.

"Okay" I chuckled "if I find you to be starting to get a little soft, I'll get you upset and a few weeks later, you'll look in the mirror and thank me."

"Kurt, I was thinking the other night while you slept." She stated. "You said you needed me." "Do you remember what you said to me?"

"You'll have to tell me; I don't know what you're asking."

"I told you I could take you to the cleaners." "Do you remember that?" She asked.

"Yeah, that was when you proposed a contract to me."

"I thought you were an easy mark" she said "and I really wanted you to see that I wasn't like the person you thought of me as." "I told you that if I was a con artist, I'd be in jail." "You're not the meek lamb that you presented yourself to be."

"Bailey, I liked you the moment you sat down across from me at Becky's diner." "Lay down with me." I said to her. When she did, I continued. "We spent very little time together, and I almost lost you." "You and I were headed off in different directions at the time, and I wouldn't have ever gotten to see you again." "I would have gone into seclusion like I did at my suite at the hotel, but a tiny little thing like a battery, changed all that." "Our lives would have been over before it even began." "The real truth was you didn't trust me, and for that reason you were cautious." "You're not anymore." "You have all you need to put every ounce of faith you have in me, that's a powerful feeling." "It took me three days to show you that, but I also had to see who you were too." "And once I saw you as being true, I needed you more than I needed you when we met." "Bailey, I need you forever, not just now, or an hour later." "I need to see you sitting next to me on the couch ten years from now just like I told Sarah." "There's only one way that'll ever happen; we'll have to wake up in the morning, and go to bed at night." "All things that happen along the way in between those times, we'll have to work to get through them." "Not everybody can do that, I'm hoping we're different." "But Bailey forever means you'll have to feel the way you feel about me now." "That's asking a bit much, don't you think, I've seen the mean side of you when you lose your temper."

"That goes for you too Buster." She replied.

"Have you ever been to California Bailey?" I asked.

"No"

"I've been there twice" I said "once in Los Angeles, and once in San Francisco." "I can't tell you anything about them; they both looked the same to me."

"What are you doing Kurt?" She asked.

"In the business world, it's not what you say but the way you say it." I said to her "All questions that's going to be asked a candidate or a CEO of a corporation are known beforehand, and the answers that are given by them contain nothing but positive information." "Celebrities are treated differently." "That's what happens when news media's support candidates, they report on the positives." "They give me the same information I need to place a bet." "I need to throw some red meat out there and see who fights for it."

"I didn't understand one thing you said." She commented.

"Bailey the only time politicians work is when their campaigning." "That's the easiest time to read a person." "They're so involved with telling the people what they want to hear that they ignore a simple equation." "When they do a lot of talking, their mouth is like their butt, when it's open nothing but crap comes out of it." "They get large financial contributions to get elected." "Once elected those that gave those large sums of money expect to be rewarded." "That's the way friends are made, and new friends are introduced." "In business you have sectors." "Transportation, housing, pharmaceuticals, fossil fuels, precious metals, real estate, banking, technology and even money is traded." "It's like that book about poker I read, place you're bet and spin the wheel." "But, in this case I hear incorrect information being fed to the people, and that's a problem." "Bailey, I took over my father's business six months after I got out of school, not college, high school." "I just turned twenty five, and my trust fund was released to me." "Before that, I was a mail clerk." "I wanted to try and work my way into the system." "No one knew I was the son of the founder of the firm." "That was the wisest decision I ever made." "I learned that the best way to do business was talk to the people that were doing the actual work." "Lawyer's make mistakes and they have legal assistants that are supposed to catch them." "They talked at the lounge and I'd listen." "Some of the people talked stocks." "I was surprised to hear they gave their money to a firm to make money for them, but they were confident." "I began researching portfolios on how they performed as far back as the company went." "They had their ups and downs." "But one of the chief factors contributed to elected officials." "These people worked for me, but I couldn't understand how they thought the way they did." "You learn a lot sitting in a lounge and listening to people voice out their frustrations." "One day I got on the elevator and rode to the tenth floor and started to go into the room and was stopped by the secretary." "I told her my name is Kurt Bryant and I own this Corporation; please open the door for me." "She didn't, she called security, and I was escorted out." "The next day, I walked into the office with the Mayor by my side." "She was more sociable towards me than what she was the day before, I thanked the mayor; he went on his way and changes were instituted in the way business was done." "The mayor was rewarded with a contribution."

I heard the door open, and chairs squeaking. Then I heard silence.

"Bailey and I are leaving for Los Angeles in two weeks." "Let me know tomorrow if you're going with us." I told Sarah and Steven.

"Mister Bryant, everything's gotten all twisted around." Steven said.

Bailey interrupted. "Steven, I don't interrupt in Kurt's affairs, he told me he moved because nothing stayed the same." "I didn't realize what he was saying then, you have to understand I didn't know him at the time, and it didn't hit me until now." "He's telling you that your life is going to change whether you want it to or not."

"We talked." Sarah said. "Steven said no one would have ever done anything like that for us, and I agree with him." "Mister Bryant."

"That's Kurt" I corrected her.

"Kurt, was it difficult for you to leave here?" She asked.

"I thought I'd have my problems and I did." "But I met Bailey and everything started falling into place." "Don't get me wrong, New York is in my blood, but I won't be moving back here." "I can walk and not meet anyone for hours in Skinland." "I miss that, and I miss hearing the kids on their games." "Sarah and Steven, I told you that I don't want you around me if you don't want to be around me." "I feel like I may be pushing you into making a decision you might regret, and all of us would end up suffering from that mistake." "The offer I made is breakable by you at any given time." "I won't offer you a contract; I only give contracts to people that work for me." "I'll know how you feel." "Whenever you need a break, you can charter a jet, and send us a postcard." "Cindy learns quickly, and Bailey does a pretty good job of keeping up with me." I told them. "We need you, but we don't need you so bad that we can't get along without you."

"Mister Bryant." Sarah began.

"That's Kurt." I repeated.

"Kurt, Steven and I did a lot of talking and needless to say we didn't get much sleep when you first asked us to work for you."

"That's working with me." I corrected her again.

"Anyway, we didn't know what to think." She stated. "I have to admit the money that was offered to us did keep coming up time and time again."

"You won't have that problem anymore, at least for a while." I said "If you choose to stay here, you'll be compensated for your troubles, and when it comes time to sign the papers, you'll be called for an appointment."

"Stop it." Sarah said. "I'm trying to be serious here."

"So am I." I told her "Sarah, I'm with Bailey for one reason, we connect." "We can talk." "There's only one way to put an end to this." "And you know what that is."

"I'm nervous." Sarah said.

"Now you know what Bailey was feeling the first night in my house with me without any electricity."

"You know, at first I thought this was a bad idea." She began with a lighter attitude than she had been displaying. "I mean the money was too good to pass up." "Travel, and living in luxury, that was way beyond my" "well let's just say that I'm still not believing this." "You know what made me think about you, you weren't the short chubby old man that wanted to get his jollies." "If you were, Steven and I wouldn't even be considering about going with you and for that matter, we wouldn't have anything to do with you."

"I know" I said "I was alone in my thoughts, Sarah; tell me, what does a blind man see in his dreams?" "I can only tell you that I can't see faces." "What does it feel like when the only person in the room that can tolerate you is yourself?" "I listen and I hear what people say." "Why are people so critical of other people, and yet they see themselves standing at the pearly gate of heaven" "You said you and Steven split up after three weeks." "You contacted him and things were patched up."

"I didn't tell you that." She stated.

"Yes, you did, not in those words but you did just the same, Sarah; I know Steven, and Steven wouldn't have initiated any contact with you." "He only has one goal, and that's to satisfy you." "I'm going to have to be honest about this." I spoke. "You and Steven are struggling now to stay together." "Sarah, when I met you, you were a totally different woman than the woman I'm talking to now." "You said you and Steven had a talk about my offer." "I'm thinking that maybe you've said more to each other in the last few days than what you've said to each other in the last three months." "Am I wrong?" I asked.

"I told you I'm a bitch." She reminded me.

"Why" I asked her.

"I don't know why."

"I can answer that for you." I told her. "Women are bitches only when they're unhappy." "If you find out what makes you happy, you'll find out that you're not a bitch anymore." "Sarah, keep your apartment here, you can always tell what a bitch looks like, she's the one that isn't wearing a smile." "You can come and go as you wish, that was the same contract I gave to Bailey when I asked her for help." "If you feel confined, then leave." "I told you, I don't want people around me that don't want to be around me." "I loved New York, but not anymore."

We were interrupted by my door opening. "That's all right." I heard my nurse say. "I've got a couple of pain pills for you."

I took in a couple of breaths. "You smell good." I told her.

I talked to the girls." She replied "You were right, they said they never noticed." "You've got quite a good sniffer on you." She commented.

"It breaks down when I'm in a room with a person that has a flatulence disorder." I commented and they all started laughing.

"Then don't ever ride in a car with my husband on a cold night." She warned me and that comment had everyone rolling in tears.

Somewhere in the night I fell asleep.

I felt my arm being lifted and a cuff being put around it. Bailey began stirring.

"I need you to take these." A woman said.

"What are they?" I asked.

"Pain pills" "The doctor increased the dosage to counteract the morphine."

I heard the door open and close.

"Did Sarah and Steven leave." I asked Bailey.

"Yeah, when you passed out." "They went to get some sleep."

"Kurt, my mother called while you were asleep." Bailey said sounding apprehensive.

"How much does she want?" I asked.

"How did you know that?" She questioned.

"Your voice, now, how much?" I stated.

"It doesn't matter" "I told her I wouldn't ask you for money." "Kurt, I haven't talked to her since I went to live with my father, and that was twelve years ago." "She seen me with you on T.V and wanted me to ask you for help." "I just turned seventeen when I met Tom." "That was when I realized I was nothing more than a mistake to my parents."

"Bailey, my father worked all the time." "He was a professional, and as a professional he was infatuated with his work." "That was his life he chose to live." "Somewhere along the way your parents had troubles and the end result was divorce." "Your mother and your father found others to spend their time with." "You're a big girl now and all that's behind you; or at least it should be." "I was angry with my father for a long time." "I was still angry with him when he died, but everybody has a lifestyle, and sometimes we're not a part of it."

"You said that to me when you got out of my car and left to go home." She stated. "That's what you meant when you said everybody has a lifestyle."

"Bailey, your mother and father must have had something that drew them together." "Chances are you'll never know what it was, and if you ask them, they probably wouldn't be able to tell you why either." "Something happened to break them up, and it wasn't your fault." "Your mother and father started a new life and their lifestyle changed."

"It doesn't matter" she said "she got mad at me and called me a whore and hung up on me." "Kurt" "If I would have asked you for some money to give her, she would have called me again."

"We've already had that discussion." I told her.

"Now, lie down and hold me." I said to her. "I'm tired, and sleepy."

"Kurt" "I love you."

I was awoken by my nurse bringing me a tray of food.

"What's this?" I asked.

"Breakfast."

"You eat it." I told her.

"I can't, it tastes horrible." She stated. "Here we are with sick people in the hospital and they serve food I wouldn't eat."

"I know." "Bailey, hand me my clothes." I told her.

"What are you doing?" The nurse asked.

"The doctor's going to let me out this morning." I said to her.

"Did he say that?"

"He said if I feel the same way as yesterday, he'll let me go." "Now, I need some help putting on my clothes." I told the nurse. "If you don't mind, could you step outside for a minute?"

"I'm a nurse young man and I've seen my share of naked men before." She replied.

"Stand up." She said as Bailey and her helped me.

"This is embarrassing." I commented.

"Mister Bryant, you need to let Bailey help you out as much as you can." "This is one of those times that you need all the help you can get, and I do mean everything." "We have more patients return from getting in and out of the bathtub than any other problem that came up." "So, consider yourself warned." "Getting dressed is the second most repeaters." "So don't get all macho and argue." "Bailey, they make brooms for people like Mister Bryant, don't use the straw end, use the wooden handle, and once is usually all it takes." She stated. "Sick men are like spoiled babies; you have to punish them when they don't listen to you."

"Trust me; that's the least of my concerns." I told her.

"What's that supposed to mean?" Bailey countered.

I took a deep sigh and held my tongue. The nurse was aware of my silence and she knew my words weren't meant for her.

"If the doctor asks you if I had anything to do with this, don't tell him I helped." The nurse said.

"Ma'am, it doesn't matter what the doctor decides." "I'll take his professional opinion under consideration, but I have to go." "I'd like for you to tell all the nurses that cared for me, I owe them my utmost respect and gratitude, I like it when you can have a pleasant conversation with the people in charge of you; they helped make my pain tolerable." I stated.

"Mister Bryant, I don't want to see you back here." She said as she turned and walked away.

"Ooh, you are one smooth operator." Bailey commented. "You tell people what you feel and apologize for it."

"Do you know when you take pain killers, it knocks you out and you feel like you're dead." I said to her.

"Don't talk like that, and what did you mean about reinjuring yourself as being the least of your concern?" She asked.

"I don't really know where to start." I told her. "I didn't go to school; I had a different kind of training." "The doctor that was in charge of me died of a heart attack." "I was twelve at the time." "I later found out that he performed unauthorized experiments on twelve boys." "His goal was to."

I heard the door open and the doctor's voice. "I see I don't have any say in the matter." He chuckled.

"The media's out there, aren't they?" I spoke.

"They've been there since you've been here but the nurses run them out when you came out to get some exercise." "Mister Bryant, I've been under a little pressure so they've started building their forces back up." "My wife and kids drive thirty miles away to go eat pizza now." He replied.

"Doc when we first met in the ICU, I admit I didn't remember much of our conversation." "But I do remember you saying a little something about having your days of glory." I began. "After a while, I'm sure it began to wear off and there were moments that tempers flared and discharged." "I know what you went through." I told him. "When you give your statement, tell the press that I elected to leave against your professional advice." "If they ask you anything else, the words you say won't be printed." "Paper's sell more papers when reporters are creative." "To say it simply, questions were asked, but not answered, and to a reporter unanswered questions only means the truth is being hidden." "Keep watching for the tabloids in the line at the grocery store you said you went to."

"I don't have to" he said "my wife picked up three different ones with my picture on it yesterday." "Did you know I was battling the flu when I operated on you?" "And one of them reported that we left a pair of alligator clips in you and had to open you back up."

I heard the door open again and I caught a whiff of the current of air it created.

"I'll sign the papers." He replied. "You can leave when you're ready." "Mister Bryant, I'll need to see you in about a month."

"Can we like do this during non business hours." I asked him.

"I don't do that" he stated "but I don't think I really care about going through all of this again." "When you were in the ICU." "You said something like I was in a damn if you do and a damn if you don't type of situation." "Now, it seems that I don't have much of a choice in the matter, I really don't want to go through all of this again." I then heard the door open and close.

"Sarah and Steven, today is judgment day, you never gave me confirmation on how you sway." I said to them.

"I need to ask a question first." Sarah said. "Yesterday you talked about my husband and me." "I need to know if you aren't telling me something."

"What did you see in Steven when you first met him?" I asked her.

"He was kind." She stated.

"I know, see that's Steven, he's kind." "Now I want you think back to the first argument that you had." "You did the arguing and Steven did the listening, he's not a fighter, at least when it comes to you, you'll win every argument every time and Steven will be Steven." "When we first met, you had a lot of anger about you." "Later, I heard you speak kindly." "This way there's a chance." "Sarah, do you do crossword puzzles?" I asked her.

"What are you getting at?" She replied.

I began my answer. "I was sitting in the lounge eating a sandwich when I was working in the mail room." "I heard one of the men talk about one of the puzzles." "There were four men there and soon all of them began coming up with answers trying to help solve the clue." "One of them was the correct answer, and for around fifteen minutes everybody was involved with working that man's crossword puzzle with him." "He didn't care; his goal was to answer all of the questions to the puzzle and it didn't matter if he had help in doing it, in fact it was accepted gladly." "The next day, I was eating my sandwich and listening to the same men working on the next day's puzzle." "After that, more people offered clues and that puzzle found a home on the lounge table." "Everyone that used the lounge for a break became involved."

"I still don't know what your point is." She said to me.

"When people have arguments, those arguments escalate until a point is reached where aggression is used, it may be unintentional or intentional, but aggression leads to fights, and fights lead both parties to lawyers." "If that's what you want in life, then you'll get what you asked for." I told her. "Those men used team work to solve the puzzle." "You have only one way of doing things, and that's your way." "We have a problem there." "Since Steven first talked to me, he was always attentive to my needs." "Never did he display and attitude of being non compliant." "That meant to me to him my concerns came before anything else, and Sarah, I'm sad to say, that meant even you." "I found that out the next day." "That was when I realized the first night you and him had a fight about me." "Steven was doing his job the only way he knew how." "Have you asked Steven what he thought?" I said to her.

"Yeah, we talked."

"No Sarah, you did the talking and he did the listening." I said "Steven, tell Sarah what I know."

He didn't say a word.

"What's he saying Steven?" Sarah asked.

"Sarah" I said "he can't tell you, but I can." "In two year's time, you'll be divorced." "You're bored with your life."

"You've got a lot of nerve." She said to me.

"Steven, how much would it cost you for a divorce." I asked him.

"Sir"

"You heard me." I said and waited.

"Twenty thousand"

"How do you know that?" Sarah asked.

"Sarah, it only takes one time to kick a man when he's down." "And you don't support your husband in what he does." "Instead of talking to him, you talk down to him; Sarah you're going to be finding yourself living alone." "It doesn't have to work out that way though." I told her. "You can't live two lives and live in harmony." "Steven can't do what you ask of him." "Together you're a team, and as a team, all problems you face can be solved." "You work good together, but apart you make for one lousy married couple, for that, that price is going to be paid." "That's why I have a stipulation in my house." I told her. "I don't want anyone there that doesn't want to be there." "If you think my answer to your question about you and Steven was rude of me to speak frankly, then I apologize, that was not my intent." "My intent was not to tell you that you act like a bitch sometimes, but to tell you why you act like a bitch sometimes." "I'm sorry if I offended you, but I care about you and I care about Steven, and the way I see it, I'm right until you prove me wrong." "If I didn't have strong feelings for either one of you, this conversation wouldn't have existed; I wouldn't have put the rest of my friends through anything I couldn't fix."

"Kurt, you're asking us to move into your house." "We're not close." She responded.

"What do you think Steven?" Bailey asked.

"Ma'am"

"What do you want?" She asked him.

"Ma'am"

She began. "I walked into Becky's diner after I got a phone call telling me that a job interview, I applied for was canceled." "I was mad and saw Kurt staring at me in the next booth." "That's how we met." "I didn't know he was blind; he had his sunglasses on and boy did I ever lose it." "To make the story short, I became angry at him and called him a butt hole." "He told me that everyone he meets is nothing more than a flip of the coin to him, so the way I see it is he's flipped the coin and waiting to see which side you and Sarah land." "Sarah, you've got a lot to learn about Kurt." "There's things that just isn't done." "Dogs don't chase cars, cats don't seek shelter under the hood of a car; you don't kiss a man with a mustache that has a cold, and you don't ignore what Kurt's telling you." "I sit and listen in on his conversations; he can milk a person faster than you can milk a cow." "Now Steven, I asked you what do you think about becoming Kurt's manager." She said in a more deliberate tone.

There was a long silence.

"Go ahead Steven." Sarah said.

I heard him take in a deep breath. "Mister Bryant lived in his suite in the hotel but his valet for that night called in and the next thing I know, I was introducing myself to him." "When I was at the hotel, my title was valet but I wasn't really anything more than an errand boy." "That's all I was, an errand boy." "And he's right about me not arguing with you Sarah." "Nothing gets accomplished except you get madder." "You left me before and before I met Mister Bryant, you threatened to leave me again." "One of these days you're going to get mad enough to make good on your promise."

"Is that what you think?" She asked him.

"Sarah, you think Mister Bryant is talking to you, he's not, he's talking to me." Steven said.

"Are you okay?" Sarah asked.

"Sarah, I know we discussed this, but I'm going with Mister Bryant."

"Steven, you didn't talk like this when we were discussing our plans." She asserted.

"I don't think our conversation should be aired in front of others." Steven said. "Mister Bryant I appreciate you're offer and I accept the conditions."

"Steven!"

"Sarah, I love you, and I'll always love you. But sometimes you get angry and when you do, I can't say anything without you getting madder" "I get this feeling sometimes that you wish I would just go away and that would make you happy." "I can work until I'm seventy and never get a better offer than what Mister Bryant is offering me." "He's right about us ending up in a divorce." He stated. "I can't find another job making the money I make now."

"Steven!"

"I'm sorry Sarah" he said "Mister Bryant, I'll get a van and we'll have you out of here in about an hour." He said as he got up to leave.

"Steven!" Sarah commented.

"I've got some things I need to do." He said to her. "I'll be back later."

I heard silence for a long time.

"You can put all that on me." I told Sarah breaking the ice.

"What do I do now?" Sarah said.

Bailey interrupted. "It seems to me you've got two choices; you can show Steven more appreciation like Kurt says, or you can stay here." "Sarah, you and I got along pretty good together." "I had a great time with you." "To be honest, you dress good and I was hoping you could make me, you know, look nice like you."

"Sarah, she's a princess in sneakers." I said to her. "She's a flower ready to bloom."

"Kurt" Bailey was going to interfere.

I stopped Bailey. "Sarah, when I asked Steven how much would it cost him to get a divorce." "You sounded surprised, I don't know why, I wasn't; your voice sounded surprised, but it told me that you went to see a lawyer too." "This is judgment day." "I need Steven, but Steven would only be half the man I need without you."

"Kurt, I'm a bitch." She said crying.

"Then you and I can take a lot of long walks together." "You can go on and on and on, and I'll talk about how a sock feels the same to way to me whether it's right side in, or inside out."

"What's that got to do with this conversation?" Sarah said with a swollen nasal tone to her voice.

"Nothing, have you ever done it?" I asked.

"What?"

"Wear one of your socks inside out." I asked her.

"What kind of question is that?"

"Well, have you?"

"Yeah, I guess everyone has at one time or another." She commented.

"Then that means all women can be a bitch to live with sometimes, huh?" I replied. "Now that's got me scared, I thought Bailey was perfect, and now I've got that to look forward too." "You know, one day you'll be doing something and you'll learn what the secret of life really means." I said taking a deep breath.

"Kurt, there's something wrong with you isn't there?" Bailey said.

Once again, I held my silence.

"What happened at the school?" She said to me.

I shook my head back and forth slowly. "Some things you have to live with until you don't have to live with it any longer."

"I need to know." She said softly.

"Bailey when the doctor died, another doctor took over his duties." I said slowly. "I should feel fortunate; she was the one that set me on the right path, she was the one that discovered that I didn't have autism like the doctor diagnosed me with." "I started first grade at the age of twelve and I was reading Braille by third grade, I was around fourteen then." "The day after my graduation, I was brought into the doctor's office." "We had a little talk." "I thought it was going to be one of those inspirational speeches where she would say all people can be the person they want to be, if they want to be it bad enough." "It wasn't one of those speeches I was prepared for." "I was told that Doctor Savidge" "the doctor that was in charge of me" "performed test on boys using radiation to render them infertile." "Six boys have died so far from testicular cancer, and on my last visit nine months ago to be tested, I found out that two more boys tested positive for cancer as well, that leaves four of us." "I bought that book on poker trying to get a feeling of what my odds were, and using the book as a guide, I would bet on my next visit to be tested and the odds were that one or maybe two more boys will test positive, it could be me." "The odds are seventy percent in favor of." I said to her. "I guess you can say in one respect, I was lucky, those other boys had six treatments and I was the last." "I had two treatments before he died." "Bailey you should have a better understanding about those suspicions you might have had about me fathering any of those children in those paternal lawsuits." "It just couldn't have happened."

Bailey began crying on my shoulder uncontrollably.

"Dam it Kurt" "you don't come out and divulge that kind of information." Sarah said crying as well.

"I do what I do to take my mind off of my life." "That's why I moved to Skinland." I said to Sarah "It played a big toll on my mind worrying." "I'd go get tested, and wait two weeks for the results." "There wasn't jubilation upon hearing the news; I worried about next year's test and on one visit, I've had to go back to be retested, it was an inconclusive result." "In three months, I have another test and two more weeks of waiting."

"Dam it" I heard Sarah say again.

"Sarah, I can't fight anymore." "Try meeting someone and in discussions you can't reveal a secret." "Mine tells Bailey she doesn't have a future with me, she deserves to know what she's involved in, and yours tells you that your future is in your hands, and you're hands alone." "The real secret to living a life is you have to wake up and go to bed every night and not let the little things bother you."

"I squeezed Bailey tight. "Bailey, when I told you I was the last of the Bryant's, I didn't want to bring this up, and I thought about it a lot." "And I really meant it when I said to be in a relationship was the last thing on my mind." "It's better to know that my outcome could change than to sit down with you on the sofa and tell you that I went to see the doctor and I've been given my clock." "Both hurt." "Besides, these pills they give me guarantee me that I'll pass pain free." "What a way to go, huh." "You die if you take the pills, and you'll die if you don't; only the latter will have you in so much pain you'll beg for the pills."

"Kurt, you're a fighter" Bailey said "I don't ever want to hear you say that you're tired of fighting again." She couldn't hold back her tears any longer.

I heard the door open.

"What's wrong with everyone; did something happen while I was gone?" Steven said.

Sarah could be heard crying; only she was with Steven, and it sounded like she was using his shoulder to cry on like Bailey.

"What's going on?" Steven said again.

"I was telling Sarah and Bailey about the real secret of life." I told him.

"What is it?" He asked.

I smiled.

"Where to Kurt?" Sarah said.

"I'd like to take home some of that pastry we had in Times Square." "I think everyone liked that place." "There is one little secret I'd like to ask for all of you to hold for me." "That hot cocoa I drank came awful close to Becky's." I said to everyone's laughter. "That means we'll have to ditch the van somewhere and take a taxi, reporters go crazy trying to find a straw in a whole pile of straws." "Then Sarah, I'd like for you and Bailey to go shopping for clothes to wear on business trips." "Men wear suits, I don't know what women wear, I never touched them to find out." "Me and Steven will be waiting at your apartment when you're through." I told Sarah. "Steven did you get the address of Doctor Marshall?

"Yes sir"

"Sarah the van is going to be watched, we'll have to play a game."

"What are you talking about." She asked.

"You'll see." I told her.

"Usually, dinner is served around five to six; Monday is a school day, so the doctor and his family should be home around seven." "I'd like to drop in on them." "Tell the nurses to wheel me out of here." "We've got places to go, people to see, and not enough time to do it in."

"Kurt, that's enough." Sarah said.

"Well, we've got things that need to be done." "How about that?" I responded.

When the nurse walked in, Sarah asked her where she could get me a walker to assist me after we left the hospital. We exited the doors to a mass of reporters and news media's that were covering my departure.

"Mister Bryant did you have Mister Reynolds killed to cover up your involvement with the sales of arms to support the rebel forces in Syria?" One reporter asked and I didn't bother to respond as I was being wheeled to the van.

"Mister Bryant, it's been reported you're building up your portfolio in the energy and precious metal divisions." "Would you care to comment?" He stated.

I put my hands on the wheels of the wheelchair to stop it and address the reporter's question.

"Judging by the sound of your voice, I would have to guess that you've heard a lot; that means you're an educated person." I said to him. "Well, I read a lot, and in one of those books, it kept referring to the people boycotting the refineries by not buying their gas." "It didn't matter; the other refineries did the same." "In one statement, a person was referring to when gas was twenty cents a gallon and when it went up to twenty five cents, she thought that was outrageous to pay a twenty percent increase in gas so she walked to and from the store, which was five miles away to prove her commitment." "Gas never came back down to twenty cents, it doubled, and it doubled again, and it doubled again, and it doubled again and it will double again." "Gas is never going to come back down once it goes up." "That's been proven time and time again." "Gas was twenty cents a gallon in nineteen seventy, take a look and see how much it is today." "Why is it so many people vote for someone to take away everything they've earned and complain about them doing it and then vote for them again?" "That gas I told you about costing twenty cents a gallon was fifty years ago." "It's simple economics."

"Sir, do you honestly believe our government would let that happen." Another reporter asked.

"I was asked a question and I answered it." I stated. "You'll all find a way to print what you heard, even if it's not what I said." "I want to give all of you a history lesson." "In the fifties, we exported fifty percent of all raw products to other countries." "Right after the world wars, we only bought American products, so we prospered." "Times have changed, and Americans don't buy American products anymore." "Foreign countries have bought our corporations." "Go home and look into your closets and pull out everything made in another country and you'll find that your closet won't have anything in it that's made in America."

"Could you respond to that statement?" A reporter asked me.

"Read the papers" I commented "you'll find dozens of responses to that answer I just gave." I said and then put my hands on the wheels to go. I didn't have to; the nurse did it for me.

I was being helped into the van when the reporters were crowding me and making it difficult for me to get all the way in without trouble. Bailey and Sarah both moved past me and shielded me so that the nurses could help me. I then felt them get in and heard the door being closed.

"That's a bunch of crap." Bailey said.

"Not really" I responded "take a note of what the price of oil and gold is today, then take a look and see how much it closes at tomorrow." "They use me, so I use them."

"They're following us sir." Steven stated.

"The first light you come to, slow down until it turns yellow and when it turns red, run it." I told him.

We were soon parking the van and catching a taxi.

"How did you know to do that?" Sarah asked.

"When you ride in taxi's, the meter runs whether you're driving or not." "I've ridden in my share of taxis that slow down to catch a red light." I stated. "Watch and learn." I told her.

"Steven, call the rental place and tell them that the van started shaking bad and tell them where you parked it, it avoids trouble that way."

Third and Broadway, Sarah told the driver of the taxi. "They have a medical dispensary there, that's where we're getting you a walker." "Kurt, you need a wheelchair."

"It's too much trouble getting in and out." "I don't plan on doing any kind of calisthenics." I told her.

When we stopped at the medical store, Sarah told the driver to circle around until he seen her standing outside. Steven and I took several trips until we stopped.

"We got you a couple of canes too." Bailey said.

"Times Square" Sarah commanded the driver. "Drive until I tell you to stop." She told him.

We were driving along and I heard Sarah's voice. "You see Danielle's bakery up ahead?" She said to him. "Pull over and let us out there."

Bailey was irritated when the driver told her seventy five dollars. I laughed as I told her to give him a hundred and told him to have a nice day.

"See there, these people know no one can drive a car down here and they rip you off legally." She commented.

Bailey took me by my arm and led me into the bakery; I sniffed around and started asking what I was looking at.

"If you like we have a list of everything." The gentleman said. "Four cups of cocoa with whipped cream and let me have one of those lists." I told him.

"Are there any tables here?" I asked.

"They're all full." Bailey replied.

I turned around and stated loudly "I'll give anyone five hundred to let me have their table." We were soon sitting down.

When the gentleman brought us our cocoa, I asked him how many different types of Danishes they carried. He told me and then began to start naming each one. "That won't be necessary." I said to him. "Give us six of each kind." "You have creamed horns and Éclairs?" I asked.

Paradox

"Yes sir, and doughnuts and pies along with." I stopped him.

"Give us a dozen each of the creamed horns, and the Éclairs." I stated to him.

"That's going to take me a little time." He said to me.

"Bailey, give me two hundred." I told her.

When I handed the money to the salesman, I told him. "When you get in a hurry, mistakes are made, I'll be two thousand miles away from here by the time I find out my order wasn't complete." "Take your time, I know I have a large order and you have a lot of customers that need attention."

"Can I get anyone anything?" He asked with a softer tone to his voice. When no one said anything, I answered for the group.

"The cocoa's great." I said to him. "And we thank you for your hospitality."

Around an hour later, Steven was loading boxes into the cab.

"Give me three hundred." I said to Bailey.

"What are you going to do?" She asked.

"You and Sarah are going shopping, and Steven and I are going to his apartment, I'm going to start with the Éclairs, and I might end up having another one." "I don't know, I've been thinking about the creamed horns some."

"Hold it a minute." I heard her opening a box and taking something out. "I'm hungry too." She said as I heard her telling Sarah that she wasn't eating both of them.

When Steven and I got in the cab I asked Steven to see which box she opened.

I heard him shuffling around. "Two of the creamed horns are missing sir."

"Hand me one." I told him.

I asked the cab driver if he was hungry. "You picked us up from the bakery, and I bought a lot of pastry to take home, one less creamed horn wouldn't be missed."

"Are you serious?" He said in an accent.

I handed him the creamed horn. "Here, be careful, you may find yourself driving by that bakery everyday just to get you one."

"Thank you, sir." He said as I felt it leave my hand.

When we arrived at Steven's apartment, I gave the driver a hundred. "I have another two hundred in my pocket, and another creamed horn, if you can help my friend carry everything into his apartment, I'm not able."

"I will do this." He said to me.

When I gave him his tip, he once again thanked me as he took his creamed horn and left.

"Steven, find the Éclairs and stand back, you might get hit with creamed filling." I told him.

The first bite didn't have that connection I was looking for, but the second bite had me convinced I was going to have to have another.

"Did you charter a flight?" I asked him as I handed him and Éclair.

"Yes sir." "Sir what's this place like, where you live."

"I told Julie" "that was that thirteen year old girl" "that New York was a place you either loved or you didn't ever want to go back." "That's the kind of place Skinland is." "There's more people on this one city block than what there is in the whole county." "That's why I leave the door open and let time be a factor in your decision." "Steven, I know Sarah is your life, she does love you, you know, only she has a problem." "There's only one way to handle Sarah." I told him.

"How's that sir." He answered wanting to know what I thought.

"You do a good job of letting Sarah direct you in pretty much everything you do." "Steven, I don't know about her past, but I do know when Sarah was young, she grew up with a dream just like every kid did." "Only with Sarah, it's difficult to satisfy her dream." "She has a problem like I do." "I can't see and I'll never be able to see." "She's blind too, only she has eyes." "Who knows, maybe where I live, Sarah will change from who she is into a person that's she's not." "That'll be found out later in Skinland." "But you have to live with what you got." "If she chooses to leave you." "Then let her leave, there won't be any way you would be able to stop her, even if you tried." "No one can tell another what they should do." "You found that out when you first started going together." "I can't tell you what to do." "This is one of those times that you and her will have to work things out." "Sometimes things work out for the better and sometimes things work out for the worst." "If she does leave, she might come back to you and things might get better over time." "She's struggling Steven, and the only person she's fighting is herself."

"When was the last time she told you that she loves you?" I asked him.

"I can't answer that sir."

"Steven, you and Sarah are riding a rowboat in choppy waters." I said to him.

"Sir" "How did you know I talked to a lawyer." He asked.

"All couples have disagreements from time to time and sometimes they evolve into arguments, and people are curious." "You weren't serious but none the less you had to get a feeling of what you were looking at." "Steven, I want you to listen really good." "No matter how mad Sarah gets, you say I love you." "If she gets madder and starts throwing knives at you, you tell her, I love you." "She might slam the door on her way out, but a little way down the road, she'll be hearing those three little words that you said to her." "I love you." "That's when she'll start to recognize that she's switching into the person she doesn't want to be." "No one knows that answer." "I heard you tell her that you love her and that you always will."

"How do you know so much?" He asked.

"I had the opportunity to research divorces." I told him. "It didn't have anything to do with anything, but I had to know what my father's profession encompassed and once I found out what type of people I was dealing with" "it was a lot easier in making settlements." "Steven, people have a first year fight." "That's when twenty seven percent of all divorces occur." "Nearly all of them didn't have any money to split after the lawyers got paid." "Then there's the five year fights." "A couple has one or two kids, and child support is stiff, and health care is a burden to contend with." "In that situation, the one without the kids gets to pay everyone and ends up broke." "Then there's the ten year fights." "Now you're talking money." "Savings plans, retirement, stocks, bonds, assets, even the pet has to be evaluated." "You're told it's for their client to get what's coming to her, but it's really for the lawyers." "Both sides get forty percent of both of your worth if they have to go to court." "After twenty years you think marriage is nothing more than a ride on a sleigh." "That's a big mistake there." "A twenty year fight gets ugly, people have a lot of trust in each other and that's usually when lawyers really get nasty." "Oh, they'll slam the law books down on the table and scream at each other like this is the way it's going to be, and then they'll storm out." "That night both of them will be at a party or a restaurant, or the opera, a ballet, and they'll act as if nothing unusual happened." "It's nothing more than a job to them." "The thirty year marriages are a little calmer." "No one gets upset; it's treated more like a mutual understanding." "After all, most of them knew it was coming the first year they were married." "Forty year divorces and neither party attend the meeting." "The lawyers just exchange papers." "Bailey and I had a conversation." "It involved gold diggers." "In divorces, that comes into play too."

"Steven, if you don't mind, could you get me a glass of water." "I need to take a couple of pills and rest."

"Yes sir"

I swallowed the pills and leaned back against the sofa.

"Lie down sir and rest." Steven said.

"Steven, a woman is trouble." "It'll cost you everything you have to keep them happy, and it'll cost you everything you have if you don't." I told him. "When you and Sarah found each other, both of you thought nothing could come between you." "Now look at your life."

I was being awakened by the shake of my shoulder.

"Kurt, it's six o'clock." Bailey said.

"How long have you been back?" I asked.

"We bought the store out." "I got you some slacks and some dress shirts."

"You and Sarah were supposed to be shopping for your clothes, not mine." I told her.

"We did, but we saw some things we thought you and Steven would look good in." "Kurt, I need a boob job." "All the girls in the department stores had price tags on theirs." She stated.

CHAPTER EIGHT

"Why did you want to stop off to see the doctor before we left?" Bailey asked as we prepared for takeoff.

"Bailey" "my future is their future too" "his name will hit the tabloids again and what they went through will once again resurface." I began. "I wanted to prepare them and let them know that they can't argue with what's printed." "I did it mainly for his kids." "Things like that have a way of interrupting a normal routine and when that happens sometimes it's too much to bear." "Bailey" "a story is a story." "No matter what is said" "some people believe what they read."

"I don't know" "To me, they seem to be enjoying it when I was taking pictures of y'all." She stated.

"Did you?" I asked her.

"You mean everybody wanting to know about what my involvement with you was?"

"Bailey, I know reporters" "and I know what extremes they'll go to." I said to her.

"I'm a hussy." She commented leaning her head back against the seat. "Every paper I saw my face in, it reported that you were paying me dearly for my affections." "Momma called me back up and asked me if I would talk to you again." "I told her no and if she ever came knocking on my door, I'd have the police arrest her." "She called me a whore again and I told her that she was the one that taught me."

I leaned my head back and felt a slight bump.

"Kurt" "we've landed" "we're home." Bailey said nudging me to wake me.

"I didn't know we took off."

"The doctor said the drugs he gave you were strong." She replied.

"We've got company waiting for us." Sarah said and by the tone in her voice I knew who she was talking about.

"I knew it wouldn't be long." I said with a sigh. "They've got their rights." "How's security?" I asked.

"I see a lot of cops." Steven said after a few seconds.

"I won't ever be able to take a walk into the city again." "Bailey" "in New York" "no one notices anybody unless they want to be noticed." "Here" "you won't be able to show your face in Skinland again without everybody staring at you." "Sarah."

"Right here Kurt."

"What did the papers say about you?" "I know they got your name." "You had to fill out a report to the police." "You were involved."

"You and I have been having a secret love affair for the last two years and all of it was done while Steven took care of your needs." "I was seen coming and going while Steven was going and coming."

"Does that change anything about what you think of me when you came across my name and you read that article to see what they were saying about me?" I asked.

"It does open my eyes to why you spoke to me the way you did when I met you." She replied.

"That's the way the people in Skinland think of Bailey here." I said to her. "They look at her as a girl that's only with me because I give her what she wants and she's taking advantage of my offer." "Back in New York" "how many people even knew who you were Sarah?" "One, two, four, more."

"We didn't do the night crowd." She replied.

"Well, Sarah" "I hope I don't sound offensive but you're hardcore compared to Bailey." "I'm trying to teach Bailey that it doesn't matter what people think of you." "The simple reason is most of them do so because they only believe in what they believe in, much like you did when we met, you had a belief molded in your mind of what type of person I was from reading those articles and nothing could have persuaded you to believe anything else about me other than what you believed."

"What do you mean hardcore?" Sarah asked.

"I guess you did take offense at my statement." I replied. "Sarah" "everything with you is one way and if you don't get your way, you become argumentative." "You need to work on that some."

"Kurt" She began and I stopped her.

"See there" "you always have to have the last word.

"We're ready sir" the stewardess told me. "Would you like some help getting into the chair?"

"No"

I stood and then sat back down. When she wheeled me to the door the airport personnel carried me down.

We were driving slowly as I heard reporters begging me to stop and answer questions.

"What time is it?" I asked.

"A little after four in the morning sir" Steven answered.

"Take a look at those people and tell me what you see." I stated.

"Who?" Sarah asked.

"Anyone" I stated.

Paradox

"They're taking pictures and asking questions." Sarah said after a few moments.

"Those people out there aren't anything more than freelance photographers getting a picture and the reporters you see haven't been able to get any answers to any questions." "If you were to check the computer tomorrow and read the headlines of the papers; you'll find stories and all of them will be read by people that don't have anything better to do than judge us by what they read." "They utilize a one party conversation to deliver a voice to bolster their point." "The real reporters are at home asleep." "The papers buy the pictures and assign a writer to listen to the audio of the questions that's being asked from the other reporters to make it seem like they were the one doing the asking." "Those people out there are called Cubs."

"Yeah" "well they're following us." Bailey said.

I couldn't help myself I had to give a little laugh.

"What's so funny?" Bailey asked.

"They know where I live." "Becky had the only diner between Murray and Skinland." "None of those people following us are from around here, so that means they'll be at the mercy of dining at Barney's grocery or drive to Murray to eat, and sleep." "Bailey" "Sarah" "I'm afraid to think what stories will be written after they talk to the locals."

"Oh, my lord" "I forgot about that." Bailey seemed to withdraw. "Kurt" "when Becky got home, she called me and told me that the kids and them had to move into the house." "They couldn't keep them away from theirs."

"What about Cheryl?" I responded.

"Her father's been driving her over and taking her home." "Kurt" "Becky said she pitched a fit."

"Why" I asked.

"You gave her a responsibility when you asked her if she would take care of your pond and her father didn't want her being hassled." "They had a fight."

"Bailey" "how old were you when you began arguing with your parents?" I stated.

"I don't know."

"That's a given" I replied. "Cheryl has to vent." "I had the luxury of my scream room." "She doesn't have one and I'm going to introduce her to mine." "Bailey" "Ronnie is becoming a young man and it could be that Cheryl's parents aren't ready to accept Cheryl as a young lady." "An injury has a way of transforming a mother and father into thinking that they know what's best."

"What do you mean?" She asked.

"Cheryl's been through a lot compared to her life a month ago." "I'm willing to bet she's spent better than twelve hours a day that was associated to school." "I can only guess." "Ronnie said she was close to failing." "Bailey" "when I met you, I asked you if you were wearing a hair band" "you reached a point to where that band was about ready to snap." "Cheryl's got worse problems than that."

"Ooh" "That is deep." Sarah acknowledged.

"Has a rubber band ever snapped with you? I asked Sarah.

"Ooh" "now that one stung." She commented. "Kurt" "you're going to have to quit poking me with the truth." "You know Bailey's right" "You would have made one fantastic lawyer."

"That reminds me" "You remember meeting Richard when we were at the board meeting?" I asked Sarah.

"I remember meeting people but I don't know which one he was."

"Well, I need you to contact him; Bailey has his number, and I need you to tell him I said that I need him to subpoena all records of visual surveillance of the foyers of all their hotels dating back four years and then tell him we're going to need a roster of all employee's dating back four years also."

"Can I ask why?" Sarah followed.

"The hotel knew I was coming." "I want to see how long it took security to get there, and I want to see if any security can be seen." "If there is security visible, why did they refrain from doing the job they're being paid to do?" "Then tell him that I need to get all the guests names that have used that chain of hotels."

"Kurt" "you're talking about thousands of people." Steven interrupted.

"That's the idea" "but Steven, it won't go that far." "I just want to rub a little salt into a wound."

"What are you talking about?" Sarah stated.

"Steven when we met you made the comment about when it came to pointing fingers, I should point mine at the manager; you said it was cheap advertisement."

"Yeah"

"If I was to file a class action law suit on behalf of all of their employee's, how many do you think would testify to the fact that they were ordered not to intervene in a timely fashion?"

"I don't know." He responded.

"But there would be some, right?" I added.

"Yes sir" he replied.

"Steven" "I don't think I'll have a problem obtaining all the positive information I'll need when it comes to the employees that's been fired." "Now as far as guest" "Not all celebrities enjoy publicity." "Careers are sometimes shattered and once I inform all of them as to my lawsuit, the ones that didn't hold onto their success will come forward and blame that hotel or those other hotels for their collapse." "I don't care what happened." "I want to keep them busy fighting every single one of them." 'But like I said, it won't come to that." "Sarah" I spoke up "My corporation makes millions off of divorces from women and men finding out that their being cheated on." "There isn't any better proof than surveillance videos." "It's all paperwork after that." "I have my rights too and when someone goes to an extreme to violate those rights, it makes me upset." "I'm tired of going to my scream room."

"What" she asked.

"We'll talk about that later." Bailey commented to her.

"Bailey" "you haven't said anything to Becky about my" "you know my situation" "have you?" I asked.

"No" "and I'm not." She replied. "Kurt" "I don't know what to do."

"Bailey" "when I sat down in the doctor's office at my school." "I was happy." "When I left, I felt the way I feel now." "Weak." "I've been living with my fear since then." "In three months, I'll be tested and my future will be foretold or it'll be foretold on my next visit or the next one." "Something happened and I met a girl that took my mind off of my miseries and through her, I met a family that's giving me a reason to get out of bed every morning and when they find out, they'll treat me differently." "I don't want that" "I want sincerity." "Like you and Sarah."

"Kurt" "You don't meet people and get in fights and become friends and then drop a bomb on them like you did." Sarah jumped in with her complaint. I could hear her breathing heavily; she was trying to suppress her emotions.

I put my arm around Bailey to comfort her. Sarah's tears were infectious.

"Ahh" "we're almost home." I commented breaking the ice.

"How do you know?" Bailey said with a broken voice.

"That's easy" I stated. "We just rounded a double S curve." "That means in about two minutes we've got an uphill climb and a downhill slope and after that, we've got Barney's."

"How did you know though?" She repeated.

"Whenever I left the hotel in New York, I had to memorize my surroundings and every day I would walk a little further." "We've got seventeen curves we have to negotiate to get to Murray, so that means we've got seventeen coming back and we've gone around fifteen of them already, that leaves us the double S curve." "You have to count that one as two, you know."

"Kurt" "You didn't really need my help when we met, did you?" Bailey said softly.

"You're the one that needed help." I told her. "Bailey why did you stay in Skinland?"

She didn't answer.

We rounded the curves and I felt the drag of the limo and as we descended, I once again broke the silence. "Don't blink, we're coming into Skinland."

"You have got to be kidding me." Sarah gasped. "What is this" "some kind of a ghost town?"

"No" I replied "It's a place where people go to when they don't have any other place they can go."

"Was that intended for me?" Bailey inserted.

"No" "that's the reason I'm here." "You just happened to get here before me." I replied.

"Kurt" "I think that's why I stayed." "I didn't have any other place to go."

"Yeah" "You came here and met someone that cared for you." "That was Becky." "I'm glad you waited for me." I chuckled.

"You're a lucky man." "What if I had gotten that job?" "I wouldn't be here now." She had a hint of curiosity in her voice.

"Circumstance" I replied.

"I don't understand." Sarah spoke up.

"Sarah have you ever been involved in an accident?" I questioned.

"Duh" she responded.

"If you had left a minute earlier or a minute later, it could have been more than likely you wouldn't have been in an accident, but you didn't, and look what happened." I commented and then shifted my focus on Bailey. "Bailey" "all things in life come at you without answers" "it's up to each individual to handle how they choose to deal with what it doles out." "If someone else would have sat down where I sat in Becky's diner that day." "It's a good bet that he would have looked at you and he might have given you a second look or even a third, and I'm willing to gamble that you would have unleashed all kinds of verbal hostility on him the same as you did to me." "The only thing that stopped you was you found out that I was blind." "I wasn't anything more than a distraction that took you away from the pain you were going through." "Bailey" "You began living in a life of hell when your fiancé put one over on you." "I'm not any different." "A doctor put one over on me too and he even got my father to pay him for it." "I sat up every night in my studio and that led me too here." "And speaking of here, we're home."

"How do you know?" Bailey asked.

"There's a hole in the road." "When I rounded the turn to see what Skinland had in store for me, I heard a truck's axle protest when it ran over it." "The limo made a wide turn and the left rear tire hit it when we turned."

"Kurt" "There's all kinds of cops up ahead." "Holy smokes" "Kurt" "They're blocking the drive." Bailey stated.

"Give me a couple of pills." I said and after I took them, I opened up. "In New York it got to where I stood out in a crowd like a sore thumb." "My cane was a dead giveaway." "I wasn't anything more than a captive trapped in my own suite." "The First Amendment gives Americans the right to freedom of expression." "People believe it to be freedom of speech." "Not so" "freedom of expression includes the right to free speech." "There isn't a distinction between Speech and the Press so slander is protected equally along with the truth."

"Are you alright Kurt?" Sarah asked.

"I will be as soon as I can get to my scream room" I responded.

"No" "Kurt" Bailey quickly stopped me "that man tore you up and I'm not going through that all over again." "You can scream all you want when you get back to the way you were when I met you."

"You didn't say you lived in a mansion." Sarah said softly.

"I only know one room and that's my bedroom." "I didn't have a need to go in the others."

The limo came to a stop and I was being guided to my door when I was stopped short.

"Mister Bryant may I have a word with you later?" A voice asked.

I stopped but I didn't answer.

"It's the Sheriff" Bailey informed me.

"Have you been busy?" I asked him.

"That's what I want to talk to you about." He relinquished.

"Sheriff I know with this county being small" "your budget is squeezed." "All monies spent by your department will be reimbursed." "If you have people that want to work extra time; I'll take care of it." I commented. "Sheriff" "I'm hoping all of this will die down in a few weeks." "I have a problem though" "You can see that I'm going to have to hire a security firm." "But I can't hire someone unless I know I'm hiring the right people and I don't know how long that'll take me." "Sheriff you remember when you first started out as a rookie?"

"Yeah" "all too well." He answered.

"It was rough raising a family on a cop's salary, wasn't it?" I responded.

"Yes sir."

"Bring me a figure on how much it would take for you to run that firm and don't be shy about the men you'll need." I told him.

"Can we talk later?" He asked.

"Bailey will tell Becky and the others you're expected." I stated.

"You get some rest young man, you hear." He said and then I was once again being led by Bailey.

I heard the door opening before we got to it.

"MOMMA" "He's home." Cindy shouted.

When we entered the house, I was led to the sofa.

"Does it hurt?" Cindy asked.

"Sometimes, but not right now." I answered.

"Cindy" "Now's not the time." Buck inserted his complaint.

"We stopped and got you some of those Blueberry Danishes you liked before we came home." "They're in the limo." I told her. "You're going to need some help carrying them though." "We bought the bakery out."

I heard the door shutting when she went out.

"Kurt" Buck began.

"Buck, you don't have to say anything." "You and Becky and the kids got a front row seat of what the paparazzi are capable of doing." "You found out they can cause all kinds of interruptions in your life and you also found out you were helpless to stop them and because of that, you found out it was safer for your family being here." "You're just as much a prisoner here as what I am and for that I apologize." "I've managed to ruin everyone's life just by meeting them." "Bailey's a hussy and Sarah's cheating on her husband with me and Steven here lost his job because I asked him for a little privacy."

"Calm down Kurt" Becky said. "Reach out your hand." I was rewarded by a warm feeling. It was a cup of cocoa.

"He took some pills before we got here." Bailey commented.

"What's that I smell?" I asked.

"Bailey called before y'all left and told us you were coming home." "I found out your best dinner was a goose so I got a couple of geese in the oven baking that I'm going to stuff with cornbread dressing." "None of us ever ate a goose." She further stated. "It always cost too much." "And Kurt" "I'm the reason we're here." "One of those men wouldn't move and I ran over his foot trying to get out of my driveway." "The Sheriff had to come out and fill out a complaint." "And as far as being sorry that you got us mixed up in all of this." "Hon" "We ain't never had this much excitement in our life."

"Don't worry" I commented leaning my head back after I sat my cup of cocoa down.

"Kurt" "Kurt" "Kurt"

"What" I said feeling someone shaking me.

"Kurt" "You need to go to bed." "You're falling asleep." Bailey said as she was shaking me gently.

"Oh"

"Come on Kurt" Bailey was urging me to get up from the sofa.

When she finished pulling the covers over me, she bent over and gave me a kiss.

"You're crying" "Your lips are salty." I commented.

"Kurt" "I was thinking about."

"Bailey your tired" I said stopping her. "Get in bed" "I don't like sleeping alone." "I did that up until that day I met you and I don't ever want to sleep in this bed without you." "And Bailey" "don't pity me" "I don't want that kind of love." I felt her beginning to tremble so I held her tight. "Bailey" "I need you to get a hold of Mister Hurley and have him transfer four hundred thousand into Becky and Bucks account, it wouldn't be right with me giving Sarah and Steven what we agreed on and pay them for less." "If I did, it would show them that I really do pay for what services I ask for." "I don't want anyone thinking that anyone is more important to me than anyone else." "I'm not speaking about you." I said to her.

"You think everything out, don't you?" She whispered.

"How many thoughts have gone through that mind of yours after we met?" I whispered back.

"There hasn't been a day that doesn't go by that I don't wake up from this bed without having to go through a dozen or so." She chuckled.

"That's my problem" "Steven's read quite a bit of the news that's been reported about me." "I'm not a fan, but let's say one day you wake on the wrong side of this bed and you hear rumors about me."

"Kurt" "Go to sleep" "You don't have to tell me anything I don't know." "I'm a hussy remember" "and I'll always be a hussy." "You said so yourself." "People believe what people believe." "They sell those tabloids in Skinland too, you know."

I smiled at her remark.

"What's so funny?"

"One of these days a handsome young man is going to come into your life and your picture will be the lay out on all the magazines." "I can read the headlines now." "Kurt Bryant" "better known as a onetime flamboyant irresponsible playboy aristocrat has roles reversed as he lays on his deathbed." "Sexy young bombshell."

"Kurt" "don't talk like that." She interrupted me from completing my sentence.

"Why" I asked.

"Because you're talking about my future without you and I don't like that."

"I'm just trying to address the inevitable." I commented. "Ever since I came here, I was trying to forget about my past." "But it follows me everywhere I go."

"If you're going to sit here and talk about death, I'm going to get up." "I thought you were tired."

"I am" "Bailey" "I'm going to need some cash." "We owe back pay."

"How much" she asked?

"Thirty thousand; take Buck and Steven with you when you go." I said to her.

"Go to sleep Kurt" she said putting her hand over my mouth to silence me.

When I woke up the bed was empty. I ran the water in my tub and when I eased in, I eased the cold water to where it ran slower than the hot water. I felt good.

When I opened the door to come out of my room, I felt a hand sliding through my arm. "Hello Sarah"

"Alright Kurt, how did you know?" She asked.

"Is anyone around?" I questioned her with my question.

"No" "why"

"I wouldn't want to offend anyone" "Sarah" "Bailey is shorter than you and Becky is a little pudgy."

"Kurt" "what you've been saying to me about me is true." "I never could see myself as being someone that wanted success the way you said I did." "The last few weeks have been an eye opener for me; I guess that's because I got a little taste of what it's like to see what's on the other side." "I have to admit at first I did enjoy the attention, it felt strange being asked questions, but after a while it got old and I began to dread pulling into the hospital." "Kurt" "this morning you made a comment about destroying the lives of everyone you came in contact with." "That's not true." "I watched Becky and Buck and I didn't see anything like the people you described." "And when it comes to me" "I've been given a second chance to change my ways." "I "was" rough on Steven."

"Sarah" "I'm blind but that doesn't mean I can't see." I stopped to catch my breath.

"What are you talking about Kurt?" She asked.

"I see things" I said.

"You mean me and Steven?" "What is it, Kurt?" She asked.

"Steven is committed to his profession and you fight him because you require more affection than what he gives you." "He's not a romantic person." "You of all, know that." "Sarah if you don't accept Steven the way he is, there's going to be some friction."

"What am I going to do Kurt?" She asked.

"They'll come times when he and I will be alone." I said softly. "It's easier to have a conversation that way." "Don't be surprised if he appears to be a bit more amorous than usual on some nights." "And Sarah" "telling someone you love them does a lot to cement and fortify a relationship." "And" I paused.

"What" she said.

"Maybe he's afraid to show you feelings because he's afraid you might not want his affections." "I'm not Steven" "I don't sleep with you." I commented. "With Steven, it would be a better outcome if you were the one that were to show him the feelings you want from him, and it would make him feel better too."

"Kurt" "Your easy to talk to, Bailey told me that and that's another one of the things I had trouble with when I was trying to figure you out." She commented as she led me along.

I stopped short of the kitchen. "I need my pain pills."

"Alright" "hold on a minute." She answered. "BECKY"

A few moments later I was being switched to Becky leading me.

"He wants his pain pills." Sarah stated.

"Two" I commented "and if that don't work" "two more" "and if that don't work" "two more." "Man should never have to endure any pain with today's knowledge."

"Are you in that much pain Kurt" "I can call the doctor?" Becky said.

"No" "pain resolves from the healing process, it's an indicator informing you that your body is active to its needs." "The apogee of pain is when you reach a certain magnitude and then you begin to feel less and less." "I'm hoping I've reached my apogee."

"Kurt you're going to have to stop using those kinds of words around here." "I don't know what you're talking about some time." Becky scolded me.

"Here" "hold on a minute." She said as she took my hand and put my pills in it. "Let me heat you up a warm cup of cocoa to wash it down." She said putting two in my hand.

"Where is everyone?" I asked to no one in particular.

"Bailey said she had to go to the bank and take care of some business that you wanted her to take care of and the kids are at school." Becky answered.

"Oh" "Okay" "Becky" "I need to talk to Cheryl's parents." "I'd like for you to ask them if I could set up a meeting with them."

"That's already been arranged" she replied "they want to talk to you too." "I invited them over for dinner."

"Becky" "about Ronnie and Cheryl." I began.

"Kurt" "Cheryl's been upset." She stopped me from continuing. "I think it's got to do with Ronnie." "She won't talk to me."

"Becky" "Cheryl knows she's going to fail." "Bailey said her father brings her here and takes her home." "Is that true?"

"Yeah"

I took a sip of my cocoa and swallowed my pills.

"You look pale" Becky said. "And you've lost weight." "I'm going to change that."

"We're home" I heard Bailey's voice coming from the front door. "You're up" she said when she entered the kitchen.

"How's our guest?" I asked pertaining to the reporters.

"Buck almost got in a fight." "They started getting pushy and Buck started pushing back." She stated.

"That's what they want him to do." I commented. "I'll address that over dinner later." I said to her. "How has this affected the kids at school?" I asked Becky.

"Our telephone never stopped ringing." "If it wasn't someone saying that they were from some television station or a radio station calling, it was a reporter or someone from a charity organization wanting one of us to mention their organization to you." "I had to pull the plug out of the wall." "The police arrested some of the reporters for trespassing on school property." "It didn't slow them down one bit, the principal had to meet Ronnie at the front of the building and escort Cindy and Julie to their classes." "It doesn't bother Ronnie; he said he just walks along like they aren't there."

"How about Cheryl?" I followed her statement.

"Her father won't let her out of his sight."

I shook my head slightly.

"What's the matter?" Bailey asked.

"I've got to talk to Cheryl and I don't know how her parents are going to react to my interference."

"Here" Becky said as she put a spoon in my hand.

"What's this?" I asked.

"I'm a critic when I cook, and the kids aren't home yet." "I need someone to tell me if I need a little more salt or something."

"What is it?" I asked again.

"Cornbread dressing with giblet gravy."

"We didn't have this, we had bread dressing." I said as I spooned another bite full in my mouth. "Sarah" I said handing her the spoon. "You've got to taste this."

"This "is" good." She acknowledged.

"Honey" "you gonna fit in really good down here." Becky said laughing.

"I guess that's two yeses." I replied. "Be warned Sarah." "Don't eat her pecan pie." I said chuckling.

"Buck told you that story?" Becky quickly responded.

"He said that's how you and him came together."

"Yeah" "the truth was my momma was the one that cooked the pies." She began laughing and then calmed back down. "He went on and on about how good they were and after he left, I sat down with my mother and she wrote down the recipe for me." "I bet I've cooked over a thousand pies since then and none of them ever came out the way my mommas did." "It didn't matter though; Buck never ate another piece of pecan pie after that." "I think he ate that much just to make me feel good."

"And he still doesn't know that your mother was the one that made the pies?" I added.

"No"

"Ooh" "Now I know the story behind the story." I commented.

"What story?" Becky asked.

"Ahh" "Becky" "You put yourself in front of Buck on purpose; you did that because you wanted him to see you, you wanted some kind of recognition from him." "So, you put yourself in a circumstance to where it seemed like an innocent happenstance from an occasional run in every now and then and you did that hoping to produce a casual conversation."

"I had an argument with my mother about him." Becky said softly. "She didn't want me messing around with him because she said I was too young to know anything about love." "I took off walking to his house and he met me in his truck about halfway there." "We parked on the side of the road and I told him I'd run off with him." "He said Becky" "that's not the way things are done." "Your momma has a right to feel the way she does about me he said." "After that, he cranked up the truck and drove me home and my momma never said anything to me about Buck again." "So, what do you think?"

"I think Buck didn't have a chance." I said to her.

"No silly" "I was talking about the dressing." She commented.

"OH" I chuckled. "You should have moved to New York." "You would have made a fortune there with your diner."

"Nah" "not me" "I'm like my family." "Four days is enough." "I did like Times Square though."

"What do "you" think Sarah?" I asked.

"About what?" "Being here or back home?" She answered.

"I was implying about being here, but you made a comment at the end of your statement." "You said back home and back home usually refers to as returning there someday." "Where's your home Sarah?" I asked.

"I don't understand what you're trying to ask me." She said softly.

"That's something I thought long and hard about." "I sat in my chair and fell asleep many nights asking myself that." "Sarah" "home is where you want to be laid to rest." "Some people are homeless; they don't want be where they're at."

"Kurt" "Steven and I took a walk around and we didn't see not one soul." "We did see a deer though." "Not once did I step out of our apartment without meeting someone in the hallway before I got to the elevator and after meeting you and going through all we went through." "I found it hard to get away from some of the people I ran into." "I don't know if I'm cut out for this kind of living."

"I'd like to ask you to do something for me." I said to her.

"I'm all ears." She responded.

"I have to return to see the doctor in a month or so to do a follow up." "I'll be damned if I do and damned if I don't." "Papers will once again circulate and fictitious rumors will be once again be reported as to my condition either way." I began. "You saw the circus we had to go through this morning." "Take some more walks and try to let yourself relax and when we leave to go back, you'll be able to find the answer that you're asking yourself."

"I didn't know I was asking myself any questions." She replied. "I thought I told you I wanted to be with Steven."

"Anyone who slips in an inadvertent meaning in articulation poses."

"Kurt" Becky interrupted me. "Talk English."

"When someone is talking to you and makes a comment like Sarah just did when she said back home, it tells me that she envisions her life living there in the future." "And Sarah you just said I told you I wanted to be with Steven." "Sarah" "a little thing like that made me a lot of money in my corporation." "If Steven is the only reason for you being somewhere, then that may not be enough to sustain and suffice a relationship." "You've got to be happy being who you are and what you are and most of all, where you are; if you can do that, then all the other things that come at you in life doesn't seem to be important." "As long as you refer to New York as back home, then one day, you and Steven may have an argument and you'll be on plane headed to New York."

"Are you always so analytical?" She asked.

"People say things sometimes without thinking and it lets me know what they really have on their minds." "That's the problem I have." I answered. "I get into a lot of trouble by saying what I feel, but Sarah I say things to you because you're close to me." "If I didn't know you" "I wouldn't have said the things I said."

I heard the door open and Buck and Steven were soon walking into the kitchen.

"How you feeling?" Buck asked.

"I need some sun" "and Buck" "would you mind turning the heater on for the hot tub."

"Alrighty" "anything else?" He asked.

"Nah"

"Kurt" he said "that was awful nice of you to bring back those Danishes."

"The kids loved them huh?" I said to him.

"NO" "I did" "I ate six of them before Becky told me to get out of the kitchen."

"Buck" "go over to the counter and get one of the boxes for me." I said to him.

"How did you know they were on the counter?" Becky said.

"There's the smell of food cooking and there's the smell of the pastries in the air." "How do you think I found your diner Becky?" I chuckled a little.

"Alright" "Now what?" He asked.

"Do they have an internet location marked somewhere on the box?"

I heard silence and then he answered. "Yeah"

"Buck" "all you have to do from now on is click on that web site and order what Danishes you want and how many and they'll be delivered at our doorsteps two days later." "Or you can get on the computer and ask for the people that make Danishes and you'll get hundreds of businesses you can buy them from."

"I want to try something." Becky said "Tell me what these are."

"That's easy" "those are Cindy's favorite" "Blueberry Danishes." I responded.

I then caught a whiff of a different aroma. "Ah" "my favorite" "those are cheese Danishes and then I began to laugh. "Cracker's"

"Kurt those boxes were closed." Becky commented. "Are your ears like that too?" she asked.

"Yeah" Bailey broke in. "When he was in the hospital" "He knew who was at the door before they came into the room."

I heard a cell phone ring and Bailey's voice answered. "He's right here, hold on." "It's Richard" "He wants to talk to you."

"Hello" "I'm alright" "a little tired" "but, I'm alright." I listened and reported "I can be there." "Have their representative meet me at the airport" "Richard" "tell them I'm going to need provisions for nine people for Friday and Saturday night." "No" "make that twelve people." "Oh" "good then" "Richard, I need you to drop a leak for me." "Have our informant tell them to ask some questions regarding that suit."

When I handed Bailey back her phone, I heard nothing but silence.

"We've got four days and then we've got to be in Hollywood." "Richards got me an interview and Sarah and Steven Mister Shelton is being made aware of my intentions as we speak." I commented.

"But you said twelve people." Buck inserted.

"Have you ever been to Hollywood Buck?" I asked.

"No" "and I don't want to go there either." He complained.

"Buck" "Listen to what he's got to say before you get yourself all worked up." Becky stated with firmness in her voice.

"Buck, I heard you got upset today when you went to the bank with Bailey." "I try to use barometers to gauge my actions." I opened my conversation with him but I was speaking to all of them. "They're looking for an A Fortiori" I commented.

"A what?" Becky said.

An A Fortiori is a man that carries a limited mental vision."

"English Kurt" Becky interrupted.

"Buck has his ways of dealing with people that sometimes lets himself lose control." "Reporters love it and once they know who they can push, they'll push." "In the circuit it's known as an A Fortiori."

"What are you talking about Kurt?" Becky said.

"Becky" "none of you are educated in a field where you find yourself to be at the center of attention." "All of you are used to watching the news on television and now there's people sitting at home watching you and Buck and everyone else they take pictures of." "You are the news you watched on television." "You can't tell me that you didn't ever watch the news and not listen to what they said about you or anyone else." "I find that some of the best information you can get is from bystanders having a conversation." I lectured. "When I first started out in my dad's firm, no one paid any attention to me." "I was just some blind guy that worked in the mailroom." "I graduated from high school when I was twenty five, but I didn't start learning about life until I turned twenty five and started to work in that mail room." "Up until then I was just catching up on the past and being taught to where I could function and perform in the present." "I discovered I had a mind of my own." "Buck" "You said you don't invest in the stock market."

"That's right" he answered.

"You remember me telling Mister Laree to invest one third of my holdings in fossil fuels."

"Yeah"

"In nineteen ninety two, we allowed the sales of our oil and chemical companies to foreign investors." "They came in and dismantled these refineries and shipped them off to other countries." "We've got oil being pumped out of our own ground that's owned by foreign countries and shipped to these countries to be used there." "See when you buy out a corporation, you obtain all their holdings and assets." "That means all the leases and reserves that they own too." "With this product being sent somewhere else, it creates a shortage of supply and right now we're floating on a low level." "Our supply is equal to our demand." "Since nineteen sixty inflations grown ten percent a year." "That means our dependency on oil has increased by ten percent a year." "That's not good news for a lot of people."

"What are you saying?" He asked.

"Increases in raw materials force businesses to increase their prices." "In nineteen eighty taxes increased a hundred and fifty percent just by taking away all your deductions and instituting a scale." "Women didn't have to work then." "That all changed when a President changed the tax code." "A woman had to find a job in order for their family to live a lifestyle that they were accustomed to." "Would it surprise you to learn that you and Becky paid more in income taxes than a Billionaire did?" "Back then they said there was an oil shortage and oil more than doubled." "It was a lie; it was fabricated to increase tax revenue." "They had twenty ships waiting in the Gulf of Mexico to unload their oil, but there weren't any storage tanks to put it in." "It was a fabricated oil shortage designed to increase inflation." "You double inflation and you double tax revenue." "This whole nation was crippled by its affect." "Then there was a coffee shortage and a sugar shortage and now every time the wind blows crops are damaged and the prices increase." "Businesses filed for Bankruptcy protection." "Oil will never decrease in value." "It'll fluctuate and frighten investors that are in it for a hedge against a bet, but, it's a sound call." "Now" "let's talk a little bit about precious metals." "Gold is where people put their money in if the economy worries them." "Becky" "Did you notice any increases in the prices of the food you bought for the diner?"

"Yeah"

"Every time something went up, did you increase the price of the food?" I questioned.

"No"

"Why" I asked.

"Because around here people won't pay it." She confessed.

"Buck" "have you ever heard the term rich people always get richer?" I asked.

"Yeah"

"What are you getting at Kurt?" Buck said.

"You can't teach kids about life until they start living life." "I started at twenty five." "When did you start?" I asked.

"When I got married." He answered after a long pause.

"Buck" "I want you to think back a couple of months; you led a different life then." "I would imagine you and Becky had a few talks about what you would do if you could do it as you drove to work every morning and back home from Murray." "If you did, what changed those dreams?" "Buck" "you've got to go beyond teaching your children about the past and educate them on how to prepare for the future." "If you don't" "they'll be like you and Becky" "spending their retirement on gas in the present looking for a better job somewhere." "Buck" "This country won't be the same country when they grow to be your age" "it'll be different." "Ronnie took care of his sisters while both of you worked." "He couldn't play sports" "so a scholarship for college was limited to him." "I think you know you don't have to worry about college anymore." "Buck" "your children are starving." "They want more" "and the only way you can do that is let them live." "Me, I didn't start learning until I walked out of my room back in New York." "Since then, the worlds changed a little and I can guarantee you it's going to change after we elect a new president." "It always has and it always will." "You can't stop progress and the only thing that changes is change itself." "Those questions those reporters ask aren't always intrusive." "They're informative too." "I get insight on what attention is being given about what sector in the market is active and I evaluate who will benefit and who will take a hit." "No CEO or Chairman speaks negatively about the corporation that they hold a position in." "They get millions in bonuses whether the corporation is successful or if it goes bankrupt." "It's written in their contract." "Buck" "there was a banking institution that told all of their representatives to tell their clients that they had a tip on some hot stocks." "They made two billion off of the sales and it was later found out that the stocks were actually worthless." "The government fined them two hundred million." "That firm is still in business and people are still doing business with that firm." "How can you help people that can't be helped?" "They made ninety percent profit and was penalized ten percent."

"Buck" "come show me how to turn the heater on." Becky said.

It wasn't long before I heard the back door opening and shutting.

"I think he's mad" Sarah broke the silence.

"We'll have another talk later." "He's not said his last word yet." I said to her.

"Kurt" Sarah added "if you graduated from high school at twenty five, how come you sound so, so, so smart?" She stuttered.

"I was twelve when the doctor I was assigned to died." I opened. "The doctor that took over had to do a reevaluation of me and she was the one that ordered my care to be changed." "I never received any education until then." "Sarah" "he was a Hitler" "a doctor that used his profession to lead him to believe that what he done was done in the name of science." "He needed specimens and he got what he needed." "He died before anyone found out what he did." "Sarah" "I found myself in my scream room a lot of times." "No one listened to me." "To them I was just some kid that wanted more attention than what I was getting." "Now" "you made mention of me being a smart man." "A smart man doesn't make the same mistake twice, and you may find a lot of women are included in that category too." "Those that think of themselves as being smart are lonely; they find that no one is they're equal." "It's what others think of you that really matters." "You read the papers and listen to the news." "You aren't anything more to some people than an adulterous woman cheating on her husband." "They believe what they read and to them, that's what you are." "You read where all of my associates are feeding off of my needs for their own benefit."

"Yeah" "They called us parasites" Bailey said.

"There's only one way I can answer that." I responded. "Do you believe that they've found a six hundred pound baby floating on an iceberg?"

"No"

"There's people that read tabloids believe that they actually found one." I commented. "Do you believe after all the evidence that's been brought forward and presented that when we landed on the moon it was all filmed in a studio?"

"No" Bailey said again.

"There's people that do." I once again answered. "Bailey" "you and everyone that's close to me are who they think you are." "That's the power of implication." "In the right hands, a pen is a weapon used to capture the wicked and destroy them." "Unfortunately, it can also destroy the innocent too." "You don't have newspapers like that in Russia, or China, or North Korea, they don't print the truth." "We have those here too and a lot of news medias are misquoting the truth and they do it on purpose like the tabloids."

CHAPTER NINE

"**K**urt" "you need to wake up." "Kurt" "Kurt." Bailey's voice was soft.

"What happened?" I asked.

"Those pills you took started to make you sound like you were jabbering." She stated.

"I don't remember walking to the sofa." I exclaimed as I sniffed the air. "Becky?"

"No" "Patricia" she said "I'm wearing some of the perfume you gave Cheryl." "That was nice of you Kurt."

"Have you tried them all?" I asked.

"Kurt" "My husband thinks he may have made a mistake by letting her go with you." She commented.

"You don't sound like you share the same opinion that he does." I replied. "Patricia" "I need to talk to you and your husband, it's important." "It's about Cheryl."

Bailey sat down next to me. I felt a warm cup being put in my hands. "Thank you, Becky." I said to her.

"How did you know it was me?" She asked.

"Your hands are tender yet tough." "Bailey's is weak and soft." "Sarah has long fingers, and I'm sorry, Buck's hands aren't feminine." "So that leaves you."

"Kurt" Elrod spoke up to let me know he was in the room.

"I don't hear any of the kids, are they outside?" I asked.

"Cheryl's feeding the catfish and Ronnie's mowing." He reported.

"I have to fly to California this Friday evening." "I'm going to ask Cheryl if she wants to go." I came right out and said what I wanted to say.

"I'm sorry Kurt" "That's not going to happen." Elrod rebutted in a tone that wasn't polite.

"Alright" "then let me explain to you what's going to happen to your daughter." I began giving my testimony "I'm sure you've heard the same words from her doctors." "I was around a lot of kids that had brain surgery from an accident or from a tumor being removed or whatever and the end result was they had seizures or aneurisms from the damage they received." "Their outcome wasn't pleasant." "Tempers would flare and the blood pressure would elevate and it wasn't long before there would be seizures that set in." "Your daughter is no different from those kids." "Being under my doctor's care I wasn't regarded as having feelings like normal kids and neither were some of the kids that were with me." "Elrod" "Cheryl is better off than some of them and she's worse off than some of the others." "I hear you stopped Ronnie from picking her up from school and driving her over here." "Is that true?"

"Kurt" he stopped me.

"Please don't interrupt me." "I don't like telling people something that they don't have to be told but I feel it's necessary to say what I have to say "anyway"." "Elrod" "how long do you plan on smothering Cheryl." "Is she going to live with you for the rest of your life?" "From what I'm getting, that seems to be your intentions." "Elrod" "you're wrong." "Ronnie is her only connection to the outside world." "He's the only person that she feels she can talk to." "Elrod" "I'm sorry but I'm not going to let you or anyone else put Cheryl through anymore nonsense." "I endured physical and mental pain in the institution and I'll be damned if I stand by and see you do that to Cheryl."

"What are you talking about?" He asked.

"Have you given any consideration at all to what's going to happen to Cheryl if she doesn't pass the eighth grade?" "Ronnie said she cries sometimes so that tells me she's worried." "And if you have given consideration, then have you given any consideration as to the ninth grade?" "If it took two years in the seventh grade and two years in the eighth grade; that is assuming that she passes, then do you think she'll not have the same problems that she's having now?" "What you fail to understand is each grade is tougher on kids and Cheryl isn't like any other kid."

"I still don't follow you." He commented.

"Ronnie said the kids in her class are fourteen and fifteen." "Cheryl's not comfortable and because of that, she's not able to focus." "Elrod" "she doesn't need to be in school." "School is doing her more harm than good." "In case you haven't noticed, even you said you couldn't help her do her homework." "Kids have problems trying to learn something new and when they have problems they can't tell adults, they don't know how to explain things so, the end result is that they don't listen." "You can't tell me that Ronnie hasn't been the best thing that's come along for Cheryl." "I have ears." "I can hear what they say to each other and Elrod you may think you have your rights, and I'll be the first one to stand by your side and slam my fist down on the table and argue that you do, but there's one problem, no matter what you believe, you don't have "all" the rights that you think you have." "Cheryl has rights too." "You deny her those rights and you and her won't be talking to each other very much." "Elrod" "listen to what I say." "You can't learn anything when you're under stress and pressure, and Cheryl is experiencing all of those symptoms." "There's only one solution" "you've got to let Cheryl start making decisions of her own."

"Sit down Elrod" Patricia said.

"Elrod" "do what Patricia says please." Becky interjected after a few seconds.

"Young man" he spoke.

"Elrod" I interrupted him. "I'm going to offer Cheryl a job." "You can protest all you want." "We've had this discussion before and my views haven't changed." "The reason you accepted my proposal was because you thought it would do Cheryl a lot of good." "Now all of a sudden you seem to think that your daughter is in peril and you want to put a stop to it." "I told you earlier that you have your rights, and I also said that you don't have all the rights that you think you have." "Elrod" "you don't have the right to tell me that Cheryl can't work for me." "That decision is up to her and if you make it for her, I can guarantee you that Cheryl will be back in the hospital; you can't suppress misery." "I'm not going to let that happen." "That's why I'm going to offer her a job." "Elrod" "I told Becky that the time has come that she's not going to be able to tell Ronnie what to do in a little while." "He'll have a mine of his own." "Are you ready to have another fight with Cheryl?" "It's coming and don't be surprised when it does." "You were foretold and forewarned." "Now" "I knew I was going to have a little difficulty expressing my views to you, especially when yours differs from mine." "I have to admit things didn't go as planned in New York, but I'm sure the kids remember some things, and if they do, then it'll be remembered for the rest of their life." "So, I made plans for twelve people." "I didn't think you would like the idea of me taking Cheryl with me so I made plans for both you and Patricia to accompany us." "That's the only way you'll see that Ronnie and Cheryl need each other." "Let the kids be kids." "I never got to be one." "My child hood was ruined."

There was silence.

"Elrod" Patricia began "he's right." "You can't be her shadow."

"What are you proposing?" He asked in a somber mood.

I took a deep breath and exhaled before I began. "There's people that can do a lot of things and they can do it all well." "And there's people that can do a lot of things and do it but not do it well." "And there's people that can do only one thing but not do it well." "But Elrod" "there's people out there that can only do one thing" "and they do it well." "You've got to let Cheryl explore and find the area that motivates her drive for knowledge." "And if she finds it" "you won't be able to stop her from wanting more." "It's a hunger" "you had it yourself." "You said you sold your business after Cheryl got hurt." "And in that business, you put everything you had into trying to figure out every way you could to keep every penny you made in your pocket." "Elrod financial inspiration drove you to succeed." "You learned more after you opened your business than before you opened it."

"Amen" Becky interrupted.

"What are you suggesting?" He followed.

"Home schooling" I replied. "Julie is at the same level as Cheryl." "Kids learn from other kids." "She doesn't get help from her classmates now." "Elrod, I think you'll see a big improvement in her next year." "The difference between Cheryl and other kids aren't that far apart." "With Cheryl" "you can't push her; you have to let her learn, her own way." "I'm not saying that's going to happen" "but, kids heal differently than adults." "Elrod" "people believe in miracles and sometimes their expectations are set too high."

"You say what's on your mind, don't you?" He stated.

"In this case, the matter pertains to Cheryl." "I want her to get better just like you do." "The problem you don't understand is you never were around people that have special needs like I was." "Elrod" "you can't make her smart."

I heard a deep sigh.

"Elrod" "you need a vacation" "have you had one since Cheryl's accident?" I asked.

Again, there was silence.

"Elrod" "sometimes when we live life every day, we begin to wake up to the same routine." "I did and I'm pretty sure everyone here has felt the same way at one time or another." "That kind of life has a tendency to get old after a while." "I don't like giving advice to people because it's usually not heeded or needed but I'm going to make an exception for you." "You need to stop living your everyday life and start living your life every day." "Anyone that doesn't have pleasure in their thoughts is suffering from pain." "When is school out?" I asked.

Becky answered. "Two weeks"

"So, finals are given next week then?"

"Yeah" Becky replied.

"So, Elrod" "are you going to let Cheryl go to the Junior Prom with Ronnie?" I asked.

"There's not going to be one." Becky answered. "It's been cancelled." "They had a water leak and the gym's been closed down."

"Can't they combine the juniors with the seniors?" I asked.

"They do." Becky reported.

"How many are there?" I asked.

"Kurt" "there's chaperones and the teachers and all kinds of people."

"How many Becky?" I asked again.

"I don't know" "all I know is Ronnie brought home a letter and gave it to me."

"How did he take it?" I asked her.

"I think Ronnie could care less." She replied. "Julie said some of the kids were talking about it at her school."

"Did you have a Junior Prom?" I asked her.

"Yeah" "Buck weighed about forty pounds lighter then." She giggled.

"If you found out your prom was cancelled, would you be all that upset?" I asked her.

"I would" Patricia commented.

"Why" I asked her.

I heard silence again.

"Ah" "Cheryl" I spoke.

"What about Cheryl?" Becky said and then stopped. "Oh"

"I'm hungry" Buck said when I heard the door open. "When we gonna eat?"

"Kurt" Becky commented.

"I'm hungry too" "and Becky" "I'd like some more of that dressing too." I stated.

"Buck, go tell the kids that it's time to eat." Becky commanded him.

"I'll help you set the table." Patricia offered.

"Where's Steven and Sarah?" I said to Bailey.

"Taking a walk." She stated.

"Kurt what am I going to do?" Elrod asked.

"Elrod, you put too much emphasis on her education." "She's not at the eighth grade level." "She's more comfortable around the fifth so that might be a good place to start." "Home schooling will give her the time to gradually absorb knowledge; and she wouldn't be under any time restraints either." "Did you learn everything in life in school?" I asked him.

"No" "but it did teach me about horse playing." "Two of my friends got killed trying to pull a prank." "My father grounded me because I didn't mow the yard like he told me to or I would have been killed along with them." He commented.

"That's life Elrod; that had nothing to do with education." "The truth is if you had a thousand kids and put them all in an auditorium, you would need only one teacher and that teacher could teach all of those thousand kids." "Some kids though aren't as smart as the other kids and they would have trouble keeping up so they would have to be removed from that auditorium and put somewhere where they can receive the special tutoring they may need." "Instead, they put kids that have trouble in classes with kids that don't have trouble and then they want to medicate them because little Johnny has problems." "I bet you weren't a straight "A" student." "You can't push Cheryl" "I don't want to see her go where those other kids went to when they were pushed." "Who are you going to complain to?" "Mommy and daddy believe what the Doctor tells them" "After all their professionals." "I don't care what you think of me Elrod" "I'd like for us to be friends, but I know what I'm talking about, and I'm trying to convince you of that, but, in this case there's only one opinion that is accepted, and that's yours." "So, if you disagree with me, then I guess we'll have to agree that we disagree." "But" "it would be nice if you came with us and then you would be able to form an opinion that is based on fact and not on an assumption."

"How old are you?" He asked.

"Twenty eight" I answered.

"Young man" he began "all my life I gave orders and when I gave orders, I expected them to be carried out." "This makes our second meeting and both times you've given me a good tongue lashing." "I haven't had that since I quit work and opened my business." "I would have bid you a good day and you and I would have been of a distant relation; and that being none." "But once again I find myself being put in my place." "Cheryl's not talking to me now; I'm getting the silent treatment."

"We all have dreams Elrod" "you may have wanted to play sports but maybe you weren't big enough." "Me" "I wish I could see the person I'm talking to now." "Cheryl" "she's easy" "she just wants to be normal." "Sometimes our dreams are just dreams."

"What about me?" Bailey asked.

"You don't have any dreams, anymore."

"That's not true" "I'm really good at screwing things up." She replied.

I began snickering.

"What?" She said to me.

"You know how a blind man knows when his wife is upset with him?"

"No" she answered.

"His wife moves all the furniture around to different locations and then leaves for her night out with the girls." "Do you know how a blind man knows when his wife is upset with him?"

"No" she answered again.

"She puts motor oil in his shampoo bottle." "Do you know how a blind man knows when his wife is upset with him?"

"No"

"She takes him to the mall and tells him that she's going to try on some blouses and leaves him there." "Do you know how a blind man knows when his wife is upset?"

"No" She began laughing.

"I do" Elrod said. "She pours dye in his bath water when he's washing his hair."

Bailey started laughing again.

"Y'all come on" Becky ordered.

I was getting ready to get up when I felt a strong hand helping me. "Kurt" "you put up good arguments."

"We weren't having an argument Elrod." "When we listen to an opposing view, we learn by communicating." "An argument is where neither side listen's; so, they don't learn." "If you take my advice and you find my advice to be wrong, then you'll learn the right way from experience." "That's how we learn Elrod." "Experience" "it's the best teacher."

"I've heard that somewhere." He commented.

"It's been quoted so many times that it's considered to be a proverb." I began "Benjamin Franklin wrote in the Poor Richards Almanac that he published that "Experience keeps a dear school, yet fools learn in no other." "Simply put" "he said that experience is the best teacher." "Ten years from now someone somewhere will write a book and he'll change the words around a little and you'll have a new phrase that will sound intellectual but it'll still mean the same."

When we walked into the dining room I was sat down in my chair and told where my bowls of food was.

"Ronnie" I said out loud.

"Yes sir" he replied.

"I hear the prom's been cancelled."

"Yes sir"

"Are the kid's talking about it?" I asked.

"Yes sir" "But" "I think the teachers are the ones that's more upset." "I hear some of the kid's say that they called the superintendent up wanted a meeting."

"Ronnie" "It won't do any good." "The school has a budget." "When you don't have enough money coming in, you have to find a way to reduce the amount going out." I said as I took a bite of goose. "Somewhere along the way good teachers became teachers because something made them decide that they wanted to be a teacher." "It's not easy dealing with a group of people sometimes cutting up in class and still be able to teach and then go home and grade papers." "And in the end, everyone puts the blame on the teacher for their children's failing grade." "But" "if you went to football games or basketball games or baseball or track or swimming meets, you probably would have seen a lot of them there too." "People are strange Ronnie." "With a lot of them it's not a job, it's what they like to do, and some people feel needed and some people feel rewarded being needed, and some people like the flexibility in the work hours that teaching offers; they get the opportunity to take the weekends and summer off, and some people like teaching because they can keep an eye on their kids, and yeah there are some people that do it just for the money." "But" "there are some people that do it because every holiday that rolls around, they enjoy the spirit, and some people do it because it gives them the offer to relive, their youth." "In truth, a good teacher can only teach those that want to be taught." "I was difficult; I was angry and I didn't want to be taught." "I asked your mother how you felt about it being cancelled and she thought that you didn't care one way or another." "Is she right?"

"Yeah"

"Why" I asked.

"I don't know?"

"Cheryl if Ronnie would have asked you to go; would you have gone with him?" I switched my attention to her.

"I can't dance." She replied.

"That wasn't my question, Cheryl." "Would you have gone to the prom with him?" I asked again.

"Yes"

"Ronnie if the prom hadn't of been canceled, would you have asked Cheryl to go to the prom?"

"Yes"

"Do you know how to dance, Ronnie?" I asked.

"No"

"Becky how about you?" I asked.

"I haven't been dancing in seventeen years." She answered. "Buck didn't know how to dance either." She said trying to stifle a small laugh.

"Elrod and Patricia." "When was the last time you two danced cheek to cheek?"

"I can't remember" Elrod said.

"I can" Patricia replied "the prom."

"We went dancing a lot of times since then." Elrod said.

"He said cheek to cheek Elrod, not the chicken dance." She quickly commented.

"Mister Bryant" "can I ask you something." Cheryl spoke up. "Are those people you talked to in New York, friends of yours?" She asked.

"Yes" "but, Cheryl in a business" "friendship can't come between you and running a business, your father and Becky will tell you that." "And anything done outside of business is done in friendship." "And speaking of that" "I missed paying everyone a few weeks." "After dinner" "I need to see all of you." "That's been on my mind for a while." "I don't like not paying my bills." "I forget about them and the next thing I know" "I got a bill that's past due."

"Kurt" "You and I need to talk." Buck said.

"I don't need privacy when I'm around friends." I commented to him.

"Kurt" Becky interrupted. "Buck told me that Bailey was talking to Mister Hurley and his secretary came up and handed him a deposit slip."

"Oh" "so that's what triggered you into being upset with me Buck." "I told Bailey to put it in there." I answered.

"Kurt" Becky once again was about to speak when I silenced her.

"Becky" "I told Bailey I wanted Sarah and Steven." "It's a long story."

"We're not going anywhere." She commented.

"All of you were in the room when I asked Steven if he would keep my visit confidential." I began "I really wanted all of you to enjoy that trip." "Steven got terminated because he didn't report to the manager of my whereabouts." "That's how the press knew I was coming." "When Bailey notified the Hotel that I would be checking in, the person she talked to; notified the manager." "They have a talent" "Sarah knows how to orchestrate an itinerary of my daily functions and she's dominant in her ways." "Steven" "well the only way I can tell you about him is to tell you to ask Cindy and Julie and you'll get a good description of Steven." "His name should have been "Alfred"." "They love him and to tell you the truth" "I do to."" "Bailey talked to Sarah and Sarah gave her a price, like you and I did when we negotiated our contract." "I told Bailey to put it in there because if you found out that I gave Sarah and Steven a different amount than what I gave you and Buck, it would sound an alarm and give off a signal that I thought they were worth more to me than you and Buck, and that isn't true." "Now Cheryl" I said diverting my attention back to her. "Ronnie calls me Mister B because he said his mother doesn't like for him to call me by my first name." "If you want to call me Mister B like Ronnie and Julie and Cindy does, I would appreciate that." "I don't like my associates calling me Mister Bryant."

I told her. "Cheryl" "those people you saw me talking to in New York were "business" managers." "You're my business associate." "This is my home and everyone here are here because I need people to help me sometimes and I would rather ask a friend for help instead of an employee for that help." "You're not and employee, you're an associate." "There's a difference between the two like day and night." "None of them have ever sat where you're sitting, that's the difference between you and them." "You'll never hear me talk to anyone here the way I talked to those people." "In business" "matters come up where if someone isn't working on it." "Then whatever it is; isn't going to get finished and before long it's been forgotten about." "Everyone thinks someone else is working on it when no one is." "Cheryl the reason I'm saying this is because I need you." "Do you want to be an associate of mine?" I asked her.

"I can't do anything." She commented.

"I thought of myself that way once." I began. "But I got to listening to people as they talked." "Some people that hear me say that would think of me as eavesdropping." "What am I to do?" "If people talk loud enough to where you can hear them then maybe they don't care what people think of them."

"Like you?" She stated.

"No" "I only talk like that to people that have a narrow vision." I then heard Elrod clearing his throat. "Any way back to my story." I began. "Everyone seemed to worry all the time; lawyer's, secretaries, supervisors, everyone." "No one was satisfied; they all sought security and that security always meant that if a better paying job came along, take it." "Those who have it are a target to those that don't, and those that don't will do anything to get it." "What I'm offering to you is the same security that everyone gives me here." "Now" "will you be an associate of mine?" I asked my question to her once again.

"Yes sir" "what do you want me to do?" She asked.

"What do you know about catfish?" I asked her.

"Nothing"

"I don't either" "but Buck took me out fishing in my pond one day and I learned really quick that it has barbs." "I got stuck in my hand, but one thing I remember from that is I made a mistake." "Does it end there?" "I don't think so, I know that one day I'm going to be out there again, sitting in a chair, holding my rod in my hand and eventually I'll wind up catching another one and possibly another one and another one." "So, I'm thinking if I got stuck the first time because I didn't know any better, what if I get stuck a second time, I should have learned the first time." "If anyone called me a name, how would I be able to argue with them?" "They'd be right" "I should have learned the first time to look for something to keep me from getting stuck the second time." "Ahh" "this is where it gets complicated so bear with me." "Let's say for the sake of argument I got stuck a third time." "What am I then?"

"I don't know" she replied.

"I don't know either." I stated. "Buck" "what do they call a man that's been stuck more than twice?"

"It's not what other people call you; it's what you call yourself that really hits home." He said laughing. "Cheryl" "It's not the catfish you need to worry about; it's the hook you use to catch it." "Becky hooked me three times on one night." "That was the first time and the last time I took her catfishing with me."

"I hated to cook them things, let alone fish for them." She giggled.

"Cheryl there was something else on my mind." "Cheryl" I was interrupted from continuing by Elrod.

"Honey" "Mister Bryant says he thinks you would be able to learn things easier if you weren't under a lot of stress." "He thinks you should be home schooled."

"I do too" she stated.

"Why didn't you say anything to me about it?" He asked.

"You never asked me."

"Cheryl" he was interrupted by Sarah and Steven coming into the back door.

"Sit yourself down and dig in people." Becky told them.

I put my silverware down on my plate.

"Momma" Cindy began.

"Kurt" "you ain't through yet." She delivered Cindy's message.

"I have business in California this Saturday" I began telling everyone that was at the table. It was intended for the children. "I've made arrangements for us to leave Friday evening after schools out." "I have a taping for an interview."

"What's a taping?" Cindy asked.

"Those people that's been bothering you and everyone here" "are doing it for only one reason." "I got their attention." "Three years ago, I took over my father's firm and that's when I was noticed." "After a while it got to where I couldn't leave my suite and then I moved here because it fit my requirements." "No one knew me and I was going to do my best to keep it that way." "Around twelve or so I got this whiff of food and my belly started talking to me." "The next thing I know I'm meeting my first resident of Skinland." "And that's where I met my second resident of Skinland." "I thought by moving here that somehow I could dodge around without too much difficulty." "You know do business and then come back and then go do business and then come back." "All of that stuff out there will go away in time." "Politicians say things to people that aren't true and when they use my picture or my name for a vote, it angers me, Cindy."

"Why" She asked.

"Do you know anything about politics?" I asked her.

"No"

"They knew it angered me and I responded publicly denying any affiliation with their views." "It was free advertisement and it was used by both parties, but bits and pieces were quoted and misquoted." "Politics is like Ronnie's prom night" I began "someone is going to be elected Prom Prince and Prom Princess." "Let's say someone that wanted to be the Prom Prince used Ronnie by wanting to be his friend only for the purpose of him winning that title and once he did, he didn't want to see Ronnie again." "That's the people that become our governors, congressmen and senators, and even presidents." "They lie to get elected." "I have a corporation to run" "those people out there are only selling their papers if the headlines capture the people's attention." "What if they wrote something about "you" that wasn't true." "You know it isn't" "but everyone that reads what they wrote walks around and looks at you as if everything they read "was" true." "And one way to put a stop to a lot of that is to tell the people I don't support anyone."

"How come?" Elrod asked.

I took a drink of milk and sat my glass back down and began my answer. "No two parties of equal strength can run a country." "There will always be friction among them." "But when one of the two parties has control over our government in congress and the senate then we'll have a one party government." "There's no guessing by speculators on which direction our country is headed in." "In the market there are people that think this stock is going to go up and others that think this stock is going to go down and suffer losses in revenue." "That's an ugly word to investors." "That's the battles of CEO's; they're trained to smile when they lie." "I don't deal with companies" "I deal with sectors." "There are two fields in the market that's never going to lose in a gamble; energy and medical." "Since the first model T Ford rolled off the assembly line in 1908, oil has only increased in value." "Precious metals reflect the census of the people so if they think the economy will do good; then they invest in a broad spectrum." "If they think the economy will get worse then they put their savings in precious metals."

"What do you think?" Elrod asked.

"I'm a pessimist" I said.

"Is that what you're going to say?" He commented.

"No" "Elrod are you an investor?" I asked.

"I have a financial institution that handles my investments." He stated.

"Okay" "do you know that there's lawmakers that own financial institutions?" I asked.

"Yeah" "Our representative is one of them." He replied.

"Then tell me why anyone in that firm should give out erroneous information if they are dealing as a representative of a representative." "Elrod" "you can't get any closer to inside information than that." "And if you think that none of his investors are utilizing that opportunity then you better be careful about who you let control your money because they're using your money to invest in areas that you aren't and all you've got to show for it is paper." "When you let someone deal with your money, you're dealing with two businesses not one." "A financial institution that handles your investment and the corporation that they invest in." "You make money off of your investments, and they make more money investing you're money on something else." "If one of those businesses fail then you're the one that loses, not them, they made twice as much money off of you than what you made, but you lost yours, they didn't." "There's thousands of corporations with billions of shares of stock that's no longer doing business as a business and now all those billions of shares they sold are worthless." "In the last ten years, dozens of corporations that's been in business for over a hundred years have gone bankrupt."

"So, you think gold is where I should invest in?" He stated.

"Are you a pessimist?" I asked.

"Yeah"

"Then I would invest in gold."

"You did." Cheryl spoke up.

"What" her father asked.

"He told a man that he wanted him to put his money in gold." She answered.

"What else do you remember about New York?" I asked.

"Sarah took us out to a supper club to eat when you were in the hospital." "We got to watch a show while we ate." "I liked that." "I thought it was neat."

"Well then if you look up what tourist attractions there are in Hollywood then maybe everyone can all agree on where to spend your free time." I said to her.

"Where are you going to be?" She asked.

"I'd be a party pooper." "I'm not much of a sightseer." I chuckled.

"Then what are you going to do?" She asked.

"I used to do a lot a reading." "I found out that words of wisdom are wasted when they're not read." "Television didn't really do too much for me and I never listened to music unless I got to attend a Symphony."

"You like Symphonies?" She asked.

"My ears are sensitive and I can't hear what the performer is trying to say when they sing." "For some odd reason singers seem to want to reach a note that no one has ever achieved, and every instrument used in the band seems like they want to be heard above all the others." "Symphonies tells stories" "they give everybody that listens to it a feeling of being in a battle or a fight of some kind and then the music begins to calm down and the feeling of happiness overwhelms you, but not for long." "A tragedy snaps you out of that feeling and gives you sorrow." "A time passes and then the end of the story is revealed to you." "That's the power of music." "Bailey and I was in Murray looking for furniture one day, and when we stopped at a light, I thought we were in an earthquake." "But" "it turned out that a car pulled up next to us with these speakers booming." "He had his likes and I had my dislikes." "It wasn't that far up the road before Bailey was telling me that a policeman had him pulled over." "Hmm" "that makes me wonder if the first time he gets a ticket for disturbing the peace." "Will the second ticket make him think about getting a third ticket?" "Anyhow" "that just goes to show you what music can do to a person." "That kid got his enjoyment the same way I got mine."

"Kurt" "eat" Becky commanded.

When we got up from the table, I asked the kids if they would meet me in the living room.

"Cindy"

"Yes sir"

"We agreed to a hundred dollars a week." "Didn't we?" I asked.

"Yes sir"

"Schools going to be out soon and that'll mean you'll be doing a lot more work around here than what you're doing now." "I missed roughly three weeks of pay at a hundred dollars a week." "That comes to a three hundred, right?"

"Yes sir."

"When school lets out, I'm going to give you two hundred a week." I commented. "Bailey, give me three hundred please."

When I felt it in my hand, I handed it to her. "Remember" "your mother is the boss and not your mother when you work." "You take orders from her."

"Yes sir"

"Julie"

"Yes sir"

"We agreed on two hundred a week." "Bailey hand me six hundred." And once again I felt it in my hand and gave it to her. "You're old enough to know what the value of money is." I said to her. "When schools out you'll be working all day, five days a week and sometimes longer, that's what a worker does." "If you work like a worker, I'll pay you like a worker." "I'll give you four hundred a week then."

"Yes sir"

"Ronnie"

"Yes sir"

"Bailey, give me six thousand please." I said and after she did, I gave it to him.

"Cheryl"

"Yes sir"

"Bailey, give me six thousand please."

When she did, I handed it to her. "I've got a lot of time sometimes and sometimes I don't." I began "Bailey told me that you've been helping Ronnie." "I'd like for you to keep on working with him." "When the time comes for school to start back up you can come here and work on your assignments and I'll help you out with your work." "You won't be working in your books all day long, you'll be reading and doing a little writing and stuff like math and history, but you won't be doing it like you were doing it in school."

"Thank you, Mister B." She spoke.

"No Cheryl it's me that should be thanking you."

"Why" She asked.

"I gave up Cheryl" "I quit" "When I went to New York" "I went there to sign the papers on my father's estate, but I also went there to give notice I wasn't going to be in charge of my father's firm any longer."

"You changed that" "I got to thinking about you as I laid there in my bed in the hospital and the more, I thought, the clearer the answer was that came to me." "You never gave up" "and that taught me a valuable lesson." "You're going to fit in just fine around here."

CHAPTER TEN

"Here's your cocoa" Becky said.
"Becky"
"Yeah Kurt"
"Could you get a cup of coffee and sit down with me?" I asked her.
"Alright" "give me a minute."

After waiting for a short while I smelled coffee and then felt her sitting down so I began my conversation.

"I'm going to talk to the principal this morning and tell him that the Proms back on so I'm going to need you to spread the word to everyone that I want them to accompany me."

"Why" she said sitting next to me.

"I don't know" "but I was laying in my bed this morning while Bailey slept and I got to thinking with all the rumors that's been floating around here for the last few weeks or so" "it would be best to give the people something sweet with all the bitter that they've tasted lately."

"You mean like putting sugar in coffee, huh?" She stated.

"Have you talked to anyone lately?" I asked. "I mean like when you go to Barney's or get gas or something."

"It's not the same anymore Kurt." She began after a few seconds. "Used to" "people would walk down the aisle checking out this or reading about that." "I don't know why" "most of them didn't pay much attention to what they were buying anyway judging by the way they looked." "They were certified country" she said. "Anyway" "you couldn't pass anyone without someone bringing up a juicy tidbit about someone else." "I was in Barneys before y'all came back home and I could see out of the corner of my eye people stopping and staring at me." "Cindy and Julie ask me a lot of questions now so I pretty much know what everyone has on their minds." "Why do you ask?"

"One time Bailey and I were talking and I was asking her about some of the people she dealt with at the grocery store and she started laughing." "I said what?" "Kurt" "these people would line up for a handout without knowing what they were getting." "All you have to say is there's a grand opening at the new resale shop and their giving away free snacks to people that come in to look around." "That's all it takes" "word of mouth and soon several cars are parked there and when other people see that many cars, they know they're giving something away."

"Yeah" she replied "and".

"When I first met Bailey, we were talking and she said that Barney's had sales to try and keep shoppers from going to Murray."

"Yeah" "and" she continued.

"Murray is fifty miles away and the only reason to go there is because like Bailey said" "there's nothing here." "We stopped for gas about a month ago and when Bailey paid the bill, she was griping about paying thirty eight dollars to fill up the tank." "I started laughing and then telling her" "what are you complaining about" "you've got cash and you've got a credit card." "Then I got to doing a little thinking and I remembered what you had said about tourism being dried up because of the lake."

"Yeah" she stated.

"Bailey's comments were reflecting the views of the people that live here." "I want you to imagine if the price of gas was to double in price" "what do you think would happen to a town like this?"

"I never thought about it." She answered. "Why?"

I paused and then spoke. "Well, when I opened the door to your place and only heard a couple of people, I was saying to myself this will probably be my first and my last hamburger here."

"Kurt when you and Bailey came walking in that next day." "I had my mind made up." She stated "I was past due on my mortgage and we were down to me finding a job in a month." "When I told you I could work for a lot less, I meant it." "I would have been saving money if I paid you to work, that's how bad it was." "Hon" "Buck and I talk a lot now, before we didn't" "both of us were too tired when we got home and all we wanted to do was sit down." "After the doctor got killed" "I didn't have much going for me so I knew I was going to have to find a job." "I took a walk down the road for a good piece and came up with a brilliant idea and told Buck we needed to take a chance and see if we can operate the diner, but back then we had a nice little flow of traffic." "It didn't take me long before I began to feel the pinch." "You've heard the term "chief cook and bottle washer"." "Honey" "I was the janitor, the book keeper, the cashier and the waitress all rolled up in one." "But that's not the point." "Buck told me he didn't think it was a good idea and I argued with him and I argued with him some more until he finally gave in." "I spent almost everything we had trying to prove to him I was right." "But I was wrong and when you came in and changed my life" "well" "you can't find the words to tell someone how you feel."

I smiled. "Kind words often go unrewarded but they never go unappreciated." I spoke.

"Who said that?" She asked.

"Me"

"No" "I mean" "who said that?" She stated.

"I've never read it anywhere, but somewhere along the way I'm sure somebody's said something like it."

"What's this all about anyway?" She said taking a sip of her coffee.

"Nothing" "I was just thinking about these people that live here" "that's all."

"What about them?" She asked.

"Becky" "People that live on a fixed income have problems adjusting to any type of change in their finances." "No one can cut prices to defray the increase in manufacturing cost and if they don't go up on prices, they have to cut costs somewhere." "Labor is the first area of concern and after that comes a change in command." "The end result is to raise the price of your product and hope that the people have to have what you're selling or file for bankruptcy protection." "That way the board of directors can remain intact and get a bonus for liquidating all assets." I chuckled.

"What?" She stated.

I then went on with my conversation with her. "There was a whiskey maker that hired a consultant to come in and see if he could tell them a way that they could sell their product." "They said we know we've got a good product but we must not have the right marketing." "They showed him around and he came walking in one day and said fellows, what would happen if all that whiskey got sucked up by a tornado?" "They said what?" "He said you have to reduce the supply and increase the cost and people will buy it." "Today their stock has increased in value over four hundred percent."

"What are you getting at?" She asked.

"Becky" "if these people around here are living payday to payday now." "What about next year, and the next year, and the year after that." "Buck said he doesn't understand how Barney's has stayed open this long." "Bailey's hours were cut back so she enrolled in college hoping she could get a better job."

"Yeah and" she commented.

"I moved here because I have a bleak outlook for the future and I wanted this place to stay the way it is." "I guess in hindsight" "I was being selfish." "Becky" "there's thousands of small businesses out there that's going to fail in the next administration." "It doesn't matter who wins, there's going to be changes made and changes always affect the little man." "Fees are generated from induction of new standards and the little man is left to contemplate his outcome week by week." "Larger corporation's benefit because small companies fold up and the larger companies can increase their prices." "The consumer is helpless." "They're forced to pay higher prices." "I got that from talking to you." I said to her. "In the seventies they had gas stations that pumped your gas, and while they did that, they checked the air in your tires, your radiator, windshield washer, oil, transmission, and washed your windshield and they did all that for twenty five cents a gallon." "They had bays for cars that needed oil changes, lube jobs, and small mechanical repairs." "You could get a new tire, a new tube or have a flat fixed." "They employed seven people and paid them all two dollars an hour and they were able to pay all their living expenses on that for two dollars an hour without their wife working." "That's no longer the way of business, everything now is specialized." "Changes in administrations did that." "This isn't the world your parents grew up in, like it wasn't the world, they're parents grew up in when they were growing up." "Becky if you were to do the math and compare the two dollars an hour the people got back then and with inflation you would find out that that two dollars and hour should now be thirty two dollars an hour." "Not all people have enough understanding to be making statements that they don't have the knowledge of what they're speaking about."

"You're not painting a very pretty picture, Kurt." She stated.

"You said it didn't take long before you started to feel the ramifications of an economic decline in tourism." I stated.

"English Kurt"

"You said when I asked you if your prices of the food went up, that it did." "The reply was when I asked you if you increased prices, you said no, and the reason was no one would come in and eat if you did." "Becky" "no one was coming in anyway, to them your prices were already too high." "You were desperate and reaching out trying to grasp on to a patch of straw hoping you could hang on until help came along." "These people don't have any straw left; they've pulled it all up trying to keep from drowning." "When a multitude of small businesses dry up; it's not long before big businesses begin to feel financial stress the same way as small businesses." "All people that work pay taxes, you put people out of work and they become servants of the public servants." "In the twenties families were misplaced from the drought, like now, and in the thirties, the depression made a lot of wealthy men poor." "Businesses along with banks shut their doors to be opened never more." "All signs point one way to me." "We're going to go through a serious correction in the market." "Becky" "I made a statement about a fabricated oil shortage in nineteen eighty. Gas went up here to over a dollar and people were lining up to get gas." "It got so bad that you could only get gas on odd or even days depending on the last number of your license plates."

"I remember that." She answered. "I was a young kid and my father lost his job because he couldn't get gas."

Paradox

"Well, then it went to where you could only get ten gallons and then five gallons."

"I remember that too." She answered.

"If you remember that, then I doubt if you remember when gas cost twenty cents a gallon in nineteen seventy." "That was a two hundred and twenty five percent increase in inflation in ten years." "People voted for that man again." "Mark Twain stated that there's no amount of evidence you can use to convince and idiot."

"Is that why you want the interviews?" She stated.

"No" "I was talking to a man of the streets one day." "He only charged me for the information he gave." "I said how much." "One dollar" "he answered" "I gave him that dollar" "He said, now if want another question you owe me another dollar." "I said what" "and he said you asked me how much I charge and I answered your first question and if you have another question that'll be another dollar." "I gave him another one and he said "son if a man only had a half a brain, and he only listened to half of the things I tell him, it would improve his intelligence one hundred percent." "I said" "what!" "And he said, that's another question" "one dollar please." "I handed him that dollar and gave him five more and told him, you owe me five more questions." "See you next train." "But I didn't."

"Did something happen to him?"

"No Becky" "I'm blind" "I can't see anyone."

"Damn you Kurt." "That isn't funny." She began laughing and after a few moments she began collecting herself. "Why "are" you doing this then?"

"I tried to live my life as best as I could." I began "When I walked into my father's office and took over the firm, I was rejected and when I returned there were changes and redirections in allocations."

"English Kurt" she said.

"I was an introvert, not an extrovert." I stated. "Like Steven."

"English Kurt" she repeated.

"I was punished a lot of times for being over demanding and it was hard for me to break that fear." "The best example is what people do here; they put a shock collar on a dog to make it obey." "That's about the way it was for me."

"But Kurt" "you have a way of getting what you want, and as far as being demanding, you'll not hear none of that from us." "You've got a tool up there in your head that's pretty sharp."

"Well Becky back then I wasn't a people person and I was withdrawn." "I was lucky, my father was a rich man." "You won't have to worry about money either, and neither will your kids." "I'll see to that." "My vent was to extinguish the untruth that was said and correct it." "All I did was pour gasoline on a fire every time I made a comment so I got to where I didn't speak in public, I didn't know if the person talking to me had affiliation with a news media or not, so I was labeled a rude and arrogant spoilt brat and after the elections everything went back to the way it was." "I had my peace and quiet." "If I share and state my opinions publicly, they generate countless frivolous law suits." "Businesses on the verge of failing find fault for their failure." "Like you did" "you blamed the lack of rain and for that, the lake level was down and tourist went elsewhere." "Corporations have wolves patrolling outside and inside other corporations looking for a weakness and when they find one, allegations will fly and the stock plummets." "You would think that would be bad, but it's not." "Opportunity abounds if you can eliminate a competitor." "If you reduce a supply to a commodity, you create a demand, just like that whiskey maker and the sales of our refineries and chemical plants." "You make more off of your product." "I invested in those corporations that were primed to gain and I was the wolf that caused people their loss." "They blamed me because I made money even though I had nothing to do with anything other than seeing an investment opportunity."

"So why are you wanting to have interviews then?" She asked.

"There's a lot of people that read magazines and tabloids and like you folks say down here." "Outhouse news" "after you read it" "dispose of it in the proper fashion." "But because of those magazines and tabloids" "people also want to see the person that they've been reading about and witness for themselves what they read." "If you've ever bought a product because you saw it advertised on television and found out the product wasn't what the advertisement presented itself to be, then you'll understand that when it comes to politics and big business." "You'll discover that they're identical twins and they both make money from each other." "But be that as it may" "I need exposure" "my comments they hear not written as I quoted will have an impression on what they read later." "We do have some unbiased news media's left, but not many." "One of these days they'll be like the sixties when you took the family out to see a movie at the drive in and lit a mosquito repellent that didn't work." "Extinct" "But exposure also helps to bury a subliminal suspicion."

"I remember those when I was a kid." Becky commented.

"Where's everyone" I heard Bailey say loudly.

"In here" Becky answered with the same decibel level.

"What's up?" She said when she came in.

Paradox

"I think Kurt's pills are affecting him again." Becky said. "He's talking in a foreign language like those people do up north."

"I told Becky I was going to talk to the principal and tell him I'd like for the kids to have their prom."

"What" Buck said as he walked in.

"Becky and I was talking, and the more we talked, the more she convinced me that the kids needed this whether they know they need it or not." I replied.

"Kurt, you're talking that kind of talk again." Becky commented.

"Do you have school pictures of yourself when you went to school?" I asked Becky.

"They're in some old boxes up in the attic." She answered.

"Buck" "how about you?" I asked him.

"Not all of them" He answered.

"Bailey" I asked.

"I don't know where they're at." She replied.

"I didn't have any school pictures" "we didn't have a yearbook." I stated. "People that resided there usually didn't leave." "This morning when I woke up, I couldn't go back to sleep." "I got to thinking about my last three years and I found that I was evolving into a person that sought success and when I blossomed, I bloomed into a self centered snot nosed egotistical loudmouth jerk." "Bailey didn't know it but she opened my eyes when she called me a butt hole and the more, I got to thinking I guess we all have a little bit of a "Doctor Jekyll or a Mister Hyde" as our alter ego." "With me" "I seem to have a low tolerance level so Mister Hyde seems to have had a lot of control over me." "I'm not the person I saw myself as and I have to change" "if I don't, I won't have my sanity left when I need it the most."

"I think those pills are starting to work on you again." Becky said.

"No wait a minute Becky." Bailey stopped her. "What do you want to do Kurt?" She asked.

"A lot of people are going to be affected from the cancellation of the prom." "I want to make sure something like that doesn't happen again." "But for now, I want to go to Ronnie's school and talk to the principal."

"Where we going?" Sarah asked walking in.

When we got ready to turn out the gate, Buck eased the car forward and then sped up at a normal rate.

"We seem to be losing some of the reporters." He stated.

"People make the news." I said to him. "You have the famous and you have the infamous." "Between them both you have news that's worthy of a headline." "Buck" "believe it or not" "that reporter Becky ran over; could have stuck his foot there on purpose." "They make steel toe boots, you know." "They're very good at provoking someone not familiar with their ways." "I found out by experience that the best way to treat them is to ignore them."

"I looked that word up the other day and it's a fancy way of calling a person an idiot." He said to me.

"Buck" "all they want is a story" I replied.

After I introduced myself to the secretary, we were led into an office to wait for the return of the principal.

A short time later I heard the door open and a chair being slid under a desk.

"Mister Bryant" "I'm Bill Byres" he replied.

"Mister Byres it's come to my attention that the prom's been cancelled."

"Yes sir" he stated.

"Are you against me having a party and inviting guest?" "I'd like to call it a prom."

"I don't understand your point." He replied.

"I'd like to sponsor the prom." I continued. "Would you let me talk to everyone in the auditorium one day soon, time is of the essence?" "I'd like for everyone to hear what I have to say and not from out of the mouth of someone else." "With me, the truth isn't always spoke or written and I don't like it when people don't show up because they didn't hear what was said, they only heard what wasn't said and Mister Byres, there's so many things said about me that I didn't say that I find the only way to defend myself in that type of libel is by taking the side of "offense"." "From what's been going on around here" "I bet I wouldn't be that far off from formulating a suggestion that you've also formed an opinion of me from what you've read too." "So, to me I have a problem when it comes to articulating to anyone in an honest fashion." "I don't feel like I get full representation of my intentions and I become frustrated and usually after I speak to a higher authority, I seem to find myself eventually talking to someone that can tend to my needs." "I don't like wasting time talking to people that don't have the power to tell me no." "Do you sir have the authority to grant my request or am I to seek out the next person in the chain of command." I asked him.

"When would you like for me to arrange this?" He asked.

"I'd like to do it now" "I'm sure everyone has stopped they're preparation for the prom and some of them can't start new ones." "And Mister Byres" "I'm not just talking about the seniors" "I want the freshmen" "the sophomores" "the juniors" "their teachers" "the cooks" "everybody to be in attendance." "What I have to say has to be said to them all."

Paradox

"I can have everyone in assembly in thirty minutes." He replied.

"Fine" "If someone could guide me to where we need to go" "I'd appreciate it." I replied.

Bailey and I were discussing my intentions when I heard voices beginning to filter in.

"Here they come Kurt" Bailey satisfied my thoughts.

"Take a number of ten and count how many come in on one side and we'll double the figure" I told her.

Soon the noise became louder and then calmer.

"I count fourteen." She answered "but don't take my word for it."

"That's alright" "I just wanted a round figure."

The auditorium became silent and after a brief introduction by Mister Byres I stood and Bailey began guiding me to the podium. I waited a couple of minutes before I began to speak.

"I'd like to thank Mister Byres quick response to my request." I began "His quick attention to this matter is responsible for you being here." "First off" "I'd like to introduce you to some of the members of my associates" "a couple of them aren't here because they're in a different school." "Their names are Cindy and Julie Roberts." "Now I'd like to address the problem of the cancellation of the school prom." "Mister Byres and the school board didn't have any other option." "Some of you will come back here and take over the jobs that's left vacant from other teachers, just the way they did when they were young." "You'll get married and have kids and they'll go to school here just the way you did and maybe they'll follow in your footsteps and become a teacher too." "Another thing I've learned is say what you have to say and get to the point." "I'm going to sponsor the prom." I had to wait until the auditorium became silent again. "I have a problem with that though." "The rule is freshmen and sophomores don't have a prom of their own." "Yet freshmen and sophomores can attend a junior or senior prom if they've been invited as a date." "I find that to be a form of segregation." "In big cities" "tax dollars support a higher education." "In smaller cities" "sports support academics." "In Skinland" "well" as you can see the school system can't support a prom and after the school gets the bill for the repair of the Gymnasium, they'll be looking for a way to pay the bill and run this school." "I have a problem with that, I can't see any of the figures adding up." "The school board didn't have any other way" "they had to do what they done." "I'm going to open my house to you as my guest." "I have rules" "I like punch" "please don't spike the punch." "Now" "I may not be speaking to everyone here, but to those that would like to attend" "I need a student body formed to decorate my back yard starting next Monday and the following Saturday will be prom night." "I think we're going to have a little problem with the dress code and I'd like consideration to be given in that field." "Due to the cancellation of the prom" "suits and dresses were put aside." "Not everyone in this room can go out and buy what they need." "Murray's a big town, but it's been picked clean." "I don't want anyone not coming because they couldn't find something to wear." "In my eyes that's a form of segregation too and in this case, it could affect a lot of people." "No pun intended." I had to wait until the auditorium became silent from laughter." "I didn't have a prom." "I went to a special school so; I don't know anything about a prom" "and that tells me that a lot of you might not know anything about a prom either." "For some of you" "it's going to be your first one and your last one" "and for some of you it'll be your second or your third or maybe your twentieth." "I need your help here" "join the student body and volunteer your help." "They need it" "and I need it." "My understanding is after the prom kids usually go off to a party somewhere and continue celebrating." "I don't see why that isn't going to happen here" "but" "to those that don't have a party to go to" "I have a pool and after the prom, it's going to be open to those with bathing suits." "Now" let's talk a little about food." I continued "Murray is an hour's drive away and that all but rules out eating in a nice restaurant to bring a close to an evening." "So as this year's proms sponsor" "we'll bring the restaurant to the prom and in order to do that I need to keep things simple." "Lobster", "King Crab", "Salmon", and for those that are allergic to shellfish there's going to be "Prime Rib." "But" "some of you are vegetarian" "and some of you are allergic to gluten and some are diabetic." "I can't do this without help." "Some of you have a parent that's a volunteer firefighter or a policeman." "And some you have a grandparent that provides supper on the ground at the church they attend once a month, and there's the VFW post." "Those are only to mention a few for an example." "All of these people cook and sell food trying to generate revenue to keep their equipment updated." "I need you to tell them I would appreciate it if they could lend me their help." "Everybody should have a good time and not suffer because they have a reaction to a food item." I then turned around to Mister Byres "I would like for you to personally extend my invitation to the school board and it's administration." I said and then turned back around. "When the committee of the student body has addressed a plan" "I would like for the entire student body to come to my house and have a cup of hot cocoa with me." "That way everyone can hear what was said and not related to you by someone else." "Things always seem to come out differently after a person hears what he heard and when he repeats it to someone else it's not the same as he heard it told to him." "I'd like to address a matter that I find important." "It's difficult for me to navigate and live a life without having to rely on assistance." "I have a business staff in my corporation and I have personal business associates to look into my private affairs." "I wouldn't be here without the intervention of one of my associates "Ronnie Roberts"." "I wouldn't have known anything about the cancellation of the prom." "There's been a lot of things said about me and my associates to a lot of people." "Be careful what you read in the papers today." "The articles you read are fabricated and they're not true, like the rumors you hear." "When it comes to sin" "none of us are born with it; but we lose our innocence when we learn what sin is." "That's all I have to say." "I hope to see you at the prom" "And uh" "no pun intended."

I began walking towards Bailey when Mister Byres stopped me.

"That comment hit home when you said be careful about you what read." "You were right" "I did have an opinion of you." He stated.

"Mister Byres" "this is election year" "there's two parties running for offices in the Government." "Nothing is against ethics when campaigning." "I want you to think about this." "What if the wrong man was elected because of a lie?" "By most standards this is a small school that's absorbing millions of dollars from the State's budget." "How long do you think the State will take before they start bussing all of these kids to other schools?" "If that was to happen" "do you think you would be given another principal's job somewhere, or would you be willing to go back to teaching at another school?" "Mister Byres" "There's been a lot of people that were told that their job was secure, but the next day they received a pink slip." "The people that told them that were lying, and all of those people they told got their information from a paper or the news." "When you fall to the bottom" "sooner or later someone will come along and sweep you away." "Mister Byres I find that no one listens to what I say" "they're too busy with their own thoughts." "I hope to see you at the prom" "oh and" "no pun intended."

"You're a good man Kurt." Bailey commented.

"You didn't go to a prom either, did you?"

"How do you know that?" She replied.

"You said you ran off to be with Tom when you turned seventeen and he went to college." "You didn't graduate with your class so I'm guessing you got a GED."

"You seem to know more about me than what I know myself." She commented. "You would have made a great lawyer."

CHAPTER ELEVEN

"**M**ake sure the doors are locked Buck." Becky commanded. "I've checked them twice already." He spoke. "Then check them again." I heard him mumbling as he walked off.

"Well, what does everyone have planned?" I asked as we got underway.

"I called Richard and asked him what time you're taping was." Bailey began. "And then I told him we wanted to see a symphony and he called someone and got us tickets."

"Hollywood is a city of glamour" I stated "and I'm sure there's a lot of other things you can be doing other than going to a symphony."

"None of us have ever been to one." "Sarah and Steven have but none of us." She replied. "Besides no one wanted to go anywhere unless you were with us." "Kurt" "there's something we all talked about and we were wondering why you always called Richard by his first name and not Mister or Misses like you do everyone else." Bailey said.

Everyone settled down and became quiet to hear my answer. "Elrod and Patricia" "Bailey's referring to a man I have on my staff in New York." I said letting them in on her question. "A corporation is like the body." "You have vital organs in the body and you have vital organs in a corporation." "If any vital organ of the body was to get infected, it could end a life." "A corporation is no different." "Everyone thinks that their department is needed more." "We had people that enhanced their life style from financial rewards that was gained by utilizing certain bits of information and sold to media's that reported fiction along with fact." "It was cheaper to buy out a contract than take them to court."

"English Kurt" Becky interrupted.

"Well, Richard and I had talks and, in our talks, he expressed a comment relating to me to the effect of not putting too much faith in retiring." "We both worked in the mailroom together." "He didn't know who I was" "he had his life and I had mine." "We never socialized outside of work." "I preferred it that way." "People don't talk to you the same way after they find out who you are." "Anyway" "I asked him questions and he answered them." "I knew the truth and he never told me one thing that didn't match." "I may be blind but I'm not deaf." "When I walked in and took over my father's firm" "I sent for him and told him to sit down." "He's been my eyes in my business and he had some serious knowledge of my operations beforehand; he turned out to be an excellent choice." "The others stay in line thinking that others are reporting what they see and what they hear." "Everyone is suspicious of everyone so trust isn't given to just anyone."

"What" Elrod grunted?

"English Kurt" Becky commented.

"He said" Cheryl began "he likes people that like him."

"What" Elrod repeated?

"He isn't talking mean to people when he talks to them" she began "if you talk nice to him" "he talks nice to you and if you talk mean to him, he talks mean to you and when he does those people get upset with him, like that man did, he made him mad at him."

"Do you know why?" Elrod asked her.

"He acted funny like and Mister B wanted to see if he was sick." Cheryl answered.

"That man took something to make him act like that." Cindy interrupted with a clearer view of her own.

"Ahh" "we're having our first board meeting." I chuckled.

"We're coming into Murray." I announced.

"You were able to count the curves while we were talking?" Bailey asked.

"No" I answered "Murray has a distinct odor and when the wind blows out of the west it's more pungent." "Sometimes when you get sidetracked it's better to have a backup system to depend on."

"That's how he found our perfume and that bakery." Cheryl once again asserted her observations.

"You remember those things?" Her father asked her.

"Sure" "there was a man he talked to because a woman was writing stuff on some paper and didn't want to wait on us." "He told the man he wanted someone that would help him and if he wasn't that man, he wanted someone that could." "He wasn't mad at him" "he just told him that he wanted someone to help him."

"What about that man that said something mean to us while we waited for Steven to get the van and Mister B almost got in a fight?" Julie said.

"That man was being rude Julie." Sarah commented. "Kurt was just letting him know he wasn't someone he could mouth off to."

"No" I interrupted. "People sometimes run into problems that they can't overcome and when that happens some of them vent that anger or aggression on anyone that happens be in their way." "When frustrations are vented verbally; tensions are released and peace allows a person to make sound judgments, and when frustrations are vented physically" "a person like that man will eventually run into someone that has more frustrations than what he has and both of them may discharge their frustrations on each other." "You never hear thunder unless there's lightning."

"English Kurt" Becky once again interrupted.

"Mister B do you have frustrations?" Ronnie asked.

"I did" "and it got so bad that I wanted to stick my head in the sand." "But I got to thinking long and hard about it and when I did, then I got to thinking if I done that, I would be unknowingly wishing that all of my uneasiness would go away, it did for a while, but unless you face and encounter what life throws at you, you'll never be free to live your life." "Ronnie" "no one can live a life without fears." "You can't hide in a closet in a fire" "so I was fortunate and met Bailey and she gave me my reasons to face my miseries." "Through her" "I've found friends." "I flipped a coin and found out that she didn't know who I was and she took me to your mother and that led me to your father and that led me to you and your sisters, and that led me to Cheryl and that led me to Steven and that led me to Sarah and that led me to Elrod and Patricia here." "I never had a family and now, I feel close to all of you."

"Your smooth" Patricia commented.

"When you feel what you say and say what you feel" "you don't have to worry about saying anything wrong when among friends." "If someone doesn't like to hear the truth, then they'll end up learning the truth the hard way." I replied. "Buck" "that's why I ignore reporters" "there's two types of media's" "fiction and nonfiction." "I didn't do interviews so I was sought after and after about six months of it; I had to leave my father's firm for a while." "Pictures were taken of me and superimposed in papers standing next to a politician." "It gave people the impression that I supported that politician."

"He went into seclusion" Steven commented.

"What" Sarah followed?

"Food was left for him outside the door of his studio and sometimes it was left untouched."

"How do you know that?" Sarah asked him.

"His valet was reassigned and every now and then I picked up his tray that was outside his door, it was untouched." He stated. "We're at the airport Kurt."

"You knew about me Steven?"

"Yes sir" he replied.

"Is that why you helped me?" I asked.

"Sir" "I saw what was happening to you and when I saw you when you came into the hotel" "you didn't look like the man you were when you left." "I helped you unpack your clothes in the boxes and when I introduced myself to you" "you didn't remember me."

"Steven" I began.

"That's alright sir" he stopped me "You couldn't remember anyone else's name either."

"Is that why you moved to Skinland?" Bailey expressed her view.

"There's a place that everyone calls home and that's where you want to be buried." "The institution I was in was my residence for twenty five years and I never called that place home." "When I moved to the hotel, I never called that place home either." "I've been alone all of my life." "When I came to Skinland, something happened to me and I've never felt alone anymore." "I'm going to die in Skinland" "it's my home." I said as I felt the limo as it came to a halt. "Ahh" "no reporter's" "good" "let someone else share the spotlight."

"Don't talk about dying." Cindy quickly expressed her anger at my answer.

I could hear Buck moaning and groaning as he sat next to Becky. "This is a mistake." He announced.

My thoughts were interrupted by Bailey whispering in my ear. "Cheryl's holding Ronnie's hand."

"Tell me if Elrod's noticed it too." I whispered back and after a few minutes she gave me my answer.

"You know" "Cheryl's the one that wanted us to take in a Symphony." Bailey whispered. "You're making a big impression on her."

"It's my cane" I chuckled. "Ronnie" I began after we were in the air "has anyone come forward and volunteered their services?"

"Yes sir" "the fire department" "the police" "and three churches along with a lot of other people." He replied.

"Good" "we're going to need police" "that's for sure." "We're going to need portable toilets too."

"Elrod's got all of that taken care of Kurt." Buck said.

"What about tables and chairs and" I was interrupted by Becky.

"Sarah's taken care of all of that Kurt." "She was the Prom Queen at her school."

"Oh" "Okay" I uttered.

"I don't think I like the way you said that." Sarah said.

"I have my thoughts." I commented.

"You said you say what you feel and feel what you say when you're with friends, so say it." She continued.

"There are reasons for our being who we are; motivation isn't a utensil that's utilized by everyone" "sometimes it's implanted."

"English Kurt" Becky interrupted.

"Sarah's an outgoing young lady" "energetic and quite set in her ways, but she has a reason for that." I relinquished.

"Go on" Sarah stated.

"Sarah" "you were voted as the most likely to succeed, weren't you?" A long silence followed and then I continued. "Sarah, sometimes a person wants to prove to the people that thinks of them as being successful, to have made an accurate assessment." "When I was discussing my plans on going to New York and taking everyone with me" "Buck made a comment about him thinking that all of the people that lived there were a bunch of stuffed shirts." "Buck" I said turning my attention towards him and then back at Sarah "that's what Sarah thought I was before we met." "She thought I was going to use her and her husband like I did everyone else." "At least that's what the paper's description of my character portrayed to her of me as being." "Later I found out that Sarah and I were having an affair while poor Steven was tending to my errands that I sent him on in order for me and Sarah to be united." "Sarah" "those people that thought of you as becoming successful are most likely to believe that you really are having an affair with me." "They thought you would do anything to achieve success at any cost" "you can bet and it would be a safe bet that you are who you are because that's what they thought of you as being when they voted; a person that will use any means necessary to achieve her goals."

"That makes three times now you've pointed out my ugly side." She said "I've lived with Steven three years and he doesn't know one tenth of what you found out in a month and we haven't really talked all that much."

"Sarah" "everyone on this plane lived a different life before we met and since then we've made adjustments." "You're having difficulties because you don't like what you hear." "Bailey doesn't either and I'm sure everyone here has read an article pertaining to me or heard a comment where their name entered into the conversation, or maybe it was the way the people looked at you when you saw them looking at you." "That's the power that money has over people because that's what "they" would do if given the opportunity to be in your shoes." "Nothing is sacred and once they've achieved the goals that they set out to achieve then nothing is sacred." "They'll write a tell all book and they'll have plenty of articles to use as a reference to expand statements that were written and I can guarantee you, they would be the centerfold in the next issue of a magazine somewhere." "You can trust me; I've been there and done that." "The girl who filed my first paternal lawsuit did just that, and when she was found guilty of attempted extortion, she was once again displayed in the magazine with a different caption." "They made good money and they did it all legally." "There's a difference in people that people can't see because they aren't looking." "Self driven motivation is separated from implanted motivation" "but each achieves the end results."

"English Kurt" Becky interrupted.

"Sarah" "before Bailey knew who I was" "she said that she wanted to be a doctor and I asked her if she wanted to be a doctor or marry one." "At the time she was only telling me of her dream because she worked for a doctor that was rich, like Becky." "When he was killed, their dreams were killed along with him." "You might have kissed a frog when you were little too."

"I did" Cindy said.

"Eeeewww" the chorus of the rest of the kids sounded their disapproval.

"Anyway" I said laughing "Sarah I was success driven" "I know what it can do to a person." "Sometimes you get involved so deep that you lose focus on your surroundings." "That's why I handed the reins over to Mister Laree after I signed the papers on my father's estate." "I had to find someone I trusted to run it after I left." "Richard was that man and after I saw that in him, I knew it was time for me to go." "My drive was self driven." "You're driven by what others perceive you to be." "You want success but not the way they think." "Sarah" "if you go back to where you graduated from and take a good look at some of the people you went to school with, you'll see a lot of them treat you like they had been your friend all their life."

"You can't change what people think of you." Bailey added "That's what Kurt said to me when I told him what the people were saying about me."

The pilot's voice came over the loud speaker informing us that we were landing in twenty minutes.

"It's nine o'clock and it's still daylight." Buck stated and then I heard. "Awe Naw" "there's way too many people down there."

"It's seven" I corrected him "we gain two hours".

I felt the plane as it descended, and as soon as we landed, I heard a gasp of air coming from Buck.

"Buck as long as we're in the air, you don't have worries." "It's the sudden stop that gets you." I chuckled.

"People jump out of perfectly good airplanes too." "I was in training to do that when I broke my leg and I got a medical discharge." He began as we taxied down the runway. "Kurt" "Some men just ain't cut out to be a rope jumper; or a mountain climber and it didn't take me long to learn that I wasn't one of them." "My first repel had me upside down hanging on my toes like a bat and when I looked up the drill instructor smiled a big ole smile and kicked my feet away from the wall." "I ain't got me no reason to go none too soon, and I ain't in no hurry to get there neither."

The loud roar of jet engines from a plane taking off was deafening when we exited the jet and there we were met by the producer's representative.

"I hope everyone had a comfortable flight." She began. "We've taken the liberty of scheduling dining at Sebastian's."

"What's that?" Buck asked.

"They specialize in French cuisines sir." She stated.

"Oh" Buck replied. "Do they have steak there too?" He added.

"Yes sir" she answered politely. "Now sir" she directed her comments toward me. "Breakfast will be served at Landry's at nine, and you wanted to do a little sightseeing." "The producers would like you at the station one hour before the interview and then dinner at Marco's and the theater at seven." "If there's anything you find to be unacceptable you can let me know at any time and we'll make the necessary changes." "Is there anything you wish sir?"

"I'm not going to be able to do a lot walking, I'll need a wheelchair." "I'm not half the man I used to be." I said chuckling. "I can't stand for a long period of time." "I have my personal associates with me that's never been to California and I wanted them to see a little bit before we left." I said to her.

"That's not a problem sir." She quickly assured me.

After we dined and was escorted to the Symphony Hall, we were soon being escorted back to the hotel." Ronnie took special care to see that my ride in the wheelchair was comfortable. When the Limo came to a stop she got out and she told us all to follow her and we were soon escorted to our rooms.

"I've arranged for a six o'clock courtesy call in the morning" "will that be alright sir?" She asked.

"Can we have two cups of hot cocoa?" Bailey asked and within fifteen seconds she had cocoa ordered for everyone.

"Riley" I said.

"Yes sir" she promptly answered.

"You wouldn't happen to be an actress, would you?"

"Sir!"

"Are you an actress?" I asked.

"I used to be an actress that was struggling" "now I'm a struggling actress." She commented. "How did you know?"

"You're rigid" "I couldn't have written a better script for you than the performance you gave to my associates." "They really ate it up." I chuckled.

"What's going on Kurt?" Bailey asked.

"Riley here is better known as being a moonlighter" "she holds a full time job as an agent and tries to put her foot in the door to be an aspiring young actress, but she's slowly waning away from that field." "When was the last time you had an audition, Riley?" I asked her.

"Last year." "Mister Bryant" "how did you know that about me?"

"You have a hint of depression about you and being in Hollywood, I could only guess that a person that labors when speaking is trying to control movements of the syllables to disguise a dialect; and they only do so for a purpose." "Do you love acting?" I asked her.

"I've been having sessions with a speech therapist." She confided to answer my statement about her dialect.

"I'm sorry if I sound offensive Riley" "but you can't take a natural and change that natural." "You will always have the accent you grew up with." "If you take a tape recorder, you'll find that it never gives the sound's you hear from your ears, it's the best administrator for education though" "those that listen, hear the truth." "Your therapist should have given you that information on your first visit." "I'm only telling you this because you would save a lot of money, but I'm not you." "I do things because that's what I want to do." "You're in control of your life and if you're like me you'll listen with an open mind and take all things said in consideration before you take action on whatever it is you want to do." "Right or wrong, sometimes your decisions are permanent." I then paused a few moments and began. "Do a skit for me and let me hear you recite a part." I told her.

"You mean here?" She asked.

"You said is there anything I wish and right now I'd like to hear you act out a scene for me."

"I can't do that" She declared.

"Oh" "that's not good" "you're not out going and you don't have a devil may care attitude." I began "In Japan" "all executives must prove themselves to be worthy of a position that's being offered." "And as a test to that testimony there's some that's told to stand in front of a busy location and shout out to the world of why they're the best person for the job." "They're judged by how far they can go before they have a mental meltdown." "Riley it's not something I would make any of my associates endure." "But there is one thing about it" "they do get the best people" "I may not agree on their ethics" "but they do get the best people."

"Mister Bryant" "I have a job." She stated.

"You're lucky" I began "a lot of struggling actors and actresses are out of work "and" out looking for a part in a play or an extra on a set in a studio somewhere." "Take my advice and don't quit your day job or you'll be joining those people too." "Riley" "you have one thing going against you" "I didn't have to hear you acting" "I knew what one of your weaknesses was when you spoke to us at the airport." "That doesn't mean you can't pursue a career" "those that can't do, teach." "You may learn that you might be able to learn more by teaching others."

"You think so?" She commented.

"You really did give a good performance to my associates earlier" I replied "and I would imagine that all of the other guests of the network you nursed, also found you to be quite attentive." "If you satisfy them then that's all that really matters." "They are your audience and every time you meet one at the airport you step on the stage and begin performing." "Like I told you earlier" "you couldn't write a better script than the one you performed." "But outside that script" "you don't portray yourself to be anything other than an agent pacifying her producers, guests." "Being an actress involves a lot more than someone delivering a line." "Take a good look at me Riley." "I can only act in scenes where it takes a blind man to perform so I'm limited on the roles I can play." "To Bailey here and all of my friends" "I'll always be a Yankee, and for that I'll get a few laughs from people that think I talk funny" "but, I also receive encouragement from them by knowing that I could pursue a career as a comedian just by going on a stage and telling a joke that I memorized and everyone would laugh" "not because of the joke, but because to them I talk funny." "Of course, I wouldn't do well in New York, they all talk like me." "Riley" "we all have limitations" "and when it comes to acting" "there's only one man that can play a lead role in a movie and all the other auditions didn't meet what someone was looking for." "It could have been his voice" "or the way he moved." "The same goes for a leading lady." "We just met you today." I said "Knowing what you know of me" "who would you want to play me if a movie was to be made about me."

A knock came at the door and the lady opened it. "Thank you." I heard her say and soon I was taking a sip of cocoa.

"Becky's is a whole lot better." I said when I sat it on a table and smiled. "Thank you, Becky." I commented.

"You knew I was here, didn't you?" She laughed.

"I bought each of you five different types of perfume." "Bailey's wearing one and you're wearing one of the other four." "Lilac" isn't it?" I chuckled.

"You're a devil Kurt" "but I still don't know how you knew it was me." "You got Sarah and the kids perfume too."

"Riley ordered the cocoa from our room" "so it was brought here and you had to meet him at the door." "I've learned that you're a sneaky one Becky." "Now" "Are we ready to go?" I asked.

"We're waiting on "you"." She stated.

I fell asleep in the limo on the way back from the restaurant and was awoken when we got to the theater to hear the symphony." When we returned to the hotel, I felt Bailey sliding into the bed next to me.

"Everyone really had a good time tonight." Bailey commented as she gently gave me a tight squeeze.

"I think Buck's more used to eating at home." I said "He didn't think the portions he got were adequate."

"That's because when Buck goes out to eat, he likes to eat at a Buffet." "He's gained a few pounds though and now his pants are getting tight." "I heard him telling Becky that." "He doesn't understand that a seven course meal has to have enough room to fit it all in, but in the end, he had trouble downing the Crème Brule." "Kurt" "Julie wasn't the only one that kissed a frog."

"I know" "you told me that a little after we met" "had I known you meant it, I might have rejected you back at Beck's diner."

"I'm trying to be serious here." She said as she struck me on the arm.

The next morning, I was tying my tie when I heard Bailey's voice and then I felt her begin to twist my shoulders followed by a command. "Turn around for me and let me see what you look like." "I've never seen you in a suit before." "You have a certain air of distinction." She said after sizing me up. "I believe you could walk on water." "Come on" "Riley said, we've got a busy day scheduled."

We were on the way to the studios when Bailey got a call on her cell phone. "Kurt" "its Richard."

"Hello" I answered "what's the average time" "then notify their attorney's and we'll proceed from there." "And Richard" "let our leak be known about the tape too." "What" I said taking a deep breath "get me an appointment and get back with me." "You too." I said hanging up.

"Is everything all right?" Bailey asked.

"Sure" "sure" I said and became quiet.

"Something's wrong Kurt?" Sarah commented.

"Nothing" I said ignoring the question. "So, did everyone enjoy last night?" I asked.

"I want to go home Kurt." Buck stated "Becky caught me eyeing the women and when I told her if I lived here, she would have competition." "I got sick when Riley told me that they were men." "Kurt" "there's just so many ways to shame a man." "What's wrong with all these people and by the way" "let's not bring this up again?" "Everybody got that?" He was angry with himself.

"Could you follow me please?" Riley asked everyone as a lady's voice introduced herself to me when we entered the studio.

"Mister Bryant" "I'm Truth Phelps." she said taking my hand and shaking it.

"I'm familiar with you." I answered.

"Are you a fan?" She asked.

"People don't like me very much." I told her.

"Are you referring to my show?" She asked.

"My comments are private." I stated.

"You can speak freely" "I heard it all before." She commented.

I paused and collected my thoughts. "Ma'am" "Your ratings are falling and you of all people know that." I said to her. "You could do better."

"I'm always entertained by suggestions." She commented.

I hesitated before I began. "I don't have sight" "so I depend on whether the person I'm talking to "like you" a reporter has morals." "Miss Phelps" "Truth isn't your first name" "I'm assuming you changed that after you left for college." "I have to admit" "it does bring favor to you" "and Miss Phelps" "reporters are like lawyers" "they don't have morals either." "It's clear to me by the way people talk that some of your guests are coached on their answers." I stated. "And I find that you don't treat all guests as you do others, that's why you're losing your ratings, you're not a neutral hostess." "You've drawn a line in the sand." "A viewer has opinions of their own and when you go against their opinions" "you lose a viewer" "you become labeled and for that your producers suffer and when they suffer, it isn't long before this program ends up having a changing of the guards." "Ma'am" "if you go from prime time to not so prime time" "I don't think your salary would be questioned." "You've become a high priced contract that only draws sponsors willing to pay less." "Ma'am" "from what I hear" "I find that you go beyond getting a story to defending a personal belief." "That's my opinion and like every person I talk too" "theirs is the only one that matters."

"Twenty minutes" A man's voice rang out above the others and then I felt a hand guiding me in a direction.

"This way Mister Bryant" "we need to put a mic on you sir." A man said.

"Quiet on the set" "five" "four" "three" "two" "one"." "Welcome to "We the People"." Miss Phelps began her introduction and afterwards she turned her attention to me.

"You don't do interviews" "would you tell us why you chose to do one now." She asked.

"I don't endorse any candidate and if the public sees me in a picture with one or on an advertisement to make it look like I support that candidate" "those candidates are lying" "they're using a tactic better known as propaganda." "This is important so let me repeat" "I DO NOT SUPPORT ANY CANDIDATE."

"Mister Bryant" "We the People" "want to know are you or are you not planning on making bid for the Senate" She began.

"That would be a definite no" "I can't vote on any bills being passed." I commented.

"Can you give us a for instance?" She pleaded.

"I can give you plenty, but your time allotment won't allow it." I stated.

"We'll see about that" she commented. "Now" "please."

"First off" I began answering her question "a bill only has one purpose for it to be presented and voted on and that's revenue." "Every bill that's being passed hurts some people, but it doesn't affect others." "The only outcome of that bill is to generate revenue and that revenue ends up going into the State Fund to spent elsewhere and not for the purpose the bill was signed into law for." "It's clear to me that people are spending less and taxes are falling short" "inflation is setting in and the higher the price of the product the higher the taxes that are collected." "I hear that unemployment is at a record low, if so, why are taxes increasing every year ten percent." "The government is the only one that benefits from inflation." "I don't think anyone would want to have a conversation with me" "others would blackball others because of suspicion." "I'd like to add to that." "I mentioned revenue in the form of taxes." "Gas driven cars are being diminished by the introduction of Electric cars." "That means less taxes will be collected from oil." "To offset that tax, oil will increase and by doing so, gas prices will rise." "There will be a bill that will be introduced charging mileage taxes on electric cars and when that bill is introduced, it will contain an additional tax on gas driven cars." "Money Miss Phelps." "Not all Americans pay their fair share of taxes."

"You said you had others." She followed her questioning.

"Yes ma'am" "I do". I replied.

"Could you tell us?" She asked.

"Ma'am we need jobs to support our economy." "When the circulation of tax dollars becomes stagnant then it's being spent in places that don't do the people any good." I commented. "If there were bullet trains built

Paradox

on every interstate North, South, East and West, from coast to coast, we would eliminate three fourths of all the airlines." "Sub stations could rent electric cars for travel and we would save thirty percent of all our fuel." "But" "that would be voted down quickly" "every gallon of fuel has City, County, State and Federal taxes on it and right now without those taxes" "we'd be in a depression." "That's why those that have electric cars will be taxed on the mileage." I then added. "Since the inception of Social Security by "Herbert Hoover" it's been fought over since its birth." I began "There's a constant that's working against it." "There's more going out than what's coming in." "Simple economics proves that it can't sustain the load and nothings being done to fix it." "Statements to the effect of reforming, overhauling, or improving Social Security aren't anything more than telling those that's smart enough to listen that you're not going to have the same things you used to have after this bill passes." "Insurance is nothing more than a Ponzi scheme." "Most people can't meet the deductible they have and add other forms of shortages such as only paying for one lab work at fifteen hundred when you may need four or five or more lab work done, they end up paying fifty percent of their cost of hospitalization." "Not to mention Mother Nature's wrath that wipes out their home." "Miss Phelps" "Corporations employees are self insured by their corporation." "They only pay insurance companies to handle paper work and in some Corporations, employees can't meet their out of pocket expenses." "I can assure you; you won't have enough money in your savings plan when you retire to cover the cost of hospitalization if you're dying." "And in the field of oil, it's cheaper to pay for a death than to shut a unit down from leaks in pumps." "That's called Capitalism "A million dollars isn't anything anymore; especially when it involves doctors and hospitals, I know that for a fact."

"What would you do if you had the power to change the way things are being done." She asked.

I began "Insurance companies are guaranteed a three percent profit every year." "Miss Phelps we can self insure all of our city and county; state and federal employees just like corporations do and not raise taxes one percent, like I said, insurance isn't anything more than a Ponzi Scheme." "But" "we're at another roadblock there too" "some law makers own insurance firms." "And in the past, some have received a healthy compensation for their efforts in fighting for their cause through lobbyist." "I'd end lobbyism, it's nothing more than thievery, a politician isn't doing what he's elected for, he's doing what a corporation pays him for." "I'd put an end to the cap on Social Security and I would cease businesses paying social security on their employees." "That would allow businesses to hire more people." "Right now, employees that work for a fast food service doesn't work a forty hour workweek." "That's because a corporation is required to provide them with insurance." "A CEO that gets a bonus of five hundred million will write out a check for seven point six five percent like everyone else that pays their fair share and tax payers on Medicare wouldn't be paying hundreds of Billions of dollars on those that reach their cap on Jan the first at twelve oh one midnight." "That's the beginning of taxing all Americans fairly."

"And you're willing to do that?" She asked.

"I don't draw a salary" "I live on my expenses." I pay my personal tax on the amount I took for expenses." "Even at that I write out a check to Social Security at midnight January First." 'I reach the cap at one minute after." "I don't have Medicare, I can draw it because I'm blind, but I'm fortunate, I don't need it." "But" "that wouldn't last long" "the reason Social Security is in the trouble is because it's been borrowed from in the first place since its birth; we overspend our budgets and the only way they fix it, is by borrowing from Social Security, that's when we began having trouble in Social Security and we'll soon be in trouble again with our economy, we're still overspending." "Under inflated numbers are used because if you use a real number, chances are, a politician wouldn't be reelected, or elected." "The odd thing is the people that clap for that man to do that, are the same people suffering because of that action." "Miss Phelps" "there isn't any money in Social Security" "that's why we have inflation, money is being printed that we don't have." "If I was a teacher, I'd be worried, from my understanding a teacher can't draw a spouses Social Security if they died." "Due to the amount of people on fixed incomes increasing, the rich will be in trouble financially?"

"Are there more?" She continued.

"There's areas that I find offensive." I stated.

"Such as" she said?

I wet my lips with my tongue and answered. "It costs a sizeable sum to adopt a child." "Yet it costs the government" "that's "We the People" Billions of dollars a year to provide unadopted children with medical, room and board and an education." "There's millions of people that want to adopt, but they can't afford it" "yet the government pays people to be foster parents." "Our regulations don't do anything more than promote "child trafficking"." "We can pay the legal fees and save Billions of dollars and there would be more than half of the children waiting to be adopted" "be adopted." "Miss Phelps, we pay more to house prisoners than we pay for orphans." "That's why I can't run." "If one party thought my ideas were good" "then since that one party sided with me" "then there's got to be a reason why the other party should side against it." "We're a house divided Miss Phelps." "This nation is going to fail." "There isn't anyone thinking about what the people lose when a bill is passed." "I'm going to repeat what I said because some of your viewers may have tuned in after I made my opening statement." "I DON'T SUPPORT ANY CANDIDATE" "and when my name or my picture appears on any advertisement promoting my endorsement or a smear campaign or otherwise, is only being used when a lie is being told, I DO NOT SUPPORT ANY CANDIDATE." "None of them support the people and by doing so, we'll turn into a socialist government.

Can you tell us why?" She asked.

"Well, Miss Phelps that's a difficult answer to relay because not everyone is listening, but I'll try my best." "I was listening to a debate once, and a speaker was adamant in his speech about the voice of democracy." "His opponent was silent until he was asked a question and during his speech, he was interrupted multiple times to keep him from speaking" "and each time the moderator stopped the debate and asked for him to give his opponent a chance to answer." "Had his opponent had been telling lies I wouldn't blame him" "but he wasn't, so It would seem to me that the voice of democracy apparently only has "one" voice." "To him" "we only need one party running this government." "Truth" "he was reelected and after he got elected" "he vacated his seat." "His opponent would have beaten his party's candidate." "This country is moving towards a new government of the people and those that vote for that government will find themselves a victim of ignorance." "There won't be any more of "We the People in the future." "Progress has many names." "I would like to see everyone not act like I don't care what you say, I'm against it purely because the party I'm affiliated with is against it." "These members were elected to be diplomatic and it would seem that diplomacy has a partisan attitude." "Every time the right bill is voted down" "the people become a victim." "Why, because a bad bill generates revenue that finds its way into the pockets of the politicians that passed it."

"You don't seem to have a high regard for our government." She added.

I smiled before I continued. "Not all politicians are in politics for the betterment of the people" "they have a different reason." "When I hear complaints from Statesman" "I'm reminded that if you own a business and you have to lay off half of your people and you continue to have the same problems that you laid off half of your people for, then you've laid off the wrong half." "I'd like to hear more about how that Statesman's going to go about changing the problem the people have instead of complaining about it; after all that's what he was elected for." "We have a problem and it's so simple that no one wants to admit it."

"What is it?" She asked.

"We can't beat slave labor." "Half of the people vote for one party" "and the other half votes for the other party" "it's got to be a fact that half of the people that vote are wrong in what they believe in and judging by the people that's being underpaid or out of work, this country depends on slave labor." Miss Phelps, the rich will pay the same price as the poor." "History is going to repeat itself." "You can go on the internet and have what ever you order delivered to you in two days." "They have distribution warehouses that store products from foreign countries as we speak." "They'll be a day when corporations will suffer from a lack of customers." "Malls aren't needed anymore." "Progress consumes all those that stand in the way."

She then began talking to her viewers telling them that we had to take a station break and that we would be right back.

"See I told you that you didn't have the time allotment." I chuckled. "Miss Phelps" "you and I have a lot in common except you believe in what someone you have trust "in" says, I think you should pay a little more attention to what they did if they were in office already and if they didn't do the job they should have, then you'll reelect a person that won't accomplish anything on his next term either." "Your job is in jeopardy and you are the one that's jeopardizing it." "Should I feel sorry for you." "No" "you did it yourself." "When you point the finger of blame, you can point at yourself." "Is that why people vote?" "No." "They only vote for a candidate because they don't like the other candidate." "Progress is stalled miss Phelps and it's not that hard for me to see that you pull a one party lever when you vote too." "If the party was to succeed in becoming the party in which you're in favor of" "where would you fit in in all of this?" "I'll give you a little hint" "you'll be reporting on some things that you know aren't true, just the way they report the news in North Korea and other countries." "I'm willing to bet you've had people on your show that's made comments that you later found out it was a lie." "But" "you still have your beliefs and no matter what I say" "it won't change what you think."

"I have to know something." She said to me. "Are you planning on making a bid?" "I'd vote for you and I'd tell my viewers I support you."

"Ma'am" "my pictures and my comments have been on every single tabloid in the business." "I've been reported to have made a lot and I do mean a lot of statements that I didn't make." "I don't do interviews and I don't mingle in the mainstream of being a socialite." "A smear campaign doesn't have to be aimed at someone" "all it takes is to be pictured with a celebrity or a foreign dignitary and people associate those pictures as being what the caption appears below." "If it's not the truth" "then what do you call a smear campaign?" "Miss Phelps" "you have eyes but you have bad hearing." "I listened to people give interviews in sports and competitions where ranking determined how much money you made competing and everyone stated that second place didn't matter to them." "Although every one of them that took second place accepted the check and smiled for the cameras." "We had a speaker of the house that stole money from the government and had to borrow money to pay it back." "He ran for president." "Money is a drive that all public servants have in common."

"Quiet everyone" "five" "four" "three" "two" "one"."

"Welcome back" "our guest is Mister Kurt Bryant of Bryant Enterprises." "Mister Bryant" "You were basically unknown until three years ago." You were in an institution" "weren't you?"

I folded my arms and answered. "Yes" "My mother was killed when she was six months pregnant and they did an emergency surgery on her and I was born." "I was diagnosed as having a form of autism and my father had me committed."

"Doctor Savidge was your doctor, wasn't he?" She asked.

I took a deep breath and exhaled before I answered. "For a while and then he died" "I was put under another physician's care and when she reassessed my records" "she formed a different diagnosis; through her I am who I am today."

"Doctor Savidge was found to have performed unauthorized tests on some of his patients." "Did he perform test on you too." She asked.

I stalled.

"Mister Bryant" "I'm sorry" "I have to ask this question." "Did he perform test on you too?"

I had to clear my throat before I answered. "Yes"

"Are you sterile Mister Bryant?" She asked.

"Yes"

"Mister Bryant" "The test that Doctor Savidge performed gave some of his subjects' testicular cancer." "Six boys have died from it and two more boys have been diagnosed with it" "do you have testicular cancer? She asked.

"I go in once a year for a test and so far, I haven't tested positive." I began "Miss Phelps" "Doctor Savidge has children and grandchildren and they all became victims the same as all the kids the doctor tested his theory on."

"Every person that's diagnosed positively reignites their memories of him." "I feel for his family." I stated.

She then turned away from me and told her viewers that we'd be right back after these messages.

"How come you didn't say anything in any of those lawsuits you had?" She asked.

"Miss Phelps" "I feel I have my rights to privacy the same as every other American that lives in America, that includes you." "Besides" "I never lost any of them or I would have then." "I don't like liars and I don't like the people that tell them." "That's another thing reporters don't care about" "if someone's saying it" "it's not liable to the papers."

"Mister Bryant" "I am sorry." She stated.

"No, you're not" I began "if you were, you wouldn't have brought it up in the first place." "To you its ratings" "that's why you're divorced" "you have only one commitment" "and it's not to any man."

"Quiet on the set please" "five" "four" "three" "two" "one"."

"Welcome back to "We the People." "Our guest today is Kurt Bryant of Bryant Enterprises." "Mister Bryant" "the FBI considers you to be a suspect in the murder of one of your executives." She began.

"Let me stop you right there" I said interrupting her "I can't comment on that" "I haven't been interviewed so I don't know if I'm a suspect or not, and I don't answer questions based on assumption or hearsay." I stated to her.

"Will you tell us what happened to lead up to that incident?" She asked.

"I was in New York to transfer my father's estate and I wanted my personal associates present." "I have a random drug test installed to where I test everyone periodically and the only way to show everyone in my firm that I meant what I say was to show them that no one was exempt." "To my understanding" "he had drugs in his system and he retaliated against my policy." "That's all I know about what happened; I'll be like everyone else that wants to know that answer and I won't know that until I'm notified, by paper or the news." "I might even be listening to you and hear you break the news on your program." "I don't know."

"Well, that was a pleasant indication that you watch us and for that I thank you." She quickly relayed her message to her viewers.

I smiled and said to her. "I'll listen to any news program that brings me the truth" "I won't ever listen to it again if I find out what was said was false." "It's just a program that's only got one interest" "and that's ratings."

"Our sources tell us you've entered a legal battle with "Morton's hospitality corporation"." She commented.

"I'm not at liberty to discuss that matter."

"But you're not saying you aren't filing a lawsuit." She added.

"Business is business and details aren't given to what business transactions are being performed." I stated. "That's an unwritten rule." "I'm sorry but I don't comment on my business transactions."

"Mister Bryant" "is it true that you have an associate that was terminated because of you." "You hired him" "can you tell us why."

I hesitated once again. "I wanted to show my personal associates the sights of New York" "they hadn't ever been there and we were mobbed by the media." "I didn't tell anyone we were coming and I knew my plans were worthless after that, and I asked him if he could give me secrecy and he did." "He went against managements orders and was given his termination for it."

"Is that what the suit is about?" She continued.

"I'm not at liberty to discuss that matter." "He hasn't given me an answer yet." "You asked me a question about a man that was fired for helping me and I gave you an answer."

"Why is it you've subpoenaed past records of employment and all the guests that were guests at the hotel for the last four years?" She continued her question.

"I'm sorry but I'm not at liberty to comment on legal matters."

"So, you do have a suit filed against them then." She once again stated.

"I'm sorry I can't answer to matters relating to my legal department." I repeated.

"Mister Bryant" "a hundred million isn't that large of an amount."

"I'm sorry" "I can't comment on that." I repeated my statement.

"You put a large sum of your holdings in gold and fossil fuels and pharmaceuticals." "Can you tell us why?" She asked.

"If you want to know what the people are thinking you've got to get out and walk amongst the people." "I'm an idiot and I don't pretend to be anything else." I told her.

"Mister Bryant and idiot doesn't increase his father's portfolio by five hundred percent in three years." "I wouldn't call any man an idiot that did that." She reported.

"I heard a reporter comment on the news that now their starting to affect the real people." I began "I had to ask myself who are the real people." "The man that made that comment was in his forties or maybe early fifties." "I wonder if he voted for the man that affected him the way he commented, or was he like everyone else and blames the wrong party for his demise." "I later heard a candidate that was being asked a question." "The candidate said "and I quote" I don't care what the American people think, it's what I know." "They shut the mic off on him quickly." "I'd like to know what he knows that "We the People" don't know." "That makes me think that to him everyone is better off only knowing what he wants us to know." "He's got a seven point lead so when he's elected the people won't be getting someone that has, they're best interest in his mind." "Would it do any good to speak my mine and tell everyone what I know?" "No" "they would think that I'm in favor of his opponent and I'm just saying what I'm saying to try to get the people to vote for him." "It only takes one man to bring down an empire, so, I don't invest in individual businesses." "There's too many people involved with only one objective and that's to improve their chances of obtaining a monetary reward." "If I was to invest in technology" "then I would have to invest equally into those products that keep that new gadget that was intentionally designed with a flaw from crashing and being destroyed." "You buy one" "you have to buy the other." "Viruses are manmade so everyone will have to buy antivirus to keep their investment from being wiped out." "I don't invest in anything that any other investor can't invest in."

"I'm sorry Mister Bryant but that's all the time we have." She then turned and began ending with the monologue of what her show pertained to next week.

When everyone began walking around, I stood up.

"This way" Miss Phelps said. "Mister Bryant" "I'd like to extend to you the invitation to come back."

"I don't think I can do that." I responded. "Miss Phelps" "you can expect comments from some of the guests you'll have on in the future pertaining to my comments that was heard tonight and when you do" "you won't hear those comments quoted the way you heard them today." "It's nothing more than free air time for them." "Some of them you will ask questions that you want the people to hear and some of them you will ask different questions." "The only thing that matters to you is ratings Miss Phelps." "Trust me, you'll be rewarded by being replaced."

I felt a hand grasp my arm to lead me.

"Right this way sir." A man's voice said and soon I was reunited with the rest of my group.

"We've got an hour before dinner." Riley said as she ushered us into the limo.

We rode for a good way in the stop and go traffic.

"Are you sick?" Cheryl asked when we came to a stop.

I didn't answer and Ronnie continued. "Mister B" "Are you sick?"

"That's not an easy question to answer." "When Bailey and I met we were having a discussion and one of the first things I told Bailey was having a relationship with anyone was the furthest thing from my mind." I began "It was the truth" "I didn't want to hurt her, and I didn't want anything to do with anybody but not all things work out exactly the way you plan." "That telephone call I got from Richard earlier was a follow up on a legal matter that I'm involved in on Steven and Sarah's behalf." "And as for as me being sick, what you heard tonight happened a long time ago when I just turned twelve." "Professionals aren't considered to be criminal minded." "Richard was also calling to let me know that another boy was diagnosed with cancer." "I can't sit and wait for my next appointment." "I did that at my suite in New York." "I told him to get me and appointment." "Ronnie" "Cheryl" "I think you should get on the internet and look it up and read about it." "That way you can get a better understanding of what you want to know."

"How come you didn't say anything to us about it?" Becky asked.

"That's not an issue one brings up during a course of having a conversation." I answered her question, but it was meant for all to hear. "None of my staff even knew about it." "Becky at the time I didn't know anybody that close to me." I began. "Everything was all abuzz around Skinland when I arrived and we were all trying to get everything all sorted out and for the first time in three years, it wasn't involved in my thoughts, I forgot about it." "I used to wake up in my bed soaking wet from sweat in New York." "Since I moved to Skinland, not once have I dreamed about my visit to the doctor." "They kept recurring time and time again." "Becky" "when you get like that your mind can play tricks on you." "I told Bailey I don't carry a cell phone because people got my number." "That's true but I really got rid of it because in my dreams I hear a phone ringing and I know who it is." "Besides what was I supposed to do." "You don't walk up to someone and say hey" "you got some time to kill" "I got some things on my mind that haunt me and I can't find anyone to tell me how I'm supposed to work my way through it." "No psychologists can talk to you to make you feel better." "When I came here" "I gave up and I was ready to accept my fate." "I was tired and I was ready to stop fighting an unfightable foe." "That was before I met any of you" "I asked Bailey not to say anything." "Sarah was present too." "I asked them because I knew none of you would treat me the same as you treat me now." "There's a right and a wrong and it's a brother and sister to good and bad." "I thought I was doing the right thing at the time and I still think I did the right thing." "The problem is my secret isn't a secret anymore."

"Kurt" Elrod spoke "you told me that I need to stop living my everyday life, and start living life every day." "That stuck in my craw driving home." "I didn't understand any of that" "but I do now and I'm going to give you the same advice." "We're all going to be given news one day that we may not celebrate another birthday." "I wake up some mornings with a pain and I think to myself what if something's wrong with me."

"What's that supposed to mean?" Becky asked.

"Mister Bryant had a nervous breakdown." Steven said.

"Why do you say that?" I asked him.

"My father had one" "he took his life." He stated.

"You never said anything to me about that." Sarah retorted.

"I didn't know too much about it either" He began "I was in Korea at the time and flew home and people did a lot of talking about him." "I had trouble putting the pieces together and after listening to Mister Bryant today, I've learned there's only one person that can tell me the reason for why he done it."

"Who?" Sarah asked.

"My father" "but he's not around to tell me." Steven answered.

Riley intervened. "Mister Bryant" "I listened along with everyone else in the sound room and the answers you gave were nothing short of a man that's a genius."

"Riley" "Steven is right" I replied to her as if I was talking to them all. "I was having a nervous breakdown but not from anything other than suffering mental fatigue at the mercy of knowing what my outcome may turn out to be." "The doctor died before anyone knew anything about what he done." "He got away with doing what he was convinced in without suffering any penalty." "I believed myself to have been cheated and I left my life back in New York and wanted to start a new life without my old life that I was living." "I thought I found what I was looking for" "you know" "peace, quiet, and calm." "Then I got to thinking" "the institution I was raised in was peace, quiet and calm." "Now Elrod" I turned my attention to him "I read a book about poker and the only thing I got from the book was poker was a game that was played by people that didn't know how to play poker." "The object of the game was to be ahead in a race to win money." "A pair of pocket aces up against a pair of pocket deuces seems like a celebration is in store." "But" "the river turns another deuce and that pair of aces you thought was a victory ended up sending you out the door." "A pocket pair of kings makes you feel comfortable when you have an opponent that goes all in with you with a seven of clubs and a jack of diamonds." "There's a funny thing about poker" "three clubs can be dealt on a flop and another club can be dealt on the river and kill a pair of kings." "If you read the book" "you would know that poker is a game of luck." "There aren't any winners until the river card is turned over." "Life is a lot like the game of poker."

"What's that supposed to mean?" Bailey asked.

"In cards" "any hold cards on pre flop are winners" "skill has very little to do when up against luck" "luck will beat you every time." I answered her "If you look at life, you'll see that there's some days when nothing goes wrong, and on some days, you'll see that nothing goes right." I said "Elrod plays poker for entertainment and he's been beaten every which way a man can be beaten." "He knows what I'm talking about but he still gets angry because the man who called him didn't have anything to call with" "but he won." "That's when he should have gotten up from the table and went home." "He was given an omen of what his future held for him that night."

"You're talking in riddles." Becky commented.

"No" Elrod spoke up. "I understood everything he was saying." "If you played poker, you'd know what he's talking about."

"We're here sir." Riley said.

When I stepped out of the limo Bailey was on one arm and Sarah was on the other.

The kids became excited listening to a piano player and watching girls swinging as high as they could to kick a bell for a small fee."

"You didn't eat very much." Bailey commented.

"I didn't have much of an appetite." I told her as she pulled the covers over us.

"Kurt" she began "you can will yourself sick you know." "People that have hypochondria think that every time they sneeze, they need to go to the doctor." "What good is it going to do to run your tests and three months later you'll want to run another test?" "You keep acting like knowing you have something is better than knowing you don't have something."

I took a deep breath. "When I was walking from the car and you came running up to me to stop me." "I told you that you didn't know anything about me." "Your reply was that I didn't know anything about you." "A relationship isn't supposed to begin and end only after a few years." "I told you I'd apologize to you after we were still together after fifty years."

"You remember that?" She asked.

"Bailey" "when I told you I was the last of the line I didn't have anyone to leave what my family worked to get." "I'm giving you the house and you'll never have to worry about the price of gasoline again."

"I told you I wasn't a gold digger when I met you." She replied. "It was my dream but if you're not there with me" "it wouldn't be my dream anymore." "I wouldn't ever set foot in it again."

"Well anyway" I continued "I don't think I'm going to have fifty years" "I lied to you."

"Kurt, you said that those other boys had six treatments" she replied "and you said you only had two." "There's hope and where there's hope then that's something." "I think you made quite an impression on the kids tonight." She commented changing the subject.

"When you were young were there certain foods you didn't like even though you never tasted it before? I asked.

"Spinach" she replied.

"Do you eat it now?" I asked.

"You're going somewhere with this aren't you?" She said to me.

"Music changes every generation and the music most people listened to when they were young is still listened to as they get older." "Dead artists are worth more now than what they were worth when they were at the top of their career." "Today they can digitally blend in fathers and daughter's singing a duet together even though her father had been dead for twenty years." "I was listening to music that claimed to be the new generation." "I must be getting old." "I didn't hear one instrument" "everything was computerized and synchronized to give the sounds they wanted." "You said that none of you have ever attended a symphony" "music is appreciated only if it captures the listener." "Back home country music is the only station they have so a little change might do them good." I responded to her. "Besides" "debutantes need to experience what debutantes do."

"You're starting to talk like dying again." Bailey commented. "Stop it."

"Bailey" "if I don't have a will" "the government seizes everything I own and sells it."

"Stop it Kurt" She put her lips on mine to silence me.

CHAPTER TWELVE

We sat in our seats preparing for liftoff.

"Has anyone given any thought to how many people we're looking at?" I asked.

I heard silence and after a few moments I began explaining my actions.

"One of the reasons I want to hold a prom at my estate is because it'll help to put an end to any kind of rumors that pertain to a fabricated conversation."

"English Kurt" Becky commented.

"They'll be city officials, county officials, school officials, and a few Judges too." I reflected "They'll be a lot of hand shaking and even a few remarks directed between adversaries but on the most part" "chivalry will prevail." "I mentioned lobsters at the auditorium" "how many pounds do we need? I asked and again there were silence. "Does anyone have a pad and pencil?" I asked.

"I do sir" Steven replied.

"Get on the internet and see if you can find anyone that can deliver us five hundred one pound live lobsters by Friday." "You may have to visit several sights." I stated.

"Yes sir"

"We need five hundred pounds of cooked king crabs and I need to see if that can be delivered by Friday also." "Two hundred pounds of fresh filleted salmon with pin bones removed and ten whole loins of rib byes."

"Becky, I need you to search for diabetic foods and order some and also foods that are gluten free."

"Kurt" "that's a lot of food." Becky stated.

"Good publicity puts an end to bad publicity, and right now everyone needs a little good said about them instead of all the negative things everyone says." I replied. "All of you have had things said about you that wasn't true" "sometimes the best remedy for those kinds of statements is to let other people that think of you a different way protests a statement with their own version."

"I'm beginning to believe Riley was right." Patricia commented "you are a genius."

"Patricia" "everyone needs a reason to do what they do." "Some are activists fighting a company that wants to destroy the habitat of a frog that's on the endangered species list and they do that because it means that much to them, and some people find their mission in life is to protest whatever it is they find that offends them." "That's their right as an American" "take away those rights and soon other rights will be taken away also." "Progress has taken away a lot of our rights we once had when the Constitution was signed" "take a look and you'll see how many amendments have been made since seventeen seventy six and you may find in the next few years, they'll be a couple more amendments added." "I'm not an activist" "but I do find myself preoccupied in my battles." I replied.

"Like what kind of battles?" She asked as we taxied down the runway.

"Money is power and some people are never satisfied with the power they have." "It's like Elrod and his gambling; that's why they call it poker" I said "he's happy when he wins and he gets upset when he gets beat on a hand he was supposed to win with." "You look and you see that you're the high man on the board and you've got good spirits, that gives you an indication that you're going to win, because you feel you've got the lead in a race" "after all your opponent checked on every hand" "you go all in thinking confidently and the next thing you know you were beaten by a man that played you for a fool." "You can't blame his opponent" "all he did was check and had he have checked too" "he wouldn't be out of the game, but he went all in so who do you blame?" "I deal with people that have money and to them a battle is nothing more than playing a game of poker and in the game of poker a bluff wins you a lot of money when your opponent can't call." "I don't bluff when I play." "When I have the best hand on the flop" "I'm going all in" "if anyone wants to gamble, I'm going to make them pay for the cards they get."

"I didn't understand any of that." Patricia said.

"I did" Elrod commented "He was talking to me."

After we took off Becky asked if she could trade seats with Bailey.

She kept her voice down low.

"Becky there's something I've been wanting to talk to you about." I said to her.

"Me too." She answered. "You want to go first?" She asked.

"I've noticed a lot of the media's attention has been slacking lately and that gives me thoughts about you and Buck is thinking about going back home."

"We were going to wait till after the prom." She replied to me.

"Becky" "I need a staff with me twenty four hours out of the day." "Bailey told me that when I asked her if she could work for me." "She said with what I wanted; a wife couldn't give me all that I asked for." "I don't know if you're happy about going home or if you feel like it's time to move on." "I do hear a lot of laughter from your kids and that gives me a feeling that there's enjoyment among everyone."

Paradox

"English Kurt" She commented.

"When was the last time you went home?" I asked her.

"I haven't been home since we came here." She expressed.

"When you and Buck have a talk, I'd like for you to tell him that it wouldn't be the same around here not being able to listen to his way of dealing with the problems everyone faces today." "And you, you're up and cooking at five in the morning." "I can smell your biscuits a mile away and you seem to know my habits too" "My cocoa is always hot and it seems like it never has to be reheated."

"How do you know I'm up at five?" She asked.

"I don't have a glass covering the hands on the clock." "Becky" "When we were riding in the limo, I told everyone some of the innermost secrecy's I had." "Did I want them to become public?" "No" "but since they did, I'm faced with a life that's filled with uncertainty and I've been dealing with that problem since I was told about the experiments Doctor Savidge performed." "I never had a close relationship with anyone" "and one of the reasons became public yesterday and now I'm being faced with a lot of questions that I don't know how I can answer them." "That brings me to Ronnie, Julie and Cindy." "They've gotten a taste of what it feels like to live a life differently than the life they lived." "Do you think anyone of them would be satisfied working as a cashier at Barney's grocery store now?" "Becky" "In Skinland" everyone wants to grow up to be something that isn't around there and the odds are they'll wind up like Riley" "chasing a dream."

"What are you getting at Kurt?" She asked.

"Becky" "You'll never be able to call that place you lived in home anymore" "Your life you once lived isn't the life you'll live again." "We've all become a family and if y'all go back to living like you used to, it won't be the same." "I never had a family and with all of you, I feel as if I have one."

"What are you saying? She asked again.

"I like the arrangement we have now." I said "I know it's not your home, but to the kids they think of it as theirs." "I'm just saying I wish you would think about staying a little longer and if everything works out to your liking, I'd like for all of you to stay here."

"I don't know Kurt."

"I'm just saying I want you to think about it." I commented.

"What about Sarah and Steven?" She asked.

"Steven is Steven and Sarah wants him to be a little more of a thrill seeker but what she got was a man that only knew how to serve others." "Strange thing about love, sometimes you settle for less than what you bargained for." "When you married Buck" "did you ever think he would be successful?" I asked.

"No" "Buck is a little behind when it comes to making decisions." She commented.

"So, you knew what you were going to get when you married him huh?" I stated.

"I didn't care" "Buck never treated anyone with any kind of anger unless he didn't have a choice not to and even then, he tried to calm the situation down." "He wasn't a hell raiser like my momma said he was."

"Becky" I began "two people can't stay married and not have fights" "I know" "I get new customers everyday wanting to file for a divorce." "I defend the plaintiff and I defend the defendant" "either way I make money from two people having a fight." "But none of that is going to do me any good." "I don't have an heir and if I die without a will" "the government gets every penny that all of my ancestors worked for." "I want to teach your children how to live as wealthy people" "I want to teach them to expect the unexpected."

"What are you saying Kurt?" She repeated again.

"My biggest problem turned out to be confidence; I don't have an optimistic view of my future as having length to it."

"English Kurt" she commented.

"I lied to her Becky." I told her. "I didn't tell her everything I should have and I still can't find a way to tell Bailey what she meant to me."

"Kurt" "when I used to go to church, I didn't really get a lot from it." "I prayed and I prayed and I prayed some more but it didn't seem like I was getting any answers but I never gave up praying that everything would get better." "The truth is we all may crash before we got home." "Do you know the reason I love you so much?" She asked.

I kept my silence.

"Kurt" "You've got control over everything you do in your life." "Instead of thinking about yourself I find you to be more concerned with what's going to happen to everyone when you're not here to take matters into your own hands." "And when someone crosses you, you let them know when you're unhappy" "but the odd thing is" "when you talk to people" "you don't pull punches, and everything I've heard you say to everyone I was with when you were upset, you were honest and said the truth." "I got to thinking one day about me going to church and praying." "I lost faith, but you came along and all my prayers were answered."

"That's why people say I'm not politically correct." I responded "I don't like calling anyone a liar but I will." "Becky" "A man can say anything he wants to say about anyone, but he better be right when he does and have the fact to back it up." "I'm not very good at putting puzzles together and when it comes to art" "the only thing I'd be good at is taking a can of paint and throwing it on the canvas and hope I hit the canvas" "if not then I'll have to have the room repainted or turn it into a room of collected arts." "When I took over my father's firm, I reinvested my father's investments and my own." "People called me crazy, a fool, and idiot and a young lunatic set out to destroy a corporation, that wasn't investors that said that, that was my own people talking about me behind my back." "Richard told me that." "I'm lucky" "because I'm blind doesn't mean that I can't focus on how words are stated and when I hear those words, I can tell whether I'm being told something other than the truth." "My investments grew and those that claimed me to be a lunatic began talking about me with a different point of view." "They were discharged like I'm going to discharge Mister Laree" "all they were doing was coming to the office to drink coffee and flirt with the secretaries." "Becky" "Some people have a hobby and some people exercise to relax and unwind." "I couldn't do that" "and that's why I withdrew to my apartment." "I need help Becky or I wouldn't be asking you for it" "and your family gives me the help I need."

"I don't know Kurt" she replied.

"I was only offering the invitation in case you find that your home doesn't feel like your home anymore and I thought you could talk to Buck about what we discussed." "Now" "would you ask Elrod if I could talk to him?"

I soon felt him sitting next to me. "You said you're not an optimist when we talked one time." "Why" I asked.

"When I first started out in my business I couldn't keep up with offers" he began "I kept all of my records and I looked at them when I got home when you and I had our little chat when we first met." "I paid good money to listen to men that claimed they could help me make money by eliminating my overhead cost." "I stopped going to those kinds of seminars." "They didn't seem to do me much good, all it did was I was able to claim it on my taxes." "When Cheryl got hurt" "I couldn't do my business anymore and I settled for a lot less than what I wanted, but the man who bought me out ended up going bankrupt, so I did the right thing." "Why do you ask?"

"I told you a pessimist invests in gold." "Every year there's always a football player or basketball player or whatever getting a record contract." "Gold is the same" "it doesn't matter what the cost is" "if my baby wants it" "then my baby has got to have it." "Did you put any thought into my advice?" I asked him.

"After hearing that lady say you made five hundred percent profit in three years, I called and told them I wanted everything I had put in gold." He commented.

"What'd you get it for?" I asked him.

"Four hundred and sixty eight dollars an ounce." He replied.

"Elrod" "I got it for four hundred and twenty two dollars an ounce and I expect it to go a lot higher than that." I chuckled. "The strange thing I find is that you did that not knowing whether I was right in my beliefs or if I was wrong?" "That's a gamble most men don't take." I stated.

"What is it that you see?" He asked.

"Ah Elrod" "That's a question that no one asks a fool." I chuckled

"Kurt" "I'm not talking to a fool." "I found that out when I first met you." He answered.

I paused "The middle class supports the lower class and the upper class." I began "From what I see, the middle class is going to be affected the most in the next administration and a large part of it will be eliminated." "They aren't needed" "overseas labor can be gotten for one tenth of the cost then what it can be gotten here." "No vacations, no sick leave, no maternity leave, and no holiday pay." "You die and someone will replace you before you're hauled off." "In other countries they don't have EPA to bother them and they don't have OSHA and they don't have safety standards to worry about, or Unions to contend with." "Someone gets killed and there aren't any lawsuits." "Is that bad business or good sense?" I asked. "Budgets will come under strict scrutiny and monies will be transferred from departments that will be eliminated in order to strengthen security." "Elrod if you look in the past, you'll see that all the empires that failed, failed because money was spent that they didn't have."

"I'm listening." He stated.

"A country without a middle class is a third world country." "You have the rich and you have the poor."

"You honestly think that's going to happen?" He asked.

"Elrod" "the Federal Government is the largest Union, no one can be fired, they can only be rehabilitated." "They removed the Postal Service from the government jurisdiction for wanting to unionize." "Private sectors are being bought out by foreign investors." "All profits from these foreign investors end up going out of the country and it's not being spent here." "You ran a business" "tell me something" "you said when you sold, the person that bought your business filed for bankruptcy." "If you hadn't have sold out, would you have had to file for bankruptcy." "And Elrod why is it everyone wants a machine gun to protect their family." "In the Constitution, it was written that everyone had a right to bear arms, they had muskets back then." "Today, children carry guns to school that can kill dozens of people with a pistol that holds a clip that contains a magazine of one hundred rounds and slip in another magazine and kill more." "Do they execute them, no." "No politician wants to take on gun control, we have too many politicians taking money from lobbyist not to." "That means that mass shootings will only get worse, and guns will be able to carry more bullets to be fired." "That's what progress means today." "But there's something else I wanted to talk to you about." "I want to work with Cheryl." I said to him.

"Come again." He replied.

"Cheryl's been studying poetry and she wants to be a songwriter."

"What" He quickly reacted?

"She's been working on trying to put the words she wants to say in a song." "She listens to music and changes the lyrics." "That might be her way of trying to say the things she wants to say but she can't." "She has problems when she thinks and a distraction causes her to shift her attention elsewhere." "Sometimes when I had to give a speech to my staff in New York I listened to a symphony like the one we heard last night." "As I listened to the music, I didn't seem to have the problem I had trying to bring out what I wanted to say without sounding overbearing." "But you have your problems there too." "Anyway" "I think if I can work with her a little bit, she'll learn what I learned and if it helps her like it did me" "then we may find our way in and bring out what's inside of her." "She has feelings too." "Bailey told me Cheryl and Ronnie were holding hands" "how do you feel about that Elrod?" I asked.

"I'm her father" he commented.

"Yeah" "and as her father you know you can't say anything about it either." I chuckled.

"My baby's growing up." He commented.

"Isn't that what you wanted; a daughter that would grow up and marry a good man and give you grandbabies to babysit."

"Whoa" "we're not there yet." He stated.

"Elrod" "this is one of those times where you've got nothing to lose if I'm wrong and you've got everything to gain if I'm right." "Becky had Ronnie at seventeen, how old was Patricia when she had Cheryl?"

"I never knew she did any of that." He commented ignoring my question about the age Patricia when she had Cheryl.

"My hearing is a little better than yours." I replied. "Sometimes when people have things on their minds they don't listen to the sounds of the world." "They're preoccupied."

"What do you want me to do?" He asked.

"When you want to get something across to someone you can't just come right out and say this is what we're going to do." "You'll find that you'll receive rejection immediately and no one's even heard a word you've said about what you intend on doing." "Sometimes the best approach is using small subtleties to make a point." "I don't want anyone around me when I talk to Cheryl and if that's going to be an issue with you then we're once again at a point where we might not have the same belief." I stated.

"Can I ask you why?" He questioned.

I took a deep breath and exhaled. "Cheryl knows she has difficulties and she also knows a lot more than what you think she does." "Her problem is by the time she can begin a conversation; her attention gets diverted; that's why I think she wants to be a song writer and if she does" "I'm going to give her all she needs to be who she wants to be." "Who knows" "she may change her mind and want to be something else, but from what I understand" "that's what all women have a right to do." "Elrod your daughter is slow to answer but if you give her time, she'll give you an answer." "Cheryl's quiet" "that's because she can't process her answers before another obstacle comes up, she loses her focus." "That's one reason why Ronnie's good for her, he listens to her, it's a one on one conversation like me and you are having now." "I'm going to have some benches built out by my pond and her and I will spend some time talking about catfish and well "Elrod" I'm hoping she'll accept me as someone she can go to whenever she needs someone." "Ronnie's there for her now" "but sometimes Ronnie can't answer all of the questions she has." "It's a lot like me and you." "You can always come to me and we'll sit out by the pond and cast a few lines and who knows things might get said and there might be answers to questions that weren't even asked."

"Kurt, I found out they're not going to repair the gym." He stated. "They're going to combine two schools and shut the one in Skinland down."

"How far away is the other school?" I asked.

"About thirty miles." He responded.

I held my silence.

"Are you okay?" He asked.

"Is the school where they're going to, big enough to handle the extra kids or are they going to have to expand it?" I mentioned.

"Why?"

"Elrod sometimes decisions are made because someone owns a business in another city and that business prospers from a decision like shutting down a school." I stated.

"What do you mean?" He asked.

"Elrod someone could be receiving a bribe." "If you think about it, you'd find that if they have to improve the other school" "why not improve this school and shut the other one down." "Public officials have relatives that do business with other businesses, that's nepotism." "I'm not saying that's happening here" I stated "but I've learned from past experience that it's a way of saying if you don't scratch my back then you'll not get another contract." "It's nothing more than strong arm tactics but if you look deep enough, you'll find that somewhere along the line" "there's always favoritism being shown in some form or fashion to every contractor that's being contracted by the government." "That's government and you and I and anyone else that comes in and thinks he's going to change the way things are done to make it better had better be ready to retire." "The first rule of Congress is you don't make changes in a law that affects you" "That's another unwritten rule." "If you remember Brutus stabbed Caesar too."

"I never thought about that." He replied.

"Elrod there's one thing about people that we've all got in common, whatever it is you can think of, someone else has already thought of it before you did." "I can tell you another thing too" "you won't need any of those resale shops or Barneys or any of those gas stations, or those banks" "oh yeah and the realtors too." "Skinland will die without the school." "All Skinland has is city, county, state, and federal employees." "And if you shut down the school, you won't need any city, county, state or federal employees." "They won't be needed because they've already got people at the other city that do that job." "I asked you if you were a pessimist" "do you think any of those offices they leave vacated will be used for anything?"

I heard him as he exhaled. "I never thought of that." He commented.

"Elrod" "money is always a major deciding force when making a decision." "Skinland is dependent on tourism but with the lake being low" "traffic has slowed." "You take away the school and when you find yourself in need of a loaf of bread" "you'll have to drive fifty miles to get it." "What do you think it'll do to your taxes?" "You may find it cheaper to move into Murray" "they've got plenty of taxpayers there." "But you may find that it may be a little difficult to sell your property here." "The real kicker is Elrod" "all of the city and county councils will end up approving themselves a nice raise and retire and have a better retirement." "That's all that happens when budgets can't be filled and departments are done away with."

"You used an analogy on me earlier" he commented "you know playing poker and you said something that really put everything I thought in the right prospective but I done forgot about what you said." He commented.

"Elrod" "I'm blind but that doesn't mean I can't read people." "I said that poker is a game that's played by people that don't know how to play poker." "Everyone that knows anything about playing the game knows that you don't gamble when you're behind in a race unless you're trying to pull off a bluff." "Gamblers are a rare breed and some of them think their good because they got lucky on the river and busted his opponent." "But it happens, and that's why I say that poker is a game that's played by people that don't know how to play poker." "Skill is good to have but on any given hand, luck can beat skill and if you notice the gamblers always seem to leave the table early." "In a business" "you meet people every day and all of them are doing their level best to play a hand with you only they're not doing it for pleasure, that's where I come in." "I've never played a hand in poker so, to me my game is those that want to prosper from me." "I made that taping for only one reason and that was to tell everyone that was listening that if they saw a picture of me with a candidate or heard my name mentioned along with one, then they were using propaganda, and Elrod, every party has members in their party that uses propaganda." "When someone knows something that's printed or used intentionally to make it look like their opponent is actually doing the exact opposite of what they say they're doing, is an act to deceive the public, and that's the viewer." "That's an evil word" "propaganda" "it used to refer to being used by the communist" "today it covers socialism" "but none the less that form of communication is being used by both parties here, today, just about every speech I've heard up to now, a fact was misquoted in the news medias, but you never hear the word propaganda stated by either party." "It's always stated as erroneous or overly creative in expressing a statement that was totally false." "Like in politics." "You can't call a politician a liar without suffering some form of retribution from politicians. It's a word that's forbidden." "That way they can protect themselves." "It doesn't matter, voters only listen to the man they like." "Elrod" "I kept to myself mostly." "But lately that's changed and now it's beginning to taper off and one day all of this attention will be gone and then boom, the next thing you know in two years" "they're all back out there like they were when we came home." "I told Buck the best way to handle it, was to ignore it, and keep on walking." "If you stop, they've succeeded in doing what they set out to do." "Now" "I mentioned Cheryl" "if I was her father, I would tell her that the things I thought were important aren't important to me anymore" "and whatever happens next week doesn't mean anything to you." "Elrod, she doesn't need the pressure of pleasing you on her mind" "she's got enough to deal with." "You've got to tell her that" "you have to be the one to break the ice." I stated.

The pilot came on the intercom and said we'd be landing in thirty minutes and I soon felt Bailey sitting next to me.

"Is everything all right?" She asked.

"I just got information that their closing the school down and moving the kids to another school." I commented.

"I know" she replied "Ronnie just told me."

"Did he say anything about how he felt about it?" I asked.

"He just said that everyone was talking about it at school." She answered. "Elrod didn't look happy when he left" "did you say something to him?"

"No" "I just told him that when the school closes" "Skinland will lose all of its government workers and with the loss of that kind of revenue" "Skinland will die." "Nothing bothers you until you can see what would happen if that came to pass and Elrod got a good picture of what I was trying to explain to him when I told him what I thought." "Bailey, that's what I moved here for." "I didn't want things to change."

"We had a good time Kurt" "everyone wanted me to let you know that they enjoyed themselves." She said to me.

"That's not true" "Buck didn't." I commented.

"How do you know that?" She stated.

"He couldn't get comfortable in his seat and I kept feeling him changing positions and when I heard Becky whisper to him to sit still" "I knew he wasn't liking it."

"Kurt" "If it isn't country music" "Buck don't care for it." "Buck said something about they're talking about building a pipeline to pump water out of the lake to a city." She reported.

I took a deep breath and exhaled.

"What's the matter Kurt?" She asked.

"Bailey I just got through telling Elrod with the drought the lake level has kept the fishermen away." "The lake is a hydroelectric reservoir that's controlled by the river authority and they can pump all the water they want to make electricity until the lake level drops to a point where they can't generate" "and then the revenue from the electricity the turbines produce is lost until the lake level once again reaches a level to where they can once again generate." "A pipeline from a major city would take more water from a reservoir than what they release to generate electricity." "The people aren't ever told the true amount" "One million gallons an hour doesn't sound as bad as ten million does." "A city of a major size requires a major portion of water for business purposes." "No water" "no businesses and no taxes." "That means no lake and if that happens, I can guarantee you that nothing was in the contract regarding regulations to stop them from pumping all they need." "Hey" "those rose bushes need love too." "Now let's talk about downstream of the reservoir, they'll be affected too." I said "People downstream need water for irrigation of crops and businesses that depend on that water supply too and with no water in the lake, that means no businesses downstream will be able to operate and crops will be wiped out along with all the residents that that water supplies to them." "Another commodity comes under pressure and due to a shortage, prices increase." "Anomalies of nature occur every so often" "much like the drought we're having" "and then you have to ask yourself how long is it going to last." "If a pipeline was in place right now the lake would be a lot lower than what it is." "That's a fact." "If they're successful in being able to run a pipeline" "you will one day see this lake without water." "That means that this lake will be useless and they'll be looking for another water supply and that means no more turbines to generate electricity will be needed also." "If they do this, they're blinder what I am." "There's more voters in the city that's running the pipeline than what they have here." "Who do you think the Governor is going to listen to if that lake level is threatened and the water needs to be cut off?"

CHAPTER THIRTEEN

"Everyone's starting to set up tents and bringing in their cookers." Buck said as he handed me a cup of cocoa.

"How about the salmon and." He stopped me.

"Kurt" "The lobsters are here and the king crab is in the refrigerator and I personally picked up a dozen rib roast in the butcher shop where I worked at in Murray." "Becky's got everything going the way Becky wants it to go." "I found out a long time ago not to get in her way when she's got her mind on something." "You know me and you didn't really have us a good talk except at the pond." "You know I had my opinion of you too, but after I got to know you" "I felt ashamed."

"Buck" "that's human nature" "I'm suspicious of everyone I meet." I began. "The real truth to life is you never really can put your total trust in someone." "Or so I believed." "That was my views because those were the people I was dealing with in New York and to tell you the truth, there's not many in Skinland I trust either." "How many people do you think is going to show up tomorrow?" I asked.

"I don't know." He replied.

"Okay then" "do you think I ordered too much food?" I once again asked my question.

"Yeah" "Me and Elrod both." He commented.

"Bailey told me that people would line up for a handout." I opened "When we went to the school and talked to the kids and the staffs and I told them I needed help." "You can see the help setting everything up." "Tonight, will be a night of preparation by everyone." "Kids date kids from other schools and word gets out by someone talking to someone else and the next thing you know" "you've got people that show up because everyone else will think that they were invited." "That's okay" "that's why I ordered as much food as I did." "You heard what I face and I have to look at things realistically." "What I do is going to depend on what everyone agrees on and that's not going to be an easy job."

"What is it?" He asked.

"I can't say" I commented. "I need you to tell everyone to be prepared and when Cheryl and Ronnie get here, I need you to tell Cheryl that I need to talk to her."

"Alright" "Kurt don't you be worrying none, everything is going to work out fine." He said to me. "This isn't Becky's first rodeo" "she did all this for Doctor Wilcox."

"I can't help it" I told him.

"Richard wants to talk to you." Bailey said walking into the room.

"Hello" "what's his number?" I questioned him. "What time?" "I'll be there." I paused for a moment and listened. "I'll be waiting" I said and then hung up.

"I have an appointment with my doctor Tuesday at four in Maryland." I said to them all "My scheduler "Arlen Pith" was found dead this morning." "The FBI has a man in custody" "he's a hit man and so far, they believe he was killed to silence him." I said as I began calling the number he gave me, and when I stuck the phone to my ear I waited and was about to hang up.

"Mister Shelton please." I stated.

"That's me" he answered.

"Mister Shelton my name is Kurt Bryant." "I was told that you wanted to talk to me." I listened and then gave a comment of my own. "I'm sorry I must have dialed the wrong number" I commented "I don't have time to sit here and be insulted by an individual Shelton" "you want to make this a personal matter I'll be more than happy to accommodate you." "I've got a class action waiting to be filed when I hang up, I'm going to cost your corporation a Billion before I'm through in bad publicity." "You're going down and I can guarantee you, you're going to be losing a lot of money." "You either lose that attitude of yours, or you'll find I don't do business with people that has one, nothing gets accomplished." "I'll see you in court Shelton."

I paused and waited for a while to listen to him and when he finished, I began. "Your lawyers were sent a tape showing the time of four minutes and thirty eight seconds before security came and provided their services that they should have been providing as soon as I arrived." "Shelton you and I both know the manager knew I was coming and when I was supposed to be there." "He received a bonus of millions last year, so therefore you knew beforehand about his actions." "I'm going to contact every member of your organization past and present and I'm going to find out if any of them were ordered to notify the manager of the actions of your guest, I won't have any trouble there, fired employees have contempt for the people that fire them." "Shelton" "I've got over a dozen clients that got a divorce because they were with a private party" "your manager knew about me so he also knew about them." "I'm going to contact them and let them know what you did to me and tell them that you did the same to them." "You're going to be fighting a lot of legal battles and I can guarantee you that your corporation is going be filing for bankruptcy when I'm through with you." "We're talking years, Shelton."

I paused for another moment and listened and like before I began my conversation. "A hundred isn't anything to me" I said "and it isn't anything to you either" "especially when I get through with you." "You've turned this negotiation into a principal Shelton." "Besides the money isn't for me" "a man was fired by your manager because he refused to divulge information that pertained to me and my guest." "I asked him for help and he gave it to me and for that" "he was fired." "Your manager pissed me off Shelton and as far as I'm concerned" "you're the one that's going to pay for the manager that pissed me off because I know you're involved also." "See you in court buddy." I said with animosity and once again began listening to Mister Shelton. "Are you proposing in making an offer I responded?" "I'm willing to entertain a conversation, but if you insult me, I'm hanging up." And once again I listened. "That's a little low and you know it but you're beginning to catch my ear." I then listened again and responded. "I want this matter taken care of immediately." I said to him. "I'll contact Richard and he'll contact you and set up the meeting." "Yes sir" "it's been a pleasure doing business with you too." "You have a nice day." I commented and then hung up. I heard silence. "Steven's getting fifty million."

"You don't play when you talk to people Kurt." Buck said.

"Buck when you got mad at those reporters" I began "you were releasing your frustration against their being pushy." "I can't do that" "I only have one way to fight and that's with my brain." "Before I was twelve, I was treated like I didn't have one, I was a patient and that's all." "No one is going to treat me like those people treated me again and that man I was talking to was treating me that way." "Had he of talked to me in a civil tongue" "I wouldn't have remarked unkindly the way I did, but he was offensive and I countered his punch with my own." "When you deal with legal arguments and have fact to back it up" "you don't really have arguments" "you just have someone that's frustrated wanting to vent a verbal comment." "Once he realized I wasn't someone that was afraid of him he went back to doing business." "When I had a talk with Elrod on the ride home last night" "I spoke to him in a way where he could understand my meaning." "He's a competitor in all that he does so, I knew he had to know the game of poker." "I hope he never enters any big money tournaments" "he lacks the knowledge that in poker you play the man and not your hand." "Mister Shelton doesn't want this type of publicity to surface." "He knew it and I knew it and he was playing a hand he was dealt" "that's all." "He made a bid and folded when I raised."

"Where is Steven at anyway?" I asked.

"Him and Sarah are out talking to the cooking teams." Buck began "Down here we boil crawfish so we figured the best way to do this was do it the way we boil the crawfish." "A little potatoes and onions and add a little corn on the cob and a few links of sausage." "So, they're out there checking out the way we do things down here." "Kurt" "you ought to hear what the people are saying about you."

"Good or bad?" I asked.

"Elrod told them what you said about what would happen when the school shuts down." He commented.

"What do you think about it Buck?" I asked him.

"Me and Becky grew up here and we worked in Murray." "It was the only place we could find a job." "By the time we paid for our traveling expenses we made a lot less." "We did that though because we didn't want to move to Murray" "we liked it here and we stayed here" "even if we did have to work in Murray." "I agree with you" "this town's not going to make it." He stated. "People have to work in Murray now will move to where they won't have to get up at five in the morning to get their kids off to school."

"Buck" I began "when a decision is made to close a school it isn't made overnight, or a month ago." "It was made when budgets began having shortfalls." "The school that they'll be bussed too was probably located in a better performing tax based atmosphere and the decision to close a school down was introduced and that's probably when the school that the kids go here started to not receive the funding they needed." "It was kept under wraps to keep the people from panicking like they are now." "Had they had said anything to that affect" "Skinland would have felt the impact and you would have seen Barney's close their doors so they keep things secret for a purpose." "I can bet you that none of the officials can be reached." "Whenever something that causes a reaction like the school closing, they find that the best place to be is anywhere other than where they're at so, they take a vacation and let their public relations handle all the gripes and complaints."

"Kurt" "they've got Barney's up for sale." Buck stated.

I took a deep breath and exhaled.

"What's everyone talking about?" I heard Sarah state when she walked into the room.

"Kurt just got off the phone with Mister Shelton." Bailey said.

"You mean "CEO" of "Morton's Enterprises" "Shelton"?" Sarah said.

"We had us a little discussion Sarah, and there was a positive outcome." I stated to her.

I heard silence.

"Steven, we settled on fifty million." "Of course, my firm gets one third since this matter was settled out of court." I stated.

"Fifty million dollars?" Sarah commented ignoring my statement.

"You got what you wanted Sarah, a man that achieved success." "Be careful how you spend it" "you don't spend money that isn't in your hands yet."

"That's what you said when you told us when we were going to New York" Bailey stated.

"You mean you got me that money because they fired me?" Steven asked.

"Steven one day you and I'll have a talk and we'll discuss matters that you might want to hear about why your father had a breakdown." "It's not hard to happen" "a man can only take so much and that statement also applies to a woman." "I got you that money because they used me and I don't like anybody using me." "I was in a position to where I was dealing with an irate individual or I would have settled for half of that." "You asked if I got you that money because they fired you." "Yes" "I did" "you knew me and you didn't take advantage of me when you could have." "That said a lot about you and a person like that can't be bought at any price, that's why Richard is where he's at." "Sarah said you catered to a Colonel while you were in the service and you ended up in Korea with him." "That was for a purpose" "you don't hear anything except what you want to hear and what you do hear you don't repeat it to others, so the Colonel put his trust in you and that's how you ended up with him."

"You mentioned my father." He said to me.

I hesitated before I answered. "You know I can't give you an answer to that but I'll speak for me." "My father didn't have very much to do with me and that's a torch that I have to live with" "he had his life and I had mine and they didn't seem to cross paths that much." I began "I didn't know anything about my mother except that my father met her at college, so I don't know if my father really wanted a kid or if a kid just happened to come along." We never really talked, so I was left with a lot of questions that didn't have answers and with twenty five years in the institution; I didn't have any way of researching to find out about her, and time erodes memories." "Everybody is somebody to somebody Steven, or so we believe." "In my father's profession it didn't matter which side was represented, you have a plaintiff and you have a defendant." "In the end, my father made money from representing both sides of the divorce and disputes were settled either out of court or in court so, my father and I were a distant relative, like I said, he had his life to live." "One thing I learned about divorces is wealthy men aren't very smart." "Steven" "do you know what one act causes seventy two percent of all the cases my firm handles pertain to?" I asked him.

"No sir." He replied.
"A smile" I answered.
"Sir"
"He's talking about a gold digger Steven." Bailey answered for me. "He used that same kind of talk on me and now he's using it on you."
"I don't understand." He stated.
"Steven" Bailey began "there's something that he's not telling you and I know what it is."
"Are you going to tell me?" He asked her.
"No"
"Mister Bryant?" He said to me wanting to know what Bailey was talking about.
"Money does things to people Steven" I responded "Sarah this pertains to you." "If someone knows you have money, they treat you differently and some are successful at achieving a goal they set out to do, seventy two percent of them to be exact." "Less than thirty percent of all couples that get married end up staying married, so the chances of you and Sarah staying married has decreased to less than eight percent because when you get that money, your marriage will turn into a different marriage than the one you had before you had the money."
"You keep talking like I want divorce." Sarah stated.
"It takes two Sarah" I said "It doesn't matter which one causes the divorce" "it all started over a little ripple in the water and escalated into a bigger wave and from it, a tsunami developed, that's when they came and saw my father." "It takes two."
"You're going to have to explain yourself" "I'm not following you." She stated.
"Buck" "you and Becky's been married for seventeen years and you went with Becky before that" "did you and her have arguments and fights during your relationship?" I asked
"OH YEAH" "And we still have our moments." He replied laughing.
"Bailey" "When you and Tom were together did you and him fight?" I asked her.
"A lot of times." She replied.
"What are you getting at Kurt?" Sarah asked.
"People don't get divorces because they're happy." "They only get divorced because they can't live with one another, and that's where money comes in." "Money makes people tired of arguing and fighting and it plays a big role in deciding to end a relationship between two individuals who

can't find a way to stop their arguing and fighting." "You two have split up once already, so you know what I'm saying." "Sarah" "the reason people get divorced is because two people aren't in love anymore, if they were, they wouldn't be getting a divorce in the first place."

"So, what's your point?" She asked.

I smiled "Sarah" Bailey interrupted. "Kurt bought me my car and on the way back home, he told me that if we were still together after fifty years, he would apologize to me for not being the person he thought I was." "You have to know everything that led up to that point but what he's telling you is you won't know those answers until you reach an age where you can say we made it this far, and I want it to go a lot further."

"Well quit talking like I want a divorce." She said sternly. "I know I'm bossy but I'm working on it."

"The kids are home" Buck said.

"Good" "I need to talk to Cheryl." I stated.

I was holding onto her arm as she was pushing a wheelbarrow Ronnie got for her instead of carrying the catfish food in buckets.

I began hearing the popping sounds of the catfish as they came to the top and took the food.

"Buck bought some crawfish and released them in the pond." She began a conversation. "He said that catfish like to eat them but they can't catch them unless they come out to eat something." "Mister B." "What's wrong with you?" She asked.

I listened as the fish popped the water and began explaining to her.

"Cheryl when you had that accident" "did you remember what happened when you woke up in the hospital?" I asked her.

"No" she answered slowly.

"I was like that too" "I didn't learn to read until I was able to learn how to read Braille and I was thirteen then." "I was reading books that were written for four year old kids at fourteen." I chuckled. "I have to have someone read the news to me or listen to it on television and then at that, I get depressed because I'm not hearing something said correctly and it angers me because the people that's listening are hearing something that's not true and they believe it to be." "That's why I listen to candidates when they're making speeches." "I can tell a liar by the way he talks." "Cheryl" "I can't do things that I want to do." "I have my limitations." "I can't watch a ballgame, but I can listen to a good announcer and see what's happening on the field." "So, I have my limitations." "I was eighteen before I caught on to my surroundings and realized that my only future was to spend out the rest of my days being cared for in the institution so I set out to make some changes in my life." "I grew up quick and I grew up with a lot of anger and I couldn't find a way to fight my feelings." "A doctor did something to me he wasn't permitted to do, but he acted on his belief and for that, I can't have children, and I'm afraid every time I go to see a doctor, I'm going to get a phone call that doesn't carry the news I want to hear, and I'm scared." "I've grown to be fond of the people that I've met and for the first time I felt good."

"You made me feel good." She answered quickly.

"How" I asked.

"Ronnie told me you told him he should talk to me and he said he wouldn't have, but you made him." She said to me.

"Cheryl" "Ronnie talked about you and him sitting at the lunch table sharing his mother's pie and he told me about what happened to you." "He's seventeen and all seventeen year old boys are afraid of girls." "Has he kissed you yet?" I asked her.

"Mister B." she giggled.

"Cheryl" "if you want Ronnie to kiss you" "you have to be the one to kiss Ronnie first." "After that" "Ronnie won't be shy the next time you kiss him and then you'll find Ronnie kissing you instead of you kissing Ronnie." "Do you know how old I was the first time I kissed a girl?" I related to her.

"How old?" She replied.

"Twenty eight" "Bailey's the only girl that's ever kissed me with a reason and she's going to be my last."

"Are you talking about dying?" She asked.

"No" "If Bailey and I ever have problems to where we couldn't get along" "it would be the end for me." "Cheryl" "I'm not a man that can socialize like other people." "I don't like having a lot of people around me and I think the reason for that was because I was raised in an institutional state of mind." "When I moved here" "that kind of thinking changed and the reason for that is I have people I know to talk to." "You and Ronnie, your father and mother and everyone else are responsible for me wanting to be a different person than what I was."

"My daddy said you're too young to be so smart." She commented.

"I have my limitations, Cheryl." I responded. "We all do, except not everyone admits it."

"Mister B" "I didn't pass." She stated to me.

"That's not important anymore." "Cheryl" "after I learned how to read Braille, I read a book about a young girl that was Autistic." "She struggled like you do after you had your accident in all the things that was easy for other people, like you did, and she was alone in her life like I was." "She went to college and she changed the way things were done in her field because she proved to the people she dealt with; she was right." "That didn't come easy Cheryl." "Being Autistic, no one listens to what you have to say" "people that think of themselves as being smart, are not as smart as they think they are." "To them they've learned all they need to know to live their life." "I know, I was diagnosed as being Autistic." "So, when it came to talking to people that weren't in a frame of mind to listen, that girl wasn't without her troubles." "But" "she was assertive in her demands and got the attention of a man that gave her" "her chance to prove herself." "She changed the way they did things in her field."

"Is that why you talk to people sometimes the way you do?" She asked.

"Cheryl" "your father and mother love you very much and they're afraid." "Like you were about not passing the eighth grade, but that's not important anymore, you'll not have to worry about school anymore." "Your father is like a lot of other people that think of me being young, that I don't have the knowledge of what I'm doing, and because of that" "I find that I don't like to argue with people that don't have the knowledge of what they're doing, so I let them know my feelings and if they go on ahead and do what they do and lose their money." "Maybe next time" "they'll listen to what other people have to say and do a little more studying before they act out of a hunch." "It's been said that no one listens to a fool." "I do" "usually a fool got that way because he failed in his approach of investing" "I've invested the opposite way a fool did and I was rewarded." "Cheryl" "I hear people say that there aren't any stupid questions, but when I hear someone ask a question, I find I hear comments about that being a stupid question." "They were the first ones I found I wouldn't want to do business with" "no one knows everything so, to those people that think they do, I would end up talking to them the way you hear me talking to people that don't know what they're talking about, so there's only one way to avoid those kinds of confrontations and that's to not invest in what they invest in." "That's one of the reasons a lot of people blame me for them not succeeding." "I wouldn't invest in their corporation and because of that" "people thought I didn't see profit by doing so."

"Is that why you're going to get rid of that man?" She asked.

"What man?" I responded.

"That man that said he didn't think you should do what you were wanting to in New York."

"Oh" "Mister Laree." "Cheryl, I'm going to replace him with Richard because Richard mingles in a crowd." "He talks to me and tells me what he hears and through him I have a way of being able to see a direction of what the people are thinking and by that" "I can make my decisions on what industry is going to have trouble in and not have my money invested there." "He makes me five hundred times more than what I pay him for his conversations that I have with him." "Mister Laree doesn't make me anything" "so, Mister Laree's contract won't be renegotiated." "He'll be given a gold watch and speeches will be made about his tenure with the company and his association with my father" "which by the way" "will be his way of telling me I'm a butt hole like Bailey thought of me when we met." "But" "he'll retire and like all people" "he'll be able to do what he wants to do."

"Mister B." "I hear things said about me." She commented.

"I'm not a mind reader." I told her.

"Mister B." "The kids say I couldn't get a job and you're only paying me." I stopped her from completing what she was trying to say.

"Cheryl kids are nothing more than messengers of their parents when they say things." "All kids are honest until they learn to be dishonest." "Their parents teach them how to be like that too, so when it comes to what kids are saying, you can't blame the kids for what a parent is saying." "Tell me something" "I blame myself for bringing this grief to your family and to Bailey and to everyone else." "I know things about you and because of that, I pay you like I pay Richard; you tell me what I want to know with only honest answers." "Are you upset with me for meeting me, or are you a happier person for it?"

"Why do you ask a question like that?" She asked.

"I have my limitations and I don't want to hurt anyone for putting them through what I do." "Buck lets it be known that he doesn't like going anywhere and I think Becky does it because she thinks it's good for the kids." "I need to know if I'm one of those people I talk to when you hear me get upset that's needs to listen to what someone is telling me" "and you're the only one that will tell me what she thinks with truth."

"Mister B." she stalled and began slowly "I wanted to kill myself."

"Cheryl" I interrupted "every time I had to go give a test to see if I have what some other boys died of from the doctor that treated them" "I gave a lot of thought to that myself." "It's not an out though; it's just a conclusion to an inevitable." "Before I met any of you" "I don't think I would have had much trouble carrying out that thought if I found out that I was sick, but I can't now."

"Why" she asked.

"Cheryl" "your parents saw you suffering and they suffered along with you every second of the day." "Many nights went by without sleep from their thinking of you laying in the hospital bed worrying that you might not be able to walk or talk." "I know." "Where I was at, a lot of kids were in that condition." "Both of them blame themselves for what happened." "They think that if they had been better parents then maybe what happened to you wouldn't have happened."

"That's not true." She said to me.

"To them it is and it will always be" "no matter what you say" "they'll always blame themselves for what happened to you for the rest of their life." "Cheryl" "If I did something to myself like I had thoughts of" "I would hurt those that didn't want me to do it." "When a person passes from life naturally" "there's grief, but there's no blame given." "I blame the doctor who experimented on me." "It doesn't do me any good now, he's dead." "But he has a family, and that family has pain from what he did." "They're constantly reminded of it everyday of their life." "They're victims too." "No one wants to remember a father or grandfather or a great grandfather that killed kids." "I feel sorry for them."

"Mister B." "I'm glad I met you." "Ronnie wouldn't be with me if I hadn't, and I know everyone else likes you too."

I took a deep breath and exhaled. "Thanks Cheryl" "I needed that."

I arose from my rock that I sat on and she told me to take her arm. We began our trek back to the house when I stated. "Cheryl" "do you want Ronnie to kiss you?"

"Mister B." She giggled.

"I'm serious" I began "you're not a little girl anymore." "You're seventeen." "You're the same age as Ronnie." "When I kissed Bailey, she kissed me back and I felt good, and when she kissed me again, I felt better than good." "Ronnie wasn't going to go over to your house and ask you if you wanted to go to New York with us." "He was scared, so, I made him go, I told him he had to know if you liked him or didn't like him." "Cheryl" "that boy was miserable" "and I got to thinking what if you were like Ronnie was and was afraid to kiss him."

"What would you have said?" She asked after a long wait.

"Ronnie's shy" "you know that" "and if I was a girl that wanted to be kissed by a boy I liked" "I would let him know by kissing him." "I think you're shy to, like him." "Maybe he wants to kiss you, but he might be like he was when I told him to go over to your house and ask you if you wanted to go to New York with him." "It's like I told Ronnie" "you'll never know how she feels about you unless you tell her how you feel about her." "Cheryl" "you ended up coming over here and going to New York with him." "I think it's same thing with you, you're afraid like Ronnie was." "He took a chance and I think you should take one too."

"Kurt" Buck stopped me from going further. "There's some people that want to say hello." "I know how you feel about those things but they wanted me to." I stopped him by telling him to take my arm and lead me over to where we needed to go. After we began, I stopped and turned.

"Cheryl" I said with an elevated voice.

"Yes sir" she replied.

"There's only one way to find out what it is I'm trying to tell you and you won't know until you do what I tell you, then you'll know what I know."

I turned and Buck commented. "What was that all about?"

I chuckled. "What did Becky's father think of you when he found out you was going to be his son in law?"

"What in the world were y'all talking about?" He asked and then we were interrupted by his guests.

"Mister Bryant" a man's voice was heard and then silence fell with the rest. "We'd like to thank you for what you're doing for our kids and grandkids." He said as I heard other people began gathering around.

"I'm not doing anything" I replied "yeah" "I'm providing food and a place to have a gathering, but anyone can do that, all it takes is a little money." "What happens here tomorrow and tomorrow night is gauged by entertainment, and there's only one way to please a person when it comes to telling everyone how good of a time they had, and that's by the food they eat." "Becky's been on the computer ordering cakes and pies and breads and doing all she can do to see that everyone has a good time." "That's where volunteers like you and everyone around me that hears my voice has to listen." "Success of any event cannot and let me repeat" "cannot be achieved without people such as yourself." "Buck tells me that everyone out here competes in cook offs and benefits and for me not to worry about anything." "I told him still." "Kurt" "he said" "I've tasted just about all of the food these people cook and he told me that he was afraid to tell Becky he thought she should taste what some of you cooked." I heard laughter and after it calmed down, I continued. "All of you are out here for the same reasons as everyone else is; you want your child or your grandchild to remember their graduation, or in this case, judging by the sounds of the children's voices I hear, future graduates too."

"Mister Bryant we heard some things." He began and it ended with the water pipeline issue.

Paradox

I cleared my throat before I answered. "Mexico City is sinking two inches a year because it's built on the aquifer where they get their water supply from, there's only one way to stop it from sinking and that's to stop pulling the water out of the ground, but you don't see them doing that." "If a pipeline is successful in being able to be built, then there will come a time when this lake will be drained." "If that happens, this lake will die, and those turbines that generate electricity won't be needed and another lake will have a pipeline run into it and it too will end up drying up." "That's progress." "You watch the news and you see where boats are lying on the bottom of lakes that's suffering from a drought, like this one, and that other lake will end up like this lake." "Eventually Murray will end up losing tourist dollars that travel through like Skinland is experiencing now, and "Murray" will end up suffering from a loss of revenue like Skinland." "Murray and all cities that lies two hundred miles in every direction of this lake will be affected, good or bad." "I heard that the school is closing and the kids will be bused to another school." "I'm helpless to do anything about what is done the same as the rest of you." "Officials are elected by a majority of the voters." "I can't do anything for anyone." "How many of you have seen on the news where floods devastate towns every time there's a storm and that water travels to rivers and ends up out to the sea." "What a waste."

"What would you do Mister Bryant?" A lady asked.

I took another deep breath and held it in and then exhaled. "Right now, all everyone has is a rumor to the affect that a pipeline is going to be built." "There's nothing anyone can do until there has been confirmation as to the effect of that rumor, even then, it may be too late." "You won't get the answers to any of those questions you seek." "I can't do anything to stop it from being built if your councilmen vote to have it allowed." "I can promise you however that if it is approved, I'll have a team of lawyers here as soon as it's been made official and I'll launch an investigation on each member that votes yes to see if I can find if any official misconduct was involved." "Al Capone was a mobster" "yet the only conviction he ever got was not paying his income taxes." "All I have to say about that proposed rumor of a pipeline being built is that if any of your councilmen have holes in their laundry, they'll be dealing with the Federal Government." "That I will promise, but until then, let's all settle down and wait, rumors have a way of changing and I don't want the kids worrying about their future tomorrow." "This is supposed to be an event for the kids to celebrate graduating on to a higher level of learning."

"Kurt" I heard Bailey's voice shouting.

"I've got other matters I need to attend to." I stated and before I left, I stopped and stated further. "Tomorrow we'll see if Buck was right about him wanting Becky to taste your food." "I happen to think Becky's is pretty good." I chuckled and we turned and left.

When we entered the back door Becky handed me a cup of cocoa. "It looked like you needed rescuing so I had Bailey call for you."

I made my way into the family room and sat down on the sofa and soon felt someone sitting close. I lifted my nose up a little and gave a sniff. "Something on your mind Steven?" I asked.

"Sarah and I took a drive to get away and everywhere we went we saw nothing but trees and pastures." He commented.

"It's not New York" I said.

"Sir" "Sarah and I are having a hard time trying to figure all of this out." He commented.

"That's a question you'll ask yourself every day for the rest of your life Steven and when you find an answer, write a book and tell everyone how you did it." "You have to look at life like the weather." "Some days it rains, and some days you have hurricanes, and some days you have tornados, and some days the sun shines a warm feeling down on you and the only thing you can do is sit in a lounge chair and fall asleep." "The sad thing about sunny days is they're just as bad as rainy ones, you get sunburned a lot."

"Sir" "why did you withdraw?" He asked.

"Steven, I found out a man can be in a crowded room and still be alone." "That's a feeling a person feels when they commit suicide." "But that's a question you have to experience to be able to find that out." I replied "Every person's life has days where he walks a tightrope between sanity and insanity." "Some people can handle it better than others, that's all." "For a time, I used my father's firm as an outlet." "I took on all comers and fought my arguments in court with a passion." "I'm not a lawyer, but I do know legal issues don't have to be accurate for a person to be found innocent or guilty; evidence gets planted sometimes." "That's a responsibility that's left up to a lawyer to uncover." "They only have to convince the jury of their peers his arguments are true, and they don't have to be." "Steven" "when Mister Shelton called Richard" "it was for only one purpose and that was to see if he could take care of this matter before it went to court." "He didn't act alone" "he had a staff of lawyers telling him I was going to give him a hit that it was going to hurt." "His lawyers knew within fifteen minutes of my actions and at that time" "Mister Shelton was notified." "They have people that work for them and we have people that work for us and between us all, we know about each other's business." "When Richard called and told me that the tape showed a time span of four minutes and thirty eight seconds." "I could have called every CEO of every corporation that owns hotels and put them on the stand and every one of them would have said that anything more than one minute was totally unacceptable" "especially after I put the girl on the stand that Bailey talked to, to notify them that I was coming." "He knew what he was up against and that's the only reason we settled" "had he thought otherwise this would have gone on for years and it would have cost him Billions." "He knew he was in trouble if it lasted, bad publicity isn't accepted." "Steven it was people like him that made me the man I am today."

"But it's not my money." He commented.

"Then give it away." I said "I don't care what you do with it." "I didn't do what I did for it anyway." "When I snapped" "my personality was a lot different three years ago." "I had trouble speaking to people" "you have to understand where I grew up at" "there wasn't anyone around except adults and all they did was follow orders." "I don't like to be bullied and I have my way of dealing with bullies." "Steven a frail man can't defend himself when he's up against a bully" "but if you're a frail man with money" "you can hire someone to let everyone know you won't be bullied." "I did it because I felt good telling him what I thought of him and the way he did business." "Steven" "if he doesn't change the way he's doing his business" "I'm going to be called up on the witness stand one day and have to testify to the account of what led up to the point of me filing my suit." "Will he change the way he's doing business now?" "I don't know" "but I can tell you if he doesn't; Morton's corporation will be filing for Bankruptcy." "Mister Shelton was forced to negotiate." "As far as you thinking it's not your money" "you told me if I was to point a finger at someone, I should point it at the manager." "Up until then I was trying to put pieces together on how they knew I was coming." "The only lead I had was Bailey's conversation to let them know." "Steven" "what do I need it for?" I said somberly. "My firm gets one third of it because we settled out of court." "I received satisfaction." "Steven" "I'm the last of my name and I can't have children." "Do you know what happens to people like me?" I asked.

He answered after a short pause.

"Yes sir."

"What would you do if you were in my shoes?" I asked him.

"Give it to charity?" He stated.

"I'm not a giving person" I stated "Churches are given properties after people die." "They sell that property and put it in the stock market." "I have a foundation where my junior executives contribute pro bono to running that foundation to children in need of special attention." "I bought the institution I grew up in." "But" "after I'm dead" "if I was to leave everything to my foundation it wouldn't be long before someone would come in and make changes to the bylaws and before you know it" "executives would be making hundreds of millions in bonuses and the foundation would end up closing its doors." "That's the way people are Steven." "You asked me about the money." "If you really want to know if Sarah loves you, I would give it all to Sarah." "If she ends up leaving you, then you'll make her happy and you'll know things that you didn't." "If she stays with you, then maybe you'll find out that she does love you." "Steven" "I've got to go back to New York to do a follow up with the doctor in a couple of weeks." "My results from the test I'm going to give Tuesday should be read by then." "If anything goes wrong" "I need you to get Sarah to get Bailey and the rest of my staff out sightseeing."

"Why" he asked.

"I'm going to have to take care of some personal matters and they have to be legalized, I'll need a witness." I commented.

"You mean make out a will." He stated.

"Steven" "there's something you should know that I know about you." "You won't say a word to anyone about me." "Not even after I'm dead." "And Steven" "when it comes to Sarah there aren't any guarantees" "I think you know that" "and if you give her the money, you'll get your answers." "If the time comes, you can come visit me, I won't be going anywhere; that's for sure." "But" "knowing what I know from past experiences in the field of family law" "you can't win an argument with your wife" "you'll lose every one and if you go to a divorce court and watch the show" "you'll find that out." "Give the money to Sarah and you won't have to pay a penny to a lawyer." "If you and her split up, you'll always have a home in Skinland." "Bailey and all the rest of my group will need you."

"Kurt" "everyone's talking out there." Buck commented walking in.

"Buck" "Some of those people work for the government and some of them know where the people I was talking about are." "They'll pass the message along about what I said and through them I'll get someone's attention and when I do" "we'll have a little talk." "If the pipeline wasn't going to be installed, don't you think someone would have already dispelled that rumor?"

"Richards on the line" Bailey said coming in and putting the phone in my hand.

"Hello" I said. "Okay then" I said hanging up the phone after listening for a few minutes. "One of my employees committed suicide this morning."

"The FBI was going to arrest him and he put a gun to his head." "They've got three more in custody and there's been a confession made as to the reason why my scheduler was assassinated." "They've got warrants out on seventeen people from four other corporations in three states." "Everyone had ties with someone." I said to all those that were present. "Isn't it strange how you find out all the things that go on behind your back from one little bit of a touch of anger." "Mister Reynolds had plenty of money and being fired wasn't a threat to him." "He could have retired in comfort."

"Kurt" "that's people" Steven said. "He was a leech sucking what he could off of you or he wouldn't have done what he did."

"Well said" I commented "Steven" "I hope you don't do something rash, and do what I tell you." "She has her dream like other young ladies."

"What are you talking about?" Bailey commented.

"Nothing" "Steven just found out how money changes a person and I was just telling him to have a cup of cocoa and I could tell him some of the things I encountered" "that's all." I said chuckling

"Buck" Becky came into the room. "There's a lot of people out there wanting to know where you want them to set everything up." "You got plenty of time to chat but now ain't the time." "Now get up and get out there and show them people how you want things done."

"I better go" "she's in a mood." He whispered.

"Whoa" "Kurt" "You got yourself a heap of people a piling up out there." Elrod made his comment as he walked into the room. "And what's all this stuff I'm hearing about you calling in the FBI?" Bailey and Steven began laughing. "What?" He spoke.

"In an hour" I chuckled "go back out and listen to what people are saying because they know you talked to me and when they talk to you, you're telling them what me and you are talking about."

"Come again?" He stated.

"Elrod, I spoke to some of the people earlier and told them what I thought." They were the same thoughts I conveyed to you and I didn't tell them anything more about what I saw than what I told you." "Rumors have a way of twisting and turning a statement completely around." "That's one of the reasons I don't like talking to a gathering of people." "I'm better at a one on one type of thing."

"Why" he said "you don't seem to have a problem to me."

"I was twenty three and one of my teachers took me to a man that had a collection of old radio shows." "Back then you have to understand they didn't have the technology they have today." "Horse hooves were cans being beat against the table." "Thunder was a piece of tin being shaken and there would be radio actors reading the story with a great deal of enthusiasm." "I remember that day because one of the radio actors said, and I quote "when you have two people talking, you have a conversation." "And when you have three people talking, there's going to be a debate." "When you have four people talking, there's going to be an argument and when there's five people gathered" there's going to be a fight."

"And what if six people were there?" Elrod asked.

"A riot" I commented. "So, I don't like talking to people because an hour later when you go back out there" "you'll hear a lot of different things said than what you heard earlier." "Do you know what feeds a rumor?" I asked Elrod.

"No" he answered.

"Another rumor" I chuckled.

"Dad gum Kurt" he chuckled also.

"It's the truth though Elrod" "Rumors are fueled by another rumor." "Regardless of the way I feel, I have to make myself available and let my intentions be known publicly and I took advantage of the moment."

"Does anyone know what he's saying?" He asked and I heard silence.

"Elrod everyone out there knows something is going on and they want answers." I began "There's fear and anger and uncertainty flying around like those pesky love bugs." "You said you sold your business and invested it in a suggestion I made, that's how I knew you were a gambler." "There's a difference between you and them and that's that those people out there aren't in the same shape as all of us are and because of them not being in the same shape as we, they're dependent on an income and they feel threatened." "Going to the mail box gives them a bad feeling." "Elrod" "you ever talk to a man that got an E Mail saying he was no longer required." "It happens every day to someone, somewhere, and a man contemplates his future for a long, long, long time, and some futures aren't contemplated at all." "Where will they go" "what will they do to satisfy them until they can find something else and where will that somewhere else be." "Elrod these people are settled here and life was good." "Becky called the women countrified." "How do you tell them everything will be okay and be lying to them?" "None of that has ever come true for me."

"Are you okay Kurt?" Bailey said.

"Yeah" I commented after taking a deep breath. "I need one of my pills."

"I'll get them." She said to me.

I could hear her footsteps rounding the door and then Steven spoke.

"Are you really okay sir?" He asked

"I have my moments, Steven." I said after a short time. "Elrod do me a favor and when you walk around listening and talking to the people" "remind them that they're here to have a good time and tell them that everything will be addressed at the proper time, but until that time comes, nothing is written in stone."

"You take it easy boy" he said putting his hand on my shoulder "I don't understand a man like you." "None of those people out there had a kind word to say about you until tonight." "I don't understand." He said walking away.

"Here" Bailey said putting a pain pill in my mouth and put a glass of water in my hand to swallow it down with.

"You need rest Kurt" "You're pushing yourself too early." Bailey commented.

"I agree sir." Steven said.

"I'm not going to argue with you" "I am tired." I said to him. "Wake me if you need me." And with that Bailey led me to my room.

She slipped under the covers next to me.

"I wouldn't have ever imagined you were the man you are." She commented. "Elrod's right you know?"

"Do you know where we're at?" I asked her.

"Kurt" "is that the pill talking." She replied.

"This is any town in the USA" I began "I hear a lot of comments being said about how well a state is doing and then you see them put a Tariff on a country that owns our country and I see property taxes going up every year." "It seems to me that if this country was doing so good then why do they raise taxes every year?" "It's simple Bailey." "The people are being lied to." "Every country owns businesses and corporations here and we're becoming a slave labor force."

"And your point being?" She asked.

"The only thing out there with everyone that's made in America is the Lobster, the King Crab, the Salmon and the Rib Roasts." "How can you tell people that buy nothing but products that's made somewhere else that this is what happens when you don't have the labor resources?" "Do you know what they mean when they say that they can't get enough qualified workers?" I said to her.

"No" she replied.

"It means they can't get anyone to work for minimum wage sixteen hours a day, seven days a week for three hundred and sixty five days a year." I felt her snuggle next to me after that. "Bailey" "close your eyes" I said "now imagine fifty years from now what everything will be like." "All corporations will cease to exist, and we'll be like we were in the depression years." "Large businesses can't operate without small businesses that pay for employee's and that means they will suffer the same fate as everyone else." "What good will it do to have billions of dollars if it's worthless." "They'll hunger the same as others and die of that hunger like all others." "That's the ignorance of man." "Bailey if I was to tell people what I think the future holds for them" "I'd be called an idiot." "So, I keep my thoughts to myself." "Bailey" "you said this house was you're dream." "My thinking is thinking that one day this house won't be standing anymore and you're dream will be gone and you will be too" "nothing can withstand the forces of nature, or time."

"What are you getting at?" She said firmly.

I began "I left New York thinking that nothing ever stays the same" "I came here on a dream." "The house was yours, Skinland was mine." "I told you" "you had yours and I had mine." "I was hoping to find my peace." "I did and now it's back to being where nothing ever stays the same." I closed my eyes.

CHAPTER FOURTEEN

I heard water running in the bathroom and got up from the bed.

"Did I wake you?" Bailey said and I just smiled. "Here" "take this and swallow it" she said as I felt a pill being put in my mouth. "Kurt" "you've been out since seven o'clock yesterday and it's almost ten." "Everyone's been asking about you and everyone's been telling them you're asleep." "Becky said you need to make a showing."

"What time did you get up?" I asked her.

"As soon as you closed your eyes." She replied.

"You haven't gotten any sleep Bailey?"

"Kurt, Becky's been baking pies and cakes all night and Sarah and I and a lot of other women have been busy too." "There wasn't too much sleep gotten by anyone last night and if they did, it was because they dozed off in their chair." "That's why Becky wanted me to wake you up." "She thinks you need to mingle some." "And Kurt" "she looked at me with that look she gives me." "I'll lay out your clothes on the bed and tell Becky to start your cocoa."

"I don't think that's a good idea." I commented.

"Hey" "you wanted a party" "now you got a party." "You're the one that started this." She asserted.

"You sound like Becky." I stated.

"Kurt" "she gave me the eye." "You don't know what her eye's do to you." "Ask Buck sometime if Becky's ever given him the eye." "Between you and her" "I'd rather take my chances with you."

"Hey" I stopped her "I'm glad you got mad at me and called me a Butt hole."

"Well. I'm glad you came back to my car and talked to me." "I was having a bad day." "Now" "I told you once" "don't talk to me like that when we have to do other things." "You can talk all you want when you're kissing me."

"You can't talk when you're kissing." I chuckled.

"You are a "very" smart boy." She said laughing. "Now take a shower and get dressed and come on down." "I don't think you're going to like Becky when she hasn't had much sleep and being Becky" "she's got a clock on you and if you aren't down by the time that she thinks you should be down, she'll be knocking on the door." "Kurt" "if that happens" "answer it quickly" "or she'll pound on the door until you open it, and when you do Becky won't be the Becky you know."

"Her eyes can do that?" I chuckled.

"Hey" "that's a question you need to ask Buck" "you're wasting your time Kurt" "the clock" "remember?" She said as she walked out of the bathroom. I eased the cool water handle to a slower pace and allowed the hot water to remain at its flow.

I soon heard a knock on the door and then a louder knock. When I opened it, I knew who it was without asking. "Kurt" "How many people did you count on?" Becky questioned.

"I told Bailey when we were at the auditorium to count how many kids there were by tens and give me a rough estimate of a head count." "She told me fourteen and I doubled that because I heard two entrances being used." "That tells me that there were roughly two hundred and eighty kids and I had to guess on how many there were that had dates from other schools." "And then there was around thirty maybe forty teachers or so and by the time you throw in the bus drivers and their families and with the staff and volunteers I asked for and Bailey telling me about the people of Skinland" "five to six hundred would be a good ball park estimate." "Becky" "in New York if someone was having a party" "It was common for people to show up that no one knew." "I'd hear it on the news, so I don't think Skinland is any different."

"And you're all right with that?" She asked.

"No" "but" "you're right" "I do need to mingle."

I held on to Bailey's arm as she guided me through the crowd. I had to stop now and then and listen to a lot of thank you Mister Bryant that were coming from a lot of women and men too and when one started, it was echoed as we walked by.

"Got some Boudin Balls here for you" A voice was heard.

I stopped. "What's Boudin balls?" I asked.

"You stand right there." He said and soon I had a warm crusty piece of food in my hand.

I held my silence as I tasted the first bite and after the second bite, I spoke. "Did you do this or did you have a team that helped you to do this?" I asked.

"My wife and I set up at all the rodeos and carnivals and we're pretty much on the go two maybe three weekends out of a month sometimes." He replied. "Sometimes we travel three to four hundred miles away."

"Do you have any kids that's going to be here tonight?" I asked.

"My daughter" he answered "she's a freshman and when she came home all excited, we couldn't do anything but listen to what she said." "Mister Bryant" "my daughter travels with us and helps us out." "We don't live close to other people so when she told us about all of this we got to calling and then people got to calling us and we thought we'd do our part for our daughter like all the rest of these folks out here."

"You spent your own money to do this?" I asked.

"Mister Bryant" "these are our kids" "we all spent money to help you help us." "I've been traveling like this for almost four years now." "I've been asked for my business cards and I'm getting serious calls." "I'm opening up a small kitchen and getting ready to see if I can expand my business." "This is one time I don't mind doing what I'm doing." "I feel good for my daughter and all of these people out here thank you kindly and I want you to know that."

"Can I have one of your cards?" I asked him.

"Yes sir" he replied.

I put my hand out and took it when he gave it to me and began feeling the card. "Some business cards are printed in bold letters." I stated to all that were listening "They do that to get your attention by secretly shouting at you." "It's a little known fact, but when you see the card, it delivers to you what you want." "This card is printed the same way." "John "Wally" Wallace" I said running my fingers over the card "hold on a minute" "give me a second." "Ah" "A smile with every bite." "That's a catchy phrase." I said to him. "You said that you were going to open up a small kitchen." "I bought Becky's diner." "I'll let you have it if you pay the taxes on it." "I don't need it, and it'll save you rent money."

I heard a lot of commotion from everyone that was around. "Mister Wallace if you get some phone calls wanting to sample your product, and if you deliver to them and the public the same flavor that this one has" "I don't see you having much of a problem in getting orders." "I'd set up a web site and invest in a refrigerated truck if I were you." I commented. "I know some people that would be interested in talking to you."

"Thank you, Mister Bryant" he replied. "That's a kind offer." "I didn't expect that."

"No sir" "I thank you and I thank everyone else for everything they've done and are doing to make this prom work, it's the least I can do to repay you." "From what Bailey's telling me here" "not very many of you got much sleep." "I'm sorry I passed out, but I've been having problems staying awake with the pain pills I've been taking."

"This is going to be quite a shindig." A lady stated and then the crowd was silent. "Most folks round here never eaten no lobster or a King crab" "let alone salmon." "If it ain't fried catfish" "they ain't ate it." "The Gym wouldn't have been able to hold all these folks, not that most of them wouldn't have been there anyway." I turned to my side to confront her. "Ida May's my name" and by the way she spoke she was up in the years. "I've been to ever one of the proms" "cepten that is" "when I had my knee surgery." "I watched all of these people here grow up." "I delivered most of them and their kids too and I busted me many a butt for them being a smart mouth." "I saw you on that program the other night and you don't care much about what people think of you." "I can tell by the way you talk that you're a man that's partial to taking his own advice."

"I learn from others." I stated.

"Ooh" "Mighty young to be so sharp witted." She retorted. "Some folks been talking bout you."

I smiled. "Ma'am" "according to the news I'm in three places at the same time."

"Son" she began "I attended a seminar where I sat across the table from Doctor Savidge and we dined while listening to the speakers, I was shocked when I found out what he did and now, I don't know what to say." "Son" "they took a picture of everyone's table and everybody got a copy of themselves attending the seminar." "To tell you the truth" "I didn't remember anyone after I left." "When it was found out that he performed test on some boys, I was questioned on whether he had said anything to me about his experiments long after that picture was taken."

I took a deep breath and then exhaled. "None of this is about me" "I have some members on my personal staff and I'm trying to show them how to be diplomatic." "You achieve more that way."

"Ah" "and you like playing the game of people." She stated.

"No ma'am" "I'm just trying to teach future members of my organization that right and wrong are brother and sister to good and bad." "I hope they understand that you can't have a little of both without having issues." "You're on the school board" "aren't you?"

"What's makes you say that?" She replied.

"You said that you've been to every prom; so that means you were here when this school was built." "And you said you attended a medical seminar and you delivered most of the people here, so you must be a doctor." "Miss Ida May" "have you ever attended a seminar given by a doctor that you didn't concur with his or her opinion?"

"Yes" she replied.

"Then Miss Ida May" "I would have to assume that you thought to yourself that you wouldn't want to be one of his or her patients when you didn't agree with an opinion of theirs" "you both had a different way of practicing your profession and people die from doctors that practice bad medicine and you of all people know that not all doctors were straight A students."

"You are a conflicting young man." She stated and I continued.

"You and I both know why this school's closing down" "there isn't any tax dollars to support it." "To me that only means one thing" "someone's wanting to come in and build a business and the only way they'll do it is if the artery of the traffic is rerouted, so the more kids that go to school there, the more traffic, and once one good size business comes in, they'll be others." "That makes me suspicious" "is Skinland on the outside of that artery and if so, it can't be supported, it'll be a burden on the county." "Ma'am" "a lot of deals are done behind doors."

"So, you read people too." She stated.

"If that's your opinion" I responded "but Bailey here used to work at Barney's and she told me that Murray was giving Barney's trouble and Buck said he doesn't understand why the store hasn't already closed and yesterday I found out that Barney's is up for sale." "I try my best to only converse in matters with people that have common sense" "a degree doesn't make you smart." "Do you honestly think anyone is going to buy any property around here "Ma'am"."

"Please call me Granny young man."

"Ma'am" "the only people I know are my associates and that wouldn't be proper."

She started her chuckle.

"Someone give this young man a chair" she spoke and after a few minutes she told me to sit down and I did. "Now" "folks been telling me bout you calling in the feds" she said. "Are you a vindictive person?"

I cleared my throat and soon spoke. "I don't like anyone in a position to gain financially from a position they're elected for." "It makes me feel that all the men that's died fighting in war for your rights, died in vain." "It tells me that they only wanted that seat because they were crooks and many have proved themselves to be just that in the past." "I'm hearing rumors of a pipeline that's going to be built." "If that rumor turns out to be true." "That lake won't exist and in a year all of the councilmen that voted for it will have moved away, and there won't any need for those turbines at the dam, they won't be able to generate electricity and that'll kill every business below the dam." "You know that as well as I do." "Being on the school board" "you know that the only reason a politician can't be reached is because he's taken a vacation, so the proposal for the pipeline that's been rumored must have merit." "No more tourist" "no skiers" "no fishermen" "and no businesses." "There will only be one school" "the rest won't be needed, no people."

"Miss May" "I gave him a pill before we came out here" "I think it's making him talk funny." Bailey tried to interrupt.

"Naw hon" she shrugged her comment off "Son" she began "I was the only doctor for fifty miles around and I pretty much know what's going on with these people, I was a part of their lives." "When I watched that program" "I saw a man that knew more than what he was saying."

"Ma'am"

"That's Granny" she replied.

"All right then" "Granny" "I'm fortunate" "I have a law firm and I have ammunition to use against anyone that does anything for the purpose of putting a few dollars in their wallet." "You asked me if I was a vindictive person." "Nothing in politics is achieved without some form of influential input and you know what that input is; money, and where there's money, there's lobbyist that work for corporations." "I'll find out who benefited from the closure of that school and I can guarantee you that he or she will be spending the rest of their years in jail." "All that's needed is an accusation and you as well as I do know that all elected officials have skeletons in their closet."

"So, you are a vindictive person." She stated.

"It's a personal thing with me." I replied.

"Son" "what's you got working on in that mind of yours?"

"Ma'am"

"That's Granny son" she interrupted.

I smiled and commented my thought out loud. "Into the valley of death, they rode the six hundred."

"That's the charge of the Light Brigade." She stated. "What's that got to do with what we're talking about?" She asked.

"When that school is closed down, a lot of people are going to leave." "This town won't receive the concerns that the residents pay their tax dollars for." "It costs people dearly to move." "But they don't have any other option." "Parents that are wealthy want their children to grow up in an atmosphere like anyone else, but in an institution, that didn't exist." "My youngest staff member Cindy, tells me of the dreams of some of the kids she talks to, and Julie tells me of the dreams of the kids she talks to." "These kids go to Murray because that's where parents have to go to take them for ballet classes and music lessons, and anything else a kid wants to learn." "They can't get it here." "That's why Barney's has such a stiff competition" "that being the only grocery store it costs more to transport products here so, Barney's has to pay more and in return" "charge more." "That's why this state wants to increase taxes; everyone here will have to go somewhere else to do whatever they have to do." "When a state begins going into shock all towns like Skinland for instance, suffer." "The people that go to Murray often; end up eating there because Becky's wasn't getting local customer's, she was dependent on tourists, and in the end, people started buying their groceries there too, so Barney's ends up losing customers and the end results is evident." "I bought that institution and turned it into a foundation of performing arts for the disability impaired." "The youngest student was four years old." "She didn't know how to do anything a four year old could do" "but when you sat down and listened to her play a violin" "she had more talent than a person that had thirty years experience on her did." "Granny" I chuckled "there's a two year old boy that's been inducted into the Mensa Society." "How would you like to have a chat with a two year old that has a higher I. Q than what you have, or a four year old that has the intelligence of a twenty year old?" "That school isn't going anywhere, it'll be torn down and a private school will be built with a new football field, baseball field, soccer arena, and this city will have dozens of restaurants to cater to the visitors." "I know a man that makes some good Boudin balls." "They'll be a good selling item." "They'll be tennis courts and an Olympic indoor swimming pool too." "Children grow up wanting to be whoever makes the most impression on them." "It could be a game warden, or a lawyer or a cop, or someone like you" "a doctor." "Public schools don't provide that extra little something a kid wants to be" "but a private school can." "When we went to California for me to tape that show" "I met a young lady that wanted to be an actress but she lacked all the qualities a director was looking for" "I apologize" "I can't say all" "I don't know what she looked like" "but still, you can't take a desire you grew up with and not have anything to do with it anymore and I told her those that can't do, teach, so I'm going to offer acting classes, painting, and courses taught in college to prepare a six year old for pre med." "A private school receives a lot of funding from voucher's because they pay taxes on public schools through their property." "I'm going to accept all vouchers from anyone locally or abroad" "I don't care." "When you build a college and a private school." "Big businesses set up in a town." "Granny" "they'll all need rooms, so, dorms will be built and they'll have to be around a dozen Hotels and Motels for visitors and the same number will be applied to department stores and service stations and I'm sorry, but Barney's will have a dozen competitor's and by the time I'm through, this town will have subdivisions that will encompass twenty miles of businesses that surrounds this town." "Murray will look small and will end up losing revenue." "I could tell you of factories being built in a fifty mile radius that will employ hundreds if not thousands of people and I can go on and on." "If that pipeline goes through, you and I both know that none of this is going to happen." "I'd be making a foolish investment and Skinland would be losing tens of millions of dollars in taxes." "That decision to install a pipeline was made not to long ago." "You're a doctor and you know your heart can't beat without any blood." "Without that lake" "this town is doomed, and if that lake is low now, what will happen when it's dry." "I'll tell you." "Another pipeline will be run to another lake and it will be drained and that town will die too." "They're counting on a temporary fix instead of focusing on a permanent one." "I'm not a fool granny." "Ma'am" "I haven't dealt with a politician yet that didn't have skeletons in his closet." "In the charge of the Light Brigade" "they were outnumbered and their leader made a mistake and because of that mistake all the men were slaughtered." "They knew they didn't have a chance but they went into battle because they were given an order." "The city council will come under an investigation." "I can guarantee that."

"What if that pipeline doesn't exist?" She commented.

"I don't see myself as being an idiot ma'am." I said to her. "I'm an investor and I don't invest in anything that doesn't promise me success in my endeavors." "All those things I said to you will come to pass." I don't like being taken advantage of."

"Who's got a phone?" I heard her say. "Someone get me a phone."

A few minutes passed.

"Joshua" "this is Granny" "you can stow it boy" I heard her comment along with the others present "I'm talking to a man right now that says a pipeline is in the works for the lake." "I know what he's telling me isn't true but" "Joshua" "I want to hear that from you." After a long pause she began talking again "Joshua" "I want you to call Bill and Martha and Theodore and" "don't interrupt me again young man" she stated with a hostile tone "I want you all out here at Mister Bryant's house tonight" "there's going to be one helluva prom and I want all of you out here to put an end put to a rumor" "and Joshua, you be a listening real good boy" "you hear me" "you're going to tell everyone here at Mister Bryant's house that there will be a doctrine to end all doubts that this lake will ever be put under control of anyone other than us." "Goodbye Joshua." "Mister Bryant" "I apologize for the interruption in our conversation but my nephew just informed me that he had heard something to the affect that it was mentioned." "I don't think this conversation will ever happen again; I'll supervise the meeting myself and I assure you that that doctrine will be signed."

"I don't think you'll have to" I responded "there's a lot of people listening to us."

"That's why I'm going to supervise the meeting." She chuckled. "Mister Bryant you are one very intelligent gentleman." "I was impressed when I found out bout your past." "I am curious though" "why so giving?" She asked.

I smiled and replied. "If you watched that program like you said you did, you understand that money doesn't mean anything to some people."

"I'm the last of my name and I've got no kin" "I've got money and there's kids that need it more than I do, simply because their parents don't have any." "I heard a commercial one time that a mind is a terrible thing to waste." "I thought how true" "when I converted the institution, I seen positive results." "When my lawyers call telling me I have protection" "I'll start negotiations on the property and once that's been settled, renovations will begin and I'll begin buying all the property that's for sell within a fifty mile radius of this county." "I dream big Granny."

"You don't trust in anyone do you?" She stated.

"I have personal associates that I consult" I replied "Mister and Misses Elrod Jessup and their daughter Cheryl." "Buck, Becky, Ronnie, Julie, and Cindy Roberts and then there's Sarah and Steven Bishop." "I get insight from our conversations." "Bailey here" "well from what I understand she's been accused of being a lot of things." "I'd like to tell those people that said those things about her that they should be ashamed of themselves." "None of my staff gets any kind of special treatments and Bailey doesn't get paid." "They all give me what I ask for and not any of them give me any arguments." "I have a corporation in New York of Divorce Lawyers." "I can't run it from here and I can't run it from there, so my associate's assist's me and intervenes in the performance of my actions." "They're with me twenty four hours out of the day, seven days a week, and Holiday's." "I rely on what they tell me, I owe them my life." I told her.

"Son" "a man makes a liar out of himself when he doesn't do what he says he going to do." She commented.

"Yes Ma'am" "and people that read the truth will always remember what they read, but what you read" "isn't always the truth."

"You are a very brilliant man to be so young." She replied. "I know you to be a man of your word." "You've given me the best prom I've ever attended" "and like I said I went to them all "cepten" the time I had my knee surgery."

"Miss Ida May" "in five years, you'll see a different town than what you grew up in."

"I may not have five years." She stated.

"I know what you mean, ma'am." I stated.

"Son, I'm sorry." "You go on in the house now" "you be a looking a might peeked." "I'll take good care of folks out here" "don't you worry none" "Granny got your back."

CHAPTER FIFTEEN

"**B**uck, make sure all the doors are locked." Becky said.
"I've checked them three times already Becky." Buck reported.
"Then check them again."

I heard him mumbling as he was walking away. "You ever been to New York Elrod?"

"No and from what Buck tells me I don't know if it's a place I'd care for." He replied.

"Don't worry" Sarah tried to calm him "in New York everyone knows you're from the south and every New Yorker thinks that all you people still ride horses and carry guns on your hips, and that reminds me, why does everybody wear cowboy hats?"

"Can we go to times square again Cheryl asked?"

"You bet" I answered.

"Can we go to that pastry shop?" Cindy asked.

You bet" I answered.

Bailey's cell phone interrupted our little chat.

"Hello" "just a minute." I heard her say.

"Hello" I hesitated and then told Richard I would see him later and when I got off the phone everything became quiet. "They want me to go back to Maryland and have a retest" "my test came back inconclusive." I stated to everyone in the limo.

I heard silence and then Becky quickly ended it. "Kurt"

www.ingramcontent.com/pod-product-compliance
Lightning Source LLC
LaVergne TN
LVHW040134080526
838202LV00042B/2903